The Longevity Thesis
Jennifer Rahn

www.dragonmoonpress.com
www.longevitythesis.ca

ISBN 10 1-896944-37-X Print Edition
ISBN 13 978-1-896944-37-1

ISBN 10 1-896944-55-8 Electronic Edition
ISBN 13 978-1-896944-55-5

CIP Data on file with the National Library of Canada

Dragon Moon Press is an Imprint of Hades Publications Inc.
P.O. Box 1714, Calgary, Alberta, T2P 2L7, Canada

Dragon Moon Press and Hades Publications, Inc. acknowledges the ongoing
support of the Canada Council for the Arts and the Alberta Foundation for the
Arts for our publishing programme.

Printed and bound in Canada
www.dragonmoonpress.com

The Longevity Thesis
Jennifer Rahn

www.dragonmoonpress.com
www.longevitythesis.ca

Acknowledgments

Lavish thanks to Cap'n ABurt and his crew of Critters.

Special thanks to C.M. Kaufman, Daphne J. Riordan, Jackie F., Peter M., Tim Reynolds

and E.A. Zefram.

Thank you to two of the loveliest people on Earth, Publisher Extraordinaire Gwen Gades and Editor Magnifique Sigrid Macdonald for making the dream come true.

A huge debt of gratitude is owed to Antronos' godfather, J.D. Williams, who diligently stationed himself at his Sony VAIO for months to guide his godson through the murkiest depths of prose.

1

Awakening

Antronos was being swallowed by the Desert. He stood petrified, watching a great wall of sand heave upwards and seethe past him overhead, covering his world in red gloom. Turning to look back towards his mother's hovel, praying it hadn't disappeared, he found he was somewhere else entirely—in an instant, all had changed. The sky churned and a vortex of wind stretched down from the red, sooty clouds to touch the ground and tease the sand into a great column that tipped sideways, and slowly writhed towards him, like a great, opened maw. At his feet, stones were sliding towards that opening, becoming caught up in the spiralling wind and tumbling out of sight. He called out to his mother, his trembling, skinny hands clutching the few dried brambles he had found, as he continued to turn in a circle looking for what he knew would not be there. Hell had returned.

Sand was beginning to boil around him, sending up small spumes as the Desert's dementia cast up buried rubble and bones that had lain hidden under its surface. Collecting together in the crude shapes of headless torsos with legs, the unearthed debris stood up and marched resolutely towards the darkness at the end of the wind tunnel. The very Earth was flowing towards that gaping orifice, forcing Antronos to run in the opposite direction, or risk being dragged in himself. It began to rain. At first it was a light drizzle of grit, then small pebbles began to pelt Antronos in the face. He dropped his bundle of kindling and screamed, both arms held up to cover his eyes. His feet were sinking ever deeper into the ground as he ran, until he was struggling to pull his legs free from the sand that had engulfed him up to his knees. Something grabbed his ankles from below and dragged him down. After a few agonizing moments of breathless torment, he felt himself being ripped free from the grip of the Earth.

"Mea Haalom, mea Haalom."

Antronos stopped struggling and collapsed into a sobbing heap as he recognized his mother's voice. She was nearly smothering him in her arms, forcing him against her shoulder as she rocked back and forth, not letting him look at her face. He knew the Desert must be changing her again. After a few moments, he quieted. The magnetic whimsy of the Desert still raged outside, but his mother's magic ensured the moaning debris creatures would not enter their home; neither would the Earth reach into the hovel to sweep him into its gullet. *Lea Chaakan bestt inalan takat, mea Haalom.*" The Desert has turned to fire, my child, she began, telling him the story that always calmed him during these storms. Antronos relaxed in her arms, feeling her hands gently roam over his back and pull his crinky, yellow hair out of his face. But the fire is not all-powerful. It is held at bay by water, which has the magic to conquer its flames. There is a river called Yrati, which flows underneath the Earth and forms an impenetrable barrier that the Desert cannot cross. In time, you will learn to summon the river that protects us, as it does the people who live underground. The water is within us, and it is that which the Desert cannot conquer. You are safe.

Antronos no longer believed her as he had when he was younger. He could reason now that he was not safe, and the only people who were underground were already dead.

His mother chuckled as she read his thoughts. "These people don't lie buried in sand. They roam about in tunnels."

"Then why can we not go live underground?" he asked. He pushed away from his mother, and saw that this time the Desert had rendered half her face into a mass of writhing tissue that snaked down her neck and wriggled beneath the shoulder of her tattered, red robes. Through her tangled, dark hair, he could see her remaining violet eye watching him compassionately.

"There are two kinds of magic, *Haalom*. The water magic, which protects humanity . . ." She spread her fingers, palm down, over the floor of the hut and a small amount of water bubbled to the surface. ". . . and the surface magic, which is also necessary for life." Antronos reached out to touch the water, fascinated, although he had heard and seen this story many times before. "The Desert must be mixed with water before life springs from it. But the Desert is wild, and its magic can deliberately mislead people to their death. It mixes you with other things, and gives you a death that lets you live forever." She moved her hand over another patch of ground, and a broken skull that had petrified into stone twisted upwards to leer at them. The thing snapped its jaws, then twitched and pulled back downwards. "I have already been touched by this magic. It has made me part of the surface, and I cannot go underground. Perhaps you can, but I wish that you would not leave me yet."

Antronos pressed his face against her neck. "I won't leave," he promised.

"You will leave, *Haalom*. Just not yet."

This troubled Antronos. His mother had never spoken of their separation before and he knew he couldn't cope with the Desert's mad rages on his own. "There's nowhere for me to go." He sat up again to search her face, but she was gazing over his shoulder, the skin over her left eye now settled into what looked like a hideous melted scar.

"The Desert has come for me. It told me It would."

"What?" Antronos turned and saw that one of the stone skeletons from outside had entered the hut. "Make it leave!" he said to his mother. Sand crept upwards to wrap the fossilized bones in an approximation of flesh, and a rotted shroud pulled free from the Earth to clothe the figure. It turned its empty sockets towards Antronos and seemed to grin at him. "*Itya*, make it go!"

His mother stood up and shook her head sadly, saying, "Not this time."

* * * * *

The sand creature was horrible. He slept with *Itya* in her bed, broke Antronos' clay pots, and burned everything he could get his hands on, including Antronos' only other tunic. Antronos had tried to dissolve him with precious water, but the thing had howled his psychic laughter as he sopped up his muddied flesh from the ground, and packed it back against his bones. Sometimes he would stand silent for hours, only to crush all hope that he had died by springing back to life when Antronos tried to bury him. What made it worse was that *Itya* seemed to accept this sandy monster into her life even though it appeared to sap her strength, bleeding a little more of her away with every passing moment. When Antronos raged at her, she would only answer, "If you live long enough, *Haalom*, you will see me again."

"Please stop saying that! I'm not going to leave!" But his mother grew more and more distant, spoke to him less, and never reassured him satisfactorily.

The sand creature grew ever more presumptuous, and began issuing orders. He had acquired a thick staff from somewhere, probably regurgitated by the Earth, which he refused to burn in lieu of Antronos' possessions, and which he beat Antronos with when his commands were not obeyed.

Out into the Desert, boy. Find me wood.

Antronos glared at the sand creature. "What for?"

I am the undertaker, and I need to build a funeral pyre.

"Are you dying then?"

The creature laughed at him. *I am already part of the Desert.*

Antronos scuttled away from the raised staff, seething with resentment.

The sandy dunes were not willing to relinquish the sparse scrub, dead and twisted as it was. Antronos tugged hard on a particularly stubborn tangle of brush, partially pulling the gnarled root to the surface, and thinking he could wrench it up a bit further before chopping it off from whatever it clung to. He heaved on it again, and felt something flat and hard shift beneath his foot. He froze, his heart thudding as he waited to see in which direction whatever he had disturbed was going to leap. Nothing moved. Carefully, he lifted his foot away and peered down at the sand. Something black with a straight edge was poking upwards. He brushed the sand away gently, and found that the black substance was soft, slightly sticky, and formed a completely straight line around a square-shaped panel of clear stone. He felt around the edges of this strange object, found another one exactly like it, and another. Many of them were stuck together, with the black stuff all around the edges. Sweeping away more of the sand, Antronos marvelled at the clear stones, as he began to see tiny people moving around inside them.

A few of them glanced up at him, but didn't seem bothered by his presence. He pried up the one he had loosened, intending to take it home as a gift for his mother, and was disappointed to see it empty of people as it came free in his hands. But there were sounds now, coming from the gap he had made in the pattern, and the distinct, metallic tang of water. He looked down at the hole and saw sand falling through it, and realized that the people were down inside a massive cavern, not inside the clear stones at all. Was this...a tunnel? Was his mother's story real?

A few of the people were suddenly swiping at their necks as they passed beneath him, then looking up to where the sand was trickling through. Some pointed, then moved away. Others merely stood, staring back up at him.

Excited by his discovery, Antronos moved to another section of the panels and swept away the sand. He pressed his forehead against the clear stones, trying to make out more of what was beneath the surface. If his eyes did not deceive him, there was indeed a massive river coursing through the bottom of the cavern, without any mages constantly summoning the water.

"The Yrati River," he breathed in fascination. Bright spots of light were coming from somewhere around the edges of the water, but they were white-blue, so they couldn't be fires. Antronos took one of the twigs he had collected, and began to pry up another of the panels so that he could see better.

A sharp bang startled him so badly that he jerked to the side, painfully twisting back his fingernails caught at the edge of the clear stone. He gaped at the man coming up through a door that had been slammed open from the ground. He had never seen anyone with hair so short when he obviously had not been burned, or with so much cloth to wrap around his body. This man wore magic cloth that encased him almost like skin, without having to tie the edges in knots over his shoulders.

"Get away!" he shouted at Antronos. "Go on!" He picked up a stone and threw it, nearly striking Antronos' head. "I said, go, *Pachu!*"—*filthy creature.* Antronos got to his feet and stumbled back a few steps. "Your kind's not welcome here!" The man pulled out a series of metallic links from his sleeve and walked forward threateningly. Antronos had never seen so much metal in his life. The man must be incredibly rich.

His amazement was halted when the man swung the links over his shoulder and hit Antronos across the face with them.

"Get away!"

Antronos finally turned and ran.

* * * * *

Flames were teasing the sky without any shifting of the Desert. The fire was real. Antronos squinted as he approached, trying to make out what he was seeing more clearly. Why had he bothered to collect kindling if the undertaker could summon enough wood from the Earth to generate such a blaze on his own? And why did he choose to place this funeral pyre so close to *Itya's* hovel? The bruise on Antronos' cheek throbbed as the realization hit him.

He wouldn't have dared...she wasn't that sick. Just tired. It was someone else.

Antronos dropped his bundle and began running, his feet sliding in the dusty grains. He was almost at the pyre when he hit a pocket of slipsand. His hands flailed out desperately, trying to catch hold of something, anything, as the sand beneath him gave way and his body was sucked into an immobilizing swathe of grit. *Itya* was clearly visible now, just beyond his reach, steadily burning out of existence. He stopped struggling and tilted his head upward as far as possible, straining to watch her these last few minutes as he slowly sunk deeper. He squeezed his eyes shut to force away the tears blurring his vision, and focused again on his mother's scorched face; it would have to be enough.

As if marking an ending, the sun dropped to the horizon, sparkling through the dust coating the sky. The Desert moaned in protest, shifting sand and rocks around Antronos' head and launching plumes of grit into whatever forms suited its magnetic whimsy. Incomprehensible pillars of sand shot out of the ground and collapsed; far away boulders drew closer, then grumbled as they burrowed back into the dust. An entire stone building surfaced in a thunder of unearthed debris, only to tip sideways and crumble a few moments later. For once, the prospect of being swallowed whole by the Desert's writhing didn't terrify him.

Rage swelled up inside Antronos. The sand creature could have waited. He could have allowed Antronos the chance to say goodbye. Somewhere behind him, he could hear the unreal man shuffling towards the fire.

This wasteland eats all comfort. Takes it for itself. It doesn't care anything for you. Pointless to cry and waste your fluids.

Antronos shoved the words out of his head, twisting his face away from the undertaker's proffered staff as much as he could. What made the disgusting thing think he'd want to live after this? Being alone in the Desert would slowly drive him insane.

Your defiance is meaningless. You're willing to die out of anger against me? After this moment, I won't even think of it, and you will lose your chance for whatever misguided vengeance you want to take.

The staff fell away, and the creature's grey, skeletal ankles came into view from under a frayed robe, as he tottered towards the fire. His feet barely sank into the sand.

I will tell the Desert to release you anyway.

A buried pillar of sand pushed up against Antronos' feet as it forced its way to the surface, sending him sprawling. It collapsed behind him in a torrent of dry granules. What was the point of setting him free? What would he do now without his mother? She had been the only unchanging thing in this fearsome existence, holding him close, and anchoring his sanity whenever the terrifying Desert storms struck and until they had passed. Hatred for the sand creature surged up inside him. He opened his mouth to tell the despicable being that he'd find a way to—

You don't need to tell me things I already know, Antronos. I don't bother hating you, because it isn't worth the effort. Almost gone now. Where's she gone? All back to the Desert and dust.

Antronos felt his mouth twist in futile anguish. Still covered in chalky grit, he crept as close as he dared to the pyre, trying to decide which emotion held him more strongly—his wish to follow his mother, or his wish to find a way to kill what was already dead. He pulled out of his waistband one of the three thin, precious books he had hidden from being burned, the nap of the soft vellum cover catching on his rough fingertips.

"*Itya*," he whispered. "Do you remember reading this to me? All these old water prayers?" He scrubbed away his tears, then carefully flipped open the crumbling pages to one of his favourite hymns: a sinuous lyric about the circle of life, describing how it always started again. As he read, the wind raged at his back, tugging angrily at his hair and the flames, as if trying to extinguish his voice along with the light and heat of the fire that ruined its perfection. The bed of the pyre split with a great crack, startling Antronos into silence and sending his mother's bones tumbling deep into the brambles. He caught his breath, unthinkingly reaching towards the flames.

His mother's charred corpse sat up and screamed at him. Antronos yelled and fell backwards. When he looked again, the pyre was nothing but a pile of bones and coals. No movement, but his mother's skull now rested at the top of the burning refuse, where it had not been before. The sand creature did not react, and continued standing motionless and vacant off to one side. Antronos cautiously crept back towards the pyre. Maybe, he thought, if the Desert was choosing now to exercise its power, its next shift might awaken his mother, lifting her out of the flames and back into the world.

"*Itya?*" he prodded. He searched the pyre for any sign of movement for several minutes.

The oblivious force of the Desert ignored him and continued to work change only within itself. Unnoticed by the magnetic fury around them, bones turned to cinder. Cinder crumbled to ash.

Faith splintered inside of Antronos as he scanned the dying fire through blurring tears, and still saw no movement. The book of water hymns was still in his hand. *The circle of life? Had this made Itya move?* He began to read again, this time raising his voice bravely over the moaning protest of the Desert as it responded to his call. The shifting of the sand intensified as he continued giving sound to the hymn. Pointed rocks shot up around where he knelt, yet he wouldn't stop.

But the Desert did.

Antronos looked around, scanning the pyre and the wasteland, now washed in thin, evening light. Nothing moved. Not even the undertaker. Determined, he began the hymn again. His voice slowly faded as he realized that the Desert hadn't responded to the lyrics at all; its motions had been coincidental.

His mother was truly gone this time. She wasn't lost in a sandstorm or mystically transported over the next dune. Waiting for her to come to him again would be futile. He swallowed his grief enough to pause, stubbornly searching for her return one last time, and cried out as he saw her ashes wriggling out of the coal pit in tiny streams. He shoved his hands into the ground, trying to scoop her away from the Desert, succeeding only in mixing her more thoroughly with the dusty grains.

"Don't leave me," he moaned through his teeth. The blue ash coalesced into a set of fingertips that reached out of the sand. Antronos caught his breath, staring at the unmoving fingers. Cautiously, his hands trembling, he reached out to touch them, feeling their solidity, their reality. The sand just above the fingers shifted, rose up in a mound, then fell away in a pattern which formed his mother's face, mouth stretched open in a silent scream.

"What...what's wrong?" he asked. All around him mounds of sand were rising. Antronos half stood, watching them uncertainly as they began to tremble, then started moving towards him in jerky spurts. He peered at the undertaker, who still showed no signs of awareness, leaning silently on his staff. Antronos kicked at one of the mounds, then scurried away as the sand flowed upward into a curving pillar. All motion stopped. He crept forward again, reaching out for his mother's blue-ash hand, constantly glancing around for more signs of movement.

The sand of the pillar crumbled away, revealing a skeleton made of grey, cracked stone. It stood still for a second, then writhed and screamed, lurching towards Antronos. It fell over the ash-image of his mother, then rapidly sunk out of sight, taking her with it, leaving Antronos sobbing as he dug madly, trying to once again find the ashes that had submerged into the Desert's being.

The undertaker came to life and tottered into the embers, spewing ashes everywhere, flattening the sand mounds, destroying any chance of finding *Itya* again. Antronos tried to stop him, but was thumped aside impatiently.

This is over. She will not live, and you will not die.

"Then I will go mad."

As you wish. It hardly matters to me.

Antronos wondered how long it would take to lose all perception of reality. His gut twisted with uncertainty. Perhaps all he had ever been was some deluded wraith who only thought that he lived, but was denied the reality of both life and death for a crime he could not remember.

Little was left of the pyre. The sand creature gestured towards Antronos, wanting him to fetch the rakes. Another shove and the threat of a severe beating were needed to send him running back towards the cardboard hovel.

The wind picked up and began to fling sand into Antronos' face. He stopped, unable to breathe or see, and put out one hand to find the entrance to his mother's hut. His fingers finally scraped against the door, which he shoved aside and clambered past. He stood gasping for a few moments, trying to rub the sand from his eyes. They began to burn. The Desert shifted again. He felt it inside himself this time, pouring all of its intense heat and unmerciful drought into his eyes. The ground heaved under his feet, sending him tumbling as he felt the Desert reach more deeply into him to work its change.

Antronos screamed and dragged himself towards his mother's cot, and the bowl of water he had kept there for soothing her fever. Finding it, he tried to quench the fire in his eyes, and finally felt the pain melt into a subtle, aching burn. He gingerly pulled his hands away from his face. He could see his fingers, cast in a strange yellow glow. He could see the rugs and the walls of the hovel, even though there were no candles lit and it was the dead of night. When he looked down on himself, the outline of his body was covered with a silken atmosphere that pulsated over his heart and moved in flowing waves over his body. The other objects around him did not glow as he did, but had a paler, more diffuse light, with the exception of the brightly glistening beetle he saw busily digging its way into the food supply.

He got up, lit a candle and found his mother's old polished mirror. Raising it to his face, he felt his heart sink into his stomach. His face and the frizzy, yellow hair that framed it were the same, but his eyes had changed. No longer a natural, deep brown, the shift that had assaulted him had twisted them into the purple, diamond-slit eyes of a snake, sunk deep into their sockets. The skin around them looked dark red and bruised. Gasping, he tore at the rough shirt he wore, exposing the semi-hardened scales that now covered his skin in patches. Some were dark green, others white, still others a myriad of glistening colours.

The Desert's magic had touched him, as it had his mother. He remembered her saying that while he was untouched, he could go underground, to where water protected life. It was impossible now, even if he could have crept past the man wearing magic cloth, who had chased him away from the underground door. Why should he be changed like this? Was he dreaming?

Needing to feel connected to something definite, even if only the rotted sand-thing outside, Antronos grabbed the rakes from the corner of the hut and ventured back outside to find the undertaker. The wind was still blowing curtains of sand across the Plains, making it difficult for him to find his way back to the dimly glowing embers of the fire pit. After a moment he froze in his tracks, realizing that the distance between him and the sand creature had increased. Then the pyre was off to his left. Antronos began to run. The directions shifted again. And again. He ran faster, but still couldn't reach the pyre. He paused in disbelief as the creature turned from him and walked away.

"Wait!" Antronos screamed, but with the next wave of billowing sand the undertaker disappeared. The pyre was also gone. Had it ever been there? He screamed again, only succeeding in roughening his throat.

He stood in the near darkness of the sandstorm, still able to see by the hazy aura of the sand, recognizing belatedly that unlike the beetle and himself, the undertaker did not have more than a diffuse glow about him as he had walked away. How had the creature left him so easily? Had he walked right out of existence?

There had to be a way to make himself real.

2

catalyst

Antronos spread his fingers and held them over the sand, willing the dusty grains to move until a small pile collected in front of him. Nothing else responded; no water or stone skulls came to the surface, and never would, no matter how hard he tried. He could still see living auras, but that hardly constituted magic, not the kind his mother had been able to conjure.

The stone marker he had built, inscribed with his name and a short message, had rested here for seven years, but was now inexplicably gone. It was just as well, as he no longer really believed that his mother still roamed the Desert, and that someday she might see the monument he had left her and know where to find him.

After a few moments the small mound of sand he had just made shifted sideways until it had completely flattened out. The elongated magnets he had placed in a semicircle in front of him spun in random directions, none of them aligning towards the world poles. They had pointed steadily south for over three months when he had initially selected this place, but now the Desert had mysteriously changed again.

He sat for a while longer, ignoring the prickling sensation of sand blowing against his face, his scholar's robes wrapped tightly against the wind. The hazy presence of the sun slowly rose from the horizon, illuminating the dust in the air with shimmering waves of pink and green. When he had been younger, the underground had seemed like a marvellous wonder, and finding a place there had seemed so necessary. In the tunnels, things were constant, unaffected by the random changes on the surface. He had thought that living there would end his terror of the Desert. He knew now that the world was much larger and more diverse than he had ever imagined, and that Temlocht was only one out of five States, the only place where most of the people lived underground, and were considered socially backward by the surrounding regions. He supposed that made his kind the pinnacle of social lowliness, if even the Temlochti had difficulty accepting him.

Antronos stood, feeling the sand that had collected around his legs sluice from the folds of his robes, and sighed, rubbing his fingers. They still ached from being broken during one of his early ventures into the tunnel dwellers' domain. Even though the dock hands, who worked along the river in the lowest tier of the Market Caverns, had eventually accepted him as a dung shoveller or cargo loader, they had never shown interest in protecting a surface creature from the idle sons of rich merchants.

For a moment, Antronos considered staying in the Desert, then rejected the idea. Although he didn't belong underground, living on the surface now would just be re-suspending himself in limbo, and his dung shovelling had lessened ever since he had rescued an academic adminis-trator from drowning in the underground river. That had earned him a spot in the university. His mother had taught him to read, but he had to work twice as hard as the other students to make up for his lack of formal education, and ten times as hard to impress his teachers and earn a grade that would have been handed to another student not considered the local freak. It had been and still was his best and only chance to understand life, and perhaps what he was, so he turned and began the long trek back the way he had come. His class would be graduating tomorrow, and even though there was talk among his classmates that the university wouldn't really allow him to have a degree, there was the remote chance that someone might mistakenly fill out the parchment anyway, and he might be able to pick it up from the Chancellor's office after the ceremony— when there weren't many people around to laugh at him for even asking. He supposed he could continue studying at the university without a degree, but that would bar him from entering a higher level of research with access to better lab equipment, interfering with his still intense desire to analyze what made a human being live, what made it die, and what the Desert did to interfere with that natural process.

At this time of day, the back tunnels would still be completely dark, making it possible for Antronos to slip into the underground unnoticed. A series of stone markers sat along the edge of the Plains, outside of which magnets behaved as they should. These had been placed two years ago by the University Department of Physics, which had been made responsible for periodically testing the Desert's magnetic sphere of influence and moving the markers as needed.

He found the metal surface of the door he had come through, and had to tug sharply on the ring handle to force the steel slab upwards against its rusted edges. The lock that had been placed on the other side had long since disintegrated, and no one had bothered to check if it needed to be replaced. In general, the contempt of the tunnel dwellers, along with their bewildering array of noises and colours, were enough to keep most surface creatures out.

In the dark of the underground, Antronos found his way easily by the glinting auras of the innumerable busy insects and meandering tree roots that lined the tunnel. The ground and east wall were slick from water oozing out of the river that ran alongside this passage, bringing life to the underground as it could not be on the surface. It was also why this tunnel was not regularly used, as the risk of a cave-in was high.

He heard a rustling sound somewhere deep in the cored-out mud behind him and froze, listening intently. It came again. He moved ahead to where a thick bundle of roots protruded from the wall and pressed himself behind them, looking back the way he had come. Last week he had been followed by a pack of student would-be tormentors down one of his favourite back tunnels, abandoned only because of a disease which had died out long ago. He was now afraid to use it, in case his classmates had set up an ambush there. It would be damned inconvenient if he had to abandon this one as well. At least his Desert-changed eyes would give him an advantage in the dark.

Several bright, erratic auras were moving towards him, not taking on any shapes he could recognize. They would remain stationary for a few moments, then tremble until they seemed to muster enough energy to finally move forward in rapid, jerky spurts. What were they? Cautiously, Antronos leaned past the tree roots to get a better look, and saw something like crumpled-up dwarves who were stuck to the walls and ceiling.

Did something follow me down from the Desert? Antronos' heart sped up with anticipation. If these dwarves had followed him because of his monument, perhaps they knew something about his mother, or maybe had some message. From past encounters he knew that any contact with Desert creatures was best done on solid ground where he couldn't be suffocated in mud or sand, so he began to edge back towards the university.

As he drew closer to tunnels that were more frequently used, the walls were cut in deliberately straight angles, and bricks lined the floors. No one had bothered to tend to the lighting in this tunnel, and the bioluminescent moss, overgrown and dying, shone weakly from tanks embedded in the walls. With a final look back, he hoped the strangers would not be intimidated by the tunnel dwellers' structured territory and follow him at least that far.

The library foyer opened before him in a vast expanse of diamond-shaped tiles, stretching past administrative offices and blue stone pillars that reached up twenty metres to support an enormous glass ceiling. The early morning light was stunning, catching on polished marble desks, as well as metal accents that lined the railings, door handles and chairs. At this time of day, the foyer was completely empty, with silence to match.

He paused at the mouth of the tunnel to give his eyes a few seconds to adjust. Something tickled at his foot, and looking down, he saw a flash of jerky aura next to his sandal. He jumped away from it and it flipped out of sight. The creatures in the back tunnels seemed to be moving towards him steadily now, writhing past roots and outcroppings of rock with ease. It was still too dark in the tunnel for him to see them by natural vision. Backing away, he waited to see if they would come out into the open. The creatures paused at the edge of the tiles, then somehow burrowed underground, moving forward through solid rock. Antronos could barely see their dimmed auras through the stone. He had never encountered this type of creature before, and realized that without Desert vision similar to his, the tunnel dwellers would also be unaware of these visitors. *Perhaps they are unable to break through the tile,* thought Antronos.

The dimmed bubbles of aura wiggled past him and disappeared under a door leading into the library archives. In the lower levels, not all areas were covered in tile, and the creatures might be able to emerge. Antronos chased after them and found that the side entry was locked. Determined to at least find out where the creatures were going, if not speak to them, he squatted and scratched at a section of the wall where the lacquer had cracked. The dusty stone crumbled under his nails, allowing him to gently pull a small blue beetle from its intended home. The little creature struggled briefly, then tapped the tips of Antronos' fingers with its antennae, seeming confused and curious as to where it had ended up.

Taking a pinch of Desert sand from a vial in his belt, he blew the grains into the lock, then held the beetle up to the keyhole. Thinking it had found a new lair, the little beast obligingly crawled inside. Antronos whispered to it, using the Desert's whimsy carried in the sand to influence the beetle to push the lock pins out of the way. *Such things were cluttering up its home.* The lock snapped open; the door swung inward.

Antronos quietly stepped inside and softly closed the door. The bubbles of aura were clustered together a few metres away, as if waiting for him. Without a sound, the tiles crumbled upward, and an intensely bright light seemed to peek at him before sinking back under the rock. Surprised, he ran forward and tried to jam his fingers into the spot where the thing had surfaced. It was completely solid, the tiles undamaged. The bubbles began to move again.

Antronos chased them past rows of aging filing cupboards and to the left, then got stuck as he realized that he'd wedged himself between a leaning rack of scrolls and an old chalk slate board. He froze, hearing voices approaching. Looking around, he noticed that he had left the archives and was now in a white and red tiled hallway, with alternating white pillars and multi-coloured tapestries displaying academic motifs that lined the walls. Teaching props littered the passageway like abandoned debris. He must be somewhere near the professors' offices. The aura bubbles swirled in a frenzied dance before coming to a stop, occasionally trembling but otherwise staying put. Antronos pulled back behind the slate and crouched down.

Several figures in black scholar's robes were coming towards him in a clumsy huddle. Laughing and talking loudly, half of them were holding hands, and the other half were kicking, slapping or punching each other as they strode down the hall. Antronos began to breathe again in relief. He could tell from the sloppy way they wore their robes and their long hair that these were priests from the Yrati Clan; healers known for their kindness and the only people in the underground who had not gone out of their way to make him miserable. If they caught him here, it was unlikely he'd be beaten. As they came closer, he could make out the red and blue patterns embroidered on their neckbands. They seemed completely oblivious to the aura bubbles, which jiggled excitedly as the priests stepped over them, then vanished, apparently sinking deeper into the Earth.

Antronos peered furtively at the approaching priests, feeling his heart speed up. He felt a strange mixture of resentment that his quarry had disappeared, and anxiety over his torn wish to remain hidden yet talk to the Yrati. Now might be as good a chance as any. Should he reveal himself? After he graduated, if he graduated, they might be the only group tolerant enough to accept him for higher study, and they had associated themselves with the river, which his mother had told him could halt the Desert's madness. He crept forward slowly and followed them, keeping far enough back that he might at least be able to hide behind something if they were to turn around. When they entered the office that must have belonged to My Lord Maxal, the Yrati High Priest, Antronos wedged himself behind a cracked podium opposite the opened office door, and peeked out from behind it. The room was much too small for so many people, but the Yrati seemed content to sit in a ring on the floor with some of their fellows perched on benches and bookshelves around them. They were still jabbering loudly as they passed books and parchments to each other, apparently planning lessons. Antronos had been taught about pharmaceuticals by a few of them, however, most of their postings were in the Faculty of Arts, as their medical approach was regarded as folklore rather than science.

One of the Yrati screamed as she was hit in the face by something that exploded in a great splash of water. She blinked indignantly at someone across the room, then stood up and dragged a red-haired boy over to where she had been sitting. The other Yrati laughed and pinned the youth down, as the soggy priest began to rub her wet hair in his face.

"Teach you to throw things at me," she was grumbling.

"It was a blessing!" screeched the boy. "Water is Life. So Dagnaum says! I was merely trying to bless you!"

"Old Dagnaum isn't here. Don't bring him into this." She picked up a tankard of something and poured it over his head before finally letting him go.

The boy jumped up and skipped into the hallway, rubbing his face. "Augh! Was that berry juice? Leelan, you sully the name of Dagnaum, founder of Yrati Water Magic."

"Dagnaum who now writes books for babies," said the wet priest.

"You who scoff at his wisdom shall surely be cursed."

"Go get buried, Tibeau."

"But I'm all sticky."

"Good. Maybe the ants will eat you."

Smiling at the exchange, Antronos shifted uncomfortably behind the podium. He liked the Yrati, but after all the abuse he'd suffered from other students, he wasn't sure he could cope with their rough brand of teasing if he joined them. He held his breath and pulled back as Tibeau came dangerously close to where he was hiding and rummaged through a box half-covered in the detritus of the hall. Pulling out something that looked like a wad of red and blue paper that had been dampened and squashed together, Tibeau struck a match and began trying to light the end of it.

"Earth, don't light that thing in here!" A stocky Yrati with a bushy, black beard and a glistening bald-patch erupting from a ring of long, dark hair, stepped into view from somewhere down the hall and slapped the paper-thing out of Tibeau's hands. Antronos recognized him as Ferril, who taught an alternative medicine course about brewing herbal tea.

"Why not?" Tibeau asked. "It would be funny, and I need to exact revenge."

"Exact revenge on this." Ferril put the boy in a headlock and dragged him back into the office.

Maybe I shouldn't ask to join them, thought Antronos. Despite that, and unable to resist, he wiggled to the other side of the podium and picked up Tibeau's discarded wad of paper from the floor. It smelled like firecracker powder. Starting to feel anxious that he had lingered too long, Antronos sidled a bit farther from behind the podium, painfully aware that the Yrati might see him walking away if any of them should step out of the office again. He swore silently as more footsteps echoed from the other end of the hall, and tried to make his lanky frame as small as possible, since he couldn't wriggle back behind the podium quickly enough.

The Chancellor of the Temlochti State University marched past energetically, his heavy ceremonial robes sweeping the tiles as he moved. His brown beard and shoulder-length hair made him look like some kind of aging warrior from a tavern song. The others who followed were all Sens, or professors declared as full medical scholars. None looked in Antronos' direction: all of them wearing grim expressions. A few were arguing as they walked, heading towards the Yrati office. Antronos could pick out his pharmacology and surgery professors, as well as the Yrati High Priest. My Lord Maxal wore a straight-cut black robe, was clean shaven, and his black hair was close cropped, in stark contrast to all other Yrati, who seemed not to know what a barber was.

The Chancellor paused at the door of the office, unable to enter because of the crowd of Yrati sitting on the floor, and abruptly turned towards Maxal in the hallway.

"By the *Earth!*" he exploded. "Am I being so unrealistic? All I'm hoping for is a day where interdepartmental politics are shoved aside and the faculty sits as a united front, tolerating each other for the sake of our shared achievement!"

"Yes, Amphetam. Shared," Maxal replied, "as in shared input into the format of the ceremonies."

The Chancellor took a deep breath, then put a hand on the High Priest's shoulder. "I am not trying to insult you—"

"Well, you have," said Maxal.

"You insist on taking things the wrong way!"

"I fail to see how the format of the graduation ceremony has anything to do with external funding."

"Maxal, it's the whole attitude of this university. We have to change."

"Fine. Change. Change whatever you like. There is still no reason to exclude the Yrati blessing of the graduates."

"The representative from Raulen State refused to come because of your 'mystical hokum,' as she called it."

"Who cares? It's our ceremony, not Raulen's. And my mysticism is not 'hokum,' so she is quite clearly uneducated and incorrect. Why should you listen to her anyway?"

"Earth, Maxal! Nobody believes in magic anymore—"

"That's not true."

"Nobody *sensible* believes in magic anymore. We have to raise our heads out of the sand. Even if there are phenomena we can't always explain, none of them is going to generate us any money *or* international respect. We cannot compete internationally without Raulen's funding. Our resources have emptied. Gone! There is *nothing* left."

"And I keep telling you, if Raulen is truly judging us on our academic merit, then a simple ceremony should have absolutely no impact on their decisions."

"But it does! And we as scholars who should know better, should not be subscribing to these children's tales about—"

"They just want to control you, Amphetam. They want to see how far you'll go for money. If you accept their terms now, the next year they'll push for something else. Perhaps they'll insist you perform your functions naked."

"Don't be absurd."

"I'm not. I can quite clearly see that they are trying to humiliate and dominate you. And you are willing to let them for the sake of money."

"None of the other States take us seriously because of these traditions—"

"I can see this conversation is pointless."

The Yrati turned and walked back down the hallway, leaving the Chancellor with his arm still raised. Sen Amphetam let his hand drop after a moment, then just stood there, watching Maxal push his way into the office. He released a shaky breath before turning away and striding off, looking absolutely miserable. The other Sens lingered for a few moments, some of them muttering vague apologies in the direction of the Yrati before following after the Chancellor.

Antronos let his lungs empty, wondering if his ties to the surface with all its implied mysticism would make his fears real. *Mystical hokum?* Children's tales? His Desert eyes were real and there was nothing he could do about it. If Sen Amphetam found the opinion of Rauleners so important and was so against belief in magic, he probably wouldn't want an obvious reminder of the Temlochti State's tainted history, like a snake-eyed surface creature, showing up at his office to claim a parchment.

Cautiously, Antronos stood up and began to sneak away from the office, not breathing until he had turned a corner and found the hallway empty. He hurried back towards the archives and ran into yet another Yrati as he rounded the last corner. The sandy-haired priest caught him in surprise, stopping his fall.

"Oh, it's you," he said, letting go and giving Antronos a once over. "What's that? Some Desert thing?" He poked at the paper wad still clutched in Antronos' hand. Feeling the heat rise in his face, and not wanting to be accused of stealing, Antronos moved his fist behind his back, looked down and didn't answer. He was also becoming angry. Why should everyone assume that he always ran around with only "Desert things" anyway? Even the Yrati, reputedly kind or not, seemed to be so ready to think he was some surface idiot, that this one didn't even recognize something made by his own clan.

"Right. Well, don't let me hold you up." The priest brushed past him and strode away, leaving Antronos feeling empty. It wasn't fair. He had worked harder than any other student, and he was due some kind of serious recognition. He would just have to find a way of confronting the Chancellor and insisting on his degree. If he dared.

*****

Convocation Day. Several metres overhead, the glass panes of the convocation hall ceiling were covered in sand. A clear spot was slowly growing in the middle, and coloured panels were emerging as workmen briskly swept away the grit. The light from outside glittered as it spilled into the cavern and puddled dimly in the corners, lifting the shadows to reveal the blue cast of the pillars and hints of the academic motifs embossed in the stone walls.

A few early graduands were trickling into the hall. Even though the end of the hall where they were seated was still dark, Antronos could pick them out easily by their auras, and backed himself even farther behind a pillar next to the stage. He had chosen this spot because not only would it remain shadowed once the skylight was cleared, it was also near a door if he had to make a hasty exit. Pulling the hood of his formal robe over his hair, he hoped that no one would notice him, at least for a while. He wouldn't be able to hide his eyes from the Chancellor when it was his turn to receive his parchment, assuming they would even call his name, but he hoped by then it would be too late, and that Sen Amphetam would be too embarrassed to say anything—just hand him his degree as quickly as possible and get him off the stage.

The Chancellor appeared on the front dais, signalling for the parchments to be rolled out from the offices at the back of the hall, moving towards the spot where he wanted them. Not watching where he was going, he walked right into the oversized and over-decorated ceremonial font of the old Yrati gods. Antronos winced as he watched the other man bite his lip and lift his foot in pain. The Chancellor leaned against the basin of the font, stared into it for a few minutes, then shoved it as if he wanted to push it off the dais.

The waist-deep stone basin rocked back towards the Chancellor, almost defiantly. A sound like a stream burbling came from it, and Sen Amphetam took a step back. Antronos gasped as his Desert sight showed him several bright spots of living aura emerge from the stone floor around the dais, moving in the same jerky fashion as the creatures he had seen in the back tunnel yesterday. *Will I be able to catch them later?*

The spots grew in intensity until they were painful to look at, then converged at the base of the font and trembled at the Chancellor's feet. After a moment, the auras disappeared under the basin, which suddenly overflowed with water that was caught in a trough around the bottom, and somehow recycled so that it didn't spill onto the stage. The Chancellor stared at the font for a few seconds, then shrugged his robe into a more comfortable position and turned his back on it. The bright auras of the creatures did not reappear, and did not seem to harm the Chancellor, so after a moment, Antronos allowed himself to look away.

The Chair of Hekka, another relic of the old religion, had been brought from the Royal House and was being hefted onto the dais by some of the university clerks and the Yrati. Hekka was the Goddess of Sight, and therefore symbolically important in the search for knowledge. The great hewn Eye of Hekka was positioned within the wooden back of the chair such that anyone sitting there would have it pressing against the back of the neck. Antronos' worry doubled when he saw the look on the Chancellor's face. All of these mystical symbols would probably drain Sen Amphetam's patience to the point where he would not hesitate to make a scene when Antronos attempted to get his degree.

"Sen Amphetam?" The administrative secretary was tugging at the Chancellor's elbow.

"Yes, what is it?"

"The Lady Alain is here, Sen."

"'Lady' might be an exagger—" The Chancellor cut himself off as he turned around and ended up face to face with the head of the largest merchant house in Temlocht, who was grinning at his half-formed insult. Antronos caught his breath and stared at her, wondering how much trouble this unexpected presence was going to bring. The last two times he had worked at the docks for the House of Dra and their shipping partner, the House of Dan, they had cheated him on his pay. Alaindra had casually suggested to her oarsmen that no one would arrest them for pummelling him if he didn't stop complaining. However, she hadn't even looked up from her ledgers then. Perhaps she would not remember him now. The elegant diamond- and sapphire-studded linens she wore matched the pale hue of her skin and contrasted perfectly with her curling, dark hair. She daintily offered her fingertips to the Chancellor, who paused for a few seconds before lifting his own hand, although Antronos thought he did so reluctantly.

"Madam Dra," said the Chancellor. "Thank you for coming and funding the ceremonies. I hope you will excuse my obvious frustration at having to ask for your help."

There was a hard glint in the wide, violet eyes as Alaindra gave a faint knowing smile, and demurely dropped her dark lashes over satin-dusted cheeks.

"Of course, Sen Amphetam. Nobody enjoys financial difficulties. I'm only glad I could assist. I wish you had taken me up on some of my other offers."

"Oh, I think you've done enough, Lady." The Chancellor smiled tightly and moved away without greeting the head of the House of Dan. On that point, Antronos could not fault the Chancellor.

The hall had filled with excited, chattering graduands but now a hush fell over them as the great stone doors to the right of the dais were scraped open to the sound of a bass drum, making Antronos lean forward eagerly. *Were any more of the spasmodic ground creatures going to come through?* His interest faded as the Chancellor heaved a sigh and resignedly waved his hand, dropping into a deep genuflection as he did so. Whoever was coming had to be visible by natural sight, and probably completely human.

A few strange-looking people emerged from the doorway, remarkable only because they seemed insane in their clothing choice and the amount of powder they wore on their faces. Their postures and apparent need to fan themselves seemed completely artificial to Antronos. A few armoured soldiers followed, scanning the crowd and taking up positions around the dais. These looked genuine, and the one closest to him didn't miss his presence. She gave Antronos a hard stare, but said nothing. He closed his eyes and muttered a prayer just the same.

Everyone in the hall suddenly stood up, the echoes from their movement reverberating through the cavern like thunder. Antronos peered through the stone doors fearfully. After a moment, a very tall, pale, sick-looking man came through, reluctant in his movements. He wore a blue patterned gown with gold embroidered tippet sleeves. His long, dark hair looked rather unkempt, and he didn't seem to know where he was going. He got tangled up in his sleeves, and had to be hauled onto the dais by some of the preceding retinue and escorted to the Chair of Hekka. It took a few moments for Antronos to realize that he was looking at the High Prince: My Lord Jait, Purveyor of Wisdom, Bringer of Justice and Omniscient Consort to the Head of the Temlochti State. The High Prince hiccupped, fumbled for the chair arm, and had trouble sitting down. Jait looked like he was in pain, either mental or physical, Antronos couldn't decide which. He searched through Jait's entourage, looking for the Royal Physician. Shouldn't somebody be showing more concern for the High Prince, or forbidding his presence when he was obviously not doing well?

"Stand aside!" Someone had come through the side door and poked Antronos in the back, making him jump. "I am the Royal Treasurer. Let me through!"

Antronos looked down into the face of a small man, with huge yellow eyes and a very noticeable underbite, who was holding a tray of ledgers and several pots of coloured ink. Antronos quickly lowered his own eyes and bowed politely.

"Forgive me, sir," he said, and stepped out of the way, keeping the pillar between himself and the other graduands as much as he could. The Treasurer bustled past him and forced his way through the courtiers on the stage to offer the tray to Lord Jait. The High Prince belched and pushed dark hair out of his face with one unsteady hand, then shoved aside the Treasurer with the other. The small man managed to retain his grip on the ink and parchment he had been trying to present for Jait's signature, deftly raising it over the High Prince's arm at the second swipe. He wiggled his underbite at Jait and breathed heavily for a few seconds before discreetly forging the signature and pretending to thank the High Prince.

"The Royal Award in Science, Sen Amphetam," Antronos heard him mutter as he handed the certificate to the Chancellor. "I regret that there is only one this year, but it was the only way to keep the sum large enough to allow the financing of a complete research project."

The Chancellor sighed. "Yes, of course. Thank you, Guillian."

"As you can see, I had some difficulty obtaining the signature of My Lord Jait beforehand, and he has left the name of the recipient blank. It will have to be in your hand, as only the university can decide which of the two excellent intended recipients will be given the award."

"Actually we had hoped for three this year."

"Alas, and I had hoped for at least two. The resources cannot be found, I'm afraid."

"It will have to do, then."

The Chancellor pulled three parchments from the front of one of the document carts, thumbing through them with a frown on his face, as if unable to decide which one was most worthy. He suddenly slapped one parchment into the hands of his secretary, then carried the other two over to Alaindra. There was a quiet negotiation, in which Alaindra must have had the upper hand, as the Chancellor came away looking irritated, and Alaindra pleased. The two parchments were passed to the Dra secretaries, who began preparing a set of certificates. Antronos wondered how badly swindled the recipients of those awards would find themselves.

A group of Yrati priests had climbed onto the dais, and one of them bumped into the Chancellor from behind. He whirled around, looking furious, then rolled his eyes and stepped out of the way as another of the priests circled quite close to him, bent over at the waist, waving shrub branches and softly hooting something Antronos could not hear.

"There must always be balance!"

The sandy-haired Yrati that Antronos had collided with yesterday was now standing behind the ceremonial font, raising his arms to the graduands.

"The Earth will crumble when it leans. The water will flow to equilibrium. The air will move to fill a void. In all things, there must be balance, or balance will be made." The Yrati dipped some sort of pan into the font and raised some water over his head. Letting it splash back into the font, he intoned, "As long as there is balance, there will be life!"

Something was bobbing just past the surface of the water. Something red. Something alive. Antronos stood a little straighter, trying to see over the rim of the basin as he thought he recognized the pulsations of the aura. Were the movements rather jerky? The red object seemed to turn over in the water, started to look like a skull that leered at Antronos for a few seconds, then suddenly submerged and vanished. The Yrati merely nodded at the water as if it spoke to him.

"All ye who come here today, retain the balance of the Earth and the natural surroundings. Without dark, there is no light. Without silence, no sound. Without death, no life. Let each dipole end balance the other. Be at peace."

The priest bowed his head and lapsed into silence. The Chancellor, looking disgusted, stepped forward and conspicuously cleared his throat.

"All of you who are in the Medical Sciences, please stand and raise your hand," said the Chancellor. A section of the graduands rose.

"You are the healers of our State. I ask you to pledge yourselves to the service of My Lord Jait, and promise your teachers, the university, that you will undertake your solemn duty to help those who need you, and to do no harm."

The graduands shouted the oath in unison. For the first time, the Chancellor smiled, finally looking relaxed and genuinely pleased. Antronos didn't know if that was a good sign or a bad one. The Chancellor reached over to the document cart that had been trundled to his side and picked up the certificates that Alaindra's scribes had filled out. He called out the names and beamed at the two new medical scientists who stepped up onto the dais, smiling and elated, reaching to shake his hand and thank him profusely. He then picked up the document the Royal Treasurer had given him and hesitated.

"There's no family name here," he murmured to his secretary. "Is this correct? I don't want to offend someone."

"Yes, sir. This boy doesn't belong to any clan. Haven't you heard of him? He's quite the pariah."

The Chancellor looked at his secretary with an incredulous expression.

"No clan?" He flipped through the pages in his hand. "But it says here that he's also won the Gold Medal in Science. *And* the Creative Achievement Award. That's difficult to do without family support."

"I know, sir. I could make no mistakes with this one. He's the one who redesigned all the microscopes and modified our drug extraction techniques to make them three times as efficient. He's put us ahead about ten years."

Microscopes? thought Antronos. He suddenly couldn't breathe.

"I see. So just the one name, then?"

"Yes, sir."

The Chancellor turned back to the assembly and cleared his throat. The delay had started up some speculative discussion which was quickly hushed.

"This is the winner of the Royal Award in Science, special recipient of My Lord Jait's approval. This is the winner of the Gold Medal in Science, and the Creative Achievement Award.

"Antronos," called the Chancellor. "Come receive your degree. We hereby give you the right to practise medicine and bear the title 'Sen.'"

Caught between the urge to run out the door or just hide, Antronos felt dazed as he finally decided to move towards the dais stairs. The Chancellor looked around the dim hall expectantly, then took a step back, the expression of horror on his face growing as Antronos moved forward into the light. He imagined how he must seem as he towered over the Chancellor and pushed his hood back, progressively revealing his purple eyes, angular features and long, frizzy, yellow hair. He self-consciously tugged the edge of his robe over the scales at the base of his neck.

Perhaps this was a mistake. Humiliating the Chancellor like this would probably ensure no Sen would ever give him a research position. The Chancellor pulled his mouth shut and forced a smile.

Antronos steepled his fingers and bowed to the Chancellor, who speechlessly handed over the parchment and accompanying awards. *Well, at least I'm holding my degree*, thought Antronos, while he waited for the command that he be arrested. *Itya, this is for you.*

"Congratulations, Sen Antronos!" cried the Chancellor. "Never in all my years as administrator of this university have I come across a graduate with such potential. The entire academic community will benefit from your contributions to microscopy and drug extraction. Well done."

"You honour me, Sen Amphetam," Antronos replied, startled.

The Chancellor shook a finger at him while turning to address the people around him. "You see this boy here? Here's a prime example of what I've been fighting for all week! You've chosen *real* science, haven't you, Antronos? You're not out in the Desert practising blood rituals, are you?"

"No, Sen!" *Earth, this is worse than refusal!* Antronos thought his face was going to burn off at any second.

"You see?" the Chancellor demanded. "This is a good step towards the changes we need to make. What will you do now, Antronos? Will you start a clinical practice? Can I offer you a professorship?"

Antronos swallowed hard, and took a second to force control over his wobbly legs and dizzy mind that were threatening to make him collapse.

"No, Sen. I thank you sincerely, but I, uh, wish to pursue a graduate degree."

"Very good! Very good!" The Chancellor, mesmerized, shook Antronos' hand enthusiastically and didn't let go. "What project are you planning to undertake?"

"I intend to control death," said Antronos, then grimaced. He realized how arrogant that sounded as the words came out of his mouth, and that there was a huge difference between what it was safe to think, and what it was safe to say. He hadn't meant to speak so plainly. The Chancellor merely stared at him and blinked a few times. "Or at least delay it." Antronos shrugged apologetically.

The Chancellor guffawed, and after a moment said, "Good luck to you, Sen. I will be watching your career with great interest."

✳✳✳✳✳

Control death. Antronos had hated death ever since it had abandoned him in the Desert seven years ago. Perhaps it was an allegorical comparison, but he intended to be different in every way possible from the tattered skeleton of a man who had taken his mother from him. Medicine had seemed the perfect way to exact revenge on death.

Still shaken, still waiting for the Chancellor to come after him and explain that his praise on the dais had just been for show and the parchments would now have to be returned, Antronos left the convocation hall, avoiding the other graduates who were collecting outside for the requisite party, feeling like they watched his every stride as he moved past them.

"Not joining us, Sen?"

Antronos looked up to see one of the other graduates blocking his way, feet placed in a wide stance, fluted wine glass in one hand. He was unsettled to realize that most of the others *were* staring at him.

"You don't say much, do you? Did I hear correctly that you had taken a professorship? That would make you my superior then, wouldn't it?"

Antronos licked his lips and shifted uneasily, trying to hide his certificates under his arm. "No, I didn't take it."

"Didn't take it! That doesn't make any sense! What's the matter? It didn't pay enough? Didn't leave enough time for your *research*?"

Someone muttered, "He has a forked tongue. Did you see it just now?" Antronos' head snapped around, but he couldn't tell who had spoken. That was one defect he did *not* have. The small group that had edged up to him snickered and backed off in mock alarm.

"I have work to do. Get out of my way." Antronos shouldered his way through. He was taller than any of them, and although slender, his years of manual labour and defending himself on the docks had made him more than a match for a group of spongy academics. Someone grabbed his elbow from behind, and he barely recovered from a motion that would have raised his fist as he recognized the Chancellor smiling up at him.

"Come, please, Sen! You must at least let me show you off a little." The Chancellor pulled Antronos back into the centre of the party, obviously trying to dispel any bad feelings the other graduates might have stirred up and show himself as being unprejudiced. "We're so pleased to have new blood at the university. Really. Are you certain you won't reconsider the professorship?"

"I'm certain, Sen Amphetam. I'm not finished with my studies. It's hardly right that I should teach." *Or that anyone would respect a surface creature as a teacher.*

The Chancellor clucked his tongue. "Nonsense. None of us is ever done studying. Will you at least consider holding a professorship after your graduate degree? I can arrange that right now. Perhaps set you up in an office just for starters?"

Antronos finally smiled and shook his head. "You are determined to give me more than I deserve, Sen."

"I think I know raw talent when I see it." The Chancellor was looking around for someone to make introductions with. He caught Alaindra's eye, hesitated, then pushed towards her. Antronos did his best not to resist, thinking that the Chancellor did not want to seem foolish by having the other faculty completely ignore his efforts, and so was heading for the first receptive person. Alaindra immediately put on her most glamorous posture and smiled engagingly. *She couldn't possibly remember me.*

"Lady Alain, I would like to present Sen Antronos to you," said the Chancellor.

Alaindra held out her fingertips again, which Antronos automatically took and brushed with his lips. She sidled close to him, and pressed against his arm, her raven curls curling over the curves of her...Antronos pulled his eyes upward, seeing that she hadn't missed the flush that rose from his neck. Or the scales.

"What a shame that you didn't win one of *my* awards. The Chancellor wouldn't let me choose. I think you would have made a very interesting recipient. Perhaps I can tempt you with an offer to be my personal physician instead?"

Antronos took a step backwards and tried to mask his irritation. There was more than one way to make fun of the local freak, and he resented Alaindra acting like he was not to be taken seriously. No woman of her status would stoop to dallying with a former surface dweller, and she obviously didn't realize he knew what a cheat she was.

"I'm afraid I've already made other commitments, Madam."

Antronos noted the subtle change in her face, and his eyes picked up the sudden organization of her aura into pulsating straight lines, betraying the iron control behind the relaxed façade.

"I'm quite serious," she said. "And I can be very persuasive."

"Persuasion by cheap, bawdy promises and money," somebody muttered. The Chancellor must have thought this was an opportunity to rescue Antronos, since he shoved an arm between him and Alaindra, bodily twisting Antronos away from her.

"May I present Sen Antronos," said the Chancellor to the mutterer. "This is Sen Vernus," he said to Antronos. "He's one of the Professor Emeriti."

"I am honoured to meet you, Sen Vernus." Antronos made a slight bow to what looked like a hooded pile of green and black rags shuffling past. *The colours of Desert magic!* His interest flared as he tried to peer into the Emeritus' face without seeming rude. A wrinkled hand reached out to poke him in the arm. The aura surrounding it was strange: nebulous and diffuse, yet too strong to be inanimate.

"This is the surface boy? Well, maybe he should be a geologist. Or an archaeologist. Since he knows so much about digging through sand." Vernus turned away and continued shuffling. With an appalled look on his face, the Chancellor cast about for someone else.

"This is Sen Opalena," he said, grabbing a woman by the arm and dragging her forward. "She is Vernus' research fellow, and was the last recipient of the Royal Award in Science."

Antronos smiled and bowed again. Sulky grey eyes stared back at him. Silvery-blonde hair fell straight down, perfectly complimented by the silver-gold gown. Skin so pale it was almost white. If he hadn't known better, he would have thought she was from the surface, judging from her pale colouring and the angles of her face.

"I'm honoured," he said.

"I'm not." Opalena ripped her arm free and walked off. As she moved towards an exit, she passed by the Chair of Hekka, where My Lord Jait sat. He tried to reach under the panels of her dress. She irritably smacked his hand away and kept going. Antronos gawped in disbelief. Jait did nothing but stare after her for a few seconds before returning his interest to his drink. *Would it be rude to ask after the High Prince's health?* Antronos wondered. He was about to open his mouth when the Yrati woman who had been doused with Tibeau's water trick yesterday, came forward and knelt before Jait, gently pulling at the glass in his hand and offering him something else. *At least someone seems to care.*

"Uh..." The Chancellor was looking around again. The light surrounding him swirled in agitation and uncertainty.

"Thank you for your efforts, Sen Amphetam. I do appreciate your acceptance of me," said Antronos. "But I think most people are tired, as I am. I would really like to rest."

The Chancellor sighed and smiled apologetically. "Things will change," he said. "I do hope you will not take offence. We need new scholars and the more diverse their background, the more they have to offer to the university. I must insist that people see the necessity of change. Everyone suffers when one caste or another is excluded from an academic society. There are talents there that are left untapped because of these prejudices. Pushing you out just encourages you to return to belief in—well, that is, I didn't mean—" The Chancellor blushed.

"No offence taken. In fact, your friendship encourages me greatly."

That last statement saw the tension drain from the Chancellor's face, making his smile more apparent.

"I *will* find you an office," he said.

3

Incense

The muttered words emitted from Sen Vernus' desiccated lips took on barely perceptible forms of insects that buzzed around his hands, which were placed on either side of his patient-donor's head. They settled in the man's ears, suggesting to him that he lie still, that he ignore the pain of his abdomen being sliced open, that he not protest the removal of his liver, or the rush of his blood as it filled his body cavity and spilled down through the grate on the floor of the unlit cavern. The man twitched a few times, resisting the suggestion, which had to be reinforced with various pharmaceuticals. Vernus' mouth smiled beneath the dark swath of cloth he had wrapped around his eyes to prevent his ocular senses from interfering with his perception of the Desert's power. He carried the extracted liver across the room to where his patient-acceptor lay in a bed of sand waiting to receive this gift, having already donated cash in advance, and sworn to absolute secrecy. This patient was also instructed to be silent as the new organ was placed on top of the old, and deftly stitched into place.

Vernus called on the whimsy of the Desert to force this new organ to change, to stretch and mix itself with the man it was being grafted into. The liver writhed and snaked a series of vessels into the tissue beneath it, accepting its current host's blood. This tactic was working well. Satisfied, Vernus recorded the procedure in his private laboratory journal, intending to compare his new method to earlier records, confirming his theory as to why the first few attempts had failed. It was done. The patient-acceptor's body was sealed, and his mind overlaid with a curse to make sure he never felt the need to speak of his surgery to anyone. Vernus never trusted sworn affidavits anyway. His spoken insects crawled into the patient's ears, telling him to awaken in a few hours. The newly dead patient-donor was dumped into a hole dug through the tiles at the far end of the chamber, where he slowly sunk into the edge of the Desert that stretched beneath this part of the private clinic. Vernus left the chamber and shuffled back to his paperwork.

✳✳✳✳✳

In the dim office, the parchment trembled. It was dropped momentarily on the desktop, before being scooped up again and rattled angrily. The words on it did not change their meaning. Sen Vernus fell into his chair in disbelief and looked at the words once more.

He was to vacate his office.

A few undergraduates appeared in the hallway outside his open door and peered into the gloom.

"Sen Vernus? We're here about last week's exam." They shifted nervously, unable to see him in the dark.

Boil off! Blind mewlings who need light to see!

"Is he even in there?" he heard them whisper.

Vernus did not move from behind his desk. He glared at the students shuffling tentatively towards his portal, feeling his irritation rise up in a wave which suddenly slammed the door shut in their faces. He muttered curses at them, at their mothers, and at the evening light that silhouetted their annoying, prying figures. The skylight in the hallway imploded from his anger, raining shattered glass and surface sand over the students. He heard them cry out in alarm and run off.

The scissors lying at the far edge of his desk spun across the wooden surface and thumped into his waiting hand. Without bothering to open the blades, he thrust them through the paper, shredding it. The tattered remains burst into green flames, illuminating his gnarled knuckles.

Antronos. Surface dung hauled into the tunnels. What is he? Nothing! Nothing but dried dung dug up from the sand. Does Amphetam really think this baby is going to bring more prestige to the university than me? Amphetam, who knows so much about science. Amphetam, who thinks that not believing in the old ways makes him some kind of enlightened scholar. He clamps his eyes shut and thinks that what he cannot see does not exist. Pompous, arrogant little...He thinks I am some feeble-minded old man who cannot respond when things are taken away from me and given to surface dung. Surface dung that won't even teach! What does surface-dung-baby need an office for if he won't teach? Uglier than I am, and Alain likes to roll herself against dung-boy like a mud-swine in heat.

Amphetam's message destroyed, Vernus crept around in the dark, sketching symbols that Amphetam knew nothing about and would never be able to see, on the floor, on the walls, on the desk, and on the shelves of his bookcase, with a stick of clear, oily wax that sank into the wood and porous rock. He muttered to himself as he went along, sprinkling powders onto the symbols and smudging them in with his foot to seal each curse as he finished drawing it. More than just an empty office would be waiting for the surface-boy.

Now using white wax, Vernus drew a pentagram on the floor, and flipping his robes aside, seated himself in it. He turned his hooded face towards his bookcase, blindly scanning the tomes shoved haphazardly among specimen jars, crucibles and the odd mandible.

The books he wanted fell off the shelves and spun across the floor, partially smudging the wax and violently flipping open to specified places. How lazy he had been. Complacent. He had been theorizing about extending the reach of his mind-control magic without bringing any of his modified incantations into practice. When the development of his new magic was complete, he would no longer require physical contact or intense familiarity with his intended victim in order to invade a mind. He would overcome the limitations put on him by the physical gap between himself and his target. Amphetam and his new baby were going to find out just how real the old ways were, and how defenceless their "science" was in the face of magic. This disrespect for true power would no longer be tolerated.

Vernus muttered to himself as he scanned the pages. Most of what was written there he already knew; some of it he had written himself. New symbols that he had crafted from the background information in his texts had been waiting for far too long to have their strength tested. He angrily inscribed these along the edges of his pentagram in red wax, closed his eyes and shoved a dried mushroom between what was left of his teeth. As he chewed and softened it, his awareness of what was around him heightened and folded out over the floor of his office, sweeping up the walls and beyond. He began to chant. And his mind reached . . .

Antronos was still too unfamiliar. He did not know what subtleties of consciousness would distinguish surface-boy from the rest of the mindless cretins he encountered, as his awareness roamed through the university's ancient halls. His vision was not clear. He began to panic, doubting himself. Why was this magic not working? It should! A painful sensation was beginning to build up along the left side of his head. Still angry, Vernus pulled back into his body and stared at the offending rune scrawled on the left side of his pentagram. He calmed down a bit, rubbed out one line, then another, and after a moment's thought, drew a squiggle across the entire shape.

This time Vernus extended himself more slowly, giving himself time to learn, reaching for familiar minds and using them as beacons. One of them might have seen the snake-eyed boy pass by.

He found one of his research fellows, Sephus, who was an easy mark, and forced his way into the other man's mind. He felt the instant hardening of thoughts into a cold void in an attempt at privacy. Sephus never showed his hatred for Vernus openly, but it was always there, steeped in futility, right below the surface, and no, he had not seen Antronos.

Irritated by Sephus' subtle disobedience, Vernus coiled another restraint around the part of his assistant's mind that wished rebellion, intensifying the pain that would be felt if he made another of his pathetic attempts at freedom, then left him and found Opalena. Fluttering her mind open had always been easy, but then, she didn't have as many years of practice as Sephus in attempting to defend her privacy. He felt her weary resentment and disgust at his presence, then sudden, sharp alarm as she felt her own hand crawl across her stomach against her will. Back in his office, Vernus crowed with glee. As he had predicted, the new runes were not only allowing him to enter and place suggestions in someone else's mind, he could also directly control particular movements, bypassing his victim's consciousness altogether. But his control was *still* not absolute. Opalena fought him. He became angry again, realizing that he needed to give the runes more power before he could control someone else's body entirely.

The pain was building up once more on his left side. He ignored it and used the force of his anger to move Opalena again. She resisted sliding her hand across her body with growing fear. By the Earth! He wasn't trying to molest her. She was much weaker than Sephus, and eventually gave in. Her relief was partial as she realized that she was reaching past her body, and for the set of scalpels on the tray next to her workstation.

Carrying the surgical instruments, she was willed to Vernus' office. As he made her walk, he could feel her resist him enough to force her step over the broken panes left in the hallway, until through her eyes, he could see the outline of his door form in the dusky light; carved, brown wood, cracked, worn and lined with age. Dust eddied up from the sweep of her dress hem, gritting between the bottoms of her sandals and feet, and she still moved forward, fighting to stop and brush her toes, yet completely unable to do anything but approach the door. He felt her heart pound as she wondered who and what the scalpels were for.

No, she really wasn't as self-controlled as Sephus.

The door opened, and she walked through, unable to see anything now. Vernus guided her to the far point of the pentagram and seated her roughly opposite from him. He could hear his own muttering through her ears. He paused.

"You will stay where I have put you." He reached out to touch her arm, and through that strengthened connection, locked down the part of her mind that was trying to resist. Opalena would obey.

Vernus left Opalena's mind and expanded his own, reaching out in an easy and familiar direction this time, feeling the welcoming sweep of arousal as he touched the mind of his lover, Meriamdan, who was roaming out on the surface, wilfully mixing her soul with the Desert and hunting for pleasure. He called her, and she responded swiftly, coming down through the tunnels like a phantom. He felt her hesitate at the edge of the tunnel which led to one of the main tributaries, long enough to let her ancient legs unfold and touch the ground, adjusting to the weight of her body resting on them. In this environment of non-belief that Amphetam had synthesized, allowing someone to see her floating like that would lead to unwelcome attention, and prying into research he wished to keep secret until he was truly ready. Her knees ached, she griped, and Vernus loved her for it.

He could see through her eyes, now, watching the hallways move past unsteadily, her head jerking around to look at groups of leery students and professors as her antique limbs carried her past. They accommodatingly moved out of her way.

Meriamdan's feet crackled insensate over the broken glass as she approached his office, and she cocked her head to gaze at the door with a brief flicker of amusement. Vernus felt her sense that he had made it slam in anger. She raised her feet up into the folds of her black robes that were edged with green, and laughed as she pushed aside the door and floated inside. She did not sit, but remained hovering next to him in the darkness. All he could see of her was a faint glint of white where her left eye was clouded by cataract, and the fuzzy, yellow tangle of her hair. As ever, Vernus was amazed by her talent.

"And now what?" she asked. "Have you found a way to touch, not just look?"

Opalena shuddered.

"Yes," Vernus replied. "But I need stronger runes. They still allow resistance."

Meriamdan laughed again and drifted to the floor behind Opalena.

"Easily done," she said.

She took up the chant she had helped Vernus compose over the last few years, allowing him to use the sound as an anchor as he reached out with his mind once more. He watched greedily as Meriamdan reached forward and tore a scalpel out of Opalena's grasp, flipping it and dragging the blade across the soft flesh inside the younger woman's elbow. He felt a giddy rush as Opalena's strength spilled out with her blood in a shimmering wave to fuel the power of his pentagram. The new symbols were working even better now. They freed him from his body in a tidal rush. He surged upwards, out of his office, into the hallways, into the cafeteria, through the concourse, across the convocation hall. He soared with elation. He was going to make Sephus *dance*!

Opalena faltered and slumped forward in the pentagram, greatly weakened from the unexpected draining. Vernus lost control of his flight. He was tumbling randomly, slowly being pulled back into his corporeal form. *Too soon! Not enough time! I have not had the chance to finish my experiment!* He angrily reached out as he roiled along, trying to force his spirit into the body of anyone nearby, to finally invade a stranger without first having a chance to become familiar with his victim's mind.

One student flinched at his first attempt, shoving him off. The second fainted, leaving him nothing coherent to hang on to. *Damn, Opalena is too weak!* If he just had more power, he should be able to invade and possess anyone.

Sephus walked by. Vernus grasped his mind and drew strength from it. This was familiar territory, and he already knew the handholds that would prevent his being shaken off. He laughed venomously as he wormed his way in, drawing on the very last of Opalena's strength to not only enter Sephus' mind, but to finally force his assistant's spirit aside to make space for his own.

He reeled forwards at the sudden lack of resistance. The airy sensation of being a free spirit was gone. The pull of the pentagram was gone. Confused, he whirled around, and saw a few other professors looking at him curiously. A group of students was also standing around him, looking worried and expectant. Sen Amphetam broke away from his own students and moved towards him.

"Sen Sephus?" Amphetam inquired. "Are you all right?"

Vernus lifted his hands and saw the smooth, white, young skin of Sephus' arms extending from black sleeves. He pushed a fistful of dark hair out of his face.

"Sen Sephus, we have another class after this," one of the students said impatiently.

Vernus grinned. He had done it. His runes worked and he had made the jump. Despite Meriamdan's confidence, this was beyond his expectations. He was *in* Sephus *entirely* and the people around him didn't know. They couldn't tell. He laughed out loud.

"It's not funny," the student persisted.

"Of course, my dear," said Vernus. "What was it you wanted?" He turned to Amphetam. "Yes, Sen, I'm fine now. Thank you." Amphetam nodded and moved away.

"My exam," said the student. She did a double-take when he turned to face her, and moved back a step.

Vernus smirked as he shuffled through Sephus' case and dug out what must have been graded exam papers. He gave them to the students and let them pick out which were theirs. The student who had pestered him watched him strangely, but said nothing.

Making his way back to his office, he marvelled at how little Sephus' joints ached as he moved. He ran and jumped over huddles of students sitting cross-legged on the floor of the hallways, laughing at their reactions. Flinging open the door to his office, he grinned and opened his arms to Meriamdan.

"Here I am!" he bawled.

Meriamdan's hovering form shot through the office towards him. She slapped him across the face.

"I thought you were dead!" she hissed. "Look! Look at yourself!"

Vernus leaned over his body and felt for a pulse. It was there, faintly, but he supposed it would have been undetectable under Meriamdan's callused fingertips.

The brief contact was enough to end his inhabitation of Sephus, and pull him back into his own body. He inhaled deeply, feeling as though he had been asleep. Looking up, he saw Sephus recoil and raise his fist. As Sephus' hand came down, Vernus released a bolt of energy that smashed his research assistant against the bookshelves at the other end of his office. Sephus didn't get up.

"Never mind that now," said Meriamdan. She shoved Opalena out of the way and dragged Sephus by his pant leg into the pentagram. "Try another. Try . . ." She paused to think, muttering to herself. She seemed to be enjoying the possibilities.

It *was* fun, thought Vernus. He had quite enjoyed his run in Sephus' body.

"I want Amphetam," he said. "He's been gradually forcing me out for years. I want to show him who is really in control of this university, and that he can't get away with such disrespect."

"Whatever for? Try Jait."

"Jait!"

"Why not?"

Meriamdan drew a scalpel across Sephus' ankle vein, then began the chant. Vernus felt tired, but was also curious if he really could disguise himself within the High Prince. He soared out of his body again, and somewhat awkwardly, tumbled towards the Royal House. He went more slowly this time, hoping to conserve Sephus' strength.

Jait was familiar enough to him. He had met the High Prince several times, and had even attended the Queen towards the end of her life. He found Jait in the High Prince's private chambers sitting on a pile of cushions, smoking a white and blue enamel water pipe, which ironically, Vernus had given to the Queen to ease her pain. Jait was inhaling deeply and rapidly, not bothering to remove his lips from the pipe to exhale. It was just as well, thought Vernus. He'd never find the mouthpiece again through all that hair hanging over his face.

He reached into Jait's mind tentatively. It was not like Sephus'. There was no order, no logic, no consciousness—it was like reaching into a bowl of pudding. He doubted Jait was at all aware of his presence. He tried to move into the High Prince, and as he did, he was amazed by the sudden recognition of an immense psychic power within Jait's spirit. At his best estimate, Jait was probably more than his equal; in fact, he was probably one of the most powerful wizards born into the Earth in the last generation. Why then did the man never use his magic?

Just as he was about to get a feel for the extent of Jait's complete power, Vernus moved out the other side of the High Prince's body. Confused, he moved back in—and out again. There was absolutely nothing to hang on to. He slapped irritably at the pipe, which had no effect.

Discouraged, he followed the sound of Meriamdan's chant back to his office, and slipped into his body.

"And?" she asked.

"Nothing! His mind is jelly!"

"Never mind. He's a puppet anyway. There's no real advantage to Jait. Try Dra."

Vernus' eyes narrowed suspiciously. "Why?" he asked.

"You know why! Those meddlers had me thrown out of House of Dan. I was an elder in the Family. Those outsiders had no right to interfere in my studies. Who are *they* to condemn *me* as being immoral? And what of it if I commune with the Desert? Who do they think they are, expecting *me* to answer to *them*?"

Vernus declined to point out that the Houses of Dan and Dra were intermarried to the point of inbreeding. And there was an advantage to taking Dra, he mused. They had real political leverage. He had not missed Amphetam's plea to Alaindra during the convocation, and as he had never touched Alaindra, or ever looked into her mind, this would be a real test. He allowed himself to be carried upwards by the force of Meriamdan's anger. This time, she had drawn the blade over her own wrist.

Vernus writhed towards the Lady Alain, guided solely by his visual impression of her, and was gratified to find that if he proceeded calmly and with great discipline, his runes were indeed able to let him approach a virtual stranger. He saw that she sat at her accounting tablets in the House of Dra, flanked by candles, plumed pen in ring-encrusted hand, eyes staring into space, ink drying on the nib. He aligned his spirit along the pulse of her aura, letting himself settle like dust along Alaindra's robes of pale blue and white, slowly becoming enmeshed with the thoughts she radiated. *My magic works!* He laughed as he felt her body yearn for some life renewing sensual stretch that would make it change, push it out of its current quiescent state, from rosebud to blossom. *So she wishes for a lover, does she? Well, I am here.*

Alaindra sighed, and Vernus felt her think of tradition, which had selected for her an entirely inappropriate husband, and she wondered pointlessly why the House of Dan had been so inconsiderate in the timing of their breeding. Of course it had nothing to do with any type of consideration of her feelings. Dan quite simply did whatever pleased them. Vernus coiled himself into her mind entirely, and settled down to listen further to her thoughts.

Alaindra leaned back in her chair, arms folded over her head, and dreamt of lapis lazuli and luxury, pitying herself that she did not find adultery more appealing. As her gaze lingered upon her gilded tapestries and the chalky patterns cut into the cavern walls, her fancy was caught by the shadows in the moonbeam, cast from the dust swirling over the panes of her skylight. It lulled her, and she imagined she saw women dancing in a ring, with broods of little children, singing, dancing, jumping at their feet. A single woman squatted in a circle of little children who sang and danced at her feet. The scene snapped into focus, and a crumpled old man sat in a circle with a half-beast that howled and swayed, and chanted to a beat.

Alaindra gasped and bolted upright, upsetting the inkwell at her wrist and sending Vernus tumbling from her mind. Despite his disembodied form, he felt pain radiate from where his shoulder should have been, up to where he imagined his left temple was. He fought against it and the pull of the pentagram that was threatening to snap him back into his body. Managing to stop the force of his backward motion, he clawed towards Alaindra, seeing her slowly twist in her chair to look over her shoulder. She screamed as Vernus lunged, and almost succeeded in clawing him away, as Vernus unexpectedly experienced his own invasion into her head. He felt something like icicles being shoved painfully through Alaindra's skull, bending her will, twisting her spirit . . .

"No!" she shouted, and shoved all irrelevant thought from her mind. Vernus felt something shatter. He opened his eyes. He sat at the edge of his pentagram, unhurt, but empty and powerless. He shuffled over to Meriamdan, scooped her from the floor and cradled her until she woke.

"Your runes are good," she said. "But we have little strength. You need to resolve this."

She slumped back to sleep, leaving Vernus to think. Jait had the strange combination of power combined with a weak mind. He could be controlled. Perhaps the High Prince was a worthwhile target after all. If Vernus was going to relinquish his professorship, then maybe it would be for a life in the Royal House.

Opalena knocked on the doorframe of Sen Amphetam's office and did not miss the weary disapproval in his glance when he looked up, or the way his eyes flicked over her clothing. She looked down at herself and suddenly felt foolish at how revealing her gown was. Feeling worthless, and insignificant in the light of Vernus' ever-increasing domination, she had chosen it almost as a disguise, realizing just now that not everyone would equate glamour with value.

"Forgive me, Sen," she said, lowering her head and feeling her face burn.

Sen Amphetam now seemed more embarrassed than she was, and waved her into the office.

"Never mind that, Sen Opalena. Please come in. Sit down."

She sat next to the Chancellor's desk and drew a deep breath. Would Amphetam believe her story of what Vernus had done to her last night? Meriamdan had made sure the cut in the fold of her elbow now looked like nothing more than an angry welt. Opalena's mind was bound so that she could not speak of Vernus' psychic invasions, but he had either forgotten or not bothered to block her from saying that she had been cut and bled. Despite Amphetam's apparent dislike for Vernus, it would still be prudent to be careful, she thought to herself.

"I noticed you have asked Sen Vernus to leave," she began.

"I've just informed him that his office space is to be reassigned. He'll still have his laboratory space. That's quite generous, I think, since with most Emeriti, the progressive losses are reversed—lab first, then office."

"Oh, I didn't realize that." Opalena hesitated, again questioning the wisdom of having come here. She had thought Amphetam might be the one to get rid of Vernus completely.

"Were you worried that you would not be able to finish your fellowship? I did take that into consideration. It's one of the reasons why the lab space was retained."

Opalena was about to throw away all caution and tell Amphetam, *I don't want to finish my fellowship*, when a sudden piercing sensation behind her eyes made her reel forwards. She gasped and shuddered uncontrollably, as her mind was shoved aside by an invading Meriamdan.

Amphetam grasped her arms and looked into her face with concern.

"Are you all right?" he asked. "Is there some sickness going around? It seems your colleague Sen Sephus had a similar spell yesterday."

Opalena felt herself raise her head and smile. She struggled against the involuntary movement, to somehow signal to Amphetam to be circumspect with his words. He must *not* confide anything to Meriamdan.

"I'm sorry," Opalena heard herself say. "It was just a brief lapse. What were we talking of?"

"I was just reassuring you that you would be able to finish your fellowship. Are you certain that you're all right?"

"Yes, quite," she snapped. Amphetam looked at her strangely. He withdrew his hands and sat back, leaning away from her.

"Well, then. Is there anything else?"

"No. I thank you for your assurances. And I want you to know that you're making a mistake if you think that this eviction of Sen Vernus will make your life any easier. You might be Chancellor, but you are not the best scientist in this community. It would not take much to undermine your judgment in this matter."

Amphetam's face hardened, and any concern he may have had for her disappeared from his eyes. Opalena struggled to make Meriamdan shut up, or at least stop being so rude. She desperately willed Amphetam to notice the changes in her, and to realize that he was speaking to someone else. She would never speak so disrespectfully to him. Could he not see that? He had to be her ally, he had to . . .

"Well, you seem to have regained your self-confidence. I think this conversation is over." He turned back to his papers and ignored her. Meriamdan forced her to leave the office.

The walk back to Vernus' labs was painful. Opalena continually struggled for control. Each time she succeeded in voluntarily moving a finger, or a toe, Meriamdan would smash that digit against the rough stone walls of the back tunnels. The pain made her release her control over that small part of her body. She hoped that someone would come along and see her ridiculous gait, somehow stilted and stiff like Meriamdan's, or at the very least, see her bloodied hands and try to help her.

I can take you at anytime. Your mind is completely known to us now. It's very easy. Meriamdan made her push open the lab door and walk in. She then was forced to walk up to a grinning Vernus and kiss him full on the mouth. Opalena retched so vehemently that Meriamdan had to stop. She laughed through Opalena's teeth.

So my pretty, too beautiful for us? Meriamdan made her pick up a stock bottle of concentrated acid. *We can change that, you know.* The acid sloshed over her arm.

Opalena screamed. As Meriamdan released her, the acid bottle slipped from her hand and shattered at her feet. Opalena screamed again and ran for the safety shower to wash off the splashed acid.

When the burning had mostly dulled to a nagging itch, Opalena turned off the shower and pushed sopping hair out of her face. The skin on her arm was the most severely damaged. It was an angry red and looked like melted wax had been dripped over her arm. Her legs and feet were only red and would probably heal without scarring. Vernus was standing a few feet away, his black eyes boring into her, a hint of a smug smile touching his narrow lips.

"I'll expect you to mop up this mess," he said, then stepped forward and grasped her by the chin. "And the next time you pull a stunt like that, the acid will be on your pretty, pretty face. There'll be no more running to Amphetam or anyone else to tell your little tales to. Your excitement rings like an alarm in my head. I'll always know when you're making mischief. Get yourself cleaned up. You're going to the Royal House." Vernus let go of her and walked away.

"What? Why?" Despite her loathing, Opalena stepped out of the shower and ran after him.

"Jait's son is looking to find his father a private physician. Apparently the old Prince is even worse off than when we last saw him. You'll go, and make sure you're hired. I don't care how. Just make sure it happens. You'll have a good chance. The old Prince took a liking to you at the convocation, didn't he?"

Opalena stopped suddenly. A sinking feeling in her gut told her she was about to ruin Amphetam's opinion of her even more.

"I don't think he'd find *me* very pretty, hey?" continued Vernus. "But once you're in, you'll find you need to bring me along for consultation on some of the more complicated aspects of Jait's care."

"Why don't you just go yourself?"

Vernus laughed. "As I said, I'm not very pretty. And young Prince Liam seems to hold me partly responsible for his mother's death."

"Were you?"

Vernus turned and regarded her with apparent mildness.

"Hardly," he said. "Once you've gained My Lord Jait's trust, you might ask *him* about that."

*****

The tunnel that led to the Royal House grew more impressive the closer one got to the main gates. The ceilings were vaulted here, cut right to the surface thirty metres overhead and set with angled glass panes, delicately frosted in such a way that the light from the early sunset sparkled as it decorated the white hallway pillars with its myriad colours. The tiles became increasingly elaborate as well, and were set in a gradient of colour, so that they seemed to evolve from the dusky red brick of the common tunnels into shimmering white marble. Large air vents that opened out onto the surface, rather than the river-cooled Market Caverns, increased the impression of openness, not having the dank, slightly metallic tang to it that most other caverns had.

Opalena walked down the main pathway of white tiles embossed with concentric diamond shapes. On either side of her, the walkway was framed by raised tiles with scenes of historic battles cut into them. Periodically, these were interrupted by full scale carvings of soldiers and mythical beasts that appeared to be climbing out of the ground. There were also terraced fountains that began at the skylights, and blurbled over shelves of shiny, pink stones, finally filling pools housing several white blindfish, their pale tentacles and plumed fins feeling and exploring their limited world. Several metres ahead of her were the massive carved gates that demarcated the entry into the Royal House proper.

Trying to keep a grip on her anxiety, she passed by several clusters of arguing politicians, grateful that none of them spared her a second glance. She was intimidated by being so close to these great men, even though she had deliberately worn modest clothing—her scholar's robes, in fact. She hoped that she could go back and tell Vernus that despite her best efforts, she had not been chosen. If she were to get this position, it would be on her merits as a doctor, and not because yet another person wanted to use her for something else. The memory of Jait sliding his hand under her skirt filled her with anger, and that she had actually struck his hand away made her feel almost sick with terror at meeting him again.

The palace guards took one look at her robes, and didn't bother asking for a pass. Inside the main foyer, she was relieved to see a long queue of applicants for the position already ahead of her. She slipped into the end of the line, taking solace that the man in front of her was very tall, and she could hide behind him for a few moments. She shut her eyes, trying to get her heart to slow down, and to control her breathing.

"Are you well?" someone asked.

Opalena opened her eyes and looked up. *Oh, wonderful,* she thought. The diamond-pupiled eyes of the snake-boy Antronos looked down at her. He would have to be the one she was hiding behind. She hoped he didn't expect to have a conversation.

"Fine."

She watched him eye her robes speculatively. Surprising herself, she did not become angry, but rather resigned as she realized what a mistake she had made with her clothing choices over the last few months. It was partly responsible for where she was now, and had hurt her credibility, something she hadn't realized was so important.

"Is this your second interview?" he asked.

"No. Do I need to have two?"

"Well, if they're interested, they ask you to come back. They don't take you right away."

"Oh."

"I can coach you on the questions they asked me in the first interview," he offered.

Opalena had to shut her eyes and take a deep breath to prevent herself from screaming. The bandages under her fitted grey sleeve were chaffing and burning relentlessly. She had tried to get away from Vernus and now Amphetam hated her. Her blood had been used in magical black rituals and her attempt to report it had ended in further abuse. Her mind and body had just been violated by Meriamdan. She was on her way to be the High Prince's slut. Antronos was insisting on chattering at her because he thought she was easy. Her head was about to explode.

"Look, I know you're being nice," she managed, "but I would prefer it if you would leave me alone."

Antronos turned away without saying anything more. Still, as they waited, Opalena caught him stealing the occasional glance over his shoulder with something like awe in his expression. *Men!*

He wouldn't look at me that way if he knew, she thought bitterly.

It took an hour for the line to finally creep into the next antechamber. Opalena saw that most of the applicants were being screened by secretaries, who had desks stationed just outside one of the main conference chambers. The secretaries were flipping through sheaves of papers as they talked, presumably transcripts forwarded from the university, then handing an applicant some parchment. These applicants left with disappointed looks on their faces. She recognized more than one of her former classmates. She looked down as they passed by, to avoid speaking to them. Some of the applicants, when they came to the head of the line, were ushered into the conference room: Antronos was one of them. Shortly after, she followed him.

The conference room was somewhat more practical than the outer chambers. The far wall was covered by plain red drapes, and the sides of the room had desks and shelves cut into them instead of elaborate reliefs. Opalena sucked in a nervous breath. My Lord Jait was sitting at the back of the room, seemingly sober, and watching his sons conduct the interviews. She put her head down, hoping that if he did notice her, he wouldn't remember her. After all, he had been drunk the last time she had seen him.

It seemed that Antronos was being selected from the queue. The High Prince's younger son, Liam, was shaking his hand, actually leaning forward as he did so. His expression conveyed nothing but respect. Opalena felt an envious respect for Antronos herself: he was an obvious freak, yet his burgeoning reputation overwhelmed his surface traits. And, she was relieved that the position was already filled, without her even getting a first interview. What could Vernus possibly expect her to do?

My Lord Jait had pushed himself up from his chair and was sauntering over to Antronos and Liam. Opalena noticed that he was palsied and very thin. It was no wonder that his son seemed so eager to get his father some proper medical care. Prince Liam was introducing Jait to Antronos, who steepled his fingers and bowed deeply to the High Prince. Jait nodded to him, then turned away and walked past, staring at some point off in the distance. He stopped next to Opalena, not looking at her. She suddenly became aware of her pulse hammering away in her throat. She hung her head, hoping he would continue on. From the corner of her vision, she could see his arm, the embroidered sleeve carelessly pushed up to the elbow, his hand in his pocket, the dark hair falling to his waist, the symbol of the Royal House that had been tattooed just above his wrist at his wedding. He wasn't moving away. She peeked upwards at him. He smiled down at her—a lazy, slow-stretching grin.

My Lord Jait was probably the only person in the room as tall as Antronos, which at the moment made Opalena furious, since it meant she could only look up at him. Painfully aware that she was breaking every protocol in the book, Opalena continued to stare at the High Prince, saying nothing.

"You should hire this one, Liam," said Jait. "I like her."

"Uh . . ." Prince Liam looked back and forth between Opalena and Antronos, apparently caught between disagreeing with his father and retracting his offer to Antronos.

Jait noticed his son's hesitation. "Hire them both, Liam."

"Of course, father." Liam looked relieved, the exact opposite of how Opalena felt. *Wasn't the Royal House so short of funds that they couldn't even hand out a few measly fellowships?* She was even more stunned when the High Prince took her by the hand and dragged her from the room. Thankfully, he let go and returned his hand to his pocket once she was walking beside him. They were headed through an interior part of the House which Opalena had never seen before, and probably was closed to the public, as there were no politicians or observers here, just servants and the occasional minor royalty. All of them were oblivious to Opalena's discomfort. They merely bowed to Jait as they passed, ignoring his new servant.

"Forgive me, Sen," he said at length. "But it doesn't seem to me that you're eager to serve here. May I ask why you came?"

"Please excuse my rudeness, Lord. I'm very nervous. I came on the advice of my fellowship supervisor, Sen Vernus. He thought it would be good for my career."

"Ah, Vernus. He's still around?"

"Yes, Lord."

They stopped inside a rotunda that was cut to the surface, like the exterior walkway, and again covered by the silvery frosted skylights that made the light shimmer. The walls of the hexagonal room were cut into faux archways, which Opalena gradually realized were lit from behind by glass encasements seeded with bioluminescent moss, giving the illusion that one might walk through the arches into a brightly lit room. She also became aware that no one else was around. Jait gently took her chin in his hand and tilted her face upwards. Half expecting it, half telling herself this was not happening, she tried not to recoil as he leaned down and kissed her.

The second his lips touched hers, Opalena did not care about Vernus or

Meriamdan or what they were expecting her to do, or how she was going to stop the seemingly endless cycle of their torment. She was tired, she was hurt, and every part of her being ached for some form of comfort and release. Part of her mind warned her that she couldn't stop caring or she would end up as the same defeated cynic that Sephus had become. At the moment, smothered in the warmth of Jait's kiss, this concern was losing the battle for her attention.

5

Plummet

The wooden surface of the desk was warped and pitted, but the recently applied oil and wax made a pleasant wavy texture underneath Antronos' hands as he ran them from end to end. He sensed energy within the wood, yet the hazy aura that only he could see remained diffuse, amorphous. Some runes had been carved into the desktop, but their edges were too worn to tell what they might have been. His fingertips felt like he rested them on electrodes when he touched the strange shapes.

He cocked his head to one side as he scanned the perimeter of his new office. The complete emptiness was unnerving. In most parts of the university, he could at least see some of the intensity of a live aura, whether it was from a newly discarded strand of hair, or a passing insect. This office was unusually dim. It was also strange that the skylight had been covered with paper. As this was not a prestigious office, it was not cut very deeply into the rock, so that the skylight was slanted, stretching from the top of the room to halfway down the wall. When Antronos finally stood and pulled the skylight covering away, he could see a build-up of sand covering almost half the panes.

The dark wood of the shelves that had been recessed into the sandy walls was also rather beaten up, but that would enhance the character of the books he planned to put there. He looked to the other side of the room. There was a small, padded inset where he could sleep if he wished, and the adjacent wall had been resurfaced with cork for posting notices.

Crossing over to the bookshelves, he again felt a mild buzzing from one particular section of the floor. Curious, he knelt and tried to brush away some of the dust, looking for more of the strange runes he had found on his desk. There was a definite pattern on the floor that he could sense not really by sight, or touch, but by some inner awareness. It was almost like a shadow set into the dull inanimate aura of the floor. He traced its outline, and found it had five points and ten sides. There were other, smaller patterns spaced evenly around the first. He stood and considered their shapes. They meant nothing to him.

Several boxes were stacked in the corner of the office, containing his books and other possessions which he no longer wished to keep in his dormitory room. He pulled a carton with holes bored around the lower edge onto his desk and could hear his lizard scrambling excitedly inside. It had been living in a box for the last few weeks, as it had recently developed a taste for the binding glue of borrowed medical journals, making itself sick, and the Librarians angry. He pulled off the lid and saw that Lizard had been feasting on the glue of the cardboard seams of the box. It crawled up under his sleeve, hunting for his medicinal seed pouches. Antronos was instantly soothed by the feel of scaly toes gripping his skin, and the enthusiastic, mindless, inhuman greeting. He ran a finger over the iridescent sheen that danced over the white scales of Lizard's tail, before gently pulling it out of his robes.

"You are not going to live in here," Antronos told it. He pushed aside the heavy wooden door of his office and took Lizard out into the tiled hallway. There was a recessed port just next to the door, where twenty years ago it would have been appropriate to house an idol of the old religion. Antronos reached out to brush away some of the dust and was surprised to find several small, bronze figures half buried in the forgotten crumble. He picked one up and peered at it, feeling himself recoil at the miniature depiction of a man-beast feasting on a child.

Murdek? That was supposedly a very old clan. According to myth, they had mixed freely with surface creatures, were more animal than human, drank blood and practised dark magic. It was astonishing to find such things here, and he doubted the Murdek had ever truly existed, as he surely would have met them in the Desert had they been real. He wondered who had kept this office previously, and if that had anything to do with Amphetam having selected it for him. Perhaps it had been standing empty for a long time, which was why it could be made available on such short notice. He finished clearing the space and deposited Lizard in its new home. He tossed the idols into the rubbish bin.

Pulling the lid off another carton, he started lifting out his books and arranging them on the shelves. When he came to the edge of the top shelf, he felt the odd buzzing sensation again, this time like flies clamouring to get in his ears. He shook his head and waved the imaginary insects away— looking around, he couldn't see any. Strange, he thought. Somewhat off balance, he absently put out a hand to steady himself against the bookshelves, then jerked away like he had been burnt. His head snapped around. There was absolutely nothing wrong with the shelf, but for a second it was as if he had placed his fingers over someone's face— someone who had been muttering at him angrily. Tentatively, he reached out to touch the shelf again. Nothing. It was just wood. He went back to his boxes and pulled some more books out, casting a wary look over his shoulder every few seconds. No muttering faces appeared.

At the bottom of the next carton, he found the stack of unopened mail he had shoved in there earlier. Sifting through, he was a touch dismayed to find a large envelope marked with the gold and blue insignia of the House of Dra. Perhaps someone else would have been flattered, but despite his efforts to excel, Antronos hated being noticed. It exposed him to too much opportunity for ridicule. While his position at the Royal House was high profile, he would only be serving Lord Jait in private. He greatly doubted Jait would tease and flirt with him like Alaindra had, and from what he knew of Liam, he didn't expect to be cheated on his pay. As long as he didn't kill the High Prince, or suddenly make him turn variegated shades of purple, it was unlikely many people would take note of his activities.

The letter inside was unfolded and edged with blue. Once translated out of legalese, it informed Antronos that if he agreed, his services were to be retained by the House of Dra, which was apparently having difficulty finding a private family physician. Furthermore, remuneration for his services would be as followed, provided he did not develop any undesirable political ties. His eyes nearly bugged out at the figure.

Well, at least it gives a believable reason for the Lady Alain wanting to hire me, he thought. And for that amount of money, now that he had it in writing, he supposed he could tolerate occasionally being paraded around as her pet freak, and pretend he didn't remember Alaindra from his time on the docks. For once it seemed his surface heritage would give him an advantage over the close-knit tunnel clans. He had no ties to speak of, political or otherwise. He posted the letter on his new cork board, intending to answer it later.

"Well, Physician to the High Prince and Alaindra, all in one week," he said aloud, swatting at another non-existent fly.

He wondered if he dared allow himself to feel satisfaction, perhaps even...happiness? Just maybe he was defeating the stigma of the eyes the Desert had given him. Amphetam was still pressuring him to take a professorship. Just maybe, however grudgingly it might be given at first, he might have the respect of his prospective students. After all, they would be taught by one of the *Royal* Physicians.

He thought about the other Royal Physician, Opalena. Although their last conversation had been abrupt, she had made it clear that he was not the cause of her irritation. So, she didn't really have any animosity towards him, surface creature that he was, and they would be working together. Just maybe...there was the possibility of friendship. Of no longer being completely unconnected to any other human being, as he had been since the death of his mother. Antronos smiled to himself, then attempted to push down any further thoughts on the matter. The last thing he needed was to start behaving like an idiot just when things were going well.

Opalena. She was truly admirable, the way she defiantly showed herself for what she was, not caring whether anyone approved or not. She flaunted the fact that she was a woman, a scholar, alive— something many Sens seemed to be shy about. Tentatively, although he was alone, Antronos pulled away the scholar's robes he wore, and watched as the black fabric fell away to reveal the bright orange loops of cloth underneath. On the surface, these were the clothes of mourning, and it had taken him forever to save enough money to purchase the fabric. He knew that the tunnel dwellers thought he was eccentric, not understanding the significance of the colour. He also wore his mother's prayer beads around his neck, and the Desert-style sandals on his feet.

Let them think what they wish. He would take a page from Opalena's book, and show what he was. It was time to stop being afraid.

The next box was stuffed full of references from the library. Gainfully employed or not, he still had every intention of pursuing a post-secondary degree in some discipline that would help him delay death. He had borrowed nearly everything the Librarians could find on patient recovery times, longevity and seemingly impossible reversal of disease. He paused, feeling conflicted about magic and science. It was clear what Amphetam thought, and he didn't want to disappoint the Chancellor, but was it possible that the Desert could give a life that lasted forever? Was his mother still—

Shaking his head, he pushed the thoughts away. Granted, the Desert did strange things, but he had made his choice to study science, and even if all the Desert magic was real, it was certainly unreliable, and there was no place for it in his work now. He plunked down in his chair and opened several of the books in a satisfying spread over the entire surface of the desk.

Most of the data were epidemiological statistics and did not interest him. Instead, he decided to look at recorded cases of notable longevity, hoping there would be some common condition that he could expound, perhaps finding some lead on an enzyme or drug that could prevent one or more aspects of aging. He came across a rather poetically written opinion article, predicting that within the next decade, methods would be developed to defer aging and death indefinitely. In the meantime, however, organ and tissue transplants were a realistic short-term goal that could avert the dysfunction of a single body part causing premature morbidity of an individual. Antronos' initial doubts of the author's mental state faded when the article developed its scope to cover the inevitable complications with transplant rejection and long-term requirement of immune suppressing drugs. It was the strange whimsy of the piece that made Antronos flip to the title page to look for the author's name. *Sen Vernus, Department of Surgery, Temlochti University.* It had been written five years ago, and yet, something about the style of it had resonated within Antronos' memory. It was almost as if he had read the article before, but instead of organ transplants, it had dealt with the use of mushroom pastes for reversing snake bite infections.

He got up and dug through another one of the boxes, until he found the other paper buried deep within his old undergraduate notes. He checked the author's name: *Sen Vernus, Department of Pharmacology,*

Temlochti University. This paper had been written thirty years ago.

Flipping through the article, the personality and bias of the author came through with freer reign, this time reminding him of something even more improbable. Hesitantly, he lifted the cover off a very special box, in which he kept all he had left of his mother—her sleeping shift, her mirror, her water bowl, her sandals, and her three books, including the collection of Yrati hymns he had once believed might help resurrect her. Looking them over, he selected the book of myths she had read to him as a child. He opened it and felt a cascading rush of old memories, hearing his mother's voice as he read the words, "In the beginning, there was dust, and man had to come from dust..." Holding his breath, he flipped to the front liner: *Sen Vernus, Department of Anthropology and Archaeology, Temlochti University.* The book had been written one hundred and fifty years ago. Suddenly Antronos laughed at himself. This was probably Vernus' father, of the same name. Or even a grandfather. Right? There were ways to check, although the rational part of his mind was asking why he would even bother validating something so obviously impossible.

Antronos reached for the university directory and looked up the location of Vernus' laboratory. The listings were published every year, and unfortunately gave no indication of which department a given Sen worked for in previous years. Since Vernus was an Emeritus, he only taught the second year of the undergraduate medical class in alternate years—thus Antronos had managed to miss having him as a professor, and the first time he had met the old Sen was at the convocation ceremony. Strangely, Vernus was only listed as having an off-campus laboratory with no apparent attachment to the university hospital. *A professor of surgery with no clinic? How could he practise?* Antronos looked back at his mother's book, and began to wonder. It was possible that father and son would have similar writing styles, and even carry on similar ideas, but then again, Sen Vernus had apparently been working on the nature of man, and longevity, for quite some time, and he was extremely old. And his robes were the colours of Desert magic! Could all of these documents have been written by the same person? The hair on the back of Antronos' neck began to rise.

This is silly, he told himself sternly, yet he found himself making his way to the library via the back tunnels, and sneaking into the archives, where the human resources data were kept.

The records storage cavern was poorly lit, and not very well arranged. After half an hour of rummaging through stiff, wooden cupboards, he managed to locate the staff records for the Department of Anthropology, dug as far back as they would go, which was only about fifty years, and found no mention of Vernus. He moved deeper into the cavern, found a series of ledgers encased in vellum that had the appearance and script of earlier centuries and pried a few of them open. Physycal Scyence, Chemystry, Phylosophy, Medycyn...*Sen Vernus, Professor of Medycyn, Temlochty Unyversyty.* Five hundred years ago.

Forgetting about being quiet, Antronos tore through any other records that he could find which might confirm that this five-hundred-year-old professor was the same Sen he had met at his convocation. He scoured payroll, university tax records, genealogy, vital and economic statistics, even birth and death certificates of everyone who had ever been in the university hospital. Every mention he could find of Vernus had consistent, linking records that could be followed for about forty years. There were conspicuous gaps, about fifty years in length, where no mention of him could be found; then he would reappear. There were no birth or death certificates, no transfer of funds to heirs, or even any mention of heirs. And to complete the eeriness of the scenario, Antronos was finding that the signatures on the university employment records were almost exact. Too exact for more than one person to have made them, even if a grandson were to mimic his grandfather's handwriting. At a rough estimate, Vernus was eight hundred years old.

Only one cabinet remained. Antronos had not bothered trying to open it, because it looked fairly new, giving the impression that it wouldn't hold any of Vernus' old records. But now, the fact that it was bolted shut with a heavy lock stirred Antronos' suspicious curiosity. Would it contain any more secrets?

Antronos picked at the keyhole for a few minutes, then looked around for a beetle. Finding none, he worried away at the bolt hinges, then at those of the cabinet door. He managed to get one of the lower hinges loose, and pry the corner of the door upwards far enough to push his hand in. The edges of the cabinet were slightly splintered, and scratched his arm badly, yet he continued to feel around until he managed to wiggle free one of the volumes inside. Flipping it open, he saw that it was a lab journal, and although there were no identifiers on it, the handwriting had to be Vernus'. Several pages had been ripped out. That was odd, since lab protocol, no matter how ancient, consistently decreed that incorrect information was to be struck out, never removed from a journal. The only explanation was that the author was trying to hide something. Antronos peered at the ragged margins, unable to make out anything more than half words that may have referred to some surgical procedure. He could not determine if the subject had been human or animal. He tucked the book into the folds of his robe.

Finally convinced that he had seen enough, Antronos somehow made it back to his office without remembering anything of how he got there. His hands were shaking so badly that he had difficulty opening the door, and Lizard chirruped at him cautiously.

He leaned against the inside of the doorframe for a few moments, before he gave a start, realizing that there was someone watching him from behind his desk. The figure was silhouetted from the skylight, and he had to move to one side before he could make out who sat there: Opalena.

"Hello," he finally managed, stunned to find her there. He saw that she had been leafing through the papers on his desk.

"Sen Vernus," she said, lazily letting a paper fall back to the desktop.

"You weren't considering him for your graduate supervisor, were you?"

"I take it you wouldn't recommend him?"

"Oh, that's not it." She stood up and moved around the desk towards him. Her dark scholar's robes parted from the neck as she moved, revealing a gauzy white dress and braided sandals underneath. "I just find it a remarkable coincidence. That's all."

"Why?"

"Oh, because I won the Royal Award in Science, and Vernus is my supervisor, and now you've won the same Award, and seem to be heading the same way I am."

"You say it like that's not a good thing."

"Were you going to choose him as your mentor?"

"I haven't decided yet. Would you suggest that I join your laboratory?"

Opalena looked down sharply, her posture suddenly losing some of its insouciance. She didn't answer for a few moments, and looked as though she was trying to gain control over tears. Remembering how tense she had been at the Royal House, it occurred to Antronos that perhaps she had come to him as a physician, and like the House of Dra, was looking for someone unaffiliated with certain factions.

"Why are you here?" he asked softly.

She let out a sound that was half sob, half laugh, and finally turned back to him. Her face was pulled into a grimace.

"Oh, yes. I would like you to work with me."

The words seemed sarcastic and forced. Yet she stood there watching for his reaction, her expression almost pleading. "Why?" he asked.

"We're more alike than you think."

"As scholars?"

"As outsiders. Tell me, Antronos, is there anyone that you can really trust? That you could tell anything to?"

Sensing a revelation, Antronos moved forward and sat at his desk.

"Tell me. Everything you say, I will keep to myself."

She seemed to be struggling with the decision to release her secret, whatever it was. Then she finally looked at him and shook her head, smiling.

"I'm a real cretin for even coming here. I'm sorry. This is your private space. You should have thrown me out as soon as you saw me."

"Why in Earth would I have done that? Please, sit down again. Tell me what is bothering you. Is it Vernus?"

Opalena laughed. There was a strange shift in her aura, almost like it had doubled, and the new aura didn't quite match the movements of the first.

"If you want to know about Vernus," she said, "then I think you should go see him yourself."

Antronos looked at her for a long moment, trying to decide if something about her had changed. She returned his gaze levelly, giving him a half smile.

"There's nothing you could tell me?" he asked.

"Such as?" She raised an eyebrow. Antronos was now uncertain of

Opalena's encouragement or what strange, subtle message she was trying to convey. He decided it would be unwise to ask her anything about magic, Desert-related or otherwise, having the distinct feeling he was treading on shifting sand. It could be that Vernus did not speak of his magic, especially if it were of the Desert, to avoid conflict with the Chancellor. Perhaps Antronos' best choice *was* to talk to the old man himself. After all, Vernus certainly knew much about longevity, and might be a better fit for Antronos than the Yrati and their water magic developed by the old priest Dagnaum.

✳✳✳✳✳

Before approaching Sen Vernus, Antronos scoured the library for anything the old doctor had written, then carefully put together a profile of the man. Vernus' public image was one of a stern old doctor who apparently frightened small children, and was intolerant of patients not following his instructions to the letter. He was said to be as inflexible as iron, and once he stepped through a client's door, one simply did not have a change of heart and ask him to leave. One had to deal with him. He was still an avid scientist, not content to settle back into the role of a general practitioner, as many physicians did late in their careers. Other physicians said that Sen Vernus was quite a talker once he started, and could be detained for hours by first asking a complex medical question, then buying two cups of blossom tea, and settling down for a lengthy lecture.

Despite certain unusual questions directed at himself, Antronos felt that his first encounter with Sen Vernus was going well, and he was learning a great deal from his staged query about using mushroom pastes to treat insect bites. During the interview, he wondered what exactly it was that Opalena had wanted him to see, and scrutinized the old doctor, noting the gnarled hands, the metal-covered teeth, and the age spots on his arms and bald forehead. The discolouration was so extreme that Vernus almost had a greenish tinge to him. Everything about his facial features was sharp: the black of his eyes, the hook of his nose, and the curve of his lips. And his mind—honed like a razor and frighteningly quick. Antronos knew immediately that there would be no hoodwinking his subject into letting any secrets slip. He also felt disconcerted by the intensity with which he was being examined. Even though the old doctor never moved from his seat on the other side of the table, Antronos felt as if every hair on his head had been lifted and turned over.

"So you're interested in mushroom extracts, are you?" Vernus asked. "It has been noted that you have a talent for pharmaceuticals. I'm afraid I haven't worked on them in years. The market has bottomed out for such things. All anyone wants these days are synthetic prescriptions."

Antronos fiddled with his teacup for a moment. Vernus' tone was amused, as if he knew Antronos wasn't really interested in mushrooms. He looked up at the old man, into that piercing stare. Would it be offensive to ask what he really wanted to know? Vernus seemed to have taken some pains to hide his past...assuming he really was eight hundred years old. But his published works were no secret. Those should be safe to discuss. Antronos drew in a deep breath, thinking that this could be the moment when he found the man who would finally teach him how the Desert may have influenced his mother's passing.

"Well, I've also been reading your publications on organ transplants. You have some very daring theories on how that may prolong a person's life. Yet I've noticed that all of your writing has been speculative, no actual patient data. I was wondering, have you had any clinical success?"

Vernus sat back at that, and took a long, appraising look at Antronos.

"May I ask the reason for your interest?"

"I'm still considering a graduate degree. I'm interested in longevity."

"How interesting." Vernus seemed to relax, and smiled into his tea cup. "I can take you on. But I'll have to warn you, I don't like having my results publicized before I feel I'm ready, and I expect a lot of hard work. Praise doesn't come easily in my lab, but when it does, it'll be well deserved. Also, I expect absolute protection of all patients' privacy. No names. Many of them do not want the university community to know that they are involved in experimental medicine, since that would involve admitting to some physical weakness."

"Of course," said Antronos. "I would have expected nothing less."

"Tell me, have you read much of my work?"

"Uh..." Antronos hesitated, catching himself before he revealed just how far he had dug into Vernus' background. "Just what I could find," he finished lamely.

"Just what you could find, indeed." Antronos looked up at the sharpness in Vernus' voice, and found himself shrinking before those intense, black eyes. Vernus was still smiling, and Antronos couldn't tell if that smile was knowing or not. He began to wonder if maybe he should corner Opalena into a more in-depth chat before committing to the project; then he discarded the idea. Regardless of how difficult a mentor Vernus might be, Antronos was sure he had faced worse as an undergraduate, and he was determined to learn what Vernus knew. All of it.

*****

The Market Caverns were always at their best at the end of summer. The ravaging heat from the surface subsided, the water in the rivers cooled, and the air was not quite so dusty. The faint breeze coming off the water smelled less like dead fish and stale dung, and more like the metal ores constantly being scraped from the riverbed. The slant of the sunlight coming through the skylights was a warmer colour, tending towards the longer end of the spectrum. The underground trees flourished in this bounty of light, their massive trunks twisting up from the edge of the river almost to the panes of the ceiling.

Business picked up during this season, and the merchants lined all tiers of the caverns, the most successful ones always placed closer to the ceiling, where the glass panes lent an elegance to their stalls, and the light refracted on their crystalline goods. Drinking cups sparkled, glorious fabrics cascaded in heavy drapes of wild colour, and magnificent lizards clutched their perches, warily eyeing shoppers who touched their glistening scales. Cages of blindfish with plumed tails swirling behind them, were hung up so that light filtered through the water of their tanks, scattering rainbows over their white gills. The fishmongers and dung sellers typically inhabited the lower tiers where there was not much light to set off the shine and sparkle of their wares, however, they had the advantage of being closer to the docks, and the first to greet the large distributors.

Vernus moved quietly through the bustle, smiling thinly to himself as he noted that no one jostled against him, no one tried to sell him anything, and no light fingers reached into his pockets. He didn't mind really, since this allowed him to keep his hands tucked into his sleeves where they would not dry out.

He found the stall of one of his clients, and stepped over the row of bricks commonly used on the lower levels to stake out mercantile territory. Stacks of old books, aquariums and candles that had been discarded from the library tumbled from makeshift bookcases and tables.

His patient was not pleased to see him. He stood regarding the Librarian for a few moments. The other man was tall, bald, and unusually gangly, as was typical for his clan, yet he had put on weight and seemed healthier than the last time they had met. Vernus gauged just how much of his anger he should release. It had been obvious from his noontime interview that *just what Antronos could find*, had been a fair bit more than what Vernus would have liked.

"You look as though I've come to give you sour medicine," said the old doctor.

"Haven't you?" asked the Librarian. "You aren't one to buy second-hand books, especially since you've written so many yourself."

"Indeed. And what do you imagine I might be writing about now?"

The Librarian gave a grim smile.

"I suppose it has something to do with me."

"Oh? How so?"

"Come now, Vernus. I didn't destroy a certain list of documents, as you had requested, and there's no point in pretending you don't know about it, because if you didn't, you wouldn't be here."

"Why haven't you done as I've asked?"

The Librarian sighed heavily. "You've put me in a very difficult situation. My clan would have found it strange if I had pulled those publications. They would have wanted to know why. They would have suspected censorship."

"Difficult? Then the library shouldn't insist on having copies of everything professors write. Several of those articles were from my private journals, which your clan pilfered after I clearly stated I did not want them in the library collection—"

"That was a university decision, not mine!"

"—And besides, those journals I wanted removed were not written during my current position in the Department of Surgery. They're outdated, and you can easily justify removing them on that basis."

"You did list a number of journals that were recent."

Vernus said, "Does your clan know I gave you a new heart?"

"They know you treated my ailment."

"I didn't treat it. I replaced your heart. Would you like to know where I got it from? Would you like your clan to know? You did ask me for a special favour, since your illness was so great. The procedure is not irreversible."

"You know, Vernus, each time I see you, I get the distinct impression you duped me into having that surgery for the sole purpose of gaining control over the library collections. That impression was strengthened when I flipped through a few of those records you wanted locked up. Seems to me we both have something to hide."

"If you want to play that sort of game with me, I am certainly willing. Shall we place a wager on who will win?"

The Librarian frowned and looked pensive for a few moments. Apparently he did not gamble. "What do you want?" he finally asked.

"Pull the list off the shelves. And I want any of the university records that mention me also removed. I don't even want them kept in storage. Is that clear? Destroyed. All of it. I'm finding that young Sens read a great deal, having not enough sense to fill their time otherwise."

"As they should. Very well. I'll make some arrangement."

"Thank you. You do realize that you've upset me. Do you have anything to make me feel better?"

The Librarian sighed. "The mail scribes have told me something."

Vernus raised his eyebrows, and waited expectantly.

"The surface boy, he's been offered a position by the House of Dra. Does that make you feel better?"

"Yes. It does." Vernus was calculating some other threat when his eye caught a gleam in the corner of the stall. At first it appeared to be a diamond orb set in a bowl of red clay. Then it looked like an eye that was watching him. "What is that?" he asked. He took a step forward, and the thing seemed to rattle, then duck out of sight. He poked in the shadowed corner with his toe, and rolled out six or seven small pieces of what looked like broken red pottery. The Librarian reached down and picked one up. Vernus looked at the object and found it uninteresting.

"I expect tomorrow will not be too soon for your arrangements to be made. It's only a partial recompense, you realize," he said, and stepped away from the stall.

Just what he could find, indeed.

Nucleate

Opalena had been summoned by Jait over two hours ago. She shifted restlessly in the hard-backed chair the guard had led her to in the white-tiled antechamber, wondering if she had been completely forgotten. A single red runner carpet bisected the room. Narrow gauzy curtains fell pointlessly from the ceiling at random junctures, wafting softly in the Desert breeze coming though the air vents. Opalena was tired of staring at them. Some of the household staff exited Jait's chambers, carrying changed linens and laundry. She leaned towards them, hoping to ask if she should go in, but they did not look up at her, hurrying off to their next task. The guard posted across the hall gave her a bored glance, but said nothing, evidently not caring that she had been waiting for so long. She grew angry at this treatment, and thought that if the guard was not going to make the effort to talk to her, there was no reason she should make the effort either. And if he didn't care what she did, then he shouldn't care if she were to just get up and walk into Jait's chambers without formal escort.

She stood up. The guard looked at her. She picked up her medical case and walked to the over-sized door and put her hand on it. The guard didn't move. *Very well.* Opalena pulled open the door, straining against its unexpected weight, and went inside. It was completely incomprehensible to her why anyone would need a door going all the way up to the vaulted ceiling—absolutely no one could be that tall.

The room was enormous, and not at all what she expected. Shimmering white tiles, cut square instead of the usual diamond shape, lined the floor and base of the walls. Heavily textured red cloth cascaded down one side of the room, while another was shelved with enough books to supply a small library. An elaborate canopy bed with gold and red linens was on a raised section of the floor that was covered in piled tapestries. A long desk fashioned from slender pieces of carved wood graced the corner of the room closest to the door. Despite the presence of unfrosted skylights and full tanks of bioluminescent moss shimmering from the walls every few paces, the room was dim, and it took her a few moments to realize that it was full of smoke. It had a soft scent, like dried peat, and wafted in curling, purple tendrils from somewhere at the back of the chamber.

Opalena walked forward carefully, checking behind vases and side tables as she passed them. The smoke was coming from a strange makeshift tent in a corner of the room, perhaps a tablecloth draped over a set of chairs. She carefully lifted a corner of the fabric, releasing another puff of smoke, then peeked underneath. Jait sat there on a pile of cushions, with one arm wrapped around an elaborate blue and white enamel water pipe, completely swathed in the fumes. Opalena was astonished.

"What in Earth are you doing?" she asked, forgetting protocol completely.

Jait's movements were sluggish as he leaned towards her with one hand out, as if trying to wave the smoke away so that he could see her better. She grabbed his hand and tried to pull him out of his tent, only succeeding in making him fall over.

"This is ridiculous," she said, and began folding back the cloth. Jait covered his face with his hands and began sobbing. Opalena stared at him, baffled. Her mental image of the High Prince was rapidly adjusting, and she was having difficulty accepting what she was seeing.

Dropping the edge of the cloth, she climbed under the tent to kneel next to Jait. She tentatively touched his shoulder, then tried to push him into a sitting position. "Is it just the smoke making you this way?" she asked.

"It hurts," Jait choked out.

"What does?"

"I can't stand it."

"Can't stand what? I can't help you if you don't tell me."

"I can't find Hailandir."

Opalena sighed and felt her irritation fade into pity. She wondered what would be the best thing to do. She could either let Jait smoke himself into a stupor and fall asleep, or gently remind him that his wife had died five years ago.

"She took me away from my family. She paid for me. Now she's left me alone."

"Paid for you?"

"She gave my father a lot of money." Jait had pushed himself up and was snickering through his tears, finally stopping to catch a stream of spittle on his sleeve. "My old father, he laughed at me, and didn't even try to stop me from being...purchased."

"I don't understand."

"I'm from Raulen. Did you know that?"

"Yes, I had heard."

"In Raulen, they don't believe in magic. Hailandir comes along, and tells my father that I have magic. She's gone and traced it to my grandmother, who was Temlochti. She wants me because I'm the last in a long, lost line of Temlochti nobles. That's what she says. My father, he laughs and takes the money, because he says he'll never get anything out of me otherwise." Jait snickered again. His voice was slurred and interspersed with gasping sobs, making him difficult to understand. "It's illegal to sell people in Raulen. Did you know that? You know what else? My father was right. I don't have any magic. Hailandir tried to make me believe I did, but I can't do any of the things she wanted me to. Sometimes she could reach inside my mind, and help me touch...something. But whatever it was, when she left, it left too. If it ever was really there. Neither of my sons has any magic either. So that's why Hailandir has gone away. Because I'm useless to her."

"Oh, no. My Lord, she didn't leave you." The motion felt awkward and completely inappropriate, but Opalena found herself trying to comfort Jait by stroking his hair. He dragged himself forward and pressed his face against her shoulder, leaving trails of mucus along her robes. She stiffened and tried to gently push him away. The smoke was making her queasy and light-headed, and the last thing she wanted was someone slobbering over her clothes.

"Then where is she?" Jait asked.

"She died," Opalena said harshly, losing her sympathy for him. He smelled too much like phlegm for her to be comfortable having him this close. Jait resisted, wrapping his arms around her waist.

"Hailandir," he murmured, relaxing against her. Opalena sighed again and reached up to pull aside the cloth so that she could breathe. Perhaps now Jait would fall asleep, giving her a chance to leave. She supposed she could wait.

* * * * *

Something buzzed in her ear and woke her, releasing her from an annoying dream. Her head felt like someone had tried to shove it through a grain mill, and the darkness was claustrophobic. Opalena pushed her arms free from the tangle of blankets she found herself caught in, and sat up. Confused as to why she couldn't see, she reached towards a crack of light, and finally pulled aside a heavy red curtain that had been encircling the bed. Red like the womb. By her side, Lord Jait slept.

"By the Earth!"

Opalena pushed herself away from him wondering how they had ended up in bed when the last thing she remembered was sitting on the cushions under the makeshift tent. Fully clothed.

The water pipe.

Her burns had been itching. She had wanted relief. She had wanted to forget Vernus. It was only a thought. She had never intended to give in to temptation. The pull of the soporific that she had already inhaled had dulled her senses. But this?

The blood-coloured linens were warm, cushioning and somewhat damp. Her hair had stuck to her skin, and she pulled it away, wincing when it came free from the scabs on her arm. When had she pulled off the bandages? She felt so weary. The scent of the bed, the soporifics and implied promise of sleepy oblivion were so tempting...

She glanced at the timepiece on the mantle and swore under her breath. Habit took over. She always made sure Vernus didn't notice her too much, and one way of doing that was not to give him a reason to notice her, like being late. Where the hell had her robes gone?

Jait slumbered soundly, completely unaware of Opalena's movements, and apparently oblivious and uncaring of the turmoil he was creating in her life. Pulling her scholar's robe over her shoulders and retrieving her medical case from the side of the makeshift tent, she took a last look at Jait: pale skin surrounded by dark hair spread over the red pillow, slightly opened mouth set in the midst of the delicate bone structure. He could have been cut from alabaster. On impulse, she leaned forward and kissed him. He woke briefly, gave her a sleepy smile, turned his back on her and slept again. Opalena stared at his thin shoulder blades for a moment, then told herself firmly that she shouldn't have expected anything different. *He was not here to comfort* her.

Out in the hallway, Opalena ducked her head in embarrassment whenever she passed one of the servants, even though they greeted her politely and with respect. She supposed they were accustomed to Jait's habits and thought nothing of her leaving his chambers in the morning.

Somebody stepped into her path and put an arm across the hallway to block her passage. She looked up into the face of Derik, Jait's older son, who was even taller than his father, and despite his light colouring, perhaps even more intimidating.

"There you are, Sen. We've been looking for you all morning."

Opalena didn't believe for a second that Derik hadn't known exactly where she had been.

"So how is my father's health?"

"He sleeps well."

"No doubt soothed by your gentle ministrations."

"I would like to think so."

She made an attempt to step past him, realizing at the last minute that he had baited her into a serious breach of protocol. His amusement made her want to kill him. Did everyone here think she was a toy? Angry enough to risk further humiliation, she swept past him, even raising her arm out of his grasp. She saw no point in trying to behave properly with him anyway. It was obvious that he had no intention of letting her save face, and what would he do if she were rude to him? Dismiss her? That wasn't such a bad idea.

She knew that Derik was staring after her, but decided she didn't care enough to worry about him. He couldn't possibly damage her more. A strange shadow passed over her, and she stopped, looking up at the skylight to see what had dimmed the sun. Nothing was there, and the light was still reflected in pinpoint gleams from the polished handles set into both furniture and miniature aquariums—it just seemed that she looked through a grey filter that dulled the colours around her. Something had descended over only her, like a swarm of buzzing insects trying to make their way through her ears and into her mind. She was being smothered by them, and tried to run, but she was paralyzed, unable to move, even to swat the insects away. At the last moment, she recognized the buzzing as a muttering chant, and the presence of Meriamdan. Futile panic rose up in her as she realized that this time, the possession was much stronger and all encompassing. Consciousness was slipping away from her. Vernus and Meriamdan were getting more powerful, and she wondered if she would be able to resist anything at all: if she would even be aware of what Meriamdan did while in her body.

*****

Opalena was aware.

"Are you back again?" Jait reached up to grab her by the wrist, and as his fingers closed, she felt something stir deep within him, some strange inner sense that made him recoil. She could see his pulse start to race at his neck and beads of sweat break out over his skin. As her hand reached down to touch his brow, Opalena could sense the confusion overwhelming him, a dizzying sensation of knowing something, but not what or how he knew.

"Why are you afraid?" Not-Opalena asked. She felt her smile widening to unnatural proportions, until she thought her skin was going to rip. She made a shallow entry into his mind and felt his nausea grow as he began to desperately try to force her out and organize his thoughts into some semblance of clarity.

"Who is that?" he demanded, as another figure stole into the room. Not-Opalena cast a look over her shoulder, feeling her head twist at an impossible angle.

"Ah, the guards have escorted him here on my request. I did have such trouble convincing Liam. Oh, it's nothing to be worried about, darling. Surely you remember Sen Vernus, my mentor. He treated your wife towards the end of her illness, before you threw him out. Well, he's back now. I've brought him in for a second opinion about your weakened condition."

"I am not weak!"

Jait threw off his covers, not caring that he was naked, and tried to get up. Not-Opalena shoved him back down with surprising force. True-Opalena had not been able to muster such strength last night.

"Oh, but you are. You're very ill, and you're going to be for a very long time. We are going to take care of you."

Vernus moved forward and grabbed Jait's wrists. Opalena's hands cupped his face and pushed his head back onto the pillow. The whimsy of the Desert filled her soul, and her fingers began to...change, stretch, infuse deeply into his mind.

"No!" Jait resisted, and found strength somewhere deep inside himself to push back against this assault.

"He is strong," Vernus said, and smiled as if Jait had done something to make him proud. "Let's give him something to make this easier for him."

Not-Opalena, still smiling her cracked-face grin, fumbled in her medicine case to pull out a long, thin, metal spike from a wooden tube and dipped it into an ampoule of blue liquid.

"What are you doing?" Jait demanded. "Opalena, stop! I never meant to hurt you! Is this some kind of revenge for last night?"

"No, no, no, darling. We wanted you to accept Opalena. You did nothing wrong. She was our way in, and you've opened the door wide. We thank you for taking her. Prince Liam would never have hired either of us."

Not-Opalena shoved the spike into a vein with brutal force. Jait cried out, then couldn't make any noise at all. His eyes rolled uncontrollably. His lips were slack. Not-Opalena reached inside his head, piling up blocks of thoughts, rearranging them, cementing them in place, and building stairs for Vernus to climb deep inside him.

"Ah," said the old man. "I can see your mind clearly. Yes. I know you now."

He released Jait's wrists, but it didn't matter. Jait's mind was locked in an iron grip.

Not-Opalena placed a hand on Vernus' shoulder. "Congratulations," she said. "You've done it."

"Not yet. We need a success. Help me draw the runes."

Not-Opalena tottered into the centre of Jait's chamber, and drew all the runes with clear wax, avoiding the chance that Liam might find their hidden game. As Vernus seated himself and began to chew the new breed of fungus they had cultured together, Not-Opalena dragged Jait from his bed and across the floor. Leaning over him, she nicked the vein at his elbow and began the chant.

"A stranger, Meriamdan. Who do you think we shall we find?" Not-Opalena sank her fingers into Jait's mind again, and released his power, which surged into Vernus, lifting him clear off the floor. Vernus laughed and threw his spirit out into the ether, leaving his corporeal form hovering just in front of them.

"Jait's son," said Not-Opalena. "The real Prince. After all, our Jait is merely a consort, never to be King."

"Derik," muttered Vernus' spectre. He shot upwards out of the room, riding Jait's spirit and carrying Opalena's consciousness with him. She marvelled at how clearly she could see all things. The very souls of each servant she passed were laid open before her. These people whom she had never met spoke their names to her, showed her their deepest secrets, offered her their minds. Jait's mind opened all hidden secrets, making them free for the taking. Prince Derik was alone, brooding with drink in his private chambers. As they approached him, he looked up and frowned, searching the air for what he could not see.

"Father?"

Derik struggled as they plunged into his mind, but his efforts were pointless. He had no defence. Vernus shattered his will and locked down his mind in a matter of seconds. He began to wind curses around Derik's thoughts of resistance, then paused.

"Why?" asked Not-Opalena.

"There is nothing to bind," Vernus told her. Derik was willing.

I will help you bring my father down. The Prince rose from his seat and began walking towards Jait's chamber.

Giddy with triumph, Vernus and Not-Opalena tumbled back into themselves, slick with the rush of pleasure surging through them both.

"Another!" shouted Not-Opalena. "Let's find another! Prince Liam!" She reached into Jait's mind again, and probed for the power. "What's wrong? I can't find it!" Angry, she called on the Desert with all her strength, and plunged her hands into Jait's head. "Where is it?"

Vernus was gently pulling her back. "Peace, Meri," he told her. "Look at him. He's been drained. Let's have him rest. Then we will try again. It is enough. We will have it all, but it will take time and patience. We must conserve My Lord Jait's strength."

7

Triggered

For a moment, all was quiet. Although it was still very early, Antronos was not inclined to try sleeping again. He had been kept awake by a persistent, intermittent buzzing that he couldn't quite hear. It seemed to wait until he had just drifted to sleep before penetrating his mind and waking him again. Unwilling to become angry, he had risen and sat cross-legged on the floor of his office with his eyes closed, trying to sense what had drained away the diffuse aura of the rock within the strange, pointed shape on the floor. For the briefest moment, the buzzing in his mind seemed to take on colour and shape. He perceived it as a series of grey, twisted limbs reaching towards him through a peculiar channel that flapped open and shut, spiralling towards him each time it opened. He felt the entity retreat each time he tried to focus on it. Gently, unobtrusively, he tried to follow it back to its source. A projection of a face, too distorted to recognize, grimaced in surprise as he approached, then withdrew altogether.

Frustrated and curious, he continued to sit quietly, forcing himself not to strain his senses, but patiently wait to see if the buzzing entity returned. He was almost certain now that it had been the same creature his hand had brushed against when he had leaned on the bookshelf a few days ago. Was he the only one aware of this creature? Was it trapped here? Why was it seeking him?

Gradually, he again became aware of something—different this time—that seemed almost smugly content and disinterested in him. Many entities were somewhere underneath him. He opened his eyes and immediately saw blotchy patches of excruciatingly bright aura making haphazard, jerky movements over the rock floor. Were these the same creatures he had seen in the tunnel so many weeks ago? At his graduation, they had talked to the Yrati from the ceremonial font. Would they talk to him now? Something shifted under the palms of his hands, making him scramble to his feet. The rock was being pushed upwards by whatever was moving under it. Dusty round objects randomly broke through the surface, then quickly moved back down under the floor.

"Wait!" he called to them. "I have to ask you something!" He kicked at the glowing mounds as they wriggled past him, trying to stop them, amazed to find that the rock was still as solid as it had been before, neither broken nor crumbled by the passing of whatever it was that moved around beneath it. He stomped at the mounds again, and something like a claw surfaced to hook onto his sandal. He reached down, intending to grab hold of the thing and try to pull it upward, but whatever it was let go, retreating back into the Earth. The glowing blotches collected together in the corner of the room and sank below the surface—leaving behind one, tiny, glinting smudge. Antronos went to the corner and picked it up, finding that it was a small, cylindrically shaped object. He held it up in the nascent light coming through the window and saw by his natural vision that it was a dull red colour. It seemed to be made of clay, which didn't make sense. Normally, inanimate objects did not have such a bright aura. Perhaps he should go speak to the Yrati, since the priest at his graduation seemed to be able to hear these entities. Assuming these creatures weren't supposed to be a secret, My Lord Maxal might actually be able to find out if they knew anything about how his mother—

"Good morning, Sen."

Startled, Antronos turned around, slipping the red object into his pocket. The strange fellow from Vernus' lab stood leaning against his bookshelf. Sephus, was it?

"Uh, hello." Antronos glanced at the door. It was still closed, and he hadn't heard Sephus come in.

"I'm told you'll be joining us."

"Yes, I would like to."

"Really. And why would you want to do that?"

Sephus' voice was flat. He looked like he hadn't slept for a month. His aura seemed diminished, fainter than the average person's. As far as Antronos could tell, Sephus was neither mocking him, nor trying to make him feel unwelcome.

"Why shouldn't I?"

"You have your practice, and you could take a professorship. This is idiotic and pretentious, trying to remain a student when you don't have to."

"Idiotic and pretentious?"

"Take it from someone who knows."

Was this jealousy? Extreme cynicism brought on by failure? It was well known that Sephus had studied with Vernus for longer than he would like to admit. Antronos searched the other man's face, realizing for the first time that Sephus looked much older than most post-doctoral fellows— even the ones that took longer to finish their fellowship. His black hair seemed dyed, and the creased bitterness of his face was enhanced by powder. Why would he wear powder? Was he hiding some scarring?

"Sen Sephus," Antronos began, "I am sympathetic to your...frustration with academics, but I still want to at least try—are you all right?"

Sephus had gasped and doubled over, leaning heavily against the shelves as his aura flickered and surged. It momentarily doubled, like one entity shifting over the other, before finally subsiding into just one. Antronos rushed over to help. Sephus grabbed his wrist and pushed a wad of folded paper into his hand.

"Yes...fine," he choked out. After a moment, he seemed to catch his breath and pushed himself upright.

Antronos lifted his hand, and was about to uncurl his fingers, when Sephus reached out and clamped them shut. In that brief contact, Antronos sensed another of the peculiar channels reaching into Sephus, and the other man's furious struggle to block out those grey, twisting tentacles. His scalp prickled. This entity, whatever it was, had taken on a decidedly malignant nature.

"You can finish reading the rest of your papers *later*," said Sephus with a fierce glance at Antronos' closed fist. "I came to tell you that Sen Vernus requests your presence immediately." His powdery face cracked into a smile. "Since I can't deter you, perhaps you would take my advice to be cautious, and not rush into your project, no matter how hard Vernus pushes you."

*****

Vernus' private laboratory was much larger and apparently better funded than Antronos had expected. It also had a closed off wing with all the makings of a private clinic, answering Antronos' question of how the old Sen could continue his practice. Peeking through the window of the door, he could see about ten beds, some of them curtained off as though they were occupied. Partitioned sections, which may have been small examination rooms, were covered by blue curtains and lined the back of the main laboratory. All the lighting was provided by very expensive, artificial light bulbs imported from Raulen, giving the entire room a crisp, white appearance. Antronos was amazed the old codger could afford it, and surprised at how up-to-date Vernus' equipment was. Perhaps he had been mistaken about any connection to the Desert or magic.

The laboratory was unnervingly lacking aura. Accustomed to wooden benches with at least a diffuse glow, Antronos found that looking at the benches constructed of artificial materials made him feel as though his eyes weren't working properly. He searched the lab for other life signatures, and finally noticed that there was one, glowing very dimly behind a blue curtain. It was foetus-shaped, and seemed to be hovering five feet off the ground. Was it suspended in something? If he strained his ears, he could make out a low muttering sound over the background hum of the lab equipment. The sound made his skin crawl. He moved towards it cautiously. He wondered if this foetus-thing had been what had assaulted Sephus and was now trying to get to him—

"Sen Antronos!"

He stopped guiltily and turned around.

"Sen Vernus! I didn't hear you come in. You wanted to see me?"

"The paperwork has been filed. You are my student now. Sen Amphetam was much surprised by your choice. I take it you didn't tell him."

"No, actually. I didn't expect you to take care of the forms yourself. I thought I would have time—"

"Why waste time? You had already made up your mind, hadn't you? You've read my most recent publications, yes?"

"Yes."

"Good." Vernus shuffled past Antronos and opened a drawer. He pulled out a sheaf of papers. "You will need these."

Antronos took the papers and looked them over.

"Consent forms?"

"Yes. You are a medical doctor, as this project requires you to be. To begin, I want you to go out and practise medicine, and while you're at it, promote the idea of organ donation. If you have no transplantable organs, you have no project, and I'm not interested in keeping you with me if you produce no data that furthers my understanding of longevity. I'm not going to teach you transplantation if you cannot find donors, and as I have said, I do not like to waste time. You'll be out! You know from my papers that I feel transplantation is a possible key to longevity, yes?"

"Yes, I understand that."

"But you must get consent first! And then, you have to wait for natural passing of the donors. But as I trust you are a remarkable physician, that too will take time. So you must start at once. And," Vernus poked Antronos' arm with a knobbly finger, "don't cause any trouble for me, or you'll be out!"

"Yes, Sen."

Antronos watched Vernus shuffle around and wondered why he thought such a lecture was warranted. He remembered Sephus' warning not to be pushed into anything too quickly, but so far all he had heard seemed quite reasonable. And as Vernus had said, he certainly hoped any of his prospective donors would take a very long time to die. So there still was no rush.

"Opalena, get his case properly supplied."

Antronos whirled around, surprised that he had not been aware of someone approaching for the third time today, and also, that she had his medical case with her.

"I thought I had left that in my office."

"Well, it's here now," said Opalena. She seemed sulkier than ever, and her face appeared swollen, as if she had spent the morning crying. Her aura no longer had the strange, overlapping, double shift he had seen earlier. She didn't look up at him while she stuffed vials, gauze and syringes into the various compartments. She snuffled and stopped to rub her nose. She *had* been crying. He lifted a hand to her shoulder, but she thrust the case at him, stubbing a few of his fingers.

"I'm sorry," she said. "Very sorry."

*****

"You're doing well, Shenan."

Antronos finished his inspection of the healing wound and began to replace the dressing. He was in a small, makeshift hut, constructed of mud and dung bricks stacked in a corner of the lower tiers of the Market Cavern. The air was stagnant here, cut off from the rush of the river, but Antronos found the room comfortable, as the echoes from the patrons and hawkers outside were mostly blocked by the porous rock. His patient was an old fishmonger who had accidentally gored his abdomen on a fishing spear. The injury had not been deep enough to damage his innards, but the risk of infection was still high.

"Thank you, Sen," Shenan wheezed. "It's good to have people like you being doctors."

Antronos looked up. "People like me?"

"Aye. Strange people. People who don't mind coming through the lower tiers to treat someone in these back caves. I'd never get one of those fancy doctors. It's not just that they'd get their hands dirty touching me; they'd get their feet dirty too."

Antronos smiled. No insult was intended, and he did not feel like taking offence.

"I used to work on the docks, you know."

"Was that you? I said to my wife, that Sen, he looks like that boy who used to be here. The funny one from the Desert who's gone now. That's you, is it?"

"That's me."

"Ha!" Shenan stopped mid-laugh and grasped his side.

"Please, be careful." Antronos gently pulled the man's hand away and eased him into a straighter sitting position. Over the course of the visit, Shenan had gradually slumped into a crumpled ball.

"How is it then? In the tunnels with the fancy people? You've made it big now, haven't you?"

"It's not easy. Some of them help me; others try to get in my way. I'm never quite sure what their motivations are."

"They took you at the university, then?"

"Yes. Eventually I made it through."

"Good for you! I couldn't. They wouldn't let me. I didn't belong to the right clan or guild. You know, those Librarians? Dirt poor, and they still get in, just because they're born in that clan. Fishmongers, you'd think we could get into agriculture, you know, but instead they're taking those botanists instead. No meat people!"

It wasn't true, but Antronos saw no point in correcting Shenan's beliefs—that would only hurt his feelings.

"How do you like it there? Are you a professor now? Can you teach me?"

Antronos smiled again. "No, Shenan. I wish I could, but I'm still a student."

"What? You're a Sen!"

"I'm doing a second degree. I'm studying under Sen Vernus now."

"Aw, what are you doing that for? That old man, he's a bastard. Comes down here sometimes, and people feel worse after they see him. He cures people by looking at them. They decide they're not sick anymore, just so he'll go away."

"Ah, well, I'm up for the challenge." Antronos finished washing his hands, and began to pack away the extra bandages. He dug through his bag for the vials of antibiotics tucked into a compartment at the bottom.

"How does it feel?" he asked Shenan. He loaded a syringe and as gently as he could, injected the medication into one of Shenan's veins.

"Still bothers me quite a bit. Didn't sleep at all last night. Couldn't get comfortable."

"Hmm. I can give you something for that. It'll make you go to sleep right away though."

"Let me have it. All I have to do today is listen to the wife get at me for not working. So what does that old Sen teach you that you don't already know?"

"He knows a lot about prolonging life. He's remarkably old. I'm hoping to learn his secrets." He gave Shenan a conspiratorial wink. The fishmonger snorted derisively.

"Like I said, *old* bastard. So what has he told you so far?"

"Well, he believes that replacing failing organs with healthy ones is a way to combat disease and aging." Unconsciously, Antronos swatted at the air next to his ears.

"And where would such an organ come from?" asked Shenan.

"A donor patient who is newly dead."

"Is that legal?"

"With the donor's prior consent, yes."

"Huh. Doubt anyone would want my old liver."

"I take it you wouldn't consider signing the consent form, then? You could save someone's life."

"Well, give it to me. I'll think about it." Antronos passed Shenan the form, and watched him tuck it behind his cot. He doubted he would ever see it again. So far, everyone he had asked had either outright refused or politely deferred an answer, just as Shenan had, especially when they heard that Vernus was involved. It was getting frustrating.

"Are you ready to sleep now?"

Shenan nodded and settled down on his cot, extending his arm. Antronos dug a second vial out of his case and filled a new syringe. As the medicine was injected, Shenan relaxed—a little too quickly.

"Shenan?" Antronos nudged his shoulder. "Are you sleeping already?"

Shenan's breathing slowed and grew deeper. Then it stopped.

"Shenan!" Antronos slid his hand behind the fishmonger's head and elevated it slightly, then lightly tapped his cheek. "Shenan! Wake up!" Still nothing. Antronos shoved down his panic and tried to resuscitate Shenan by breathing for him and massaging his chest, and finally stopped when the aura of his patient diffused into the weak background glow of the bedding he lay on.

Antronos was horrified. How could this have happened? It wasn't possible. Shenan should have made a full recovery. What had he missed? A blood clot? He was getting dizzy and had to sit with his head between his knees, consciously slowing his breathing. Patients died. It had happened before, and it never got easier. He had to calm down. *But this wasn't right!* This had not been a terminal patient, and his aura had been so strong—*Stop relying on that! It's not proper medicine and this should teach you a lesson!*

The vial of sedative still sat on the small bedside table. Antronos' hand shook as he reached out and turned it so that he could see the other side of the label, where it quite clearly said in bold, black writing: 10X concentrate. *It wasn't possible—calm down—I never carry 10X solutions!* The last three vials of sedative he had administered were all working solutions. He pulled the remainders out of his case. They were all diluted to the proper dosage. But Opalena had stocked his case. No, it wasn't her fault. She couldn't have known his habits, and it was his responsibility to check the labels first. What was wrong with him? The first thing they had taught him in undergraduate medicine was never to assume he had taken the correct vial. He always checked first.

He stood up, defeated, and looked down at Shenan's body. He started to laugh. Was it surprising, really, that he should have failed so miserably to promote life when he was the step-child of Death and the Desert? The buzzing in his head increased. He couldn't breathe. He didn't feel at all like himself. Who was he, anyway? *Buzzing little insects worming their way into my ears. I have visions of grandeur, just like Lord Jait, who is in my head right now.* His thoughts were refusing to be controlled, spinning madly through his consciousness, ordering themselves in ways he would have never considered previously, like someone was purposely stacking the blocks of his mind in a pattern that pleased...who? And the constant *buzzing*. It was natural for insects to be attracted to the dead, but why couldn't he *see* them? *Grey, twisting insects, coiling out of Lord Jait's eyes and nose and mouth. Swallowing my mind, swallowing me.*

The corner of the consent form was sticking out from behind the cot. Antronos slowly pulled it free and ripped it up. He could rip . . .

Earth damned consent form. *Rip it open.*

Antronos picked up his scalpel.

*****

Antronos' hands shook as he roughly shoved the stolen organ and bloodied surgical knives back into his case and pushed it under his cloak, remembering at the last moment to pick up and hide the vial of medicine as well. He was so damned tired. He tried to push long, dark hair out of his face, and was momentarily surprised to notice that it was blond and frizzy. Of course it was. It always had been.

Turning away from the body, he went outside and told the fishmonger's widow the truth about her husband's death in terms she would never understand, then tried to hurry back to the river barge without listening to her wailing. He hadn't made two steps through the straw-covered rock of the lowest tier of the underground market, before hands were reaching up from the piers, clutching at his orange robes, pulling him back, begging him to come and heal their sick. He tried to dislodge the other fishmongers, yet with each hand he pulled away, two more took hold. He almost dropped his case and felt a dizzy rush as he realized what it would mean if it were to fall open. The insects in his mind spoke to him. *No one here would ever blame you for Shenan's death. You are the rising star of the university. It is unthinkable to suspect you of murder. Go and find another donor. They want you to. We want you to. Obey your Lord and High Prince. Buzzzzzzz.* His feet turned him around. No! He twisted back again. His own body betrayed him, trying to turn back. Why couldn't he control himself?

In a rage, Antronos shouted at the fishmongers to leave him alone, and struck viciously at their hands. His own hand glowed with an intense double aura, leaving trails of shifting light as he moved it. He watched his hand in frantic enthrallment as he tried to shake off the extra light that wasn't his. Those patrons nearest him backed away, and he stood hyperventilating in a small bubble of silence. Looking up at the cavern skylight, the tiers of the market above him laden with their multi-coloured, glimmering trinkets, seemed to spin and crush him with endless waves of dagger-light and sound. *Move!*

Antronos forced himself to think about how to leave, furiously ignoring the whispers and looks of the imbeciles clustered around him. They murmured that it was difficult for him to accept his patient's death, that the old widow's selfish howling had upset him. Were they all so stupid? Could they not *see? Who am I? Am I real? Why is Jait riding around inside my head, carrying demons on his back?* Why were they begging to be his next victim? Euthanasia was one thing; deliberate killing of a recovering patient was quite another. It was driving him insane.

He looked past them towards the barge, which was just about to travel north on the underground river, and saw the hopeful faces of the passengers wanting some free medical advice. Instead he punched aside those standing too close to him and ran up the nearest skylight maintenance stairwell. He bashed open the lock and shoved the door upwards, tumbling out onto the sand.

The openness of the Desert gave him some relief. He was finally alone. The buzzing subsided and his mind began to clear. He walked slowly, his robes wrapped tightly around him, his eyes closed against the grit carried by the wind. If the organ were to be useable, he should hurry. The ice container would only last so long. What should he do? What had he done? *By the Earth, what have I done?*

Desert

Antronos was completely lost, feeling stupid, and the Desert was playing games with his mind. He didn't think he had wandered more than a few hundred metres from the skylight maintenance door, but all he saw in any direction was endless sand. He strode angrily in what he thought was the right way, occasionally spinning about when the sun seemed to change position in the sky, then turning back to his original heading, determined not to let some hallucination confuse him further. He could still feel the intense heat of the real sun burning his face, and let that guide him instead. He also knew he could find his way out of the Desert by following the gradual change in the dusty scent of the wind, which had an increasingly metallic tang to it as he neared the Yrati River.

Then again, maybe he shouldn't leave the Desert. There was a good chance that by now Shenan's murder and theft of his heart had been discovered, and a mob had formed to hunt down the freak who wanted to be a doctor. Why in Earth had he taken the heart? It didn't make sense. He was thinking of insects and Jait and then...he couldn't explain it to himself. It was almost like Jait had invaded his mind and shoved him out of his head with such ease that he hadn't quite noticed when it had happened. But why? On his last meeting with the High Prince, he had sensed no animosity from the man, and certainly had not felt any of the strange, coiling, grey entities coming from him. But what was the point of agonizing? There was no way the tunnel dwellers would accept him as "normal" now. His office, his placement at the House of Dra, his fellowship...all lost. He hadn't really been that eager to start his project without further consideration, and yes, Vernus had pushed him, but he had been prepared for that, because Sephus had warned him that Vernus would push—

He stopped walking, suddenly remembering the folded paper Sephus had given him. As he fished it out of his pocket, he felt something small and hard within, so he sat down in the sand, turned his back to the wind and carefully pulled open one corner of the packet. A small vial was inside and some writing was on the paper itself. He pulled open the cap of the vial. It was filled with coarse, grey powder that smelled a bit like mildew. He strung the vial onto one of the ropes of prayer beads he wore around his neck, and completely unfolded the paper. The words were handwritten, and the paper looked like it was ripped out of an old lab journal: perhaps the same one he had stolen from the archives.

"*Herein fynde the recipy for powder that can blocke peruysal of the mynde by persons of the outsyde...scrypted by Sen Vernus, Professor of Medycyn, Temlochty Unyversyty.*" A formula for medicine that could prevent invasion of someone's mind. The date was just over five hundred years ago.

Antronos doubled over and swore violently. Sephus had known about Vernus' age and had been trying to warn him about—what was it? "Peruysal of the mynde," which must have been what those peculiar buzzing channels were this morning, coming from "persons of the outsyde." But why was Jait trying to get inside his head? And why hadn't Vernus warned him, especially since he had formulated this blocking powder ages ago? Vernus...it wasn't right. That muttering foetus-thing behind the curtain, Vernus pushing him, specifically warning him to get consent, Opalena crying, saying she was sorry...

Too many pieces were missing, but one thing seemed certain: poor Shenan had been the pawn, and had been sacrificed for nothing. The ice container was not designed for long periods in the daytime heat of the surface, and Antronos had been leery of opening it for some time now. There was no point in taking the heart back. It would only incriminate him further, and was completely untransplantable. He dug a hole in the sand and tipped the messy contents of the ice container into it. After a few seconds, the magic of the Desert made the heart wind its way below the surface, just as his mother's ashes had.

Antronos stood and wondered what he should do now. The recipe Sephus had given him might allow him to return underground and prevent another atrocious suggestion from being planted in his mind, although the ingredients were disgusting and he wasn't sure if he actually wanted to use it—they included mould grown on a human cranium. And even if he did go back and fight to regain his position, was it really worth it?

He folded the paper and returned it to his pocket. His fingers brushed against the other object there—the funny red cylinder. He took it out and looked at it, wondering about the underground creature who had deposited it in his office. His office. How strange that he still thought of it as his. He decided that he had to go back, if he were ever to make sense of what he had done and be able to live with himself. He continued to roll the little red piece between his fingers as he again began to walk.

He sighed in relief when the tip of the slanting glass skylight of the library attic came into view over the next crest. The barrenness of the Desert would soon end at one of the piles of rubble erected by the

Department of Physics. Just ahead, his path was blocked by a gully where the Yrati River had broken through the surface of the Earth for a few miles, before plunging back underground. Water trundled past: absolute desert on one side, and lush oasis on the other. The surface plants on the far side were sheltered from most of the wind and dust by a short cliff that edged the water. Antronos stared at it, wondering if this strange patch of vegetation was newly formed, or if it was one of the phenomena the Desert liked to move around. As he prepared to wade across, Antronos mused that knowing this oasis had been here decades ago would have made his childhood so much better.

Mist was on the ground as he stepped out of the shallow water on the other side, and he bristled at the unfamiliar sensation of humidity. It made him think of a dank sewer cave. He was distracted for a moment, and the world seemed to swarm and reshape itself. When it settled, it looked exactly as it had before, except everything appeared much more alive and vibrant. Blossoms sprouted everywhere in unbelievable colours, their scented petals floating on the mist. Some unidentifiable animal called through the foliage, and another hooted in return.

Strangely, the otherworldly sense of illusion did not end, and as Antronos walked farther into the oasis, it seemed to increase in strength. His mind became rather muddled, and remembering where he was going took considerably more effort. His body became filled with such a complete peace that his limbs felt impossibly heavy. He needed to sit down, yet if he sat, he knew he would not get up again. He trudged along a small creek, which somehow ran uphill, as he climbed to the top of the cliff. The mist did not dissipate, but rose higher off the ground to obscure his view, as did the surface plants, sometimes sticking out leafy branches that caught him in the face.

The mist faded as he came to a small clearing where the creek expanded into a shallow pool filled with multi-coloured rocks. Lord Jait was there, bending to the pool for a drink, his long, dark hair trailing in the water. He looked different, and it took Antronos a moment to realize that Jait's limbs were stretched so that they looked thin and elegant. His body was shortened and curved, ending in a small, upright tail, and his face was also stretched into a pointed snout. His ankles and wrists bore hooves. He moved with careful grace as he drank, now and then pausing to look up at Antronos.

Slowly, Antronos became aware of two figures on either side of the clearing. One was a priest from the Yrati Clan of healers, and the other was Vernus. Both of them were mesmerized, not moving and staring at nothing. Both held crossbows. Jait sniffed at the Yrati, then ducking his head, began to move towards Vernus. Antronos felt certain that Jait was going to die.

"No," Antronos whispered, and kneeling down in the water held out his hand. His heart raced. "Come here. Come." Jait's head came up as he looked at Antronos. He ducked his head again and took a step forward, sniffing the path ahead tentatively. Another step. If he would only come! Antronos was filled with a confusing dread, convinced for some reason that Jait was going to die, and that he had to prevent it. *But didn't Jait make me kill Shenan?*

Jait became nervous and his nostrils flared, the little tail flipping about wildly. A crossbow cracked loudly and he fell down dead.

Antronos was enraged. He looked at each figure, but his vision was too muddy for him to tell which of them had fired, so he struck both of them down with his fists. The Yrati fell over and crumbled into rubble, while Vernus looked surprised and hurt. Antronos noticed that Vernus was bleeding badly. He ran forward to take up the body of Jait, but within a few strides, nothing looked familiar and he was no longer where he had been. He was running though very tall surface plants, and they were growing up everywhere, blocking his view in all directions. He was running downhill now. Had he passed the cliff? Impossible to tell. Brown, crisp leaves were beneath his feet, and more kept falling from the surrounding plants, terrifying him as he ran. Then, in a deep ravine before him was a temple of stone. Dusty grey, the architecture was strange and curving, yet somehow familiar.

A trough ran from a door in the side of the temple, around a pool of water in the front, and down, spiralling into a tunnel that led back into the underbelly of the structure. Shiny red baubles glinting with an intense aura bobbed and twitched in the dark water of the pool. There came a chattering noise, like the sound ghouls from children's stories were supposed to make when it rained and they left their graves to walk the Earth. Six ghoulish skeletons came chattering down the trough. Their bones were *red!* And they wore *blue robes!* The little red cylinder he had been holding flipped out of his fingers and bounced along the ground, back towards a ghoul who darted out of the pool long enough to scoop it up and attach it to its knuckle. That thing had been a bone?

The speed at which the ghouls moved frightened Antronos, for the steps they took were so tiny, and they ran in a compressed pack, as if each ghoul had its shoulder bones fused to the one in front of it. Their jaw bones clicked rapidly. Around the pool, down into the tunnel. And again, but this second time there was a seventh ghoul who had eyes in his sockets, and as he ran around the pool, he watched Antronos. The third time, he broke away from the others and came speeding up the ravine, carelessly dropping bits of himself in his haste, and grasped Antronos' robes in a bony red fist. "Water is deadly," said the lipless ghoul. "But a fish can live in water. If you make sure they don't permanently kill the fish, there will still be life afterwards."

＊＊＊＊＊

Antronos awoke. He lay on his back and the sky was moving above him. The sky turned to rock, then to glistening skylight panes. He realized that he lay on a raft that was moving down the Yrati River and had just entered a tunnel that echoed with the clipped, cultured speech of business folk. He was headed towards the House of Dra. It was just as well, he thought. He had business there.

The two oarsmen looked down at him and grinned.

"Greog's brew has a lot of kick, don't it, Sen?" said one. The other, apparently Greog, lifted the bottle to Antronos' health and took a long swig. He nearly toppled backwards and swore.

"Hafta be careful," said Greog. "Otherwise ya might fall inna water *and he drowned*. We're not like *fish*, you an' I. For us, we've got to be *balancing* the water with somewhuts, like mixing it with *Desert*."

"Are you trying to tell me something?" asked Antronos. Greog looked confused and belched.

"Ain't it obvious?" he replied.

As the raft neared the House of Dra, the river widened and slowed. Antronos looked dazedly at the elaborate, three-storied façades of the Merchant Houses that were cut into the back walls of the cavern. Pearl-shaped balconies cupped oval windows. Windows overflowed with blossoming ivy that trailed down braided knots carved into the rock. Rock striated with generations of dust layers was compacted into semi-precious, polished trickles of translucent colour, like water. Water flowed past several small docks covered in blue-slate tile, already crowded with waving merchants looking for rafts to hire. Greog crowed.

"Lookit, Sag! All this out here at our end! We're goina make a *killing*!" He poled into one of the docks and hauled Antronos off the raft by the elbow. "This is as far in as we're allowed, Sen. House of Dan won't give us permits for businessing any further in. You don't give us no money, since we're happy to say you've come in our boat, but you just come back again, so other people can see, yes? Here, don't forget your kill." He bent down and lifted something from the bottom of the raft. He put it into Antronos' arms.

"What is this?" Antronos cried. He looked down at the white-spotted brown fur of a small deer.

"That's yours, Sen. You told us you killed it out by the cliff when you were setting it free from a trap. Part of your *live-long* plan, wuddn't it?" He gave Antronos a broad wink. "We'll have to be off now, and you be going to the House of Dra, yes?"

The raft pushed away. The sunset light coursing through the ceiling panes cast a red hue on the oarsmen's skin. As they drifted away in the distance, they appeared to disintegrate into tiny bits which floated on the water like pieces of a broken clay pot.

9
Flashpoint

Antronos jerked awake. He found himself in the small sleeping alcove of his office, his sandals full of grit, his chin pressed painfully against the stone wall. He listened intently for buzzing or any other indication that someone might be trying to get inside his head. Silence.

He sat up and pushed his hair out of his face. He had no recollection of how he had returned to his office, just hazy memories of wandering over the surface...and something about water. Red and blue, water surfacing...somewhere. He wondered how much of it had been hallucinations, induced by the heat and the Desert's magical whimsy. The vial hanging around his neck was still full of mouldy powder, but the paper Sephus had given him was missing, and there was no red finger bone in his pocket. Well, he could have dropped them. Looking around the room, he saw no crumpled figure of a dead fawn, so that must have been a Desert-induced hallucination. His eyes snapped back to his desk. The ice container sat there with the lid off and dried blood marking the edges. Everything he had carried into the Desert was with him on the mattress, except that container, and he had certainly closed it, not wanting the smell. Had someone been here? Why then, was he not in prison?

He got up and tried to brush most of the sand from his robes. If he were going to bluff his way through Shenan's death at least long enough to find out what was going on, it wouldn't hurt to look presentable. His mind kept returning to hazy, half-formed thoughts of water. Perhaps he should look for the books the old Yrati priest Dagnaum had written. He shook his head. Children's books about water magic wouldn't help him now. What was he thinking? He had two options: either go to Vernus for information about the "recipy," or go to Jait and watch for clues. He didn't trust either of them, but Vernus might ask questions about the organ donor consent forms that he didn't want to answer.

Still afraid of encountering an angry mob, he dug out his black scholar's robe from under a stack of papers and pulled it over his orange mourning clothes. He then left his office and wound his way through the back tunnels to the Royal House, keeping out of sight as much as possible.

The only way for him to enter the Royal properties was to walk through the main promenade past the columns and artificial waterfalls, which was a very public and well-lit place. He stepped in front of the palace guards and pulled out his pass for their inspection. If they arrested him, he might still get some information from the interrogator. One of the guards peered into his face, and he pulled off his hood to avoid offending her. Her expression immediately softened.

"Good evening, Sen Antronos," she said. "I heard about your patient this afternoon. I'm very sorry."

Antronos stared at her, stunned. *What had she heard?*

"Thank you," he said at last. "I'm also very sorry about him. And for his wife."

"It was very brave of you. Sen Vernus told the coroner how you had to use your bare hands to try to massage that poor man's heart into beating again. If only it had worked. You would have been a hero."

Antronos felt like he was going to throw up. Why would Vernus protect him after saying so clearly that he would not keep him as a student if he made the slightest mistake? And how could Vernus have told such *lies*?

"I...had to leave. I was unable to console the widow or help her with arrangements. Is the deceased with the coroner now?"

"Yes, so I hear. It is standard protocol for the coroner to step in when there is no attending physician."

Not out of the slipsand yet. Antronos wondered how Vernus had explained the complete absence of Shenan's heart, or if he had covered that up too.

"Will there be an autopsy?"

"Oh, I don't know anything about that. Perhaps your colleagues could tell you."

"Is Sen Vernus here?"

"No, but Sen Opalena is. Shall I escort you to the High Prince?"

"Yes, please."

The guard escorted him to Jait's chambers, then gave him a smile and a pat on the arm before she turned and walked away. No one came to announce him, so Antronos pushed aside the heavy door and cautiously entered. The first thing he saw was Jait writhing on the floor, puking up bile everywhere except in the bowl in front of him. His legs kept moving, as though he were trying to curl up into a ball, but couldn't quite manage it. Opalena was kneeling next to him, trying to keep his hair out of the mess and looking disgusted. Antronos rushed over to help her, and was dumbfounded when she immediately stood, and began packing up her books and outer robes without a word. Did she know? Was she angry with him?

"What's wrong with Jait?" he asked her.

"He has trouble tolerating diloxzapam," she replied.

"Then why did you give it to him?"

"He kept whining."

"By the Earth, Opalena! I can think of at least a hundred soporifics less dangerous and more commonly used. You didn't have to give him that one!"

She tried to leave and tottered to the wall, putting out a hand to steady herself.

"Had a bit yourself?" Antronos asked, then bit his tongue. As frustrated as he was, being waspish wouldn't get him any answers. "Did you hear about Shenan?" he asked her.

"Of course. I've been hearing about Shenan all week."

"What's that supposed to mean? Look, Opalena, I don't know what I've done to make you so uncomfortable around me, but I was hoping—"

Opalena cracked a smile. She seemed about twenty years older than she was supposed to be, and her normally lustrous hair looked like faded chamomile rather than its usual liquid silver. Antronos felt the gap between them widening rapidly. He rummaged through his thoughts for some way to make it stop, coming up with nothing. Opalena almost looked amused as she waited for him to finish. Finally she turned her back on him again.

"You do that, snake-boy," she said as she walked towards the door. "Keep on hoping and you'll end up like the rest of us."

The rest of who? Vernus' protégés? Could she have been affected by the grey, buzzing insects as well?

"I don't know what you mean."

"You don't know anything. Just leave me alone. You'll figure it out when you've been here long enough."

Jait pushed himself up, fell over and lapsed into dry heaves, forcing Antronos to attend to him and let Opalena leave.

Antronos dropped his outer robe on a chair, then hit a few pressure points along Jait's arms and chest, trying to relax the High Prince without giving him any more drugs. Jait bolted upright and grabbed Antronos by the arms with a surprisingly strong grip and pulled him close. The smell of vomit on his breath made it difficult for Antronos to pay attention to what Jait was trying to say, and he was being dragged into the mess on the floor. Was this really the man Antronos had considered a threat just hours ago? Jait was in no condition to control himself, never mind other people.

"I can't stop . . ."

"Don't worry, My Lord. It will pass."

Antronos tried to lift Jait off the floor a few times, then gave up and tried to clean him instead. Where were all the attendants? This was their job. Opalena could at least have told him more about Jait's condition before leaving.

"You're not listening to me." Jait's hands left gooey streaks as he pawed at Antronos' clothing, managing to knock several vials out of the loops of orange cloth.

Antronos sighed and stripped off those robes as well. It was easier to work in his fitted grey clinic scrubs anyway. He didn't know if he had the authority to summon the attendants. He would have to clean Jait properly by himself.

"My Lord, I'm prescribing a lavender bath for you. It's very soothing. Please, let me help you up."

Jait finally made an effort to stand, leaning heavily on Antronos.

"You think I'm stupid," said Jait.

"No, My Lord. Just tired and overtaxed. We'll set you right."

"I'm too stupid to have seen her and them in her head. I couldn't see them in her head. Liam wouldn't have let himself sleep with her with them in her head. Hailandir will be furious because I'm still not seeing things the way she wants me to."

Antronos dragged Jait into the adjacent bathing chamber and deposited him into a wicker chair. He looked around, flabbergasted. Even the toilets in the Royal House were extreme. The white-tiled room was excessively large, the ceiling set with a fractal-patterned skylight, and trees had been planted in the corners. Trees!

An empty square pool was in the middle of the floor, shallow and broad, with fish painted in enamel at the bottom. Antronos began to fiddle with the water fixtures at the edge of the square. How in Earth did the confounded things work? He finally banged against one of them with his fist and was satisfied to see water run out. At the moment he didn't care what the temperature of it was, or that there wasn't any lavender in the cosmetics tins placed at the edge of the bath. Jait was still babbling, one hand swatting alternately at his face and the air. Antronos stared at him, completely perplexed. *No, definitely not a threat.*

Jait was beautiful by conventional standards, but the contrast between how he looked and how he behaved was striking. Antronos was frustrated by Jait's lack of self respect. As much as he was beginning to understand Opalena wanting to drug Jait into a stupor, he thought that perhaps he could do something about the High Prince's longing for medicines. Maybe then he would be able to take better care of himself.

"He's making noise inside my head," said Jait.

Antronos stared at the High Prince for a moment, trying to decide what exactly he meant. Perhaps he was referring to grey, buzzing insects, or perhaps he was delusional. Or still completely doped up. Jait lapsed into repeatedly plucking at a thread from his shirt.

"Who is in your head?"

"Little black and green man in my head."

So that was it.

"My Lord," said Antronos, "there's no one inside your head, but I would like *you* to get in this bath."

Jait stared at Antronos like he was the swill-brain.

"Vernus is trying to use me."

Antronos swallowed hard, forcing down the sudden tightness in his throat.

"What did you say?"

Jait rubbed his face against his messy sleeve.

"I..." He seemed to be having trouble breathing. He gasped and doubled over, cradling his head in his hands. "Grey buzzy insects in my head," he moaned.

The vial of Sephus' powder was still strung around Antronos' neck. He opened it. The mouldy scent wafted up, suddenly seeming like a promise. Gently, Antronos eased Jait's head back and sprinkled some of the powder into his mouth. Jait choked on it and coughed so violently that Antronos hurried to fetch a basin, afraid that the High Prince would vomit again. He knelt next to Jait, whose eyes snapped open with startling clarity.

"Thank you," he rasped.

Antronos' hands began to shake as he realized the implications of the powder working. The mind invasions were real. No alternate explanations were possible.

He licked his lips, working up the nerve to speak the dreaded question. "My Lord," he started, "did Vernus use you to...get to me?"

"I don't know. He just took my mind away. Like Hailandir, he said I had power and he was going to use it. Says he doesn't have to touch anymore, when he uses me. Just jump. Into anybody he wants. But once he was in my head, I don't know what he did."

"Do you know why he's using you?"

Jait didn't answer. He was much calmer now, but still shaky and pale. If Vernus had managed to get to the High Prince, he could probably overpower anyone. But why was this happening? Why use Jait? Because of this power he spoke of? And why had Vernus lied about Shenan?

Had Vernus used Jait to force him to kill Shenan?

Antronos was getting an inkling of just how much trouble he was in.

Jait began pulling off his shirt and making moves towards the bathwater.

"My Lord, shall I call your attendants?" asked Antronos.

"I don't trust them," said Jait.

"Why not?"

"It isn't safe anymore. I thought I could do anything with anyone. See now, I've made a mistake."

When Jait said nothing further, Antronos prodded gently, "Would you like to tell me what happened?"

"I took Opalena to my bed. She brought Vernus with her, carried the others in her head. That's how they got into mine. Touched me and reached in with grey, twisting worms." Jait slid into the water without removing the rest of his clothes.

"Opalena?" Antronos felt an irrational stab of betrayal and jealousy. *Stop it*, he told himself furiously. Opalena was trapped, as was Sephus, as he was becoming himself.

"She's spreading like a disease. Now she goes to Derik. First me, now my son. I couldn't stop her."

"Derik?" Antronos' voice sounded very small in his own ears. Vernus' sphere of influence was rapidly expanding. And Opalena was being used like a whore. No wonder she had been so testy when he had tried to get close to her.

Jait was no longer talking or paying attention to him, and thankfully, had begun to dump water over his own head. A sharp bang nearly made Antronos jump out of his skin. The dream-memory of a fawn being shot by a cross-bow flashed through his mind.

Jait had dropped a metal decanter against the edge of the bath. Antronos muttered something about finding clean clothes and excused himself.

The red bedding was rumpled and formed mounds, reminding Antronos of the skulls of the red ghouls as he imagined them moving under the floor of his office. For some strange reason, the memory of his Desert-dream meeting with the fairy tale ghouls comforted him, and he wished he still had the little red piece of bone that had been one of their fingers. What should he do now? Confront Vernus? Take Sephus' advice and quit graduate studies? Run back to the empty Desert? *Is any of this real?*

Lost in thought, he pulled open the great carven doors of the wardrobe and rummaged through Jait's clothes. It was a huge walk-in closet with at least seven rails of hangers and mirrored from end to end. Instead of being lit by bioluminescent moss, imported electrical lights from Raulen had come on when the door was opened. Unlike those in Vernus' laboratory, these cast a soft, yellow light.

Jait had a lot of very nice clothes. Antronos wondered if the High Prince even knew what he had, or if he ever got a chance to wear all of these. Considering how sick Jait was, Antronos didn't want to pick out another of the elaborately embroidered white shirts, and managed to find a plain sleeping robe instead. Now what? His mind felt numb, and he absently told himself that he was slipping into shock-induced fatigue and should find something to eat. He began to hunt for some slippers, the simple action giving him some reason to delay sorting out his personal mess.

Digging into a back corner, he heard the rustle of packing papers somewhere to his left. He froze. Had he made that sound? Cautiously, he began to search again, ears straining. He pushed aside a stack of shoe boxes, and caught the glow of a human aura hiding under a mound of tissues. It was small: a child. He relaxed.

"I don't suppose you know where I could find some slippers," he said. "All I've been able to find are dress shoes and hunting boots."

A small face peeked out at him. Brown eyes, shaggy blond hair. Features similar to Prince Derik's. Was this his son?

"Who are you?" the child asked.

"I am Antronos. A doctor. Who are you?"

"Leod. Are you going to help my grampa?"

"Do you mean My Lord Jait? Is he your grandfather?"

Leod didn't answer, apparently having thought better of speaking to Antronos, and covered his face again.

"Why don't you come out of there?" Antronos asked.

"I'm not supposed to be here," said Leod.

"Then why are you here?"

"Grampa is the only one who is nice to me. I don't want him to be sick."

The only one? Antronos had always thought his own beginning in the Desert was the worst experience a child could have. Was Leod not the Crown Prince after Derik? This was a strange upbringing for a prince.

"Come out, Leod. There's no one else here, and I won't tell. Why shouldn't you be here? You're a prince, aren't you?"

Leod finally pushed the papers aside and sat up.

"I'm not supposed to be born."

"Excuse me?"

"I'm not real. I'm a bastard." He drew out the last word, saying it as if he had only heard it spoken, but didn't really know what it meant. For a second, Antronos felt as if he were looking at himself, during one of those awful times when the Desert had spirited his mother away, leaving him uncertain if he would ever find her again. "If my father finds me here, he'll hit me again. Can you make sure Grampa is all right? Things would be awful if anything happened to him."

Antronos was horrified, and at the same time felt a strong affinity for Leod—the light hair, the brown eyes, the abandonment. He wanted to pick the child up and protect him from all the things he had suffered himself, growing up without a caring father. If Leod was telling the truth, that is. Very gently, he took the boy's hands and extended his arms. The child was extremely thin and small for his age, which Antronos guessed was maybe five to seven years. He had bruises and nicks all over his limbs. His hair was not evenly cut, his clothes were too large and dirty, and there was a deep, oozing sore on the left side of his head. It looked as if someone had grabbed him so hard that his ear had almost been torn off.

"By the Earth," Antronos whispered. He reached for Leod, wanting to pick him up, but the child scurried away.

"Leod, I only want to help. Let me put some medicine on your ear. It will hurt less."

Apparently that was still considered a threat, as Leod slipped away into the endless rows of shirts and gowns. It was understandable, Antronos thought, that the child would want no one touching him.

"I will help your grandfather," Antronos said.

Back in the sleeping chamber, Jait had slumped into bed, still wearing his sodden pants. Antronos did his best to undress him and ease him into the robe. Jait was a little more helpful this time, and seeing Leod creep to the side of his bed, he scooped the child up in his arms and collapsed with his face nestled in the boy's hair. Each of them seemed to comfort the other. Antronos was confused.

"Leod," he whispered. "Did your father hurt your ear?"

Leod nodded.

"Why doesn't Jait stop him?"

"He can't," Leod whispered back. "Most of the time he's too sick."

Or doped up, Antronos thought.

"Where's your mother?" he asked.

"I didn't have one. I have to hide now." Leod slipped out of Jait's arms and ran towards a panel behind a tapestry. Somehow he opened it and disappeared through it.

"Leod, wait!" Antronos hissed. He scuttled after the boy and was relieved to find he could also fit inside the narrow tunnel.

"Are you coming with me?" He heard Leod's voice from somewhere up ahead.

"Yes! Wait for me." He shuffled along in a squatting position, his head bent at an uncomfortable angle because of the low ceiling. Dust spilled in from various cracks in the walls, and he could see the aura of the odd insect carried with it. Leod's small shape finally glowed in front of him as he turned a corner.

"I can show you where *they* hide," said Leod.

"Who?"

"The new people. I hate them. I thought they were so mean that even my father wouldn't like them, especially when he caught them hurting Grampa. But I was wrong."

Leod's aura pulsated with distressed anger for a moment before he scuttled ahead on hands and knees. After a few turns, he pushed open another panel and crawled out into a dimly lit room. It was a tall, circular chamber, with no skylight, but the occasional brazier and tank of biolumi-nescent moss. Five spiral staircases were spaced around the perimeter of the room, leading upwards to several circular tiers, all lined with shelves of folio books. They were in some sort of archive.

"Come up here!" Leod ran up one of the staircases and disappeared between the shelves. Antronos ran after him, following the glint of Leod's aura that gleamed between the books. They stopped at the edge of a raised walkway that led into another chamber. Leod crouched down, as did Antronos. Voices were coming from below. They crept forward cautiously, trying to stay concealed as much as possible by the carved stone railing.

The room was roughly hewn, not at all decorated like the finely tiled chambers that characterized the rest of the Royal House. Lined patterns and the odd symbol were etched into the walls, and a fire cast flickering shadows on the sandy rock. Antronos peeked over the railing as far as he dared. Several people were sitting in a ring around Prince Derik. He recognized Sephus and Vernus. Opalena was not there. The others were unfamiliar to him. They were strange looking, distorted somehow, and half of them had an odd, depleted aura that was hazy grey or blue, unlike anything Antronos had seen before.

"He is trapped," Vernus was saying. "The fishmonger's body has been quarantined by the coroner, and questions are being asked. One word from me, and they will perform the autopsy. There are several witnesses to testify that he was at the docks. We have him now."

"But will he participate?" That came from an ugly creature with frizzy, yellow hair, who sat with her crooked limbs curled up in an impossible lump. "He may defy you yet."

"Then he will die," said Derik. "The penalty for such a heinous murder can easily be arranged."

Antronos realized that they were talking about him. He suddenly understood what Opalena had meant when she said she had been hearing about Shenan for an entire week. The whole thing had been planned. And all Vernus' talk about not tolerating mistakes had been a distraction. The old goat never had any intention of letting Antronos leave his lab, never mind throwing him out. His legs felt prickly and cold. He tried to shift them without making any sound, to get up and get away as fast as he could without his rising panic making him do something stupid.

"Try to take him again. It's time you controlled him properly," said the folded-up, frizzy thing.

"Jait is not well enough. We will have to wait until he regains his power," Vernus replied.

"You and your stupid wish to jump from long distances. Enough with your idiotic *experiments*. They're making you dependent. Do it the old way, by direct contact. He's your student. Summon him."

Vernus looked choleric. "I will decide how—"

"I can substitute for my father." Derik cut himself with a dagger, along the length of his wrist, and watched his blood run down his arm. Vernus still looked angry, but made some gesture with his hand. The others began to chant, swaying, hypnotic...low muttering...grey, twisted entities worming out and reaching in. So much louder now.

Antronos grunted and pressed his hands to his head. It was painful this time, not just an annoying buzz. It was more like someone trying to rip the top of his head off with giant pincers. He cried out in pain and saw Leod run back into the archive. He fumbled at the beads around his neck, trying to find the vial of mind-blocking powder. His hands were leaden and numb. His mind and vision went black. He couldn't even see the diffuse aura of the rocks. Padded footsteps on the walkway told him that someone was coming.

"Well, look who we have here. Sen Antronos. How convenient." Vernus reached down and grabbed him by the arm.

10

Resist

Antronos dug in his heels and twisted against the grip of the brute pulling him into the cavern. The creature gave him a rough jerk, flipping him over and scraping the skin from his arm before continuing to drag him down the stairwell and through the coppery dust of the stone floor. He shook his head to clear it, staring up dazedly at his captor. The monster might have once been a man. Its teeth were rotted, one eye was desiccated, its skin was a mummified mottled brown, and the sloped disjointedness of its shoulders didn't affect its strength. No aura radiated from it, not even the reflected candlelight. Its face made Antronos think of dead things rising to the surface during a raging magnetic storm, of a creature pulled apart and put back together by the Desert, of the tiny bronze figures he had found in Lizard's nest. Murdek.

"Leave him there, Caros," said Vernus. The thing obediently released Antronos' arm and shuffled out of sight, while the other Murdek shifted to close around him in a circle. Most of them looked either dead or well on their way. Some of them had misshapen limbs that may well have been fused with those of surface animals: human flesh tones, but twisted and stretched so that heels ended where knees should have been, and toes curved in black talons. Vernus crouched next to Antronos, leaning over him slightly. "What did you do with Shenan's heart?" he asked.

Antronos pushed himself up from the floor and away from Vernus. "What did you want with it?" he spluttered. The old man's mouth twitched, his black eyes unwavering.

"You're mine now. Your every action, every thought, every moment. We were part of you when you killed Shenan. You felt it."

Antronos swallowed hard. He needed to believe he was still in control of himself, not the crazed thing he had been when he had ripped open Shenan. He panicked at the thought of his free will being trampled like

95

that again. But perhaps he could resist them now that he knew what was happening. They had tried to take him a few moments ago and failed. Perhaps it was only because they had stopped the chant, but he pushed that thought away and tried to believe he had an advantage.

"You can't force me to do anything without Jait! On your own you're nothing."

Vernus chuckled. "That's hardly the case. I only needed Jait to control you when you were far away. The reason I did not bind you immediately was that you've been very useful as my little test subject. Once I've bound your mind properly, it won't matter where you are." He stood up and regarded Antronos for a moment. "Oh, did you think this was going to protect you?" Vernus took a paper from his sleeve and waved it in front of Antronos' face, showing him the "recipy." "As I'm sure Sephus can tell you, it loses its efficacy with repeated use. Certainly, I had wondered for a time how he managed to resist me so well, but that was only ever a partial resistance, and it isn't doing him much good now, is it?"

Antronos looked over at Sephus, and caught his breath as the other man raised his head, revealing severe bruising around his face and neck. His hands, twisting in the folds of his black and green cloak, were bound at the wrists, and his aura seemed drained, faded until it was an odd green colour. Sephus met his eyes for the briefest moment, then looked away, seeming to stare bitterly at something on Antronos' chest. He didn't have to look down to know it was the vial that carried the mould powder.

"I hope you appreciate how much it cost him to make that useless gesture towards you," said Vernus. "Now you've both been caught." Pulling a stiletto from his sleeve, he grabbed Antronos' arm, yanked it straight and tried to force the spike into his vein. Antronos twisted away, the pointed metal scraping the inside of his elbow. He broke Vernus' hold with his other hand and scuttled up against the wall.

Vernus again looked at him speculatively; then with an agile turn, he strode away. He stood completely straight, regardless of his gnarled limbs, looking more nimble than he made people believe with his public façade of old-man doddering.

"Try it once more, without contact," he said to the others. The buzzing chant rose from their mouths like a swarm of black flies. Antronos convulsed with pain as the sound pervaded his mind and the twisting, grey tentacles pushed against his will, into his head. This attack was more brutal than any he had felt in his office, at the docks, even most recently at the top of the stairs, but it was somehow tangible, lacking the insinuating liquid form of Jait's mind, and Antronos was able to resist it. The chant grew louder, more persistent. Some of the creatures hedged towards him, and with closer proximity, their assault grew more intense. He felt them seeping through his skin, slithering up his legs like coiling ropes of sand, but this was surface magic, and he was a child of the Desert. He could fight this. He knew the very source of this power—

A sharp pain erupted at the base of his neck and he pulled his eyes open to see Vernus stepping away from him, needle and syringe in hand.

"NO!" he shouted, and forced them out of his head with every bit of will he could muster. He slid along the wall to get as far away from them as possible. Vernus held up a hand, and the chanting stopped.

"Interesting," he said. "This one is definitely stronger than most. My apologies, Prince Derik, but it seems that you *cannot* substitute for your father."

"Enough! I will take him this time." The frizzy-thing rose up off the ground to hover over Antronos' chest. The creature's robes ruffled with the wind of her movement, carrying an unwashed stench from underneath them. He stared at her in amazement, unable to believe that she was actually floating in the air. She reminded him of the pickled foetus specimen his professors had used to test him during his undergrad work—the semi-developed face pressing against the glass jar had given him nightmares.

"You've given him the drug! It will weaken him, and we'll crack him like an egg."

"Patience, Meriamdan. This one is different. His mind is like a fractured mirror with only shards to hang on to. Let me think a moment." Vernus began to pace, ignoring Antronos as if he were an oblivious laboratory rat.

"Think later," the seaweed-haired creature growled. "I am not afraid of his shattered thoughts." Her hands shot out and clamped around Antronos' head. He screamed at the burning pressure of her hands and the influence of her spirit that she forced onto him. She was inside him in a second and tore open his mind.

For a moment, he saw his hands flailing, a double aura echoing their movements, before the pain transcended into a searing white nothingness. He floated in it, lost. The entire world had been shut out. No sound was here. No sensation of the rock against his back. No scent or colour.

It was a moment before he came back to himself. Vernus had pulled the thing away, but Antronos could only focus on what he was saying mid-sentence.

"...see now, you've rushed in and hurt yourself. You must wait for the drug to work, and you need our help."

Vernus was holding a kerchief to the tiny trickle of blood that seeped from the foetus-thing's ear.

"Do it your way, then," the yellow clot-head spat. "But *hurry*. You always waste time *thinking,* and I have waited a very long time."

Antronos' lips moved but were too uncoordinated to form the sounds he wanted. His arms wouldn't push him away from that hovering, filthy creature. He could still feel the unsanitary presence in his mind. It made him afraid to breathe, in case he inhaled more of it. He wanted to crawl out of his skin. Anything to get away.

"You'll never find Shenan's heart," he managed to force out. It was the only protest he could think of at the moment.

Vernus looked at him contemptuously. "That's hardly important. Besides, it has already served its purpose. Danos! Come here."

One of the Murdek jumped from a dark corner of the room, landing cat-like in front of Antronos. Again, it might once have been a man, dark curly hair, relatively handsome features, regular formation of body and limbs, but the eyes were incongruous with humanity—empty white orbs with only the blackened, wide pupil in the centre. Its grey-blue aura swirled about like polluted water, as it stared at Antronos while its lips twitched and nostrils flared, as if it were taking him in with all senses at once.

Vernus bled the creature, which didn't flinch as its skin was slit with the knife. The muttering chant did not enter Antronos' head this time, but surrounded him like an impenetrable wall. He stared at the Murdek in amazement as they swayed around him, the monosyllabic sounds falling from their mouths like stones to fill up the floor in front of them and pin him down where he lay. He struggled against the tide of sound, but his legs wouldn't move under him, his arms wouldn't press against the ground to lift him up. He squirmed to cover his ears, then screamed in fright and pain when the creature Danos bit his ankle, gnawing away the skin, trying to force his spirit into Antronos' body. He kicked at it, finally free of the paralyzing spell. The Murdek directly opposite him momentarily stopped their chant, falling back as if having been pushed. He gasped desperately, feeling like he had come very close to being suffocated.

"Let's kill him," Meriamdan said.

"Later," said Vernus.

"NOW! Sephus can do this thing. We don't need this little reptile, and YOU cannot control him."

"The Lady Alain is not taken with Sephus. She doesn't write him letters, offering him money to come visit her."

"It doesn't matter. She cannot keep him out."

"That would take time, my love. You have already been in exile these last two hundred years, and you are the one who doesn't want to wait for Jait. Besides, I'm beginning to understand why snake-boy intrigues Lady Alain so much." Vernus carried a small cage into the centre of the circle and reaching in, lifted a squirrel from it. The tiny ball of fur hid its face, its body heaving rapidly in terror.

"I'll tell you what, Antronos," said Vernus. "You do a little something for me, and I will hide your secret about Shenan a little longer."

"I don't care who you tell! I'll tell everyone myself!"

"You'll be skinned alive for murder," said Prince Derik, who spoke with quiet, threatening intensity.

Antronos' mind raced. What "little something?" What were his options? How badly would it hurt to be peeled? Why did they want *him* to do it? Vernus was experimenting with him now, but for how long until they killed him?

Vernus' chant erupted into a long string of gibberish, with the occasional word recognizable as Old Temlochti. The tiny squirrel squeaked pitifully, then struggled and scratched as Vernus squeezed the life out of it. The creature Danos leaned towards the squirrel, mouth opened and straining, as if it would vomit. As the golden aura of the squirrel spilled out and dissipated, the unnatural blue aura of Danos flowed from its mouth and coiled around the squirrel's body.

The chanting stopped. Danos collapsed. The squirrel fell silent. Presently, what was left of Danos fouled itself, while the squirrel sat up and preened, exploring its body with newfound curiosity. Vernus stroked the small creature's head. He held it out to Antronos.

"A gift for the Lady Alain. You will take it to her."

Antronos stared in revulsion at the squirrel as it was placed in his hands. Its eyes were completely white, except for Danos' black dotted pupils leering back at him.

"Take it. To Alain."

He flinched away from the words that were hissed directly into his ear. Looking around, there was no one nearby.

"You've shown with Shenan that you're just as skilled in murder as everything else you put your mind to," said Vernus. He smiled as Antronos cringed at the words. "So I expect you to kill Alaindra first. This is to be a permanent transition, and it wouldn't do to have both her and Danos living in the same body. You know I'll make sure you do it, so whether or not you resist the inevitable is up to you."

The Murdek were silent now, staring at him. Waiting for him to move. He got to his feet, pretending acceptance, trying not to let his trembling show, and wanting to get out of there as fast as possible. He closed his hands over the squirrel, half expecting it to bite him.

"Is that all?" he asked. "Then I'll leave now."

"You just remember, Antronos," leered Vernus, "that one word from me will win public support for your execution. I'll say how convincingly you lied to me. No one will miss you, or wonder where you've gone, because they'll all know, and all approve. There's no rescue for you, and no incrimination for me."

Antronos shakily started breathing again, then turned and walked out of the cavern, damned if he were going to let his legs wobble, tensing in anticipation of an attack by the creature Meriamdan, imagining her teeth sinking into the back of his neck in another attempt to take over his mind.

When he was relatively certain that they could not see him, he began to run. The tunnels grew increasingly rough until they were little more than natural hollows eroded through the rock, untouched by human implements.

Antronos finally had to slow down. He slumped against the rough walls, chest heaving, some distant part of his mind noting that he was about to cry, something he hadn't done in ages. Helpless anger was far more frustrating and infuriating than anger alone. Vernus had made it clear he was playing with him, a cat lifting his paw for the sheer pleasure of pouncing a second time. Meriamdan had just ripped him apart and he had been completely unable to resist. Her parting glare had left him with no doubt that she would devise a way to overcome his "fractured" mind. How was he going to keep his promise to Leod when he was up against that? Should he give in? Become like Sephus? No. He hadn't escaped the

Desert to wind up a prisoner of terror again. He had to fight until either he won or they killed him. Being dead was better than being controlled, and he wasn't going to let them use him to rip up another fishmonger. Rage finally swelled up in him, giving him strength.

He didn't know where he was, but the archive had to be somewhere in this direction. He winced and pulled the squirrel away from his chest. The damned thing had chewed a hole through his shirt and had started to gnaw away at his skin. What the hell was he going to do with it? If he didn't play along, he might find himself barred from the Royal House or worse, unable to help Leod, and knowing what he knew now, he could never leave that child here. He had a brief flashback of the undertaker walking away from him in the Desert. *No more abandonment!*

His mind was his own for the moment, but if he were to have any chance of controlling his next move, he had to keep it that way. He pulled open the vial of Sephus' powder and tipped it onto his tongue. The stuff was putrid. He clamped a hand over his mouth to prevent himself from spewing it back out and did his best to swallow. He stood with his back against the tunnel wall for a few moments, breathing heavily, and trying not to drool as he waited for his nausea to pass. He didn't notice any immediate change in his mental state, and even if the powder did become less effective with repeated use, it was the only potential defence he had. He would have to reformulate it the first chance he got, to make it last longer. Pushing away from the wall, he continued down the tunnel.

The ceiling finally began to show cracks with shafts of light coming through from some overhead chamber, and water dripped from the ceiling. Antronos cautiously chipped one of the cracks open further, but his view was blocked by leafy green foliage and ferns. He crept along the tunnel until he saw a low, wooden door. The wood was very damp, and had swelled so that the door was jammed shut, but after a few frustrated one-handed tugs, he managed to yank it open, a few inches at a time. In a squatting position, he shuffled through a narrow tunnel, then was able to stand up in a miniature stairwell that was situated in the middle of a grandiose arboretum, packed with imported surface plants. The entire ceiling of this cavern was made of glass, increasing Antronos' sensation of exposure. A few gardeners were tending this cavern, but they were content to ignore him as he slunk past, searching for the fastest way out of the Royal House.

* * * * *

The Lady Alain didn't keep Antronos waiting very long. Her caverns were on a smaller scale than those in the Royal House, but competitively decorated. The main antechamber was tiled in pink-hued mother-of-pearl mosaics, the spiralling designs sweeping over the floor and up the pillars supporting the amber-tinted skylight. Antronos had spent the last few moments seated in a plump cushioned chair covered in floral tapestry, positioned between strange decorative boxes full of sand that had been combed into intricate lines, with the occasional translucent pebble redirecting the flow of the pattern. He had been staring at them curiously, feeling the patterns calm his agitation enough to allow him to think, yet when Alaindra swept up the stairs from a deeper chamber in a flourish of plum-coloured silk, he still hadn't decided what to do with the squirrel. Perhaps he shouldn't have come here, but he needed to pretend obedience, at least long enough to figure out what to do, and this was the safest place for him to mull over his options.

Alaindra's dark hair had been ironed straight, lips and eyelids painted shiny violet, skin powdered lilac-white. She barely gave him time to stand, before pretentiously offering her fingertips in greeting.

"I'm so glad you've come," she gushed. "I was worried when you did not answer my letter that you weren't going to accept."

"Forgive my rudeness," Antronos said automatically, and leaned closer to her, making a shallow bow over her hand. He couldn't miss the delighted flush that immediately washed over her face. Why in Earth was he letting her play him? For Leod's sake, he had to keep his wits about him. *Well, she started it*, he thought angrily. He released her hand and took a polite step back. "I never intended to reject your offer. Unfortunately it has been a rather hectic week, and I haven't had time—"

"Oh, yes! That poor fishmonger! And how was your sojourn in the Desert? Such a pity that you have to resort to such measures just to get a bit of peace! That is such a vibrant shade of orange you're wearing. Is it common among the Desert folk?"

Antronos felt himself becoming more angry and forced it down. He already felt grossly violated by the Murdek without having it dumped on him that the Dra were keeping such close watch on his every move. Like he was property. He wished she would keep it to herself and not flaunt it like some intimidation tactic. It made him think that she was feeding every tidbit about the new pet freak she was going to get to her gossipy high class companions. He wondered how much Alaindra knew about Vernus. Perhaps she would be prepared, and he did not need to worry about her. As if it could sense his thoughts, the Danos-squirrel rattled inside the metal canister Antronos had slung at his side. He instinctively covered it with his hand and watched Alaindra's eyes follow the motion of his hand downward, lingering at his mid-section, before finally creeping back up to his face. She said nothing. He found her stare irritating and disrespectful.

"So," he began, turning away from her. "What business do we have today?" Feeling rebellious, he unslung the canister and banged it down on an ornate tabletop. *Let her ask what was in it.* "I expect you have some contract for me to sign?"

"Perhaps we could talk?"

"About what?" He immediately regretted the terseness of his remark. Alaindra had been giving him the same look he had seen in Leod's face— trapped, wanting, trying not to hope. Now she looked angry and upset.

Her aura was also distressed.

"I get plenty of viciousness from absolutely everyone around me every single day. I thought that you of all people would understand how unpleasant and hurtful that can be. I thought you were different from tunnel dwellers. Are you going to show me now that I was wrong?"

He looked away from her and took a few seconds to force calm over himself. Considering what he had brought into her house, at the very least he could be polite. *By the Earth, I am a pachu. Such pettiness over a few coins that won't amount to even a fraction of what they've offered to pay me now. You're no longer a dock hand; you're a doctor. Start acting like one!*

"I'm sorry, Lady. You're right. I do know about being hurt." He held out a hand to her. "Shall we start again?"

Alaindra didn't completely lose her angry expression, but reached out to take his hand.

"I suppose you've had terrible hardships as well. I'll forgive you." She led him back to the cushioned chairs, and thankfully curled up in one separate from his. When she dropped the spoiled noblewoman act, she seemed much younger and more insecure than would be expected from a lady of her rank.

"You know I'm getting married," she said.

He hadn't known but was not surprised. "I take it you're having second thoughts about the gentleman?"

"He's half my age. Only sixteen."

That did surprise him. "Did you choose this partner?"

Alaindra raised her head from the armrest and gave him a cynical look. "No one in my family has chosen their spouse in over thirteen generations. We're all cousins, you know. I have to marry my cousin from the House of Dan. Herodan. Traditionally, I would marry the first male of his generation, his older brother, Dano, who appeals much more to me. But you see, Dano has no sister to lead his House, and he is older than I am, which means he would outrank me and thus take over the House of Dra. We would all be Dan then, and my elders won't allow it. Since there are no others, I have to marry Hero, and I have to do it soon. They're worried about my ability to breed properly if I wait any longer." She gave a defeated chuckle. "So much for me. Great patron of the university. Great head of the big merchant house. Nothing more than a breeding cow."

Alaindra waited a few moments for his response. Antronos was too derailed by her revelation to say anything. *Her sixteen-year-old cousin!*

"What would you tell my family if they told you to give yourself up like that?" she prodded.

"I'd tell them to go boil in Earth's Volcanic Bowels!"

Alaindra gave a delighted laugh. "I've never heard that one before! Tell me another!"

Antronos felt himself turning various shades of purple and self-consciously tugged his collar up over the scales on his neck. He hadn't meant to swear in front of her.

"Um. Perhaps I'd better not."

"Oh, come on Antronos! Please!" Alaindra reached over and tugged on his arm, very much like a child. *Like Leod.* He looked at her wonderingly. So different she was from her public persona, but if he had learned anything in the last week, it was to be more cautious with whom he trusted.

After a long moment of returning his searching gaze, Alaindra asked, "Were you born with those eyes?"

"No. The Desert changed me."

"I don't understand."

"Have you ever been out on the surface?"

"Once, as a child. But it was only so that my teacher could show me that there was a horizon. I've never been to the Desert. I've heard that it can trap you. Make you see things that aren't there, so that you'll never find your way out."

"Well, I don't quite understand it myself. It does change things. People, the landscape, anything. Some of the physicists at the university say there are very powerful magnetic forces out there which can twist metal into all sorts of convoluted shapes. They talk as if that explains everything." He gestured toward his face. "My eyes are not metal. How did the Desert change them?"

"Did it hurt?"

"Yes. I thought I had gone blind. It happened suddenly, just after my mother had died."

"And the orange robes?"

"The Desert colour of mourning. For my mother."

"I see. I think I understand you a little better."

Likewise, Antronos thought.

"Thank you," he said.

Alaindra looked surprised. "For what?" she asked.

Antronos smiled as he thought about the squirrel waiting in the canister. "You've just helped me decide something."

*****

Antronos left the House of Dra several hours later after giving Alaindra and a few of her aunts a clean bill of health, then taking generous liberties with the Dra cosmetics laboratory to compound what he predicted would be a more reliable version of Sephus' powder. He had expected nothing more than perfume bases and colorants, but discovered that their skin care products were based on remarkably solid science, and the lab was well stocked. He remembered most of the components from the lost piece of paper, guessed on others, and made a few modifications that should make it stronger and more palatable. With due consideration, he had also added an analgesic to the "recipy." Though he had clearly sensed a storm brewing among Alaindra's elders over her excessive friendliness towards him, he felt unburdened and even a little happy. If he were perfectly honest with himself, he had wavered in his resolve to defy the Murdek, and had considered "forgetting" the canister at the House of Dra, leaving them to open it or throw it out; thus their contamination by the creature would not have been by his direct actions. But now that he had access to a lab off campus, his chances at mounting a workable resistance seemed much easier. Before realizing Alaindra was not also his enemy, he had first considered sneaking into Vernus' laboratory, or failing that, asking the Yrati or Amphetam if he could use theirs, but concluded that either his "murder" of Shenan would come out when they began asking why he was not working with his supervisor, or he might inadvertently pull more people into the trap that he, Opalena and Sephus had found themselves in. Besides, his confidence was rising the longer he analyzed his situation. Vernus and his Murdek were going to be formidable enemies and could quite easily kill him. But it was unlikely.

They obviously wanted to use him, and Vernus had flatly refused to kill him when they could not immediately bind his thoughts, so hopefully they would be unwilling to play their execution ploy so soon. Besides, they would have to catch him first. If they couldn't always use Jait, their ability to search for him over long distances and conquer his glass-shard thoughts would be limited. For the first time in his life, he sent a mental prayer of thanks to the Desert for whatever it had done to him that had restructured his mind. At least he assumed it was the Desert that had changed his psyche.

The outer common tunnels were quiet, as most of the people who might have frequented these passages had probably gone home for supper. Antronos opened the metal canister he carried and flung the squirrel against the rock in disgust. It smacked against the ground, squealing in pain, its limbs flailing desperately. He drew up his leg and stomped on it. *How's this for skilled murder, Vernus?*

"I will still keep my promise, Leod," he whispered. He'd keep it for both the child and Alaindra.

11

Atonement

Antronos carefully felt his way around one of the thick wooden bookshelves, his hands trembling, as they had all the way from the House of Dra to the university library. He stared at his fingers, trying to force his eyes to see the golden, pulsating aura that he knew should be there. He managed to focus on it for a moment, then it faded into hazy grey nothing. His heart skipped when his vision faded into complete blackness, then reawakened in a blurred flash. What was happening? Had he poisoned himself with his new formulation? Two of the new powder capsules he had made in the Dra cosmetics laboratory were softening in his other hand. If he took them and was unable to see auras at all, it might disable him to the point where he would not be able to distinguish the Murdek from ordinary people. It was now clear to him the meaning of Opalena's double aura, and his own when he had been manipulated through Jait. He was also watching for the dull blue-grey aura that marked those Murdek who seemed less than human, and the diffuse yellow of those who were simply incredibly old.

The back of his neck prickled with some instinctive warning sense. He turned around and peered through the books, blinking rapidly. Two aisles down, someone was pacing rapidly, quiet and hunched, as though hunting for more than books. Antronos' vision sank, then flared to life, letting him see a clear double aura. He held his breath and snuck through the bookshelves in the opposite direction. He hadn't made it very far when his vision faded to the point where he couldn't keep moving. Cursing silently, he felt his way to the floor and curled up, his back pressing against the books, hoping that no one would find him. The darkness lasted for what seemed like an eternity, and for all he knew, his pursuer was standing right in front of him. What in Earth had he done to himself? The giddiness he had felt when he had imagined he could improve on Vernus' formula now made him feel stupid. Did he dare take the medication again? Did he dare not take it? Could he fix the unwanted side effects? He had to, if he was going to keep them out of his head!

Lightning flashed across his field of view a few times. Then a tiny circle of glittering lights appeared in the blackness, slowly growing larger, the middle of it filling in with a hazy image of the library around him, until his vision had cleared except for a misty ring of peripheral grey. His head felt like the front of it had been ripped off and someone was mixing his brains with a wooden spoon. Gradually rising to his feet, Antronos managed to take a few steps without vomiting, and covered his eyes with one hand, the other feeling his way along the shelves. Now it hurt to see, but at least he could glance around every few steps to make sure he was still alone.

Coming to the next call number location, he again found that the book he wanted was not there. Of course it wasn't. Every single reference that carried any academic weight at all was signed out, being re-catalogued, or mysteriously missing. He had only been able to find one book with any specific information about magic in it, and that was the child's storybook written by the old Yrati Dagnaum, about ghouls and water magic. Perhaps it was pointless to even bother with it, for if it had any value, it surely would also have been missing. But within its pages was clear animosity for the Murdek, so Antronos had tucked it into his robes anyway.

Finally accepting that fairy tales were all he was going to get, Antronos wound his way back up to the top level of the library, and slipped out through the back archives, completely bypassing the circulation desk. The tunnels leading to his office were almost empty, and he managed to walk in a fairly straight line to his door, without going blind or being unable to smile politely at the few other Sens he passed. Once inside, he flung the papers off his desk and flipped open Dagnaum's book. He impatiently dragged his eyes through a silly explanation of where ghouls came from—they were people who had suffered the stiffening disease—until he found the page of spells he wanted, and began hunting for what was needed. In frustration, he pulled out all the drawers of his desk, emptying them on the floor. It was such a simple thing, just a stick of red wax. He was sure he had hundreds of them. A metallic glint caught his eye, and he reached for it with one hand, while the other continued to sift through the mess on the floor. At least he had found one part of what he needed: a brass-handled haemostat, and now...of course, all the wax used by professors was purple, not red, and Amphetam had ensured he was given all the stationery due a professor along with his office. No wonder he couldn't find red wax. He clamped the haemostat onto a tie which could be used to hold shut the office door, and hooked the rings of the handle on nails set just behind the latch.

This is all so stupid, he thought, yet Dagnaum's baby-entertainment spell promised it would protect him, so he lit the wick of the wax stick and proceeded to seal the edges of the door with it. The Murdek were using magic, and if he were going to fight them, he would have to learn to do the same, and it would have to be far more reliable than just moving a few sand grains around. Even so, this was ridiculous, and while he didn't believe it would work, he couldn't stop his mind from accepting the possibility that it might. A blob of purple fell into the orange folds of his robe and he swore violently.

"Aren't you supposed to use red wax for that?"

Antronos spun around and saw a skeletal figure backlit by the skylight that formed the sloping ceiling of his office.

"Sephus! How did you...have you been here the whole time?"

"More or less. Vernus is furious about Danos." Sephus moved forward and leaned against the desk. He was barely recognizable. He looked shrivelled, even desiccated, like someone who was starving to death on the surface. *Or had been drained of all his blood.* Antronos blinked and strained his senses for any muttering sounds. He could hardly see by natural vision, and his Desert sight was not responding at all.

Antronos tried to swallow the dryness in his mouth. "He already knows?"

"He knew the moment you did it. Of course. What did you expect?"

Antronos blinked again. There. Sephus only had one, faded, weak aura.

"You didn't really think that wax would keep any of us out, did you? We wouldn't be able to come in through the door, but then there are other ways in."

Us? We? Antronos looked at Sephus suspiciously. Apparently he wasn't here to offer any more powders, and hadn't come after escaping from the Murdek.

"What do you want?"

Sephus came forward and Antronos backed up, nearly tripping over a stand of essays. Now that Sephus had stepped away from the window, it was obvious that his aura had completely changed. It looked grey.

"You are very handsome, Sen Antronos." Antronos said nothing, but stared numbly into eyes that were as glassy and dead as insects caught in ice. "This body of mine is almost completely useless. And I'm tired of this colouring. Meriamdan says black hair suits me but," he sighed, "I think I like your hair. And your eyes."

"How many times?"

Sephus lifted an eyebrow. "How many times what?"

"How many times have you stolen someone else's body? Were you ever really Sephus, or did you just steal the body of Vernus' student and pretend to be Sephus?"

Sephus' face became taut, as if he might weep, then cracked into a bitter smile.

"Oh, I was born in this body. I haven't been with Vernus *that* long."

"How many of your organs have failed from old age and been replaced?"

"Three. But not because of old age. Or by my choice."

"So have you given in to them now?"

"Who?"

"The Murdek. Did you finally let them get the better of you?"

Sephus gave an unhappy laugh. "Antronos, I *am* Murdek. Haven't you figured that out yet?"

"That isn't true. You were trying to resist them. Why don't you tell me something I'll believe?"

"What do you want to hear? That I'm really Sephus who you can convince to be your ally? I never intended to help you form some sort of "faction." I've always known that was futile. I was just trying to give you a chance to stay out of all this. I gave you what you needed to run away, but you knew better. You wanted to be part of Vernus' little gang, so now here I am, offering you exactly what you wanted. So come. Be a part of us."

"That is *not* what I wanted!"

Sephus took another step forward and Antronos stumbled backwards until he struck his head against the wall.

"You slimy little dung worm," said Sephus. "Crawled down here from the Desert. I *gave* you that formula, and you took *everything* from me! Every last trace of my freedom, my dignity, my life. And you just handed it all over to Vernus. Why didn't you *hide* that paper? By the Earth, you're an idiot. Well, I suppose I am too, for giving my defences away."

"Leave me alone!"

"Oh, it's far too late for that. I wonder what it'll be like, being you. I wonder what it'll be like when I go to visit Alaindra in your body. She'll trust me. Let me get her into the most vulnerable positions. And she's rather lonely, I hear."

"Sephus, you didn't want any of this. That has been clear all along. What has changed? Why are you going along with it now?"

Sephus smiled: "Because I'm tired. I'm sick of constantly fighting Vernus. And now, I realize how much easier and better my life can be."

"Better? Listen to yourself! You know very well it won't be better. That's why you resisted Vernus in the first place. And look at you! If you choose to prolong your life in this way, you'll be walking dead. Is that what you want to be? Stop this, Sephus."

Sephus was silent for a long moment. Then he screamed, "*Do you think he'll let me?*" His posture immediately changed, became relaxed, elegant, and he re-settled himself at the desk. "Tell me, Antronos, for I am curious. Here you are telling me I shouldn't prolong my life and yet, your motive in all of this is that *you* don't want to die. Why should *I* die? Because you tell me to?"

"That's not what I said. I said you can't have *my* life and you can't have *my* body."

"You owe me. I gave you mine. You give me yours."

"You gave me a damned piece of paper!"

"You still owe me. What's left for you, Antronos? Why can't I have your life?" Sephus' expression said that he was deliberately playing stupid. Apparently he was enjoying this game.

"Because it is *mine!* You've had your chance to live, and your chance to gain what satisfaction you could out of your life. You have *no right* to claim someone else's. Sephus, you're not dead yet. Don't let them kill you. You can still heal."

Sephus scratched under his chin. He looked unimpressed. "That's it?"

"Yes."

"Even though throughout my "chance to gain" I never came across any satisfaction? Perhaps therein lies your "why." I will continue to take life after life until I get my just due of "satisfaction." And as for me *healing!* Can you imagine my despair, Antronos, at finding that none of what you say is true? Do you think that I never had your youth, that I never listened to and believed those damned stories of my promised and wonderful life to come? Do you think I never wept and struggled to claim the achievement I trusted was mine to receive? Do you think I have not lived, waiting for the friend who did not break my heart, or the lover that did not push the knife in my back? All those years of never being as good as I was promised I would be. Liars, all, with thoughtless tongues. There is no such thing as a loyal companion. No such thing as a successful career. You're such a wise one, Antronos. It's only a matter of time before you realize how *pathetic* your life really is."

Sephus had risen and moved to the side of the desk. Antronos moved in the opposite direction and tried again: "Vernus doesn't want me dead. He already refused to let that flying thing kill me."

Sephus cut him off, laughing loudly. "You're full of dung! You know what, Antronos? You'll never enjoy your life because you don't know how to have fun. And by the way, it seems you do agree with me that having more than your fair chance is worth striving for, since wasn't your chosen research topic *longevity*?"

Antronos ducked and skittered across the room as Sephus came forward, slamming his fist into the wall with surprising force. He didn't even flinch, although his knuckles were peeled and bleeding.

"You're right. I'm not going to kill you. I'm here to bring you under control." Sephus pulled a long, metal wire from his sleeve. He struck at Antronos with the wire, this time laying open the cloth and skin across his back. Antronos refused to scream. He would not call anyone else into this fight.

He heard Sephus begin chanting, saw his own aura double, triple, as the pain of having the Murdek force their way into his head started once more. His modified mind-blocker was not working. He could feel Jait's presence so strongly that it was as if he were looking the High Prince in the eye, seeing the Murdek that rode on his back, inside his mind, and around his neck. He felt Meriamdan *shift* Jait's soul farther out of the High Prince's body and into the ether. Knowing he could not hold up against that level of power for long, he wondered if he could use Meriamdan's tactics against her, perhaps *shifting* Jait out from under her control. Instead of resisting, Antronos let them in, then imagined shards of light cutting the Murdek's thoughts into ribbons. He was about to grab hold of Jait's spirit when Sephus struck at him with the wire again, breaking his concentration with pain. Antronos gasped and felt Meriamdan's presence grab and hold on to him, mental shards and all. He grit his teeth, moaning and tried to force her out. He was too weak.

Sephus stopped his assault and stood back. He was breathing heavily, and wore a satisfied smile as he knelt and pushed Antronos' hair back. He pressed his lips to Antronos' ear and whispered strange words in Old Temlochti that caused a tightness in Antronos' chest, followed by a panicked fluttering of his heart, and finally a crushing pain in his abdomen.

Antronos flailed and managed to close his hand over a stylus that had been dumped on the floor with the other office supplies. He mustered together all the strength he could to shove the pen into Sephus' side.

"Get off me!" Able to breathe again, he shoved Sephus away, not at all sorry to see the other man clutching his side in pain and anger. It didn't faze Sephus for long. He grabbed the discarded desk drawer and swung, the corner of it catching Antronos at the temple. Meriamdan began to break off shards in his mind, and each one that broke felt like a snapping limb.

Having no other option, and feeling that he was about to lose this battle, Antronos slipped both of the powder-filled capsules he still had in his hand into his mouth. Section by section, the double dose of medicine shut down his mind, closing out Sephus and Meriamdan, and their bitterness.

Paralyzed and barely conscious, he had the vague impression that the assault had stopped. Muted sounds and visions were still available to him, so he was aware of Sephus flinging the wire aside, kicking him in the groin a few times, then leaving. Antronos was sure he would come back later.

12

Yrati

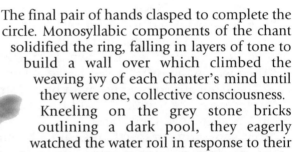

The final pair of hands clasped to complete the circle. Monosyllabic components of the chant solidified the ring, falling in layers of tone to build a wall over which climbed the weaving ivy of each chanter's mind until they were one, collective consciousness.

Kneeling on the grey stone bricks outlining a dark pool, they eagerly watched the water roil in response to their call, bubbling red like blood. Eyeless, red skulls surfaced and slowly twisted back into the depths. Several black fish appeared in the water, bodies twitching as they darted through columns of red bone. The pluming white fins and tentacles of a single, lost blindfish stood out against the dark water as she reached desperately, grasping at weeds and bones, unable to determine her way.

The chattering of the ghouls was clearly audible over the splashing of the water. *Sickness is coming through the fawn,* they said. *To free the fawn, you must help the fish. The snake killed the squirrel, and that helped delay the sickness, but sickness is still coming. If you make sure they don't permanently kill the fish, there will still be life afterwards.*

One of the Yrati broke the chant.

"What sickness?" he asked.

Ask the snake.

"Which snake?"

The water became still. The red colour disappeared.

"What the hell was that supposed to mean?" Ferril demanded as he looked over at the High Priest. My Lord Maxal sighed, as he wearily rolled back his hood. "Did you get anything out of that?" Ferril persisted.

"Boiled if I know," said Maxal.

Fara twisted her hand out of Ferril's thick fingers and winced as she shifted into a more comfortable position. She pushed the tangle of dark hair from her face and stretched. Beside her, Leelan yawned, not bothering to cover her mouth.

"Well, we were asking about Alaindra, and whether or not we should accept her petition to market some of our pharmaceuticals," Fara said. "Either she is sick, or she's going to make us sick. But they didn't say we should reject her, just block the sickness. I think."

"So, does she have a pet fawn?" asked Aren. Ferril looked over at his priest-brother, who was scratching at the sandy-brown stubble he hadn't scraped from his face yet. His eyes were barely visible under an unruly mop of slightly darker hair. *Why is everyone so much younger than me?* Ferril wondered privately. *Well, Maxal is older, but he has more hair. Such a shame that he always cuts it so short. It's almost as if he wants to be bald.*

"Maybe she has a pet fish," said Ferril out loud.

Maxal rubbed his eyes and snickered. His dark brows wiggled over his fingers. "That's going to sound dumb. 'Hello, in order to determine if you're worthy of our medicines, we need to determine if you have a pet fish.'"

"Maybe we're taking this too literally," said Aren. He tugged at the red and blue embroidered collar that marked him as Yrati, finally unfastening it and pulling it off. "Maybe she is the fawn, and there isn't an actual animal."

"Then who's the fish?" asked Locke. *Again, with an unjust allotment of hair!* Locke unconsciously blew light brown strands out of his eyes.

"Well, you're the fishbrain," said Fara. Locke tried to push her into the pool. Maxal grabbed their robes.

"Hey, show some respect! This isn't a bathing tub!" His rebuke didn't stop Locke from scooping some of the water into Fara's face.

"Get you for that!" she said.

"The fish and the fawn don't matter," said Ferril. "We're supposed to ask a snake anyway. So who's the snake?"

"Maybe that refers to Alaindra," said Aren.

Maxal's expression turned to amazement. "Hey, you're right," he said. "She *is* devious."

"Can we get a private audience with her?" Fara asked. "Where we could talk to her without all her advisors misinterpreting everything we say?"

"Probably," said Maxal. "If she really wants this deal, she could arrange it."

"What would we ask her?" asked Aren.

"About her pet snake," said Ferril.

"Alaindra has a pet snake?" asked Locke.

"Well, that turd, Antronos," said Ferril.

"Hey, now, just because he's different—" Maxal began.

"I don't like him either," said Aren. "Especially because he studies with Vernus. And he's always sneaking around in the dark. And he's weird. I've nearly tripped over him a few times in the library, and once when I asked him a direct question, he wouldn't talk to me. Wouldn't even look at me."

"Give him a chance, you two!" Maxal glared first at Aren, then Ferril.

"I know, I know," said Ferril hunching his broad shoulders and holding up his wide palms. "You and Amphetam love him. I'm just irritated that he's taking up office space when he refuses to teach. And as far as anyone can tell, he hasn't made any progress at all in this big 'death control' project of his."

"Nobody from that lab publishes much," said Leelan.

"Well," mused Maxal, "so long as their supervisor doesn't complain, it's unlikely anything will happen to them, the assumption being that their work takes a long time to complete, and they'll publish when they're ready."

"But except for Sephus, they don't even teach," Ferril persisted. "I've been teaching for ten years, and I'm still working out of the cafeteria."

"Tough roots, baldy," smirked Aren. He had a professorship in chemistry, office included. Ferril slapped him lightly.

"I still have *some* hair."

"But it's on the wrong side of your head!" Aren reached over and tried to tug on Ferril's dark beard.

A loud, muffled thud was heard from somewhere in another cavern, followed by angry yelling. Tibeau's laughter was punctuated with squeals of pain. Ferril sighed and squeezed his eyes shut in exasperation, hoping the boy was getting a good thumping.

"That would be your student, Ferril," said Aren.

"Since he's my student, why did you teach him how to make explosives?"

"To make sure that your reputation stays so low that Amphetam never gives you an office."

"Amphetam won't give them to us because we don't teach 'real' medicine," said Fara with a cynical smile.

"You two have made yourselves perfectly at home in my office," said Maxal.

"What do you mean your office? That's our office," said Fara. Maxal gave her an aggravated look.

"Can I push her in the water now?" asked Locke.

*****

Afternoons were free for eating and trips to the university. Fara and Ferril loaded themselves with books, tablets and pens, and made their way to Maxal's office in the faculty residence. Flame-haired Tibeau followed them, made a nuisance of himself by teasing Fara and earned several slaps in the process.

Ferril calmly endured all of this, knowing that as soon as Tibeau saw the shelves of books in Maxal's office, he would sit still and become attentive. As the afternoon wore on, Fara settled down for a nap, and Tibeau was engrossed in learning the fundamentals of plant-based pharmaceuticals. Ferril stared at them wistfully, wondering about their future, and how far-reaching the sickness the ghouls had spoken of would be. He couldn't see any of the Yrati turning away from Alaindra, especially now, knowing that she might need help.

Thinking of the latest, annoyingly cryptic conversation with the ghouls, his curiosity got the better of him. He stood and left the office to saunter down the hallway, speculatively eyeing one of the doors in particular. As expected, he shortly heard the familiar pattern of Tibeau's footsteps behind him, and braced himself in case the younger priest decided to pounce.

He approached the magnificent reptile that crouched in a nook outside one of the less elaborate offices, and stopped to admire the glistening oil slick of colour shading its white scales. The animal matched the white tiles and wall hangings that lined the tunnel, and Ferril thought its display was to intimidate those who thought they could be as impressive as its owner. This creature was the pet of that over-promoted fellow Antronos, the orange-toga-wearing, poppy-headed dandy who was such a master of the medical arts, yet eccentrically refused to teach. Anyone who truly had a firm grasp of medicine would not hide from the examination of his students and peers. Ferril had wanted to test Antronos' knowledge for quite some time now, to see if he was really as good as everyone said. It was probable that the surface boy hadn't learned that much in a three-year program, just met the right people, smiled into the right faces, and now needed to bluff his way about to hold his position. He hadn't submitted any of his writings to the library since taking this office, probably because he didn't have any. It was only a matter of time before Amphetam saw through him.

Ferril started guiltily when the black door panel of Antronos' office slid aside to reveal the young doctor, the slit pupils of his funny, purple snake eyes dilated, most of his pale, crinky hair held back in a green clip, and his veiny hands resting in folds of orange cloth. Ferril regained his composure, and selfishly thought that Tibeau's hair was a much nicer colour. Such a stupid shade of orange that man was wearing.

"Hello. I am called Ferril," he said.

Antronos bowed to him. "My Lord Yrati," he replied.

Hearing that generous title applied to himself, Ferril struggled against his impulse to feel superior.

Antronos said, "I was wondering if I might have a word with you."

"Of course," said Ferril. "Perhaps you would care to join me...in the cafeteria."

"No. In my office." Antronos—arrogant little beetle that he was—turned away from the door and went somewhere inside the office, obviously expecting that Ferril would not refuse to follow him. Tibeau came and leaned his elbow on Ferril's shoulder.

"So that's him, huh?" asked Tibeau.

"Hmph. I'd like to stick a pin in his over-inflated head," said Ferril. With the sensation of being a child peeking behind the altar, he stepped through the office door, carefully noting everything so that he could tell Fara later on. He secretly hoped that Tibeau would talk circles around Antronos, while he sat quietly and smiled indulgently at his student.

A weighted mechanism slowly rolled the door shut. Antronos stood with his back to them in front of a slanted skylight, so that his hair was an effervescent aura encircling his silhouette. Tibeau and Ferril seated themselves on a low-backed wooden bench and waited for Antronos to turn. After several moments he did not, and Ferril stood up again, slowly moving around the room until he could see the young doctor in profile.

"You did mention that you wanted to speak to me, Sen," he prodded. Antronos still did not answer him, the purple eyes now consumed by the fully dilated pupils, the orange robes heaving with irregular breaths.

"Sen? Are you feeling well?" Ferril ventured to touch the faded hair, and seemed to jolt some inner workings that had become stuck.

"I am in so much trouble," Antronos gasped. "I don't know what to do anymore. I can't," he faltered. "Can't do this anymore." His face suddenly went shock-white, and he put out a hand to prop himself against the wall. Tibeau was by him in an instant, gripping his shoulders to ease him to the floor. Ferril took one of Antronos' hands and felt the pulse.

"You must tell me in precise detail what you have been eating. I don't know exactly what is wrong with you, but I know a case of poisoning when I see it. I don't believe for a second that a medical scholar of your calibre would be unable to taste poison secreted in his food."

Antronos was having such difficulty breathing now, that Ferril began to unloop the orange robes in preparation for a chest massage. His heart skipped in panic as Antronos' eyes rolled up into his skull, and his head twisted strangely in Tibeau's grasp, but it was only an agonized blink.

"It was the...coffee and papaverine...and mescaline and aconitum...and turpentine...some radishes, tetrodotoxin, lithium, sodium pentobarbital, atropine, different species of mould that...produce beta-lactam ring structures..."

"Had lunch at the hospital cafeteria?" asked Tibeau.

Ferril gave the younger Yrati one of his best shut-up-right-now looks.

"Why?" he asked Antronos.

"I had to keep him out of my head."

Ferril was intensely worried. No doctor should self-prescribe for a self-diagnosed psychotic condition. Radishes and turpentine!

"I'm going to refer you to another doctor who is a specialist in this area..."

Antronos began to laugh. "Who? Vernus?" he spluttered.

Both Yrati stiffened. There were a few moments of pained silence.

"You see, I know," said Antronos. "I've read the children's spell book by the old Yrati priest, Dagnaum, all his ways of blocking Desert magic, which is what the Murdek use. That's why I wanted to talk to you, as the Yrati are also trying to take him on, and you haven't suffered."

"Dagnaum? He's senile! And we're not trying to take anything on. We've taken steps to defend ourselves, but otherwise we *avoid* the Murdek. We're not about to go *looking* for trouble."

Antronos looked surprised. "Please tell me you're joking."

"Why would I joke about this?"

"You must know more! I need to know more! Now! Don't you understand? You must do more than just defend yourselves! How long have you been at it? He's been tormenting me for months. Trying to make me do things. But he leaves you alone. You must have ways to combat him! Or is it that I ask for privileged information?"

Ferril could have slapped him.

"If I knew anything that was truly effective, I'd tell the entire world! The older Yrati say the Murdek have been dormant for about fifty years, but they've always been a latent threat. I don't know why they've been silent, but if they were to become active again—"

Antronos glared at Ferril. "They already have!"

"What?"

Antronos struggled to sit up, retrieved a notebook and pen from his desk drawer, and began scribbling madly.

"Hey! That's mine!" Tibeau reached for something that looked like one of his wadded-up paper explosives that was lying in the opened drawer. He nearly got his fingers severed when Antronos slammed it shut.

"I will write down for you everything I know," said Antronos. "Perhaps using that as a base will allow you faster advances in your research."

Ferril took a deep breath. "I'm not sure we want to get so involved in all this."

"You have to. Someone has to. The number of Vernus' 'recruits' for the Murdek Clan is going to increase rapidly."

"How do you know this?"

Antronos laughed like he was insane, rolling his head around.

"I'm old Vernus' student, remember?"

"Do you know anything about a fawn?" Ferril asked.

Antronos choked and spluttered. "I suppose next you're going to start spouting rubbish about fish."

"How did you know?"

Antronos stared at Ferril for a few seconds, then shook his head. "Boil *me*," he said, and turned back to his frantic scrawling.

As Antronos wrote, Ferril picked up the pages to scan the description of the Murdek's mind invasion powers, and lists of pharmacological agents, subsequently passing them to Tibeau, and found himself growing warm with apprehension. It was sounding exactly as had been described in the ancient Yrati texts, written in private books that Antronos could not possibly have read, which meant...all those impossible stories must have been real.

"Sen Antronos," he began, "if you have any journals already written, I think perhaps we should take them now, and get further details from you later."

"I haven't written any of this before. I never dared give Vernus the chance to find them and read about my defences. He has sent Sephus here five times now, and each time I have had to modify my medicines and come up with something new."

"How did you reproduce these compounds without journals?"

Antronos paused in his writing to give Ferril a vacant stare. "Well, I've just had to remember everything."

Three knocks sounded at the door.

"I don't suppose that would be your lizard," said Tibeau. Antronos swore savagely as he snatched up all the pages and dumped them onto an open brazier, nearly toppling into the flames himself. He took Tibeau by the arms and gave him a rough shake.

"How much do you remember? Did you have time to read it properly?"

"I got it all as you wrote it," said Tibeau, trying to squirm away.

"You'll have to take it home. Now. Go!" Antronos took him by the neck and propelled him through a hole in the back of a cupboard. He turned to Ferril. "You, at least, will have to be seen leaving through the door. I hope they weren't watching too closely. I will act like I've told you nothing. If you do the same, you might not become one of their targets."

"Target? Wait a minute! I just told you that we don't—"

The black panel door slid open.

"Antronos, I can't be kept waiting all day." Black eyes turned towards the disintegrating paper on the flames. Ferril gawped at the woman who moved into the room as though she was afflicted with chorea, horrified at her slow, unnatural motions and the mummified cast of her skin. Her frizzy, ochre hair made her look like a gorgon. His awe registered in those black eyes, and she pulled her lips away from her brown teeth in merriment. Peculiarly familiar, she was.

"I strangely find you in the company of the Yrati," she said.

"I was not feeling well," Antronos stammered. "My Lord Yrati was kind enough to help me to my rooms." It was at least partly true; Antronos had retained his greenish pallor.

"And burn your papers, I see."

"He...suggested that I have an allergy to dust, and that I should tidy my office."

"Oh, *well*. You are certainly quick to believe him. And I'm certain the *ashes* will help your allergy." She sat, never looking away from Ferril, and had to bend her neck at a disturbing angle to do so. His skin crawled as he began to think that he recognized her. Antronos grabbed his arm and shoved him towards the door.

"My Lord Yrati, you should leave now. I must see to this patient."

"My Lord Yrati," the visitor parroted, twisting the words around her tongue with sarcasm, "what are you called?"

"Ferril, Madam. And you?"

"*Go home!*" Antronos hissed. Ferril shook him off, annoyed at being pushed.

"Ferril. I shall have to remember that. Antronos, my knees ache." Ferril grew angry at her rudeness, but said nothing further, noting with interest the manner in which Antronos poked at the woman as if afraid he might get his fingers dirty. Hardly proper bedside manner. Her knees did not easily bend, making her appear like some grotesque stick doll. He was again surprised when Antronos practically yelled at her.

"You haven't been taking care of yourself!"

"I have!" she snapped back.

"There is nothing I can do! The joints are quite simply worn out. There is no more cartilage between the bones. Short of cutting you off at the knees, I don't know what you expect from me!" The stick-woman immediately rolled her sticky, obsidian eyes towards Ferril.

"And your diagnosis, Ferril?" she asked.

"I defer to the Sen's greater experience with you as his patient." She began to laugh, or perhaps she tried to clear her throat, but Ferril understood that she meant to be insulting. Assuming unnatural positions to get her stiff limbs to provide enough leverage to lift her body out of the chair, she stood, her head again twisted at an appalling angle towards the two men. She reached out, her fingers barely touching Ferril's face, then smiled and sighed as if finding something she wanted. Abruptly, she pulled away and headed to the door.

"I shall seek better doctors. Perhaps Sen Vernus can solve my problem, eh, Antronos?"

The door slid shut behind her.

"Please tell me that wasn't Alaindra's Aunt Mirodan." Ferril turned towards Antronos to find him standing rigidly with his eyes shut.

"No," said Antronos. "That was Meriamdan. And she knows."

"Who?"

"Meriamdan. She was exiled from the House of Dan, oh, maybe two hundred years ago, for unethical research practices. Now she knows I've told you things. That was why she came. To look you in the eye, to give herself a close look at the path that leads into your mind. Jait's been down a lot lately, so they haven't been using him. She thinks she can force you to tell her about my methods of resistance that they couldn't squeeze from me. They probably weren't ready for you; otherwise she would have taken you right away, but they'll come for you later. Now she's gone back to Vernus to tell him to look for your boy."

"Tibeau? But she never saw him. And by Jait, do you mean My Lord Jait?"

Antronos punched Ferril on the arm. "Of course she saw Tibeau! She saw him in your mind! She is Murdek! *Earth!* You Yrati really don't know anything! Why didn't you leave? I could have kept her here while you ran! Now you'll have to watch your back all the way home!" He moved towards a basin and ewer and began scrubbing frantically. "You were right not to touch her. She can jump into your body that way, and I think she might have the stiffening disease." As surprised as Ferril was to hear that old superstition come out of the mouth of a modern medical scholar, he nevertheless found himself believing that the woman he had just seen had stiffened until she should have been dead, but her body was too stiff to release her soul. It was supposedly a contagious condition.

Antronos' skin was turning red from his scrubbing. "Please, go home and make sure your boy got there safely. If I can pass along any more information, I'll try to find a more discreet way of getting it to you."

13

Lure

Ferril stepped out of Antronos' office, trying hard not to constantly look over his shoulder. The Yrati teachings had warned about the Murdek, but the stories of their sinister magic had always seemed so outrageous, and Ferril had privately considered the more extreme of Maxal's admonitions to be based on old grudges: perhaps ill-reasoned competition with old Sen Vernus. By the Earth, he never truly believed Vernus was a member of the ancient Murdek clan. Deceit, he believed. Theft, he believed. Murder, he believed. But inhabitation of the dead had always been folklore to him. Now that he had seen one of the Murdek up close, he wasn't so sure.

The hall outside seemed darker than usual, the inset red tiles suddenly looking like diamond-shaped blood drops, spilled on the white marble of the rest of the floor. He asked himself why he was afraid. The woman—Meriamdan—she had really disturbed him. He tried to shake the feeling of being watched as he walked through the empty corridor, hearing the sounds of his footsteps clack back at him as they bounced off the walls.

He turned down the hall that led to Maxal's office, wondering where all the other professors were. It wasn't that late in the day, yet there were no students or anyone else present. Fara was not in the office. She must have been planning to come back though, as her books and outer robes were still there—*unless she had been snatched away*. Ferril pushed the thought down. Why had such a notion occurred to him? Fara had probably just gone to get something to eat. But then where was Tibeau? Shouldn't he have crept out of those back passages somewhere nearby and returned to the office by now? Had he become lost? Damn it, this game wasn't worth playing. Antronos had shoved Tibeau into a series of tunnels that led who knew where and Ferril had stood by and allowed it.

He didn't doubt Antronos' warning that something was seriously wrong, and his mind was now fully ready to believe that the Murdek were orchestrating it. But where was Tibeau? His heart pounded heavily as he raced back towards Antronos' office. The eerie sense that everybody in the Temlochti State was missing only increased when he shoved aside Antronos' door and found the office empty—and despite the unshuttered skylight, the light was as dim as it had been in the hallway, some dust storm apparently having blocked out the sun. But he could hear no wind.

Ferril shouldered his way inside and ripped the door off the cupboard to reveal the hidden passage. It was too dark to see past the opening, so he frantically looked around for a tank of bioluminescent moss or something he could use as a torch. The brazier still had some burning coals. He scooped a few of them into a drinking tankard, and finding a bottle of solvent and some rags on the shelves, managed to fashion a lamp. He returned to the cupboard. As far as he could tell, the passage immediately behind it was newly hewn—or perhaps bashed through—to an older series of tunnels. The cupboard hole was not large enough for his broad frame, so he grabbed the edges of it and splintered the wood away until he could step through, the rough sides scraping his legs. The imprints of Tibeau's sandals could still be made out in the grey dust.

The tunnels behind the passage were cut quite deep. They looked as if they had once been quite elaborate and frequently used. Remnants of public houses, perhaps retail establishments, lined the back wall, their bottom halves pushed aside by a hardened magma flow. He had to stumble over rubble from a partial cave-in, an invasion of the Desert into the underground, as he passed an inactive font and animal pen in the middle of a series of caverns that might once have been used for commerce. They were silent, grey and damp. All the skylights were hopelessly buried in what must have been decades worth of sandstorms. Ferril muttered a prayer of thanks for the puddles of muck that made any new footsteps obvious. His anxiety increased as he saw another set of new footprints, and then another, join into the path that Tibeau had taken. At first he thought they were human, then began to worry even more as he found a clearer print that had the distinct toe and padded heel shape of a surface feline predator.

"Tibeau!" he yelled. Nothing.

Ferril tried to run, then had to slow down as the increased impact of his feet made him sink deeper into the muck.

"Tibeau!" he yelled again, his voice breaking. Still no answer. Damned dampness!

The trail led to a narrower set of passages that were cut at completely square angles and eventually he found himself in one that no longer branched—just continued forward. Tibeau's sandals must have dried out at some point, as his footprints had disappeared, but he had to have gone this way, since there were no alternate paths. A little farther along, Ferril's lamp died, and he dropped it in the passage.

A draft brushed against his face, then cobwebs, and he emerged with a great puff of dust into a wider space. He still did not have enough room to stretch out. He shoved against the clutter around him, and cried out when something toppled, striking him on the head and arm. It was a book.

He waited a few moments for his eyes to adjust to the weak light, trying to make out where it was coming from. The diffuse dimness made it seem like he was moving through a fog of smoke. Carefully, he shifted his way past an enormous pile of rolled maps, a broken astrolabe, a mounted globe and a rickety old bookcase from which the book had fallen.

He finally had enough room to stand without his shoulders angled, and feeling rather irritable, shook the dust from his receding hair and robes. Bookcases towered around him on every side. He must be in the library then, but on what level? The texts looked very old, and were not written in any alphabet he could read. He wandered for a few minutes, looking for the main aisle, which should lead to an exit. He couldn't find one.

Ferril heaved a sigh, and felt the burden of impatience add to his irritability. This couldn't be right. If he were in the library, then surely Tibeau would have eventually been able to find his way out and go back to Maxal's office. He was a smart boy. It shouldn't have taken him very long. Or had he made a mistake? Had there been another passage? Or had Tibeau's footsteps ended for some other reason? *Stop it!*

Someone behind him also sighed, oily breath blowing against his neck. Ferril whirled, and saw no one.

One hand clasped to his neck, he pressed his back against a bookcase and scanned the area in front of him. No one was in the empty, silent room. Only the dust and the books were there to confirm that the world still existed.

"Hello?" he said quietly. The word did not travel far in the heavy air.

Peering between bookcases before he passed them, Ferril inched forward, rapidly checking over his shoulder every few seconds. Was that a shuffling? He froze and listened, eyes straining to see past the gaps in the bookshelves. Nothing.

"Hello," someone breathed.

"All right! Where are you?" he demanded. His anger was fuelled by fear, and he marched up to each new aisle, glaring down it to find the other person.

"I want to see where you are!" he yelled. He banged his fist against a few of the shelves, only raising dust, and still found no one.

"Come on, where are you?" he shouted.

"I am here," came the feathery reply, and when Ferril turned to face the speaker, something dark swept across his face so that he couldn't see at all.

14

Offence

Antronos crouched far back in the hallway leading to his office, concealed by the darkness. He had spent the afternoon and early evening in the Dra laboratories, finally perfecting his mind-blocker formulation. Over the past three hours, he had watched five of the hazy Murdek auras, either blue-grey or doubled up, patrolling the passage in front of his door or wandering in and out of his office, waiting for him. Both his natural and Desert visions were perfectly clear. He could sense the probing of the Murdek's minds, and had to suppress his desire to gloat over their inability to detect his presence. Finally most of the Murdek left, and there was just Sephus. His aura had changed to a strange metallic blue, glinting feebly as he paced the hallway. The last light faded from the skylight, forcing Sephus to stop his pacing, and lean against the wall. Antronos got up and silently crept to Sephus' side. The other man apparently could not see in the dark, and was probably expecting that Antronos would need a lantern of some sort, which would give warning of his arrival.

"Are you still happy with them, Sephus?" Antronos asked.

Sephus flinched, and turned blindly towards Antronos. He pulled a small glass sphere of bioluminescent moss from his pocket and held it up. His dried face cracked into a grin.

"I admire you more each day, Antronos. Why do you ask after my contentment with the Murdek? Are you planning to start your own clan? Do you want me to join?"

"And if I did?"

Sephus hung his head and started to laugh.

"We've had this conversation before. I know it's useless to have such dreams. And you? Well, you're still learning."

Antronos regarded Sephus' profile for a long moment, calculating just how far he could trust the other man, or even more importantly, if he could forgive him.

"I have a new formulation," he said, reaching into one of his pockets and retrieving a glass ampoule. He snapped it open with his fingers. "Here," he said, passing it to Sephus.

The Murdek took the vial and held its contents to the glass sphere, as if trying to visually determine its composition. "You've changed the mind-blocker? Ah, I thought so. You've been impossible to track these last few hours. Thank you," he said, and started to turn away.

"Sephus," Antronos called. "Why don't you take it now?"

Sephus looked back over his shoulder and hesitated.

"Once the ampoule is opened, its contents rapidly degrade," Antronos lied. "If you don't swallow it immediately, it will be useless to you. There really is no time for you to carry it back to Vernus, have him pat you on the head and promise to reward you with a new body, so you may as well use it."

Sephus stared at the vial for a few moments, his mouth twitching. Then he smiled at Antronos again, lifting the powder in salute. "You are truly admirable, Sen Antronos," he said, then tipped the vial onto his tongue. He swallowed, leaning against the wall to keep from sputtering and losing the medicine. His breathing became laboured, then he dropped the vial and glass sphere, his hands going to his mouth. He turned towards Antronos and coughed twice, before sliding down the wall and collapsing as his mind shut down entirely.

"Well," said Antronos, "That *will* keep Vernus out of your head. I didn't say it was my newest or my best formulation." He watched for a few seconds to make sure Sephus' aura didn't fade completely, then turned and entered his office.

Dumping his outer robe in a corner, Antronos moved towards his cabinets to collect a few ingredients he had been unable to find elsewhere. He looked wistfully at his desk, thinking that he would probably never get a chance to actually complete a thesis, and wishing he had never met Vernus. If he did break free from the Murdek, would he ever get a chance to sit there and write? He stepped forward to open a drawer, wanting to find a sachet, and noticed a small, golden aura winking from under his desk. Not wanting to frighten his visitor, he lit the brazier, then sat next to it on the floor.

"Hello, Leod," he said. A small face peeked out at him.

"Don't like you anymore," said Leod.

"Why not?"

"Didn't keep your promise. Grampa's still sick."

Antronos regarded the child for a moment. There was no way he could give an adequate answer.

"I have been trying," Antronos said. "How did you get here? There were other people here, the ones you showed me at the Royal House. I'm worried about what might happen if they ever see you. I'm glad you've come to visit me, but I don't think my office is a very safe place."

"They don't care," said Leod. "They saw me. I followed them here."

Antronos nodded, feeling relieved. It did make sense. Leod's powerlessness afforded him some protection. If the child could stay here, then at least he would be away from his father. Getting him a constant supply of food might be a problem, however. Perhaps Alaindra might consider sheltering him. Leod crept out from under the desk and surprisingly crawled into Antronos' lap.

"I know you're not very good at this," Leod said, "but I have another friend who's sick." He held out a blue and red embroidered collar. Antronos gasped.

"Where did you get this?"

"A man. I found him in one of the lower caves in my grampa's house. He gave that to me and asked me to give it to some..." Leod thought hard. "Reetee," he said.

"Yrati?" asked Antronos. Leod just looked at him. "Does your friend have a name?"

"Ferril. He's very sick."

"Oh, Earth." Antronos took a deep breath and put his hand over his face for a few moments. His resolve was starting to crumble under the weight of his frustration. He should have left Ferril alone. He didn't dare ask Leod what had happened to Ferril's red-haired student. How long would it be before some action of his also led to the capture of Alaindra? The death of Jait? Or Leod? His mind flashed back to the dream of the fawn, where either the Yrati or the Murdek had killed Jait, and he hadn't known which, or been able to stop it. He didn't know what to do.

Leod started picking at Antronos' fingers, trying to peer into his face.

"Do you know any Reetee?" he asked. "Ferril said they would know what to do."

Antronos gave a choked laugh. Well, at least that had been Ferril's decision. Antronos supposed he could be the messenger. And maybe in a group, they would be able to resist the Murdek.

"I hope you're right, Leod. Come." He shifted the child off his lap, then stood and took him by the hand. Maybe the Yrati could also shelter Leod.

The way to the Yrati tunnels was uncomfortably public. Antronos had never visited their home before, so he had not picked out a route through the back passages. A gigantic cavern in front of their private chambers doubled as a main commons and informal clinic. Even at this time of night, a few Yrati were still tending to street urchins, and other homeless people who preferred roaming in the dark rather than in the day.

Ceremonial fonts towering three times the height of a man stretched haphazardly through the space of the cavern. Made of grey stone, and shaped as surface trees with extraordinarily thick trunks, they spouted water from somewhere at their tops, constantly spilling it over their stone leaves. Knots in the carven bark stretched up into splattering pools, and various species of blossoming fungi crept up the sides of the faux bark, sharing their space with bromeliads and insects purported to have medicinal value. Moss covered the entire floor of the cavern, making uneven any tile that might have once been placed there, and the bioluminescent species grew randomly, uncontained in glass tanks. Some funny little rune stones jumped next to his sandals wherever he put his feet down. Water-filled stone troughs also inexplicably criss-crossed the mossy terrain. Hiding behind a font, Antronos stared at one of these, mesmerized by the apparently random flow of water, which seemed to change direction as it pleased. He shook himself out of it. He had no time for daydreaming.

With Leod tucked under one arm, he skirted his way from font to font, trying to make his way to the entrance of the Yrati private caves. If he were going to talk to them again, he would make damned sure it was where there couldn't possibly be any Murdek.

The inner tunnels branched into a multitude of dim caverns, none of them containing skylights, just the irregular growth of moss. Antronos saw the auras of several insects crawling over the walls, and froze in amazement when he realized that they were moving in the same patterns he had seen in the water troughs: three pulses in one direction, then a pause, a turn in a quarter circle, then another three pulses. He shook his head again and moved on, forcing himself not to be hypnotized by the soothing effect the insects' motion had.

Peeking down one branch of tunnels, he saw several caverns in which Yrati were sleeping, cuddled together like small rodents burrowed in nesting shavings. Just looking at them made Antronos feel sleepy. Rationalizing that he didn't want to disturb them, he turned down a different tunnel, and found himself walking past empty study rooms. More of the little rune stones lay along the floor and tossed themselves around as he walked past them. He eventually came to a series of brightly lit caverns that turned out to be laboratories. They were also empty.

A chemical cabinet set above a lab bench caught Antronos' eye. A bottle of papaverine was sitting right behind the glass door. Just waiting for him. He needed more of that. Surely the Yrati wouldn't miss one bottle. He ventured into the laboratory, letting Leod slide to the floor. He reached towards the cabinet.

Someone grabbed his arm from behind, spun him around and kicked out his feet, sending him sprawling on the floor. Before he could get up, a blunt weighing spatula was wedged under his chin. He looked up into the face of the sandy-haired priest leaning over him, the same one who had caught him holding the stolen explosive in the archives so many months ago. As trained as the Yrati might be in fighting, he really wasn't all that intimidating, since he was using lab equipment as weaponry, and since Antronos had learned there was much more to be afraid of than someone's bad opinion of him.

"Hello," said Antronos. He cautiously pushed the spatula away with the tip of his finger. The Yrati allowed this, but did not change his angry expression.

"What do you want here, Murdek?"

Antronos guffawed. "I am *not* Murdek!"

"You think I don't know who you are? You study with Vernus and you set off our ward stones, which are specifically set to detect Murdek."

The Yrati turned in surprise when Leod ran up and grabbed onto his sleeve. He had apparently missed the presence of the child.

"Give him the collar," said Leod. He excitedly pointed at the Yrati's neck, recognizing the blue and red pattern.

Antronos winced as he shifted into a sitting position. He had fallen with one of his hands tucked under him and the skin had been scraped from his palm. He gingerly fished Ferril's collar out of his pocket with his injured hand and passed it to the Yrati. The other man's eyes immediately widened.

"This belongs to Ferril. He never came back." He slammed both hands against Antronos' shoulders. "Where is he, Murdek?"

Antronos frowned. "I have told you, I am not Murdek. If I were, would I have brought that to you?"

"Of course, to make demands on behalf of your superior, Vernus."

"By the Earth! You're being stupid. I hate Vernus. I'm trying to get away from him. I know the Yrati have been enemies with the Murdek for generations. Ferril was trying to help me. That's why he was taken. I'm sorry, but I didn't intend it. You want him back, and I want to be free myself. We have a common goal, and we can help each other."

"You were the reason Ferril disappeared, and now you *dare* ask us for help? Get out!"

"Aren, wait."

Antronos gave a start. He had not noticed anyone else in the room, and involuntarily recoiled from the shadow that pulled away from the wall to become a hooded man, who was at least as tall as he was. Leod ran and hid behind a table.

Antronos steepled his fingers and bowed his head in respect. "My Lord Maxal," he said. The Yrati High Priest nodded back.

"Sen Antronos. Why don't you tell us exactly what has happened?" Maxal pushed back his hood and sat down on a bench, gesturing to another beside it. Antronos gratefully got off the floor and sat on the other bench, stretching out his aching knees.

"Vernus, he's—" Antronos waved his hands helplessly. "This is going to sound unbelievable."

"I know. Just tell me."

"Well, I suppose you do know," Antronos blathered. "I mean, I read the book the Yrati Dagnaum wrote, but it was a child's book, so I thought perhaps some parts of it were exaggerated to make a good story. Although, now, I think..."

Maxal just watched him patiently, his eyes so dark they seemed to have no pupil. Antronos took a deep breath.

"Vernus is trying to become more powerful. He's in league with Prince Derik. They are using My Lord Jait's power to...place suggestions in other people's minds. To control them. They have done this to me, and now they are trying to use me to get to Alaindra. Every time they use Jait, he weakens. So that limits them, but it's only a matter of time. Right now

Vernus is still experimenting, but I'm afraid that he may eventually figure out how to jump into a person's body without Jait and then be unstoppable. Right now, they must let the High Prince rest before using him again. Anyway, I was trying to break free, and had asked Ferril for help. The Murdek found out and I believe they are holding him somewhere beneath the Royal House."

Maxal sat back, looking as though Antronos had explained a great deal.

"May I ask exactly what they've made you do?"

Antronos opened his mouth, but couldn't say anything. Not with Leod around. His eyes met Maxal's, and something told him that if he lied, the fragile trust he was sensing from the High Priest would be permanently broken.

"I...a man called Shenan...his heart. They confused me into taking it. They're holding that over me as blackmail to force me to help them get Alaindra. So far I've been able to resist. I don't know when they'll try to use Shenan's death to have me executed. I don't know why they haven't already." Antronos glanced at Leod. The child showed no comprehension of what had just been said.

"Actually, they have," said Maxal.

Antronos looked up. "What? When?"

"Oh, it was a while back. An anonymous tip came through the coroner's office. From what you've just said, it must have been Vernus trying to have you punished for disobeying him. It didn't work, obviously. The Murdek are apparently unaware that the coroner's pathologist left our clan one generation back to study conventional medicine. He did the autopsy immediately. It was so unlike Vernus to praise anyone, and we were curious about your purported "heart massage," so he didn't wait to perform a full examination, but delayed writing the report until we understood the significance of Vernus' attempted deception. I trusted Vernus less than you, so I didn't believe for one minute that you had lied to your supervisor, and that his report to the coroner was based only on what you had told him. We think they haven't pressed the issue because at the moment, they don't understand why the coroner's office hasn't reacted. Prince Derik made one brief inquiry, then let it drop."

The priest called Aren huffed derisively, and leaned against the wall with his arms folded. "Why does none of this surprise me?" he said, glaring at Antronos from underneath his messy hair. "You've given him far too much leeway, Maxal."

Antronos blinked at Aren for a few seconds, then turned back to the High Priest in disbelief. "So, if you knew, and if the coroner has been notified, why haven't I been arrested?"

Maxal didn't reply, just sat looking at Antronos speculatively. "Did you kill a squirrel?" he asked finally.

"Yes. How did you know?"

Maxal just smiled. "Why did you kill it?"

"It—I mean, Vernus, he somehow put the...spirit of one of the Murdek into the squirrel. I was supposed to carry it to Alaindra, and give it to her. When Jait's too weak for them to use, the Murdek can only 'jump' into someone's mind by direct contact. So the squirrel was a disguise for one of them."

"How do you know this spirit was in the squirrel?"

"I can see their auras. Murdek appear...diminished, or a strange blue colour. Everyone else's aura is bright, golden. When they jump into me, I can see two auras surrounding my skin. One is mine; the other has that strange dimness to it."

"Why do the Murdek want Alaindra?"

"I don't know. Meriamdan is one of the Murdek. She's exiled from that family. I think she hates Alaindra, or is jealous of her." Antronos paused to think. "There's also political influence. Maybe financial power. Alaindra does have a lot of contact with people in high places. If they had her, it might give them access to just about anyone."

"Yes," Maxal said nodding. "It would give them access to just about anyone." He exchanged a meaningful glance with Aren. "And the fawn?"

"Did you have the dream too?" Antronos asked wonderingly.

"Perhaps. Tell me about the fawn."

Was it safe to tell Maxal? In his dream, the ghouls had told him to make sure "they" didn't kill the fish. But who were "they?" The Yrati or the Murdek?

"I'm not sure," he stammered.

"How about the fish? Do you know who that is?"

"I have no idea."

"But you do have an idea about the fawn?"

Antronos hesitated.

"We can't help each other if we can't even talk," Maxal said gently. Antronos studied the High Priest's aura, hoping that it would give him some clue as to the Yrati's intentions. It told him nothing. At the very least, the Yrati were known for healing, not hurting, and Antronos needed to trust someone. He just hoped he wasn't endangering anyone else.

"Can you look after Leod?" he asked. Maxal turned and smiled at the small blond head, partially concealed behind the table.

"He's Jait's grandson, isn't he? We can take care of him." He turned back to Antronos and raised his thick eyebrows expectantly.

"The fawn, I think, is My Lord Jait."

"Does Jait participate in this 'jumping' willingly?"

"Absolutely not."

Maxal nodded and stood.

"Ferril said you would know what to do," Leod piped up. Maxal turned back to the child, smiling.

"Yes, *Haalom*, I do." The High Priest took a step towards Leod with his hands out, but the boy ducked away from him and ran into the tunnels. "He'll be safe here," Maxal promised Antronos.

*****

Antronos lay on his side in the small, padded sleeping cavern the Yrati had lent him. He was infinitely grateful to have a resting place where he could feel safe closing his eyes for more than five minutes. It was a huge relief after what seemed like ages of constant vigilance. Leod had taken up residence in his chamber, playing with a small aquarium Maxal had given him. Antronos smiled as the child chattered at a little turtle, promising he would build it a house of leaves.

Leod was reaching into the water now, gently pulling at the white, slowly wriggling tentacles of a tiny blindfish at the bottom of the tank. Either the creature was sleepy, or it just wasn't threatened by Leod, as it showed no distress from the boy's touch. Antronos watched the lulling movements of the fish's pluming, white fins, thinking about what Maxal had told him of the clue given by the ghouls. Who was it that Jait would be freed by? It wasn't him, and it wasn't Leod. He had also been surprised to hear that Jait had been unable to use his magic on his own. According to the Yrati, the ghouls had told them on Jait's ascension that his mind was locked in his own disbelief. Maxal felt that the Yrati were meant to somehow help the fawn, or Jait, and Antronos had been told that a fish could live in water...so was he supposed to turn Lord Jait into a fish? Or...maybe he had to introduce Jait to water magic? Or teach him to swim! What was he thinking? He could barely swim himself and knew nothing of magic, and almost a year ago had been ready to give it up completely. Perhaps he should try talking to the ghouls again.

Antronos got up and wandered through the Yrati tunnels, no longer finding the patterned motion of the insects disconcerting. He didn't know where the prayer pool was, but assumed it wasn't near the laboratories or sleeping chambers, so he meandered down a third branch of tunnels, and was gratified to see a shining bubble of ghoul-aura resting off to the side on the floor of one of the tunnels. It trembled intermittently, but did not move away. Antronos crouched next to it, brushing at the dust that covered it. Bony red fingers reached out of the rock and grabbed his sleeve. Antronos attempted to tug the fabric out of the creature's grip, but it sank below the surface, pulling the cloth into the rock.

"Hey!" Antronos tried to break free, then became alarmed when his sleeve was pulled down until his wrist scraped the floor. The creature tugged again, bouncing Antronos' wrist against the rock a second time, then let go. Antronos watched his sleeve with fascination as he pulled it free from the rock. The floor did not crumble.

The aura moved now, in the characteristic jerky dance, heading down a side tunnel that led into a widened space. Antronos followed it, curious at the lighting change. In most of the Yrati tunnels, the predominant colours were brown and yellow, influenced mainly by the light reflections off the soft brown of the Earth, and the yellow clay of many of the Yrati pots. In this space, the light seemed blue. As he entered the room, he felt a draft coming from above, and looked up to see a paneless window, cut as a circle in the ceiling. The white shine of the moon fell coolly into the cavern, illuminating a wide ring of stone bricks that encircled a dark pool of water.

Antronos knelt at the edge of the pool, stroking its surface with his hand. A few bubbles ruffled the water, but otherwise nothing happened. He searched for the ghouls' aura, and thought he was beginning to see one of them coming to the surface, but instead of gold, this aura was white, and angular in shape. It spiralled upwards in a lazy motion, finally taking on the slim shape of a blindfish.

Was it real? Antronos put his hand into the water, feeling the slender tentacles that reached from the tiny creature's underbelly gently coil around his fingers. The white mouth and whiskers explored his knuckles. Looking closely, he could make out two small mounds on either side of the fish's head, where the eyes should have been.

"Who are you?" he asked. The fish released his hand, the little fins back-pedalling. It hovered in the middle of the pool and spread out its fins and tail like petals of a flower, the graceful tendrils at the edges of its limbs trailing delicately in the water. Then it folded in on itself and darted downwards.

"By the Earth," said someone behind him.

Antronos turned and saw that Aren had followed him into the cavern. He stood up, wiping his hand on his robes. "I meant no disrespect."

Aren wasn't looking at him, instead staring at the pool as he stepped closer.

"You learn fast, don't you?" asked Aren. He turned towards Antronos with a chagrined expression.

"What do you mean?"

"It took me years to learn how to do that."

Antronos looked back at the still water. "To do what?"

"Didn't you see it?"

"The fish?"

"The message. Before it disappeared, the fish transformed into the face of a woman."

Antronos looked at Aren for a moment, feeling dumbfounded. Then hope surged within him. "Was it my mother?" he asked. "Was it a dark haired woman wearing Desert robes? Did she have a scar down the side of her face?"

Aren looked at him skeptically. "Why are you asking? You summoned the vision."

"But...I didn't see it. All I saw was the fish."

"Really? I'm surprised. Or perhaps you're pretending."

Antronos frowned again. Aren was starting to irritate him.

"What have you got against me?"

"The disappearance of Ferril and his student. And I find it strange that while the Murdek are holding Ferril because of knowledge you gave him, if that is indeed the truth, they are not holding you for the same reason. Why is that?"

"They're trying to use me as a marker for their jumps. And part of it is just Vernus playing around with his new techniques. He isn't in any rush. I think he's still hoping they can reach Alaindra through Jait or me. If they stop me from seeing her—"

"So then you are their agent."

"I have told you—"

"Did it ever occur to you, Sen Antronos, that they might be using you now, to get to us?"

Antronos froze. He hadn't thought of that, even knowing full well the animosity between the Yrati and the Murdek. *How stupid I have been.*

"I will leave," he said.

"No," said Aren. "You will do exactly as Maxal tells you."

*****

Antronos entered the Royal House openly, hoping the guards would not have any reason to announce him, or otherwise bring attention to his arrival. He had to get to Jait without Vernus knowing. The courage that Maxal's support had filled him with, was quickly draining the closer he came to a possible meeting with Prince Derik. He was surprised when he was immediately ushered into a private room and asked to wait for Prince Liam.

The younger prince entered at once, looking haggard and exhausted. He came right up to Antronos and took his hands.

"My Prince Liam, what's happened?" Antronos asked him.

"I don't know what's going on, Sen. But this morning, my father attempted suicide. Sen Vernus intervened in time." Liam looked away, shaking his head. "Something is very wrong. I've tried talking to my brother, but—" Prince Liam broke off, apparently not wanting to speak against the Heir of the State.

"I have nothing against either Sen Vernus or Sen Opalena, but I don't think they are able to make my father any better. I don't see why Opalena needs her mentor here. I hired her, not Vernus. She should be more than capable of performing her duties by herself, but my brother—" Liam broke off again. "I'm afraid I am doubting Opalena's competence. And my father has been asking for you constantly."

Antronos considered that for a moment, wondering if he should disobey Maxal and take Liam into his confidence. He decided not to. It was probably true that the younger prince was still in partial denial about his brother, and would go directly to Derik for reassurance. That might cause him to be drawn in to the Murdek's circle as well.

"I sincerely want to help My Lord Jait," he said finally.

"Please see what you can do about his sadness. It only seems to get worse. I can't bear the thought of losing him before it's time."

"Of course, My Prince."

"And there is no reason to mention this conversation to anyone, is there?"

"None at all."

"I know that you will also keep my father's condition confidential."

"I have taken an oath, and I will keep it, Prince."

Antronos was delighted when Liam opened a door to a *back* corridor through which he could move around the Royal House.

*****

The hazy dimness in Jait's bedchamber made it difficult for Antronos to see where he was going, unaided by insects or moss. He checked quickly around the room to make sure none of the grey Murdek auras were present, and saw none. He could make out Jait's aura at the far end of the room, pulsating weakly, white with distress.

He pushed aside the flimsy netting that shrouded the bed, and pulled the covers off a few of the cylindrical glass chambers of moss that stood by the bedside, so that he could see the High Prince by natural vision. Jait looked bruised and desiccated. Both his wrists were bound in thick, padded bandages. His skin was hot and dry to the touch, peeling slightly along the line of his unshaven jaw. His breathing was shallow, and his eyes were swelled shut.

"My Lord Jait," Antronos whispered. No response. He tapped Jait's cheek lightly, and called his name again. Jait opened his eyes, but otherwise did not move or show any sign that he was aware of Antronos' presence.

Antronos fumbled through his pockets and managed to find the vial containing the medicine he and Maxal had compounded together. He tipped some of the powder from it onto Jait's upper lip, carefully holding the High Prince's head straight, so that he would inhale the dust.

Jait twitched slightly, then swallowed.

"My Lord Jait," Antronos persisted. Jait finally seemed conscious, turning to look at Antronos, his eyes following the line of his hair. He seemed dazed, but not in pain.

"You are a powerful magician," Jait informed him.

Antronos cast a worried look about the room, wondering how long he could linger here before the Murdek came back. He still did not see any of them.

"You must fight them," he said to Jait. "I will do all I can to help you. *Resist Vernus.*"

Jait gave him a barely perceptible look of disdain. "Resist Vernus?" he asked. "You must be a very stupid magician."

"I've given you enough extract to keep your mind clear for a few hours. It's also from poppy, but modified to have the opposite effect." Antronos fumbled with a small pot, then smeared some clear paste from it on the inside of Jait's palm. "When you feel yourself starting to slip again, try to get this paste on the underside of your tongue. Don't let anyone wipe it off."

Jait's eyes closed, and his head began to fall to one side. Antronos gently turned his head back, lighting tapping his cheek.

"Jait, listen. I need you to do something. The Yrati have challenged Derik's appearances on your behalf. He will have to allow you a public appearance to quell the rumours they have started. It will also draw Vernus into the open, as he will have to come to control you. With this medicine, you can resist him long enough to publicly denounce him, in the presence of as many people as possible. People will listen to you. He can't silence an entire assembly, and you must speak of treason, not magic. If you so much as mention magic, he will be able to play on people's skepticism and discount you as a madman, especially because he has Derik's support. Even if not everyone believes you, it will raise enough questions to allow you to order Vernus arrested before he has a chance to retaliate. Command only your most trusted men do it, and tell them they must not allow themselves to be touched by him. They must use lariats and gag him as soon as possible. Derik can be dealt with privately. Do you understand?"

Jait gave no indication that he did. Antronos sighed in exasperation, looking around the room once more. He didn't dare stay any longer and Maxal was waiting for him.

∗∗∗∗∗

The noise was overwhelming. The Yrati allegations that Jait had been secretly murdered and Derik was attempting to usurp the throne before his time, were raising an immense furor. Prince Derik appeared from a secured walkway and stood regarding the ocean of people, innumerable bodies pressed against inadequate railings which couldn't possibly hold for long. As soon as they saw him, the shouting intensified, and their arms reached out into the gangway which Derik had to walk through. The Crown Prince glared at them, and after a moment's hesitation, thrust his way through the tangle of limbs and voices.

Off to one side of the dais on which Jait would have to appear, Antronos stood wrapped in a dark cloak with the hood up, flanked by similarly camouflaged Yrati. Aren had one hand clamped around his arm, still not fully trusting him. He held his breath, hoping the ploy had worked. Vernus entered. And then Jait. The crowd fell silent.

Antronos let out his breath with a shudder. Jait was being supported by Prince Liam. He appeared disoriented and still very weak, and Antronos wasn't sure how lucid he was, or if he would be able to speak out against Vernus.

The High Prince paused at the end of the gangway, seeming unable to step up onto the dais, despite his son's help. Vernus came and took him by the elbow. Jait's jaw dropped a bit, but he made no sound and moved to where he was directed. Prince Liam's expression was controlled, revealing none of the concerns he had suggested to Antronos privately.

Prince Derik watched his father be seated in the small, ceremonial throne, then turned away suddenly and moved to pick up something which had been thrown upon the dais, flinging it away into the crowd. He pulled a dagger from a sheath strapped to his ankle and pointed it somewhere, shouting something. A man had perched himself on a railing and was now shaking a fist and shouting back. Antronos was gratified to see that although Jait was obviously still alive, the crowd was clearly not pleased with Derik.

Vernus stood behind Jait, one hand on the High Prince's back. Jait's head came up suddenly, and he shouted into the crowd.

"You will all be silent!"

Damn, thought Antronos. Vernus' control seemed real. He doubted Jait was that good an actor. Had Maxal made a mistake with the formulation?

Derik, who still had his dagger drawn, took this as his cue. He strode across the dais and again pointed at someone.

"You. Come forward."

That person did not move, but the crowd parted silently and an undisguised Yrati stepped forward. His genuflection was too polite to allow Derik to order him away.

"My Lord and High Prince Jait. I am called Locke, and come from the Yrati clan. I wish to respectfully ask for the return of my brother Ferril to our caves."

"Dog!" spat Derik. He moved forward again, waving his little dagger about. "You dare accuse the High Prince of this!"

"I accuse no one of anything," said Locke. "I merely ask for my brother's return, if his service in the Royal House is no longer needed." Antronos stared at Jait, willing him to speak.

"Come on," he whispered. Aren looked at him sharply.

Jait looked at Locke, frowning. He seemed confused. He then shifted forward slightly and nodded.

"Of course. You may take him home with you today," he said. Derik began screaming again, something about disobedience, detracting attention from Jait, whose head snapped forward as Vernus did something to him. Antronos tensed, at the same time feeling Aren's grip on his arm tighten.

Jait retched and clasped a hand over his mouth. His eyes suddenly widened and he looked wonderingly at his hand. Had he managed to get the second dose of medicine Antronos had smeared there? Smiling tightly, Vernus leaned down to wipe Jait's face and palm with a square of cloth. All the while, the old doctor's hand kept working at the base of Jait's neck, and feigning concern, Vernus leaned down to whisper into Jait's ear. The High Prince grimaced, glared at Vernus, then seemed to relax. Vernus, looking satisfied, eased Jait back in his chair, patting his shoulder in an apparently comforting way.

"It isn't going to work," whispered Antronos. "He didn't get enough of it." He pulled against Aren's grip.

"Not yet!" Aren hissed back.

On the dais, Liam put his arm around Jait's shoulders, pulling his father away from Vernus, and earning himself an angry glare. Jait's expression lost some of its glazed look, and the High Prince raised a hand to his son's cheek. Vernus turned away to dig for something in a medical bag.

"Now! Go!" Aren shoved Antronos forward.

Pushing his hood back so that the Royal Guards wouldn't try to block him, Antronos clambered onto the dais, hoping his sheepish smile conveyed the notion that he had just arrived and was embarrassed to be late. He stepped between Vernus and Jait, physically blocking Vernus from touching the High Prince.

"Having trouble, Sen Vernus?" Antronos asked cheerily. "Let me have a look." He made a show of checking Jait's eyes. "Ah yes, My Lord," he said to Jait. "You've got a little bit of bloodrot. Not surprising really. We'll have to treat it properly later on, of course, but this will help clear your mind, and get rid of the stomach ache." He took a third medication from a vial and sprinkled it on Jait's tongue, at the same time jerking back an elbow to catch Vernus on the chin. His other hand shifted too much with the movement, causing half the dose to fall onto Jait's shirt. *Damn!*

"Great Stones! I'm sorry, Sen. I didn't expect you to come up behind me like that. Well, you're not hurt. No matter then." Antronos quickly stepped out of the way, trying to leave the dais. He was stopped by several soldiers—no, they were cloaked Murdek—who grasped his sleeves. Vernus put a hand to his bruised chin and hissed.

"What did you give him?" he demanded.

"How did he get *bloodrot*?" asked Liam. "Haven't you been sterilizing your needles properly?"

Vernus put his hand on Jait's neck for a second, then turned back to Antronos, his expression livid.

"What. Did. You. Give. Him?"

Antronos glared back at Vernus until his ribs were discreetly prodded with a dagger by one of the Murdek.

"Mould grown from the human cranium," he finally replied. "I added a few other things, but I believe you invented the original medication, Sen. I read about it in some obscure, *very* old journal."

"Here, stand aside. What's wrong with him?" Derik came to grab Jait by the jaw and turn his head from side to side. Jait looked up, his expression blank, then interested, finally angry. He smacked Derik's hand away and shakily stood up.

"My Lord and High Prince Jait has been very tired," Vernus said to Derik. "Please, see if you can get him to remain calm." The look on Derik's face was now not only curdled, but smug.

"Sit down, Father."

It was all Antronos to could do not to interfere and denounce Vernus himself. He stared at Jait intensely. The High Prince glared at Derik, his stance weakened, his expression faded. He sat down.

There was a sudden movement at his side, and Antronos saw Liam move to catch Derik by the arm. Everyone in the crowd began yelling at once, as the two princes argued with each other. Derik drew his sword, and Liam stepped back. Jait's mouth opened and one hand reached towards Liam. He struggled against Vernus' hold, and finally desisted, without having said anything. The crowd fell silent.

Derik's eyes flicked over the assembly. Antronos hunted through the people to see what Derik was looking at, and was surprised to see armed soldiers not in the livery of the Royal House lining one side of the dais. He looked searchingly at Derik, then noticed the hard expression on Liam's face. The younger prince had not come unprepared. Those men were his. Derik seemed to be calculating his next response.

"I will not fight with you, brother," said Derik. He reversed the sword in his hands, and offered Liam the hilt. "Take my sword, and become my equal in birthright."

Antronos grit his teeth, and looked towards Aren. What should he do? It was a trap, couldn't Liam see? How could Derik play his own brother's emotions like that, without any remorse?

Liam slowly took the curved blade, and smiling with disbelief, tilted it to watch it glisten in the dust-light. Jait began to fidget in his chair, hands fumbling on the sides, trying to push himself up again. Vernus' hand never left his shoulder. Antronos wondered if he could push Vernus away without earning himself a knife in the back. Or if he should do it anyway and hope Maxal could heal him.

"Liam." Jait didn't stand, but met his younger son's eyes squarely. "Put down the sword. Now." Liam looked shocked, and did not move. Jait struggled weakly against Vernus, then finally stopped trying to stand. He looked up at Liam again.

"Or suffer," he managed.

What in Earth is he doing? Antronos wondered. He watched Liam stagger as if he were going to faint. The prince's look of confused shame said he did not understand what he had done to earn such a reprimand from his father. The sword fell to the dais with an irritating clatter, and Liam dropped to his knees before the throne, his head bowed. An unbearable pause followed, during which Jait struggled to speak.

Do it now, Antronos thought at him furiously. *Denounce Vernus!* Instead, Jait addressed Liam again.

"I want you to leave. Don't come back."

Liam ran off the dais and into the crowd, one bracer-covered arm raised to shield his eyes.

Voices were shouting again. Derik countermanded Jait—Ferril would not be returned to the Yrati. The people were demanding why Jait did not now speak. Towards the side of the dais Antronos saw a flourish of dark cloth, as the Yrati priests charged the stage and lunged at Antronos, pulling him into the crowd. It seemed that everyone was rushing the dais now, clutching at ankles and table legs. As he was pulled away, Antronos cast a last look at Jait. The High Prince was staring after him, looking defeated. Broken. Empty.

15

Blindfish

Opalena woke up next to Jait. She was lying on the floor of a rough-hewn cavern somewhere, the uneven rock pressing uncomfortably against her shoulders. She couldn't sit up. The Murdek had bled her so heavily that the very act of raising her head made her feel dizzy and sick. Her carelessly bandaged wrist still burned from Meriamdan's knife. It hurt to move her fingers. Antronos' mind had completely disappeared, making Meriamdan increasingly determined to ride Jait until she found the snake-boy again. In a way, Opalena wished her blood had given the Murdek what they needed to penetrate Antronos' defences. Then perhaps, they would leave her alone.

"Opalena."

She rolled her eyes towards Jait, and wondered if he had died after speaking her name. His skin looked blue-grey, his eyes sunken and dark, staring at nothing. He looked dead. He blinked.

"Are we alone?" he asked.

"Of course not." Meriamdan was in her head constantly now, eliminating even the slightest chance she might have to form any sort of secret alliance, or ask for help. It was only a matter of time before the old hag killed her once and for all, taking up permanent residence in her body. She was so tired; the thought of dying appealed to her. Then she would be finished being nothing more than a blood source.

"I attended a public assembly today. I couldn't finish the session. But I made sure that Liam is safe. He didn't understand, but he's away from here now. It was the best I could do. Maybe someone will have noticed that I'm...wrong."

"It's unlikely. Derik is lying to everyone. He's told people your addiction to medicines is what makes you so sick. People don't respect you anymore."

"Why?"

"You tell me."

"Derik would have inherited everything anyway. Why do this to me? Why did you do this to me? You helped the Murdek turn Derik against me. You helped them seduce my son."

"I didn't want to."

"You brought them here."

"You shouldn't have hired me."

"I thought you would make me feel better."

"Maybe you should have let Antronos do that."

"Antronos. Where is he anyway? He had that powder."

Opalena didn't want to answer him anymore. She was already so angry that it was impossible for her to fall asleep again, and his irritating prattle was just making it worse. If he had just stuck with Antronos, maybe she wouldn't have been here at all.

"There's something moving around under my back," said Jait.

Opalena didn't care. Let the beetles eat him.

"Feels warm," he said.

There *was* something moving underneath them. Bracing herself for the expected nauseating spin of her head, Opalena pushed herself up on an elbow and rolled onto her stomach so that she could stare at the eyeless, red skull that had surfaced through the rock she had been lying on. The thing blinked at her, and she noticed facetiously that it had pale, blond eyelashes. It sank back below the surface.

"It's nothing," she said, lying down on her stomach. "Just a very strange hallucination."

"That doesn't make sense," said Jait. "You see hallucinations. You don't feel them."

"There are different kinds of hallucinations. You can have auditory ones, where you hear things, then olfactory ones, where you smell things—"

"But does it make sense that we're having the same hallucination at the same time?"

Opalena's head hurt. She didn't want to think that hard. She sighed in irritation, wishing Jait would just shut up and leave her alone.

"Antronos had some medicine," Jait blabbered, "that could keep people out of your head. It was very good. I wish I had some more of it."

"You were dreaming. If he had that medicine, we wouldn't be here."

"No, I'm sure he had it."

Opalena felt Meriamdan's presence strengthen in her mind. Why was the old hag interested in Jait's ramblings? Was there something to what he was saying? Through the Murdek's mental connection, Opalena could feel Meriamdan coming closer, could feel the brush of air against the old gorgon's skin as she floated into the cavern. Meriamdan lowered her feet to the ground in front of Opalena's face. For the first time, she noticed that Meriamdan's feet were not human, but rather blunted with clawed toes. How strange.

"Jait. What do you speak of?" asked Meriamdan.

"I need some medicine," he said.

"What medicine?"

"Uh..." Jait's expression glazed over even more. "I don't know," he said finally.

"Was it the one you got from Antronos?"

"Yes."

"We'll have it, then," said Vernus. He had entered the cavern, followed by several other Murdek, and was sketching symbols on the floor with determination. Opalena groaned.

"We won't be needing you this time, my dear." He smiled at her unpleasantly and began strewing small, triangular magnets around his composition on the floor. Meriamdan tottered over to him.

"At least now you're seeing the value of a direct approach," she said to Vernus. He ignored her.

Two Murdek beasts dragged a struggling, red creature into the room. Opalena frowned and squinted at it, then realized that it wasn't another hallucination: just a boy with blood-coloured hair. The boy's hands were bound, and he was being cruelly shoved face-down against the rock, yet he still managed to pull one of his legs free, and twist enough to kick one of the squatting Murdek in the chin. The Murdek struck him across the back of his head, making his face smash against the floor and his nose bleed. Meriamdan grabbed the boy's head in her hands and her voice erupted in a staccato of noise. Her victim screamed. Opalena cringed as she felt the backwash of Meriamdan's mind crash into her own, while the boy shoved the Murdek woman out of his head. Meriamdan flinched her hands away and swore. He was strong. Disciplined.

"I told you the Yrati cannot be invaded thus." Vernus tore the boy's sleeve away, then proceeded to inject him with something. "They are also practised at mind projection." The boy's struggles weakened, and eventually he lay still.

"Idiot!" snapped Meriamdan. "He cannot answer like this!"

"I have no intention of asking him. We'll have it from the other one."

A second captive was dragged into the room. Opalena squinted again, trying to focus on a vague memory tugging at her mind. She had argued with that man, several years ago, during her undergraduate work. He wore a dark beard now, but she had known him when...he had tried to teach her something about herbal remedies. Ferril, was it?

"Tibeau!" The balding man tried to reach for the boy, but was roughly pulled back by ugly Caros. Vernus grabbed him by the collar.

"What did Antronos tell you?"

"Antronos?" Ferril gave Vernus a bewildered stare before his expression turned angry. "That you're murderers. Tibeau!" He made a second attempt to reach the boy. Vernus drew a knife from an arm sheath and crouched next to Tibeau.

"I meant about his medicines," Vernus said calmly. He pressed the tip of the knife against the back of Tibeau's neck.

"I didn't get a chance to read it. Earth! Stop!"

Vernus had begun to idly flick the tip of his knife across the boy's pale skin. Opalena imagined it drawing tiny rivulets of blood.

"Read it? Then he has a book of some sort? Where is this book?"

"It was thrown on the fire. Please, stop!"

"If you lie to me again, I will kill your child. Tell me what Antronos wrote."

"Something about mind control. Stop!"

"You are making me angry. The medicine!"

"Turpentine. Papaverine. Uh, I think he had aconitum in it. Earth, I don't remember!"

"Really?"

"I swear it! I don't know."

"Too bad." Vernus made a sudden stabbing motion. Ferril screamed. When Vernus got up and moved away, Opalena could see the knife handle protruding from the back of Tibeau's neck.

"Let him feel the death," Vernus said, and the Murdek holding Ferril let him go.

"No! Oh, Tibeau, no." Ferril crept forward and scooped up the limp boy. Opalena felt herself start to cry, watching the horrible way Tibeau's head lolled and his red hair swept the floor. At the same time, she wished that Vernus had killed *her*. It wasn't fair.

"Why?" Ferril sobbed. "What for?"

"I told you why. I want to know what changes Antronos made to my formula. He told you, and soon you will tell me," said Vernus.

Ferril looked up, scrubbing tears away with his fist.

"Earth damn you. Bastard. Get away."

Vernus ignored the insults. "Why don't you tell me what Antronos said?"

"Why don't you ask him yourself?"

"I'm asking you."

"Go boil yourself."

Vernus stood considering Ferril, then turned his gaze to Opalena. His mouth twitched, then he looked away.

"Is Jait awake?" he asked Meriamdan. She snorted derisively.

"Now you want a chant? You told me the Yrati cannot be invaded. You contradict yourself," she said.

"I do not," said Vernus. "With Jait's power, I may be able break him."

"Jait is sleeping," said Meriamdan. She staggered over to Ferril and put her hands into his hair. "Grief has weakened this Yrati. I can feel his mind opening. Yes. Help me with him."

Vernus again stared at Ferril for a long moment. With a sharp gesture he waved the other Murdek forward. Caros pinned Ferril down while Vernus injected a series of medicines into his abdomen, ignoring his kicking and his screams.

"Very well," Vernus said finally. "Try him, Meriamdan. See if he will bend to you."

The old crone hissed this time, her words palpable against Opalena's ears, nearly visible to her eyes, as she saw them fly throughout the cavern, entering every mind they came into contact with. Her own body heaved and buckled as she felt Ferril's mind twist open. It was an odd sensation, like being turned inside out, liquefied, then moulded into someone else. She was inside Ferril, part of Meriamdan, and murderously hungry. Ferril's body bounded up, pounced on Tibeau and began to feed. Stringy bits of cartilage caught between his teeth as he ripped the boy apart, swallowing huge lumps of his flesh without chewing, tearing deeper, deeper—

"Enough, Meriamdan." Vernus broke the spell, sending Opalena tumbling back into her own form. She sobbed, still partially connected to Ferril and fully aware of his blistering anguish, his retching and disbelief at the taste of blood and raw flesh still coating his mouth.

"I apologize for not believing." Vernus was gently lifting Meriamdan from the ground, then gestured towards Jait and Opalena. "Make sure they recover. Keep them drugged so they don't get anymore ideas about suicide."

One of the Murdek, Iegat, roughly scooped up Opalena, the motion making her head throb mercilessly. She tried to straighten out her neck, and found herself staring into the creature's yellow-eyed glare. Iegat smacked his lips in response. She had woken a few times to find him nibbling at her ankles, and wondered what would happen if she suddenly became useless to Vernus. Would he let this demon consume her? She wondered if Iegat would have Ferril as a snack, while he waited for his chance to butcher her.

She and Jait were taken to the upper tunnels of the Royal House and unceremoniously dumped in Jait's bed. Prince Derik had ordered the servants to stay away, so the linens were dirty. A cup was ground against her teeth. She drank what was given to her, spluttering at the metallic taste of blood. She wiped a hand against her mouth, relieved to see it come away grey. They had only given her a supplement. Of course. If they were getting blood from elsewhere, they wouldn't need it from her. She was left lying with her face towards the headboard, unable to see if the Murdek had exited the room. She supposed it didn't matter.

"Maybe we should just accept it," said Jait. "Like Sephus. He has an easier time of it now."

"It wouldn't matter if we accepted it now," Opalena murmured. "We have our roles in this game. Nothing will change that."

"But maybe, they would allow us some time together. I did want to treat you honourably, Opalena. I just never got the chance."

Opalena laughed. It sounded raspy, and it made her lungs burn. "You could have done that right from the start."

"Maybe, if we did what they wanted without resistance, they would let us comfort each other. Right now we have nothing."

"You're insane. There is no comfort in this."

Jait did not answer. Opalena stared at the headboard for an interminable time, not sure if she slept. Her entire right side had gone numb. She heard a rustling somewhere behind her, then felt something tugging at her ankle. Probably Iegat. Perhaps he would be allowed to eat her foot, since she really didn't need it to serve Vernus' purposes. But then,

Meriamdan's new body would be damaged. She was gently turned onto her back, and stared up into the hooded face of a sandy-haired man.

"Earth," said the man. "Here she is. The blindfish from Antronos' vision." Opalena frowned at him as he stroked her hair back. "Is she not beautiful?"

"Come on, we have to get out of here. We don't know how long he can keep the guards occupied." So. There was a second man in the room, and the sandy-haired one had not been speaking to her. He lifted her off the bed, easing her over his shoulder.

"Can you manage Jait?"

"He's a lot bigger than I thought." There was a metallic clinking sound. "Earth! He's chained to the bed."

"What do we do now?"

"I hear them coming. We have to leave him. Damn it. Let's go."

"We can't leave him." A woman's voice. "Look at him! Everything Antronos told us must be true!"

"Leelan, shut up! We have to go."

"Break the bed post, cut the chain or do something."

"They're coming!"

Opalena passed out.

✳✳✳✳✳

Tock. Tock. Tock. Tock.
Hypnotic.
Tock. Tock. Tock. Tock.
Soothing.

A timepiece encased in cracked wood and polished glass stood against the clay wall of...somewhere. Peaceful. An obsidian pendulum swung with unambiguous regularity, keeping pace with time.

Opalena dreamt of Jait. "No comfort here," she told him.

"What did you say?"

Opalena opened her eyes. Antronos was sitting next to her. He smiled and tugged his collar upwards. She hadn't felt this unbroken in weeks. Raising her hands, she saw that the scars and bruises were still there, but the bandages around her wrists were fresh and clean.

"How did you . . ." The question died on her lips.

"The Yrati are skilled healers," he said.

"No, I meant, how did you get me out?"

Antronos smiled again. "Stole you from under their noses."

Opalena began to remember. The tug on her foot. The sandy-haired man. Being lifted. "And Jait?" she asked.

"Ah." His expression sobered. "We couldn't get him."

Opalena sat up, amazed at how easy it was. She still felt weak, drained, but refreshed. Jait had been left behind. It made her feel...incomplete? Sad? Did it matter to her?

"Will you try again?" she asked.

Antronos shrugged. "My Lord Maxal is reconsidering our actions. Our attempt to have Jait denounce Vernus failed. Our attempt to rescue him failed. I don't know what we'll do next. There was a message, though, given by the ghouls that you would help him."

"By the what?"

"The Red Ghouls." Antronos smiled sheepishly. "Did you ever read the children's story about the skeletons that marched around when it rained?"

"And the Earth softened enough to set them free. Yes. What does that have to do with anything?" The image of the eyeless face she had seen protruding from the rock flashed through her mind. The realization must have shown on her face, because Antronos merely nodded.

"They said you would free Jait."

"Me? How?"

"I don't know."

Opalena pushed aside the blankets and stood up. Her legs were shaky, but still obeyed her. A deep anxiety was building up in her gut, threatening to consume her from inside out. She couldn't face Vernus again, not now, when she was finally away from him. She couldn't go back to the blood-letting, the constant despair. She couldn't ever let Jait touch her again, dragging her back into his psychological mire. She couldn't ever not touch Jait again. She couldn't let Jait be alone with Vernus.

"I can't leave him there." She stumbled to the opening of the chamber, and came face to face with the sandy-haired Yrati who had carried her out. He had apparently been leaning against the wall outside the small cavern, listening to her conversation with Antronos.

Opalena spluttered out a laugh. She put her hands to her mouth, unfamiliar with the sensation of glee she felt at seeing him. He smiled back.

"Thank you," she finally managed. Then, surprising herself, she flung her arms around him, hugging him tight. "Thank you so much."

"You should not go back there, Lady," he said.

"But, Jait—"

"We can deal with him."

One of his hands stroked the back of her neck, and she could feel the presence of his mind brush against hers. *Aren.* Unlike Vernus, he did not pick through her thoughts like they were his to do with as he pleased, but instead sent a wave of warmth and well being through her. She relaxed against him, feeling broken shards of her mind knit together, making her stronger.

"You are not healed yet," he said. Finally, his touch was nothing more than an embrace. Opalena lifted her head from his shoulder, feeling slightly embarrassed at how much she welcomed it. She took a step back. The Yrati looked into her eyes, with more than a healer's interest. She took another step back and broke eye contact, sweeping loose strands of hair from her face.

"Thank you," she said again, now feeling flushed, dizzy and confused. She turned away and saw Antronos standing at the other edge of the doorway, watching her with something like sadness. Still, he smiled at her encouragingly.

"I have to go back," she said, looking from one man to the other. Aren took her hand.

"Don't," he said. "You are life. The prophecy from the ghouls told us to protect your life. The Murdek are slowly killing you. Stay here."

"But...I thought I was the one who was going to have to free him." She wanted to come up with some logical explanation, some strategic justification, that leaving Jait with the Murdek would give them too much power, but the Yrati's gaze was weakening what little resolve she had.

"Somebody has to free him. He should have already been rescued," said someone angrily. An Yrati woman with light brown hair had entered from a side tunnel and was glaring at Aren. He glared right back at her for a moment before turning back to Opalena.

"With due respect to Sen Antronos, he hasn't as much experience in interpreting the ghouls' messages. The fact that you're away from Jait will end this," he insisted. Now he was trying to influence her. The touch of his mind was subtle. Had she not spent so much time with Vernus, she might not have noticed it at all.

She pulled her hand out of his, uncomfortable with the control he was trying to exert over her. She was aware that he wanted something, and she was tired of giving.

"Why am I so important to you?" she asked. "We hardly know each other."

"I've told you. We saw it in the prophecy."

Aren's steady gaze did not move from her face. It would be a mistake to try negotiating with him when she was so exhausted. *This is not over.* If anything, Aren's attempt at control was strengthening her decision to go back for Jait. She would decide what she did—not Vernus, not the ghouls, and certainly not Aren.

"I need to rest," she said, and stumbled back into the sleeping chamber.

16

Fawn

Opalena tried not to fidget as she waited impatiently for Antronos and Maxal to finish compounding their drugs. Maxal was making a larger batch of yet another formulation of mind-blocker, which excluded any kind of bone-decomposing mould, while Antronos was fiddling with something he said would remove Jait's inhibitions. The two of them were cooking up something new almost every other day, each time promising they would give some to her, then backing down on the promise, saying it wasn't ready. Each day that went by without Meriamdan finding and reclaiming her mind was a blessing, but one that Opalena wasn't going to take for granted. Aren kept telling her the influence of the communal Yrati mind would stop the Murdek from invading her here, but she wasn't satisfied—she wanted the drugs. She knew first-hand how difficult it had been to find Antronos when he was using them, and she didn't see why he wouldn't just give her one of his older formulations, not believing him when he said they were all used up.

"You know, My Lord, I almost asked to join your clan before this all started," Antronos was saying as he pounded a root to mush. He put aside the white stone pestle, and swept the pulp off the wooden lab bench and into a bowl. "I wish to the Earth I had."

"What stopped you?" asked Maxal. He repositioned the mirrors around a glass tank of bioluminescent moss so that he could see his work better. The room was basked in yellow light from several low braziers lit around the edge of the room, but it was never wise to bring an open fire close to a work bench. The light from the moss was erratic, and despite herself, Opalena was wishing Maxal would import lights from Raulen as Vernus had. Anything to speed up his work!

"I didn't think you would accept me." Antronos smiled sheepishly at the Yrati High Priest, looking like some weak-minded supplicant. Opalena reined in her urge to slam her fists down on the bench and tell them to get on with it. "But now look at me," Antronos continued. "Regardless of being old Vernus' student, I'm still studying pharmacology instead of surgery."

Maxal twisted around on his stool and sat facing Antronos. "Perhaps you should change, then."

Antronos annoyingly also stopped what he was doing. "Really? I didn't dare go to Amphetam and ask for another supervisor, or even just quit, because I was afraid of being arrested over Shenan, or that Vernus might kill my new supervisor, but you already know everything." He was grinning stupidly. "This might actually be possible!"

"Of course it is."

"Are you two done yet?" Fara and Leelan had entered the lab and were standing on tip-toe behind the bench, trying to peer over the reagents rack.

Thank the Earth, thought Opalena.

"Everyone's waiting for your magic powder. When are you going to give us some, Maxal?" asked Fara.

"Well, I have to make sure it's right. If we're going to be dosing a large group of people with this stuff, most of them unaware that they're even taking it, it better well be unnoticeable. What we're planning isn't exactly legal."

"Is that the biggest batch you can make?"

Maxal sighed. "Yes, Fara, it is."

"Not going to go very far, is it?"

"I know, I just can't get the ingredients to react the same way on a larger scale. Some of the components keep turning solid when they're supposed to be liquid. I can't get them mixed properly."

"Huh. How about you, Antronos? Got much?"

"Not really. This is specifically for My Lord Jait anyway."

"Max, when are we going to rescue Ferril?"

Maxal looked defeated, and poked at his formulation pensively. His hand shook as he pulled his sleeve down, covering up an angry red welt on his arm that Opalena hadn't noticed before. His next words were bewildering. "I don't know. I'm not sure this is the right time."

In the following silence, everyone stared at Maxal in amazement. *Not the right time?* thought Opalena. Her mind reeled with the impossible revelation that Maxal didn't seem to share everyone else's feeling that the right time was already long overdue.

"You have to get him out, and soon," she finally broke in. "After what they did to him, and that boy . . ." She stopped speaking, unable to concentrate because of the lump forming in her throat. Each time she let herself think about it too much, she ended up either sobbing for hours or vomiting. Telling the Yrati what had happened to their priest-brothers had been the hardest thing she'd ever done.

"How can this not be the right time?" Fara persisted. "He must be waiting for us. What if he thinks we've abandoned him? What if he gives up? He could end up like that Sephus fellow."

"He won't," Maxal said sharply. "He's a senior Yrati, and his mind is fully trained. Ferril would die before giving into them."

"So why are we waiting? They've already broken into him once. Surely they'll do it again. How long are we going to leave him there?"

"Just let me finish this, Fara. At the very least I want our people protected before going near the Murdek. I *will not* lose any others." Maxal's face was growing red, and his eyes were watering. Another red welt seemed to appear on his left temple. Opalena blinked, and it was gone. She shook her head. He stood up and swept out of the room without looking back at Fara, who ran after him.

"Dammit, we should go now," Leelan muttered.

"I'll go," said Opalena.

"What?" asked Antronos.

"You just got out," said Leelan.

"I know. But I'll go. I can take some of whatever Maxal has now, and some of Antronos' custom drug for Jait, and give it to him. If I get a chance, I can also give some to Ferril, but that's unlikely, since the Murdek always used to keep him separate from us. Anyway, if their minds are hidden from the Murdek, it will give them a better chance of escape. At the very least they'll have some of their dignity back."

"What if you can't escape?" asked Antronos. "They'll probably chain you down as well this time."

"Like Leelan said, we can't leave them there. We have to go back."

"I'm going with you," said Leelan.

"I don't think that's a good idea," Opalena told her. "The Murdek are most likely going to be extra vigilant where Yrati are concerned, especially now. They've deliberately been keeping Ferril isolated, like they're afraid he'll do something to spoil their control over Jait's mind."

"We can't let Aren know about this," said Antronos.

*****

Wrapped in a cloak and treading softly, Opalena entered the outlying Royal caves which were once used for farming, but had since been permitted to grow wild. For a few moments, she daydreamt of meeting a gardener she could bribe into taking some of the mind-blocking powder to Jait. She could lie, and say it was a love token from her, and ask the servant not to speak of it. Antronos had given her as much of his special formulation of mind-blocking powder as he could compound, hiding it in a hollow barrette. He had refused to come, saying that someone needed to stay behind and stop Aren from following her. *Leelan could have done that*, she thought angrily, but nonetheless had accepted his brotherly kiss on the cheek before leaving. She suspected what Antronos had refused to say was that someone who really knew what was going on needed to still be outside the Murdek influence if she failed.

It had been two weeks since the Yrati had pulled her out of the Royal House, and despite their treatments, she still felt sore and battered all over.

She secretly questioned the wisdom of returning so soon, but the longer she let Aren think he was in control of her, the bolder he was becoming in his conversation and demands. Also, her desire to see Jait again had become unbearable.

The lichen and fungi growing in the cavern were glorious in their muted shades and intricate growth patterns, climbing up the walls of the caves. It had been years since she had seen this strain, having kept a small, stolen specimen of it in her rooms as an undergraduate. Opalena approached carefully, watching that she did not crush the brims of the toadstools scattered in her path, and smiling irrepressibly, brushed her fingers gently over the surface of the lichen. This variety was heat sensitive, and small blossoms opened up in response to her fingertips. She squatted next to them, encircling the plant with her arm, and the longer her body warmth was there, the more the tiny flowers unfolded and turned towards her.

"You are welcome wherever you go," said a man's voice from behind her. She started, and ended up tipping herself over to avoid damaging the plants around her, landing half sprawled in a puddle of dank water. She looked up to see Jait standing there, and felt a rush of relief that she had to go no farther into the caves. How had he come to the outer caves? Why had Vernus allowed it? Why would the High Prince be wandering around in abandoned farming caves? She didn't care. He looked beautiful, healthy and strong. His hair, smooth and glossy, fell in dark cascades over a blue embroidered shirt. Decorative silver daggers hung in straight lines from his hips, like tusks. The Murdek had allowed him to recover, and now that he was strong, Antronos' mind-blocker would ensure he'd stay that way.

"My Lord and High Prince Jait," she said, and unable to stop herself, began grinning like an idiot. He came forward and grabbed her by the arm to haul her to her feet, an unfortunate bitterness tainting his smile. He seemed distant, and completely lucid. A worm of uncertainty crept through Opalena's thoughts. Had he given in to Vernus? Become Murdek willingly? Would he change his mind?

"What are you doing here?" he asked. Feeling rather breathless, Opalena fumbled for one of the barrettes in her hair.

"I brought you this," she said. She flicked open one end of the enamel decoration, showing him the hidden vial before handing it to him.

"You have been with the Yrati?" he asked. She nodded. "And Antronos?"

"Yes."

Jait gazed at her for a few seconds, then nodded and tucked the barrette inside his shirt.

"Thank you." He stood there, just watching her somewhat speculatively. Why did he not take the medicine immediately? Opalena began to feel uneasy. She hedged away from him. He was not the same.

"Must you leave so soon, Sen?" he asked. Opalena choked on the formality of his question. Why was he being so cold? Had she imagined all his implied feelings for her? *Stop it,* she told herself. She was unimportant. All that mattered was that she give Jait a fighting chance.

"I only came to give you the medicine." Jait still gave no indication that he had any personal interest in her, as though he had completely forgotten his drug-laced courtship and words about treating her honourably. He stared at her like she had betrayed or somehow disappointed him. "Why don't you just take it?" she asked, her voice cracking. Jait's hand shot out and grabbed her sore wrist.

"Come with me. I want to show you the other gardens, the ones that are actually taken care of." Her mouth opened soundlessly for a moment. Now what? Play some sort of pretend game?

"I really have to be going." She tried to pull away, wincing at his tightening grip. Jait grinned broadly at her discomfort.

"It won't take long. There is something I want to show you: surface plants."

Opalena swallowed with difficulty. Her mouth was dry. "What? *Plants?*"

"Yes, they come from the other side of the world, where the water always runs on the surface instead of underground. They really are quite magnificent." Jait's face transformed, becoming suffused with a ferocious kind of joy. He dragged her deeper into the caverns, until they came into one that was structured in agricultural tiers, and had several species of fruit-bearing trees hanging heavily-laden branches into the walkways in explosions of colour. When she stopped pulling against him, and allowed herself to walk at his side, Jait let go of her wrist. *Now what?*

"I'm glad you came back," he said. Opalena didn't look up at him. Jait ran his finger across her cheek, looking pleased to see her stop and recoil from his touch. He grabbed a branch of orange drop-shaped fruit and offered it to her.

"Here, try these." Opalena plucked one from the branch and looked at it uncertainly. What in Earth was Jait playing at? He smiled in her face, leaned close to her and said, "Plants are for eating." Opalena looked at the orange fruit in her hand. She had never seen its like before. She took a bite.

Jait straightened up, his face losing all expression. He stared at her blankly. "You would eat from my hand?" he asked. Opalena blinked in confusion. "Why not?"

Jait now looked frustrated. "Is the medicine you gave me poisoned or not?" he demanded.

"Poisoned?" she whispered.

"Is it?"

"No. Earth, no. It's a mind-blocker. It's to help you break free. I took some myself."

Opalena couldn't believe what she had just been asked. Didn't he understand she was trying to help him? *Poison!* Jait's face crumbled and he turned his back to her.

"Please don't be like this," she pleaded. He did not turn around.

"I thought you had brought me poison."

"Why?"

"I assumed the Yrati wanted me dead. They think I'm Murdek. They asked me for their brother Ferril, and were refused. You saw what happened to their boy. If you've told them of his death, I'm sure they're blaming me. And Antronos. I've...helped them invade his mind, so many times. If I'm dead, then everyone's problems will be ended."

Opalena grabbed his sleeve, trying to force him to turn around. "Jait, none of that's true. The Yrati tried to rescue you. If they wanted you killed, they would have done it when they took me. You can leave with me. Now. We can just walk out the way I came. Please, come with me."

"I can't leave."

"Yes, you can. Take the medicine. You'll be invisible to them, and we can just leave."

Without turning around, Jait stalked deeper into the cavern. Opalena stood there, stunned, watching his retreating back. He wasn't going to return. Not even to tell her to go away.

She leaned against the brick support of a planter, unable to grieve. After a while, she retraced her steps to the back tunnels.

She saw a group of Murdek waiting for her there. Ferril stumbled towards her, his eyes dark with bruises, his lips slack, his expression vacant. He paused in front of her for a moment, then struck her across the face.

"Jait really *can't* leave," said Meriamdan. "And neither can you."

17

Caïna

Vernus wasted no time cornering Jait in one of the far gardens. The metallic green thread embroidering his black robes caught on leafy brambles as he fought to keep up. He lost sight of Jait for a few moments, and gestured for Caros and Iegat to run ahead. Slowing to a walk and stepping out into a cleared path, he saw the High Prince standing with his back turned, gazing at a false archway filled with blooming lichen and painted with an artificial vista of Raulen. He approached slowly, carefully checking to see if Jait had managed to snatch up any gardening tools, which he might use as a weapon. Caros and Iegat crept up on his flanks. It had been risky, letting Jait loose to lure Opalena deep into the gardens to give Meriamdan a chance to check if she had been accompanied by any of the Yrati and close off all exits—it was done on short notice when his sentries had reported that they had seen her coming, and there was a chance that Jait would not have done as he was told.

"Jait. Give me the powder Opalena brought."

A hair clasp fell from Jait's hand. He didn't turn around. "I've already taken it."

"You were to give it to me!" Vernus probed Jait's mind. It was like hunting through air. No resistance, no substance to even let him know that he had made contact, as if Jait were completely invisible to him. He took a step closer, all senses straining to find a handhold on Jait's thoughts.

He finally perceived it. Jait's mind was completely open, and immense; so large that any part of it was well out of Vernus' reach. And the magic flowed freely, no longer trapped in the farthest corners of Jait's psyche.

"How have you..."

Jait turned around, the whites of his eyes bright like burning magnesium, the violet irises deep as pools of obsidian magma. Vernus stared at him in fascination. Was Antronos trying to raze Jait's power?

"What have they done to you this time?"

"This is what you've done to me. You tore down the barriers. They've just given me a chance to keep you out while those walls are down." Jait swung an arm forward, casting a wave of energy over Vernus that knocked him flat. Caros and Iegat sprang onto Jait's back, trying to bring him down.

Iegat was immediately flung to the ground, a bright light emanating from his stomach. He curled up on the stones of the walkway and screamed, as the blistering white fire gave way to an explosion of curdled blood and the overwhelming stench of burnt flesh. Iegat was not dead. He lay sideways on the ground, trying to scoop the bits of himself back towards his body.

Vernus looked up to see what had become of Caros. The other Murdek was suspended in the air in front of Jait, shuddering with fear, arms and legs tucked up in a defensive posture. Jait laughed.

"Is this the power you were after, Vernus?"

Lazily, whimsically, Caros' arms twisted upwards, then over his head, and behind his back, until with a sinewy crunch they came forward again to hang limply at his sides. Then Caros tore in half lengthwise and the dead pieces of him fell to the ground with a bloody thump. Vernus stared in disbelief.

By the Earth!

Jait started to come towards Vernus. His stride was unsteady, as if he were drunk. Still sprawled on the ground, Vernus shuffled away on his hands before realizing that he had to stand up first, if he wanted to move faster. Then he remembered that it was never a good idea to turn tail when faced with a predator. He stood up. Jait was still weak, still crippled. Still controllable. He sent a mental probe out towards Meriamdan. She had finished with Opalena and was circling round to catch Jait from behind. While the High Prince did have power, he was too stupid, and too careless to win this.

"Do you know the price of using their medicines, Jait? Sephus learned the hard way. It's always the same. You might have temporary control over your mind, but that block goes two ways. If I can't see you, you can't see me."

"Oh, but I can. And I'm going to kill you."

Vernus cast out a bolt of his own force, one that would have sent Sephus sprawling half a mile away. It was the strongest assault he could muster, yet Jait didn't waver. The High Prince didn't even seem to notice as the bolt became lost in his vastness. His power spilled from his mind in great coiling ropes of malice that twisted up the walkway faster than Vernus could back-pedal. They merged under Vernus' feet and invaded his flesh, wrenching muscle from bone, rupturing his skin, scorching his viscera. Vernus pulled in his intentions of attack, focusing all his energy on keeping his physical form from being obliterated, hoping that Meriamdan would act soon. He was vaguely aware when her inert, desiccated form fell down on the walkway somewhere in front of him. *This can't be happening. It can't be! I am the master here! How is it possible?*

"Father, stop this."

Jait faltered. Paused in distraction. "You...*dare*...call me 'Father'".

Prince Derik was stepping out of the unkempt foliage. Vernus blinked the ooze from his eyes enough to see that Derik palmed something behind his back. He approached Jait with his other hand outstretched.

"Are you going to kill me as well?" asked Derik. "Father, I may have wanted power. I see now that I was wrong. I'm willing to wait for it, if you will forgive me."

"You liar."

Derik fell to his knees in pain as Jait's anger crushed him.

"Stop," he hissed. "Or you'll never see Leod again."

Jait's expression turned to angry surprise as Derik straightened somewhat and seemed to breathe easier. "You haven't seen him for weeks, have you? Haven't you wondered why he hasn't come begging for candy for so long?"

"I don't need you to find him."

"By the time you get to him, he'll be dead."

Jait's lower lip trembled for a moment as he considered this. "We'll see. At any rate, you *will* be dead."

Derik lunged forward, sinking the syringe he held into Jait's arm. Jait's mind flung him against the stone wall, causing a wealth of rubble to fall to the ground when he let Derik go. He pulled the syringe from his sleeve, then stood watching as a small patch of blood soaked through the fabric. He staggered, and fell to the ground in convulsions, his spittle foaming at the sides of his mouth.

Cautiously, Vernus struggled to his feet, wincing at the pain of his damaged limbs. It hurt to breathe. He stood motionless, surveying the area before him, holding his breath as he waited for Jait to get up again. The High Prince didn't move. He limped to Jait's side and put a hand to the High Prince's lips. Jait was not dead. He turned as he heard rustling behind him. Derik also stood.

"What did you give him?" Vernus asked.

Derik rubbed the back of his head gingerly. "A little bit of Antronos' old mind-blocking formulation that Ferril mixed up for me. I've been testing it out on Sephus, and he assures me it's quite close to the drug Antronos duped him into taking outside of his office. I mixed it with laudanum. Potent, wasn't it? And that nasty side effect of shutting the mind down completely. Such a tiny bit, and yet it was enough to do *that*." He gestured towards Jait.

Vernus surprised himself by guffawing. He nodded at Derik. "Well done."

18

Supposition

Just inside the door of Dagnaum's chamber, Antronos knelt and bowed his head, as was required by Yrati ritual. He did not have permission to enter this cave, but could think of no one else to discuss his fears with since Maxal had gone into isolation. Aren thought that Fara had unforgivably upset the High Priest by nearly accusing him of abandoning Ferril, but Fara was unrepentant. Maxal was stronger than the lot of them put together, she insisted, and was not going to snap in two over a handful of words. She thought Maxal was meditating to find a solution to the Murdek threat.

Dagnaum had also once been High Priest, but now lived in complete darkness and seclusion, only having contact with the other Yrati when he had written something new. While Antronos' Desert vision had recovered from the effects of his early mind-blocker formulations, Dagnaum was so old that all he could see of the ancient priest was a waffling shadow.

"Who is this charming boy?" came a warm and comforting voice. Antronos heard the shuffling footsteps coming towards him.

"My Lord and Priest Dagnaum, I am called Antronos."

"How is it with you, boy?" Callused fingers touched his hair and smoothed it back.

Antronos felt Dagnaum's mind gently brush against his own. "Ah ha. You've read my children's books about the ghouls and magic using red wax. Your mind reels with doubt. Is Dagnaum an old fool, or does he hide what he knows from Vernus by writing for little ones? Everybody thinks such things, so let's never mind. There are greater problems that you want answers to."

A little embarrassed at having his opinions picked out of his thoughts, Antronos decided that Dagnaum's suggestion to "never mind" suited him. He plunged ahead with his question. "The Yrati are dying because of me. Ferril's gone, and his student Tibeau. I had a dream...or vision, where the ghouls told me something...I think I'm supposed to protect Jait somehow, but he's still going to die. I couldn't tell from the vision if the Yrati or the Murdek are going to kill him. And in a second vision, all I saw was a fish, but Aren seems to think they wanted us to protect Opalena. Anyway she's gone back to Jait to try and set him free, but she hasn't returned, and I really need to know if she's done the right thing. Or if I've done the right thing in letting her go. Could you help me understand what the ghouls have been trying to tell me?"

"Die because of you? You're not killing them. And it's only water. Some things drown, while others need it to live. Water does not kill all; it just needs to be balanced. These things have become separate, but I only described them as such because they are detached. I didn't mean that they were meant to be kept that way, because water can change the potential of the Desert, bringing life to both."

Antronos pushed down his frustration. He had been hoping to hear clear answers, not more riddles. He strained his eyes, willing himself to see more of Dagnaum's faded aura. "Have you also had the dream about the fawn? I was hoping you could tell me what it means."

Dagnaum hesitated. A soft thump made Antronos imagine the old man had sat down next to him.

"I have indeed dreamt of the chattering Red Ghouls in their blue robes, who have told me things that are not immediately understood."

"And?" Antronos prompted.

"I have prophesied."

Antronos waited. Would it be rude to ask again? His eyes picked up a faint flickering of aura. It faded. It came again, and he realized that it was not his Desert sight at all, but a dim, chemical flame that Dagnaum had struck in a clay bowl. The old priest was hooded, and his hands were gloved. Antronos could see no part of him as he moved the bowl to the side of another of the looking pools that the Yrati mediated by.

Dagnaum hunched over the pool, waiting. After several moments, he spoke.

"It was this, Antronos: Opalena found Jait sleeping in the Desert. She gave him an egg which he could have either smashed against the ground, or kept. He did not know what to do, and stood with it in his hand until it hatched and a white falcon came out of it. Inspired by the beauty of the falcon, he fed it his blood until it grew strong, then threw it up into the wind. Wherever the bird flew, the Desert became overrun with water, and the light became rich. All evil things fell away. Hmm. Another new prophecy. I've just realized I haven't written it down for Maxal. Paper, paper, paper."

"An egg? First a fish, and now an egg? Aren is right, I really don't have any hope of interpreting these messages."

Dagnaum said nothing.

"My Lord Yrati, pardon my rudeness, but that doesn't help me decide what to do. It doesn't help at all!"

Dagnaum's hooded figure weaved back and forth, as though searching the floor for answers. Antronos wished he could go back to that temple where the

Red Ghouls hid, and *shake* the answers out of their rattling bones. Finally, the old man said in a helpless tone, "The prophecy has been given."

Antronos reined in his emotions. He shouldn't have spoken like that, especially when he had asked for Dagnaum's council.

"I'm sorry. Please forgive me."

A gloved hand reached out to pull at his hair.

"Who are you?" Dagnaum asked. "Why are you here? I don't think I've seen you before. You're not one of those seed sellers, are you? I have no money."

"No, My Lord. Thank you. I'll go now."

Antronos stood up and fumbled his way out of Dagnaum's cavern. He leaned against the tunnel wall, rubbing his eyes wearily, trying to ease the headache he had developed from straining to see in the dark. Opalena had been gone for so long. Surely if she had succeeded he would have heard from her by now.

"What are you doing here?"

Antronos blinked his eyes futilely.

"Aren?"

"Dagnaum is precious to us. I don't like you skulking around his caves."

"Pardon, but if Dagnaum doesn't want me visiting him, he's perfectly capable of telling me himself."

Aren shoved against his shoulder.

"You come here, take advantage of Yrati hospitality, and we end up paying for it dearly. Now you want to fetch Dagnaum into Vernus' hands?"

Antronos groaned. "I just came to ask him about the vision."

Aren huffed derisively. "You assume you had one. You came right out and said you hadn't seen Opalena's face in the pool the last time you *tried* to have a vision."

"Why are you insisting on being like this?"

"Because of Tibeau."

"I did nothing to that boy!"

"Except feed him to Vernus."

"I've told you. I didn't want that to happen."

"I think you also talked Opalena into going back so that Vernus could trap her again, and keep her from us. We need her here."

"This conversation is useless. Leave me alone."

Aren grabbed his elbow. "From now on, you stay away from Dagnaum, *and* Opalena. If it hadn't been for you, she wouldn't have gone back."

"Earth, Aren! She went because she wanted to! I didn't tell her to. She was angry with me because I wouldn't go with her."

"Sent her to do your dirty work."

"She wants Jait, not you, so why don't you just back off?"

"You mean not *you*."

"Get off me!" No longer caring that Maxal might throw him out, Antronos gave Aren a hard push, sending him sprawling. He stood glaring at Aren for a few seconds, stunned at his own actions, then pulled his robes straight and walked off. He had better things to do than this.

19

Love

Feeling slightly ill from yet another dose of mind-blocker, Antronos crept through the Royal House, hoping the guards would heed his polite request that they not bother to inform Sen Vernus or Prince Derik of his arrival. There was no way of knowing how involved any of the palace staff were with the Murdek, or which ones he could trust. He wished he could have consulted Maxal before coming, but perhaps that would be pointless after his tiff with Aren—there was no way the High Priest would favour Antronos over one of his own. And if he wasn't welcome in the Yrati caves anymore, he was damned if he were going to sit around waiting for Vernus to find him. Perhaps he shouldn't have let Opalena come here by herself, but he really did think that the mind-blocker would have masked her presence to the Murdek. Earth, he should have been the one to come. He was the one with years of practise at sneaking around, not her. He only hoped that he could do something to help her now.

Jait was predictably found lying in bed, and Opalena was nowhere in sight, despite her previous tale that she was always kept here. The High Prince's pale cheeks were sunken, and his black hair was matted with sweat from fever. There were fresh bruises and open wounds along the veins of his arms, which oozed appallingly. Soaking wet, the High Prince opened his eyes and asked for water when Antronos pressed a hand along the side of his face.

"He's...he's not going to let it end," rasped Jait.

"We'll make him end it!" Antronos hissed. "I've brought you something different to use against him. If we keep changing your defences, he won't be able to constantly control you. Here, take it." Jait turned his head away.

"It's no good. I tried that junk Opalena brought me. He always finds a way around whatever you people come up with. It just makes it so he has to torture me longer before he gets what he wants."

"Take it. You must keep on fighting him."

"Why?"

"You must! Think of your people! Think of Leod and Opalena. You have to fight Vernus for them."

"I cannot. He's too strong. Leod and Opalena are dead. Derik told me he's killed them."

"It's not true. Leod's with the Yrati. Jait...Jait, swallow this."

"I'm tired of being crushed. You only stand me up for him to knock down again." Antronos pushed two powder caplets past Jait's teeth and poured water after them. He held his hand over Jait's mouth until he swallowed. He then began stitching a small button to Jait's shirt.

"There's one more dose hidden in this button," he told Jait. "The metal is thin. You should be able to bite through it."

After a while Jait seemed more alert, at least enough for him to push Antronos' hands away.

"You know he uses me. He can't jump into a stranger's body without me, only someone he knows well, and that doesn't interest him anymore. If he's on his own and wants a stranger, he needs physical contact, and that is not so easy for him. If you really want to slow him down, you can kill me."

Antronos closed his eyes and shook his head. "No."

"I'm your pawn. If you want to use me to make the most effective strike, then kill me! All your other efforts are useless. They accomplish nothing!"

Antronos stared at the High Prince. Kill him? Would it be out of kindness or strategy? *You've shown with Shenan that you're just as skilled in murder as everything else you put your mind to.*

"I cannot kill you. That would be treason against my country and a betrayal of my trade. As a doctor I have taken an oath." Jait shook in either a laugh or a sob.

"And you've never broken it? Not even for mercy?"

Antronos only felt a mild twinge as he lied about Shenan: "No."

Jait began to cry. He held up his scarred wrists.

"Look at this," he sobbed. "I can't even do this myself. How do you expect me to defeat Vernus?"

Antronos stood up to leave. Jait lunged upwards and clutched his robes.

"Please," begged Jait.

"You must fight Vernus."

"I've tried!"

"Try harder!"

"Kill me!"

"I will not!" Antronos broke away and fled from the room, telling himself it was because he had to find Opalena. If only Jait would cooperate! Why did he have to be the one constantly pushing? Jait was so stubborn! If only he would turn that stubbornness the other way. *Earth's Volcanic Guts!* He'd force Jait through this if he had to, *but he would not allow him to be killed.* The Red Ghouls and their vision of Jait's death be damned!

＊＊＊＊＊

A dim, dusky light summoned Jait through his eyelids, calling him towards wakefulness. His mind was too sluggish to respond, and every time he made a motion towards the grey beacon, he would sink again, muddied and mired. For a while he was content to rest, to give up reaching towards the light. After all, what did it have to offer him but Vernus? Vernus and pain. Vernus and boredom. Vernus and hopelessness. He slept, turning away from the grey beacon that would have led him to consciousness. In his repose he did not dream, did not wander through the scarred pockets in his mind. He just lay there, stuck in the mud, too weary and apathetic to free himself. It was warm there and very comfortable. He began to like it, and felt soothing relief seep through the dry cracks in his being, filling them, making him feel supple and whole. He sank a little further into the mud, felt it ooze around him, soft and warm, embracing and caressing. He felt love for the mud. Peace.

As the mud reached up and covered his head, he began to suffocate, his body automatically struggling to breathe. *Leave it alone*, he told himself. *It's all right. You don't have to bother.* He began to subside. *Yes, and now to rest again.* He experienced a few happy moments with the mud completely covering him, and he was hidden from all things...well, not quite. There was an eel in the mud, and it nuzzled against his arm, then his neck. He wished it would GO AWAY. It would not. *Rotten eel.* It came at him, striking him hard against the chest with its head, then whipping its tail across his face. Jait decided he was weary enough to tolerate this, and that he would be able to sleep anyway. He would just ignore the eel. The stupid animal became enraged that he would not respond, and bit his arm, sinking a single pointed fang deep into his vein. Jait was aware that his flesh was being pierced, but it did not really hurt, not until the idiot eel spat its fire-venom into his blood.

The silence was shattered.

Some very rude light came along and tore out his eyes, so that it could take up noisy residence inside his skull. Three-headed eels began writhing and shrieking, spattering the mud so much that Jait was no longer covered by it. His soul moaned. WHY did they have to come here? He took in a breath to tell them to SHUT UP, and instantly realized that he had made a mistake. The air in his lungs was making him lighter, and he was beginning to float back towards the surface. Already another noise assailed him, stirring up troubling little clouds of pain that had previously settled and were quite nicely out of the way. He drew in another breath. He was going to find that eel and kill it. One of the pain clouds swirled up and tossed silt across his chest, making him gasp in agony. His lungs and throat were suddenly raw, making each breath excruciating, yet he couldn't stop. His heart began pounding, and each beat shot shards of broken glass into his already tattered and bleeding lungs. His chest convulsed and he smelled the blood that filled his mouth. The mud, which had filled and softened the cracks within him, dribbled out, leaving long, tender wounds behind. Something else seeped in: profound misery. Unable to withstand the bursting within himself any longer, his eyelids surrendered and snapped open, allowing him to see the yellow, sticky pus coating his eyes.

He had awakened. He was lying in bed.

Vernus was there, holding a spike.

Opalena was there. She put a soggy hand on his face. Her eyes and nose were red. She was screaming.

"Those injections are responsible for giving him bloodrot and nearly killing him in the first place!"

Her voice sounded raw. Her throat probably hurt as much as his did. His breathing grew shallower and less painful. Opalena twisted about to face Vernus, causing her sleeve to brush across Jait's face, and he caught the brief passing of her comfortable, musky scent. How nice that she was there.

Her next words sliced away Jait's pleasure. "There are a hundred other ways you could have revived him. I could have done it for you!" *Alas. You as well, Opalena?*

Jait felt himself sink again, this time into sadness. Sleep would not come.

✳✳✳✳✳

Several days passed, and under the much gentler ministrations of Opalena, Jait again got to his feet and left the sick bed. Perhaps Vernus thought leaving the High Prince to himself for a while would keep death at bay. For weeks, the old man let Jait alone, allowing him to read or wander through the Royal House—so long as he was watched. At night, they continued to chain him to the bed. Derik had cut him off from all outside dealings, as well as any official documents and sharp objects. The servants all complied with Derik's commands, each of them resoundingly threatened with the responsibility of Jait's death, should they allow the High Prince access to anything that might upset him and lead to another suicide attempt. Perhaps it had been a mistake to give Derik this opportunity to label him as a fragile madman.

One thing he was allowed was access to Opalena. Derik didn't come after her anymore, and she was too afraid to sleep anywhere but in Jait's arms. Despite this, he knew it was temporary, and that it wouldn't be long before Vernus spoiled it again.

Waking up one morning, he swept Opalena's hair away from her ear, and whispered, "I need poison. I need you to bring me poison."

She turned towards him, her face a mask of denial. Did she really believe this peace would last forever?

"But why?"

"Just bring it. I want you to look around here for what you need, cook up the deadliest stuff you can think of, and give it to me. All right?"

"But *why*? Jait, you were so close the last time you fought them. Why don't you want to use your power again?"

"I cannot. That last time, when you gave me the medicine in your barrette, was a fluke. Antronos snuck in here and gave me another dose, and it had no such effect. I haven't been able to reach my power and Antronos hasn't returned. Perhaps he's been caught, or they've blocked his route of entry, but I don't think he's coming back. Hailandir was the only one who could let me see anything remotely like magic in myself. And she died because I..."

Opalena pushed herself up on an elbow, looking concerned, afraid, anxious.

"She died because I drained her. Trying to control this damned power. I didn't want to. I only tried to push myself so far because she asked it of me. It's been nothing but a curse. Everyone knows I was the cause of her death, but no one really understood what I had done. I've never been punished. So you see, this is right. I should die for having killed her."

"And what about me?" she asked.

Jait took her hand and pressed it to his chest. The grip he had on her fingers was making the tips turn purple. He spoke slowly and in ragged gasps.

"I am dying. It doesn't matter how hard you try. You're treating the symptoms, not curing the disease. It is very slow and painful. One day I'll be dead, and it will just be my body walking around: a dead stiffened husk with me trapped inside."

"No!" Opalena gasped, and tried to pull away at the mention of stiffening, but Jait wouldn't let her go.

"Opalena, I need poison to die while I still know myself. Can you help me?"

"I can't." Opalena was also crying now.

"Please!"

"I have taken an oath!"

Jait released her and cursed vehemently. Opalena huddled, silent and trembling, under the sheets. After a long time, she spoke.

"Is there no other way?"

"I have tried." He lifted his hands to show the scars on his wrists. "You of all people know it has gone too far. The only comfort is death." He shifted closer to her, and leaned over to press his head against her shoulder. "I'm already half dead," he moaned.

After a moment, Opalena overcame her upset and began to comfort Jait as she always did, smoothing his hair and rubbing his back.

"Shh," she whispered in his ear. "You need to rest." Jait relaxed somewhat, too tired to beg again.

"What did the oath say?" Opalena snuffled. "Do no harm? It seems life is harming you more than death would. But I don't think poison would work anyway. You have already tried your knife, not eating, and drowning. Each time they've dragged you back. What good will poison do? They'll just inject an antidote or make you vomit." Jait flinched at that last word, but nodded bitterly.

"You're probably right. Still, I had thought it worth a try."

"This is a magic thing. You need to fight it with magic."

"You cannot work magic, Opalena."

"No, but the Yrati can."

Jait's bitterness deepened. *They would be more than willing,* he thought. He pushed his hand under the base of the headboard and pulled out a tiny dagger that he had managed to hide from Derik, and used it to cut a lock of his hair, which he gave to her. "Hailandir once tried to teach me magic that could attack someone over a distance. They'll need my hair to connect that magic to me. Apparently that spell is now a favourite child's poem."

Opalena took the hair and wove it through her fingers. "I've heard it."

"It will be easier for the person who casts the spell to know where I will be at the time of the casting. On the Night of the Third Moon, I will sit upon the Chair of Hekka on the second level, in the hearth rooms that lie close to the magma flow. Please, Opalena, find someone who can do this. Go now."

"How will I get out? Meriamdan will stop me. She listens for my mind all the time."

Jait pulled a button off his shirt and handed it to her.

"Here. It is the last of the medicine Antronos gave me. Relax. Pretend you're asleep so that Meriamdan does not listen too closely. Then swallow it to hide your mind and go. You'll have to be clever to make sure that no one sees you."

Opalena took the button and twisted it between her fingers, looking at it sadly. She then wrapped an arm around Jait's neck and kissed him passionately.

"As My Lord wishes," she promised.

20

Ignominy

The Desert beyond the caves was already in darkness, unable to give light to the passage Opalena ran through. Slight afterimages of spiders who had sat on the bioluminescent moss appeared more frequently, guiding her towards what she supposed were the mystical Desert Plains.

From Jait's chambers she had slipped into his bathing room, from there into the attendants' quarters, then into the kitchens, and finally she had struggled through a coal shunt to the outer caverns. Seeing her in her nightshift, which was now soiled and torn, the guards posted there had assumed she was a beggar hunting for handouts, and had gruffly shooed her away. Now she raced desperately for the end of this last tunnel that would take her to the surface.

She caught a vague rustle on the edge of her senses, and thought she heard muttering. She froze in terror. Seconds passed, then the need to be out of the tunnel overcame the need to remain undetected, and she ran, mouth open in a silent scream as she felt shadowed forms move into the passage behind her. She saw them close off the looming opening to the surface. A fistful of her hair was grabbed from behind and she was pushed face first into a sack. Her fingers became scraped and burned as she pushed against the rough cloth. She began sobbing and gave up struggling. Besides, if the Murdek took her back, she would not have to kill Jait. Perhaps they could at least die together.

It seemed that her captors had taken her to the surface instead of back into the Royal caves. She could hear the wind and dust of the Desert battering against hoodoos, and the crunch of booted feet on coarse sand. Were they planning some dark ceremony on the surface?

After a time, there was the banging of a wooden door closing overhead, and the sounds of many voices. The echoes were dull and flat, indicating that she was in a small, low-ceilinged cave without a skylight. Someone tipped out the sack so that she tumbled onto the floor.

"Well, it seems we have ourselves one of the Royal collaborators." Whoever the speaker was, he behaved rudely, nudging Opalena's shoulder with his knee. She looked into the face of Prince Liam. Miserable rage filled her as she realized that she wasn't going to see Jait again after all.

"You awful *child!*" she fumed, stumbling to her feet. "Do I *look* like I need you treating me like this? And like it or not, you are damned *lucky* to be out of that House!" Liam flopped ungracefully into a chair and gazed at her with a sour expression. Several of the armed soldiers in the room pulled up chairs in a circle around Opalena and sat grinning like patrons at a bear baiting. It was immediately obvious that even sitting down, they were all bigger than she was.

"You piglet, Liam," someone joked.

"My apologies, Madam," said the Prince. "I feel somewhat wronged myself these days." One of Liam's companions scooped up a handful of Opalena's hair.

"Like ashes," the soldier said, letting the strands fall from her fingers. Opalena edged away from her.

"What do you have to do with me?" she asked Liam.

"What do you have to do with my father?" he returned.

"You hired me. He is not well, and I am a doctor."

"I think it's more than that. It seems to me that these days no one moves freely from the Royal caves unless they are in collaboration with the Murdek and Jait. I distinctly remember apprehending *you* from the Murdek vicinity."

"Then you know I was running away! If I were 'moving freely,' I would have bothered to wear something more useful on the surface."

Liam shrugged. "Part of your ploy," he said.

"Your father is very sick. I would think that you might show some sympathy. And it is Derik, not Jait, who is dictating what goes on in the Royal House."

"My father and Vernus are trying to undermine the Houses of Dan and Dra, jealous of their wealth and popularity, and my father, no longer interested in ruling properly, has become a *despot* and a *murderer!* I've got a pretty good idea of what he's done with those missing Yrati. And you had best watch how you speak of my brother. He was willing to let me become his equal before—"

"Your father's no murderer! And as for the Houses of Dan and Dra, they're not innocents either. And *Derik!* He was about to kill you. Your father saved your miserable bones by sending you away."

Liam's expression darkened to an almost feral madness. He leaned forward in his chair and spoke to her very softly.

"I will let that pass for now, only because there are other things I want to hear from you. Why don't you tell me on what business you left the Royal House, and why you were leaving so stealthily?"

It took Opalena a while to answer with a controlled voice. "I didn't want Vernus to stop me."

"And why would Vernus have wanted to stop you?"

"He interferes with me."

"Really. Then how did you escape?"

"My Lord Jait created the opportunity."

"Why?"

"It is a confidential matter."

"You will tell me."

"What does it matter to you anyway? Your father is dying, and you are the secondary heir, exiled or not! If you trust your brother so much, then you can crawl back to his side once Jait is dead."

"If he is dying, then why is he trying so hard to tear apart his family and his country?" Opalena chewed her lip in anger and did not look at or answer him. "If you were really trying to escape, Madam, you might be grateful to us for assisting you. In the state you are in, I doubt you would have gotten far from Vernus otherwise."

"Jait is dying. And he is afraid. He sent me to ask the Yrati to pray for him."

Liam barked a laugh. "The Yrati! This story becomes more unbelievable by the minute. I know about these so called 'Murdek,' Madam. The Yrati have told me some wild and unbelievable tales, but I do believe they would send you to con the Yrati and pierce them all with contaminated needles to infect them with bloodrot! Maybe start addictions among them to make it easier to turn their numbed brains from any thoughts of interfering with their plans."

"And wouldn't you pity them if that did happen? Wouldn't you try to save them? It's what happened to your father."

Liam glared at her, not answering.

Opalena decided that she would say no more to defend either Jait or herself. Liam obviously wanted to stick to his preconceptions, and she did not think him worthy of knowing his father's mind.

"Are you going to keep me here?"

"I'm afraid so." Liam slouched back into his chair and reached for a mug, indicating by his posture that the interview was over. The soldiers around him began to lose interest, and went back to previous activities.

"You mustn't. You are preventing me from carrying out the last wishes of someone who is dying."

"And who might that be?"

"I've already told you. Will you at least tell Aren I'm here?"

"Oh, you don't need to doubt for a second that I will."

*****

Liam didn't chain her, but set one of the soldiers to watch her constantly. It was noisy in the cavern, and Opalena found it very difficult to sleep on the prickly mat of straw with the guard's eyes on her. After a while, she sat up to stare back at the other woman. The guard smiled.

"Don't mind Liam. He's angry and confused. We don't really know how bad the political situation is, since nobody has any contact with Jait. We're all jumpy. Anything could happen at any time. You've seen Jait. You tell me how bad it is."

"I don't see how anyone can fault him. He hasn't done anything lately, since he can hardly get out of bed. I think Liam should at least consider having a compassionate thought."

"You forget that his father publicly disowned him, without warning or just cause."

Opalena could not answer her. The night had already been too long, and she needed to see Aren so very badly, not for herself, but for Jait and the promise she had made, carried in her pocket as a lock of hair. Once it was done, Liam would get the power he wanted, Antronos or Maxal would make sure the younger Prince's mind was fully protected, Vernus wouldn't be tolerated, Derik's true nature would destroy him and the Royal House would be restored. Things would be all right again, soon.

*****

Aren came with the morning, sweeping into the room like a dusty windstorm through an unshuttered window. Opalena wept in his arms with relief, horror and crushing grief. Aren simply held her for a few moments until Opalena felt him stealthily reaching into her mind. She pushed him away in disappointment, surprised to see that his cheeks were covered in tears also.

"The Yrati have prayed for your return, Opalena."

She frowned at him, wondering why in Earth they would do such a thing. Because of some silly, half-gibberish vision? Perhaps he was just being kind. She saw Liam approaching and quickly pulled out Jait's hair, pressing it into Aren's palm.

"Take it. Grant him death. He will be seated on the Chair of Hekka in the Hearth Rooms, close to the magma flow on the Night of the Third Moon. Please Aren, do it." He stared at the lock of hair, looking incredulous, perhaps dumbfounded that he had gotten it from her, or by what she had asked him to do with it. She could see unpleasant emotions chase each other across his face—kill Jait and satisfy his envy; kill Jait and avenge Tibeau; kill Jait and cripple Vernus and let Liam succeed.

"How have you dared, Opalena? It is very risky. Do the Murdek know anything of this? They'll hunt us all the way back to the Yrati caves."

"I will escort you." Liam had been closely watching the entire exchange. He still looked suspicious, as if waiting for Opalena to make a mistake and perhaps reveal some hidden agenda. "This seems to be an effective plan, but how can you be absolutely sure of where he will be on that night? It could be a trap."

Opalena grit her teeth and refused to look at Liam. Why must he insist on misinterpreting everything she said? This was no "plan" against Jait. Jait himself had requested it. It was an act of mercy, far more important than Liam and his entire world of petty triumphs.

"I'm not going back with you, Aren. I have to return to him."

"Why? You're safe now. I'll make sure of it." Aren tried to hug her again. "You mustn't go back. Dagnaum told Antronos of a horrible prophecy."

"She will stay with us as surety that Jait is where he should be on the Night of the Third Moon," said Liam. "I trust that for the sake of your own safety, Madam, you would not lie to me. I will release you once he is dead."

So be it. Let Liam think he is right. Opalena finally looked directly at him. "Yes," she said.

21

Antenora

Antronos considered waiting until after dark to return to his office, but thinking that might be when Vernus watched for him, he crept back through the university tunnels while other faculty were still around. He wondered how long Amphetam would tolerate his absences before giving his space to someone else. He paused, wondering if he could just tell Amphetam...would that result in the Chancellor being murdered or abducted? Did he dare write him a letter? Would he be believed or would Amphetam foolishly confront Vernus to verify his claims? There was no way to inconspicuously deliver the message anyhow. It was becoming next to impossible to avoid the Murdek. The bastards seemed to be everywhere.

He hadn't gone back to the Yrati caves since his fight with Aren. He wished desperately to talk to Maxal, and had managed to speak to Fara briefly in the library, but she was politely cold towards him, and told him that Maxal still hadn't come out of seclusion. When he had pressed her for more information, she had cynically asked him how his visit to the Royal House had been and if anyone else was going to walk out as easily as he had. What else could he have expected? Maxal was the only one who believed he wasn't a Murdek infiltrator, and for whatever reason, could no longer give him support. Well, fine. He wasn't going to hide behind the Yrati, taking Aren's abuse. He was going to find Opalena and Ferril, and carry out his plan to dose as many people as he could with mind-blocker, with or without Maxal's help.

His lack of progress was gnawing at his guts. What had he done in the past few weeks except run around and hide in holes like a lizard? Cut off from the Yrati laboratories, he would have to go to the House of Dra and hope he could find what he needed in their cosmetics lab. Before going, he wanted to collect the book of children's tales he had left in his office, and scour it for more clues on what to include in his medicines. It seemed that old Dagnaum's ramblings were all he had left for guidance.

He peered around a corner into the hallway that led to his chambers, and was relieved to see no one. So far, the Murdek had not risked waiting for him during the day. Thus assured, he approached the heavy wooden door and pulled it open. No sooner had he stepped inside, his head was pulled back by the hair, forcing him to look into Vernus' face. The door of his cupboard which he had nailed shut was wrenched open; the gaping hole at the back leading to the old tunnels was clearly visible. The old man was livid. His eyes were bloodshot, and his gums were receded to the point where his teeth looked like fangs. The creature Iegat was with him, watching Antronos with his yellow eyes, running the edge of a cleaver over his fingernails.

"So, my student," Vernus hissed. "You would study under me, yet resist my tuition. You are no use to me! There is no reason why I should keep you alive." Antronos fought to keep his balance, and finally succeeded in pushing Vernus away and twisting free.

Antronos protested: "If you had wanted to kill me, you would already have done it."

"I've just decided on it now. You've been nothing but trouble for me. I warned you. Cause trouble for me, and you'll be out! With you dead, your interference ends, and Dra will need another doctor, which I will gladly supply."

"Another doctor! Dra would never allow you or Sephus in their home. They picked me because I'm an outsider. You'll never get in without me." Antronos immediately regretted these last words, fearing Vernus would take it as an invitation to try forcing the Murdek into his head again. He braced himself against an attack that didn't come.

"Without you? You've shown me quite convincingly that I'm never going to get in *with* you. I don't know how you convinced the coroner not to denounce you, but his apparent bent to sloppiness is my advantage now. How willing will he be to pull your corpse out of the sewer canal? We are finished with your little games. It's time for you to die."

"No! Wait. I've been thinking . . ." Antronos hesitated. He wasn't playing this right. He had to come out with some new tactic—to buy himself enough time to get to the Dra labs. Vernus smirked at him.

"What have you been thinking? That now you're going to cooperate since the Yrati have thrown you out? Or are you plotting another turn of events for me? Thinking how you will dupe Vernus next? No matter, I'll have Alaindra murdered some other way. Iegat should be able to do a better job by himself."

Antronos could see that Vernus was aware of his indecision, and revelled in it.

"What should you do, Antronos? Try to make amends and regain what little control you have, or remain silent to avoid slipping even more?"

Antronos licked his lips and began carefully. "I can make a very effective draught . . ." He got no further.

"Of course! Of course you can! One that will no doubt give Alaindra a pleasant and painless death. What a diamond you are! Your altruistic mewlings make the heart crack! Well, Antronos, you've lost your chance. I admit these games were amusing, but now they're done."

"If you would just give me more time! I can get you what you want without having too many people harmed. And I can do it discretely. You know that if you send Iegat in, he'll have to start with killing and possessing some lowly servant, and it will take time and many murders to get to Alaindra. I have direct access. That's what you want, isn't it?"

Vernus lowered his voice. "What will you do?" He was still smiling, obviously enjoying Antronos' squirming.

"I will do as you ask."

"I don't believe you. You're thinking once old Vernus is gone, you will find a way to confound him again, to turn his own plan against him."

"You want Alaindra? Fine, she's nothing to me."

"And why would you give her to me now, when you've resisted for so long? What is it exactly that you hope to get from me?"

Antronos paused, weighing his gamble. "Let me have Opalena."

Vernus laughed. "Opalena? You expect me to recapture her from the Yrati and hand her to you? One of us is an idiot, and it's hardly me."

"*What?* How?" Antronos' mind raced. With Opalena clear, he could probably make a more aggressive strike—

"Don't play the fool, Antronos. You're not good at lying. Iegat, cut his throat."

The yellow-eyed Murdek pulled his lips away from brown tooth stubs as he raised his dull-surfaced cleaver, his fingers rubbing the handle as if to find the best grip. His other hand slid around the back of Antronos' head.

"No, wait!"

"Why?"

"I don't want to die. I swear it. I will do as you say."

"I have no leverage with you, Antronos. Once I let you go, there is nothing to make you obey me."

"I don't want to die," Antronos said again. His mind raced. He had to make an offer that was attractive to Vernus. "I'll let you put Sephus in my body. He will make sure I keep my promise. I'll take him to the House of Dra, if you will just let me live."

"If you do not . . ."

"I know, I know."

"You will kill Alaindra, then you will put Sephus in her body. This is your last chance"

"I will do as you say."

* * * * *

Antronos could hear the echoes of Herodra's voice as he railed and screamed at the Dra elders, several chambers away. It was a shame they had married after all. It would have been better if Herodra wasn't involved.

Alaindra's own voice was raw from calling out to him, and she was becoming weary from fighting off Antronos, as he constantly tried to soothe her by rubbing her arms and back. Sephus was coiled in a lump within his mind, calmly waiting for his chance to inhabit Alaindra's body. Getting her subdued was Antronos' problem. Carrying Sephus felt like an impending migraine weighing down all thought with cold nausea.

Antronos marvelled at how strong Alaindra was, still fighting against the sedatives he had given her over an hour ago. He had also slipped her a strong muscle relaxant to make her at least appear dead, and perhaps minimize the damage she might do to herself when the Murdek finally invaded her mind, but she fought that as well. She broke away from him yet again, and roughly pushed a fistful of raven hair from her face, getting her fingers stuck in the tangled curls.

"Don't touch me," she snapped at him. "I'm not insane. I don't know who told them that. Maybe it was you."

"I didn't tell them that," he said in a gentle tone. "They don't think you're insane. They're merely concerned that you're not happy. They want to rectify the problem before it interferes with your breeding. It's very important to them that you produce an heir."

"*And they think that this is going to help?*"

"Please sit down. If you calm yourself, they may be more inclined to believe that you are not going to continue to physically refuse Hero." Too exhausted to pull free again, Alaindra stumbled towards the chair he directed her to, and toppled into it.

"I trusted you, Antronos. I told you my feelings about my marriage in confidence! I can't believe you went and discussed these things with my family behind my back! If it weren't for me, you wouldn't have had a single penny from my House!"

Antronos sighed heavily and squatted in front of her chair. "I don't pretend to comprehend the politics of the business world, but quite frankly, as I understand it, they feel that both you and Herodra are too mismatched to sustain your House through the next decade. I was actually quite surprised at how ready some of them were to consider pushing you aside to avoid the collapse of this House."

Alaindra gawped at him in disbelief. "To hear such words coming out of *your* mouth! The elders would *never* have discussed such things with you!" She suddenly slipped out of the chair and crouched down, one arm wrapped tightly around her midsection. "Those manipulative, backstabbing..."

Antronos imagined that by now her guts were roiling and cramping so severely that she couldn't sit upright. He was feeling like throwing up himself. Sephus pushed against these uncomfortable thoughts, wincing as he pressed against the shards of Antronos' mind. *Get on with it*, he told Antronos angrily, and retreated to a less jagged corner of their shared consciousness. Antronos took a deep breath, then continued with his invective. Not only was it important that the Dra family have no physical contact with Alaindra while she was inhabited by Murdek, he also had to make sure Alaindra would be extremely angry when she woke up—angry enough to kill.

What are you doing? queried Sephus. Antronos walled up his thoughts as best he could, imagining a barrier of razors surrounding Sephus, then distracted him by tugging the sleeve of Alaindra's robe off her shoulder.

"I've warned them about inbreeding and its long-term effects, and have suggested they bring in some new blood. Considering that you have been under such tremendous pressures for so long, it is unlikely that you will be able to breed at all. I've also suggested that extreme rest is the only way you might recover, so that perhaps, one day, you might be able to come out of isolation." Antronos was pacing restlessly, unable to stop wringing his hands as he moved from side to side of the small cavern. "They have agreed to keep you segregated from the rest of the family. From now on, you will have no contact with any of them, and your food will come to you by a dumbwaiter."

What do you mean, no contact? demanded Sephus.

"What? Why have you done this to me?" The look of anguish Alaindra gave him really started the despair churning up at the base of his skull. "This is my House. I'm not incapable of providing an heir. I don't know why you think so. Ask another doctor! I want to see another doctor!"

"I know you're not crazy. Please don't take this personally, but they're forcing my hand. This is the best I can do to protect your family. I'm afraid I can't defend you, but I'm hoping you'll be strong enough to hold your own. I really don't think any of this is right, but it's my only option."

"Protect them from what?" Alaindra asked. "From *me*? I have no intention of harming them."

"I know. I wish I could help you keep on fighting, but I can't. This is the best compromise I can come up with. Please forgive me."

"I still don't *understand!* What are you trying to protect them from?"

"From Sephus," he whispered. "It's truly the best I can do. Sephus is the cause of all your pain. If not for him, none of this would be happening."

Stop it! You dare, Antronos! I'll have you for that! Kill her now!

Alaindra's fingers were slipping from the chair arm. Her face was growing slack, but her eyes, although becoming glazed, never left his face. He caught her as she slumped to the floor and carried her to the sick bed. There was no reason to delay, was there?

"It's done," he said to the air. He relaxed the walls of his mind and let Sephus take control. The sensation of the Murdek spirit unfolding within him was like having insects running out of his eyes, nose, mouth and ears, to cover his entire body. It lasted only for a few seconds before Sephus, hungry for the Dra money and political power, tired of the bruising experience of Antronos' mind, unhesitatingly ran up to the bed and bit into Alaindra's neck, emptying himself into her. *Trapped.*

Antronos pulled away and stepped back, spitting out blood. He looked back at the cage he'd fashioned for Sephus, watching the Murdek's hazy blue aura struggle futilely against the robust gold of Alaindra's. It had almost been too easy. She did seem dead, her wide open eyes staring back at him blankly. And just maybe, it would take Vernus a day or two to figure out what he had done.

22

Cure

Jait had a few moments alone. Jalena and Taphit were lounging somewhere by the cavern's entrance, positioned so that they would know if he tried to leave, but too engrossed in their game of bones to watch him or care what he did, and it would take Vernus another half hour at least to finish writing his latest composition. Jait sat in the great carved chair of oak with his back turned towards his keepers, thinking of the last time he had sat in it—at the graduation ceremony, when he had first seen Opalena. Seen her while with Hekka, the Goddess of Sight, the patron deity of the search for knowledge. How ironic he had been sitting in this chair, now knowing how self-indulgently stupid he had been. If only he could have courted Opalena under much different circumstances.

He leaned his back against the wood so that the Eye hewn into the headrest of the chair slowly pulled itself open, and he could feel it against the back of his neck. With the Goddess' help, he began to See. Hekka Looked where she would at first, idly gazing about the caves; there was Meriamdan hunting for nuggets up her nose, Iegat chopping up something for his cooking pot, and Vernus, bent over his books and scribbling madly, pausing only to change ink pots, from brown to green, the colours of surface magic. The old Sen unexpectedly froze, his eyes narrowing, then slowly his face bent into an indulgent smile. He took out a little brass clock from his pocket and tapped it on the face.

"It's time you went to your rest, Jait," he said to the air.

How did he always know? Anyway, he still would not be coming away from his spell writing for a while, and Hekka grew bored with Watching him. Jait nudged her out of the caves, and her Sight swung into the night sky, making the view suddenly breathtaking. There were thousands of stars! Jait had never seen beyond the atmospheric silt. He had only ever been on the surface during the day, when it was too bright to see anything in the sky, and he had never been out on those rare occasions when a hole naturally appeared in the sky dust at night.

He nudged Hekka again, and in her petulant manner, she plummeted downwards in retaliation, slamming into the Earth, and ripping through various caves at great speed. He coaxed her into slowing down, and said to her, "The Yrati. Let us Look upon the Yrati." Pleased that she was not commanded, she decided she would oblige, and Showed him exactly what he needed to see. There was Aren, holding the lock of Jait's hair. Jait had to firmly stamp down the surge of joy that would certainly give warning to Vernus. He must go carefully now, cautiously. How much time was left? Curious that something secret was going on, Hekka cooperatively swung her Eye towards a timepiece on the wall. Almost twenty minutes had passed. She waited in silent anticipation, hoping to be rewarded for her help with more of the secret. "Watch, and you shall See," Jait told her.

Aren was twisting the hair around a magnetic rod. Leelan was with him, nervously fidgeting about and chewing her fingernails off. Aren, already looking ill at ease, stopped his preparations and took a deep breath. He said to Leelan, "Please stop it. You're going to knock something over."

"What of Dagnaum's prophecy?" Leelan asked. "The egg most frequently represents a child. How can Opalena give him a child if he's dead?"

A child? thought Jait. *What a shame. I would have liked that.*

Aren rearranged the items on the table with exaggerated calm. "You yourself agreed not half an hour ago that it was too uncertain," he said to Leelan.

"But Dagnaum was sure."

"He refused to confirm anything." There was another stretch of silence and fidgeting.

"Are you sure you know where he's going to be?" Leelan nearly screamed.

"I have to try! Opalena suffered so much to give us this chance, and what was it worth if I don't at least try?"

"But you said you were going to help him. You promised."

"Trust me, this will help."

"But Aren, this sort of thing is *forbidden*. What if you get caught?"

No response.

"You know where he is?"

"I know. Opalena told me."

Leelan fretted silently for about half a second.

"Where is he?"

"Where Opalena said he'd be."

"*Where?*" The word was spoken as a plea. Aren barely caught the candle that Leelan's flailing arm had struck.

"Upon the Chair of Hekka!" Aren snapped. Leelan's expression turned apoplectic.

"Are you insane? What if he Sees you!"

"I will just have to be quick! Besides, he could very well be Looking elsewhere when I strike. Please, stop distracting me!"

"Aren, I don't think you should do this. It's not worth it. I wish you hadn't made me promise not to tell. We should try to rescue him again. That poor man."

"Leelan, please. This is all supposed to be his idea."

"But you don't really believe that?"

Panic fluttered momentarily in Jait. He clamped down on it. How much time left? Again of her own volition, Hekka glanced at the timepiece, then flicked her Eye towards Vernus. The old goat was looking up from his books and frowning. He stood up and started towards the door. *Oh, Ground and Stone, he knows!*

Hekka blinked again, and Jait railed at her to go back to Vernus. She would not. She turned to Aren who had finally started the incantations. It was soon now. Vaguely aware that he was shaking, Jait Watched Aren with growing anxiety, mentally mouthing the words with him. Aren paused and peeked at the scroll in front of him. *Drakka. The word is drakka, you idiot!* Aren had it now, and recited the spell smoothly, his body swaying slightly to the rhythm. The ritual was getting close to the end, and Jait felt his bowels tighten. He wondered for how long he would feel the pain. Aren was a little shakier than he looked, and the rod slipped out from his fumbling grasp. It made a sharp pang as it hit the floor. Jait exhaled in exasperated despair. Where was Vernus now? Hekka wouldn't Look. Aren was picking up the rod. He was definitely pale.

"I think he Saw me," he told Leelan.

"He might be suffering. Finish it quickly!" She bounced her fist off the back of Aren's head.

Come on, you bungling morons. Why couldn't Opalena have more competent friends? She could have lodged with the Mercenary Guild, by the Earth's Volcanic Guts! Aren steeled himself and resumed. *It is close now,* thought Jait. *Very, very close.*

It was too intense. Jait could not Watch anymore, and tore himself away from Hekka's Sight. The room about him gradually hazed into focus, and thankfully, it was still empty. The fire had burnt low, making it dim, and everything was very quiet. Jait felt himself become a little queasy and the room seemed to sway. Had he chosen the right spell? It would certainly be the quickest, and he was sure now that Aren could perform it, but damn! He hadn't thought about the potential pain when he'd given Opalena that lock of hair. He put both hands on the table in front of him and waited. His heart was racing, his mind was remarkably clear, his jaw dropped open, and he had to force himself to breathe shallowly and not too quickly, so that he would not faint and fall out of position. A spoon dropped from the table, almost making him jump out of his skin. He actually guffawed, then began trembling uncontrollably. He gasped as the mystical Yrati blade entered through his back, right next to the lower vertebrae, and pushed upwards into his stomach. He emitted a thin squeal. Why was it happening so slowly? After a second, the blade resumed its course, and Jait saw it come up through his mouth before he died.

23

Ptolomea

According to Dagnaum, it was only supposed to rain when the ghouls wished to escape the grip of the Earth. Water sloshed down over the surface, turning Desert dust into slimy muck. Antronos' hands shook with cold as he reached out to the slick surface of a boulder, hoping to steady himself enough to pull Leod up behind him. He could feel the child shivering through the brief contact between their hands. Finally on level ground, he hoisted Leod onto his hip and tried to pull his outer robe over them both. He hugged the boy fiercely, using him as an anchor against the rage/pity/sorrow that had threatened to sweep him under ever since Jait had slid from his grasp. He felt no relief at the thought that Vernus had been crippled, only the heartbreak of losing Jait and the scathing burn of his own failure to keep his promise to Leod. As he carefully picked his way over the top of the cliff, he thought he saw the occasional tree root that resembled a mummified bone. But he was now certain that ghouls were red with fire-bright auras, not brown, so he kept going, not looking back. Not turning to see the hooded figures of Liam's soldiers he knew would be following him up the cliff, towards certain underground entryways he had told them were lockless and unguarded.

This uneasy alliance with Liam was part of the agreement he had to make in order to be with Leod. He hugged the child close, silently begging to be forgiven for his failure. Leod hadn't spoken since he had been told of Jait's death, and acted like Aren had taken part in it. When Antronos had finally been allowed to enter the Yrati inner caverns, Leod had dodged Aren's outstretched hands and run straight to Antronos. The child had hidden his face and refused to look back at Aren when the priest had tried to say goodbye.

And now, despite all Antronos and Opalena had told him, Liam was headed back towards the Royal House, refusing to believe the full extent of his brother's betrayal of his family.

The young prince came alongside Antronos, watching him suspiciously as he now always did. "I am aware that you think me blind," Liam said. "But I have to know. I have to see it myself."

"I feel sick at the thought of seeing any of them again," Antronos replied.

"Why? You said their buzzing mind invasions stopped when Jait died. Has that changed? Have you heard their mutterings since?"

"No, but as I've said before, they are still dangerous without Jait. They just have to be close enough to make physical contact, and by going there, we're giving them the perfect opportunity. I wish your Lordship would wait until I've had a chance to make more mind-blocker." He again wished Maxal had been present when he'd gone to collect Leod. Aren had flatly refused to let him stay a minute longer than necessary, never mind work in their labs, and Dra had barred him from their laboratories and House once they had safely deposed Alaindra.

"There's no need. Derik will oust them. I'm sure I can convince him he doesn't need the Murdek. Why should he share his power with them now? Jait was his only rival, really."

Antronos made a fist in exasperation. "And what if Vernus starts to control you as well? We've all told you about Derik's compliance with the Murdek, and you've always trusted the word of the Yrati before."

"*He's my brother!* I grew up with him. He took care of me—"

"Like he took care of his son?"

Liam sighed and briefly put a hand over the small blond head poking out from the shawl. Leod blinked, but still said nothing.

"He wasn't supposed to happen."

"Were any of us *supposed* to be? That doesn't justify how he's been treated."

"If his mother hadn't left, then maybe . . ."

Antronos looked sharply at the prince. "What happened to her?" he asked.

"Ran away. She was Derik's first, and refused to marry him. One day Jait brought her back with him after he had been on a diplomatic visit to the northlands. She stayed long enough to give birth, then ran away again. A week later Derik found her body at the end of an old hunting tunnel. She had taken poison. We found out later it had been given to her by her family, who blamed Derik for spoiling their daughter's chances at a noble union with another House. They never accepted that he wasn't the one who had refused the marriage. It was around the same time our mother died, which made it all harder to bear. Derik always...well he wondered..."

"Why she left?"

"No, why she always seemed so close to my father. Jait swore to both of us that he never touched her, but I don't think Derik ever believed it."

"So Derik thinks Leod is Jait's. . ." Antronos let the sentence trail off, afraid that if Leod was paying attention, this might upset him even more. Liam turned, frowning, to look at the boy again.

"I don't know. I doubt it. Derik must be his father. Jait seemed loyal to Hailandir, even when she was sick. But the uncertainty of the possible betrayal, regardless of what level it went to, is still there."

"Ah. So this association with the Murdek was revenge."

"Perhaps. I don't think Derik even knows how deep his hurt runs. But losing Jait as well as Hailandir has to shock him into seeing that things can be different now."

"My Lord Liam, I think you need to prepare yourself for the possibility that what Derik wants may not be the same as what you want. What will you do if he rejects you? Or if the Murdek continue to interfere?"

Liam studied the wet ground passing beneath his feet for a few moments, his mouth clamped into a thin line. "I still have to see it. Even if I am just having dust dreams, there is the chance that he will want both of us back." He tried to touch Leod's cheek, but the boy tucked his face against Antronos' chest and wiggled farther under his robes. Antronos tried not to let annoyance seep into his expression. Liam had never tried to protect Leod before; this was all a doomed attempt to win Derik's favour. It was unlikely the elder Prince would find any pleasure in seeing his bastard son.

They entered the underground through one of Antronos' favourite routes, one that led towards the main foyer outside of the university library. As the "Purveyor of Wisdom," Jait was to be interred on campus, in a special cavern that had been prepared for him just next to the convocation hall.

Murmurs of shock and speculation started as soon as Liam stepped out onto the blue tiles of the library foyer. His hood was pushed back, and he walked forward with such authority that the amazed Sens surrounding him bowed and backed out of his way. Antronos let Leod slide to the ground, but kept one hand firmly around the child's fingers, the other moving his outer robe aside so that he would have easy access to the daggers he had shoved through the loops of cloth stitched to the side of his trouser leg. He noted with satisfaction that Liam's people were equally cautious.

They walked through the tunnel that headed towards the convocation hall, and found that the funeral procession was already in progress when they arrived at the hallway leading to Jait's tomb. Antronos quickly scanned the attendees, seeing many regarding them with varied levels of disbelief: Sen Amphetam who frowned, Vernus who smiled, and Derik, who looked absolutely livid. Antronos took a deep breath and did his best to resist hiding behind Liam, who was much better armed. Liam, for his part, looked absolutely calm, and bowed his head respectfully as the grey-robed, hooded pallbearers came into the tunnel.

Against a century of tradition, the pallbearers were Murdek. This was also the first time any of them were confirming the existence of their clan in about fifty years, publicly displaying their emblem of a patterned green and brown diamond on the front of their robes. Antronos could not see a single Yrati in this morbid assembly, hoping desperately that they were here in disguise.

Jait's corpse was carried on a silver-encrusted slab of sandstone, modestly engraved with patterns of straight lines that were meant to represent spiritual peace. Death runes had been inscribed on his skin in bright blue ink, tracing a line from his forehead to his collar, appearing again at the end of his white sleeve and running around his fingers before disappearing again. His hands were folded over his stomach in a gesture of serene piety. After being soaked in brine for a month, Jait's skin was a strange yellow colour against the blue of his robe-like shroud, his lips were pulled away from his teeth in a rictal grin, and his eyes were seemingly gone. Yet his hair was still gloriously dark as it spilled off the stone shelf to brush the ground. Antronos wondered facetiously what they had done to protect it from the salt.

He swallowed hard as the procession passed him, stifling his anger as Taphit leered from under a grey hood. As he passed by, the Murdek deliberately tossed some of the sand he strew along the procession path over Antronos' sandals, the whole time muttering some disgusting chant about Man's return to dust. Antronos glanced down at Leod who was hugging his leg. The child did not cry. Perhaps he didn't even recognize his grandfather. Looking up again, he was stunned to see Ferril shuffling along beside Iegat, wearing the same robes, one of his hands hooked around the short posts being used to carry the sandstone slab. The Yrati's expression was dully vacant, like a man with fever. *What have they done to you?* Feeling his heart pound and his stomach wrench, Antronos looked up at Derik, whose stony glare had apparently not left them since they had arrived. Even though dressed in formal robes and trousers of dark grey, it was easy to see that Derik had tempered his mourning garb with a threatening array of weapons. Antronos decided he would watch for a chance to catch Ferril alone before trying assess how much damage had been done to the priest's mind.

Jait's corpse was carried into a dome-roofed chamber with criss-crossing arches that met at the central point of the ceiling. The length of each arch was decorated with embedded blue rock cut into runes of serenity outlined with tiny troughs of bioluminescent moss. The entire chamber was lined with textured white tiles, and on the floor, portions of the tiles were slightly raised to make a footpath through the layer of Desert sand covering the floor of the chamber. Jait was placed on a block of white marble covered with green and black blankets that were edged with gold. The corners of these were reverently folded over his body, as though he slept.

The Murdek covered what remained of Jait's face with several strands of braided dragweed with more mutterings about loss of humanity and the rise of a new beast—some of the words Antronos could not make out. Then they left Jait to rot. Derik came to Liam immediately, his stance forbidding anyone else to approach. Face-to-face with his brother, he kept his voice low.

"Have you come to challenge my right to Kingship?" he asked. Liam blinked at him calmly, some of the hope leaving his expression.

"There was a time when you called me brother," he replied. "I came to see if you would do so again."

"You expected that, when you brought this . . ." Derik's lip curled as he took in both Leod and Antronos with a single glare. "*Pachu.*"

"We are your family," said Liam.

"I have no need of *family*. Especially when all you want is a chance to backstab me."

Antronos gasped as Derik's arm made a jerking motion at Liam's side and the younger prince winced. As Liam pushed his brother's arm away, the distinct sound of a metal blade scraping against linked armour could be heard.

"You're wearing mail. So you did come here expecting conflict," Derik murmured.

"I'm not completely stupid," said Liam. "I am, however, extremely disappointed. I'm sorry you've chosen to believe in the wrong things." Liam took a step back and slowly drew his sword. "Shall we settle this?"

The Murdek moved forward, as well as the Royal Guard. Some of them looked uncertainly between Liam and Derik, who spread his hands and smiled.

"Liam, I am the legitimate heir."

"You did offer to share your birthright with me, and I did accept it, right before Jait sent me away. My claim is also legitimate."

Derik's smile faded, but didn't disappear. "I can make this very difficult for you, little brother."

"Not if you're dead."

Derik drew another blade.

Liam's soldiers held out swords to block the further advance of the Murdek, who darted away from them and began chanting. The Royal Guard did not interfere further, apparently accepting Liam's challenge as valid, while several of the Sens flustered about hesitantly, unsure of whom they should notify of this disruption. Antronos' attention was pulled away from Liam as he felt the distinct, sharp probe of Vernus' mind slam against his thoughts. He lurched, then shoved back, succeeding in pushing Vernus out long enough that he could find Leod and pull him away from the fight. Derik and Liam's blades scraped against each other as the brothers clashed, fell back, and then struck at each other again. Derik circled Liam, constantly challenging him with rapid thrusts, while the younger prince held the same spot, parrying each attack with intense concentration, unable to make an offensive move.

Vernus made his own sudden strike, twisting past Antronos' mental barrier and delivering a blast of pain that made his vision explode in a scattering of red and white stars. Antronos fell to his knees, feeling Leod tugging at his collar. He couldn't push Vernus out—couldn't find the edges of this assault that would allow him to gain some leverage against it.

Ferril yelled and charged at Antronos, startling Vernus and making him recoil in surprise. Antronos pushed Leod away and got to his feet just before the former Yrati collided with him, and was confused by the other man's ineffectual slaps at his head. Ferril suddenly jerked away as if Antronos had struck him, crashing against Derik's back just as Liam's sword lashed forward.

Vernus was staring aghast at the falling form of the elder Prince, as Derik fell first to one knee, then both hands, until finally his head hit the ground. Leod screamed.

Liam stood for a moment longer, eyes glassy, before he also fell. Blood covered his hands. The Royal Guard rushed forward, checking both princes. Finally, one stood up and announced, "Liam lives, Derik is dead. All hail King Liam, Son of Temlocht and Rightful Heir of Queen Hailandir!"

One of Liam's soldiers jabbed a knife in Vernus' direction. "Kill that Murdek," she commanded. Vernus turned and fled. Before Antronos could stop him, Ferril also got up and ran.

24

cinnabar

The surface of the water rippled softly under Aren's hands as he skimmed the images with disappointment. The visions came so easily now, even without him falling into a trance, almost every time he looked at any kind of water, including his own bath, and he hoped his interpretation was wrong. The ghouls were constantly showing him troubling images of Opalena, her hands stretching out, a white falcon egg in her palms, and Jait reaching out from the murky sea of death to touch her fingertips. Dagnaum's prophecy was being repeated to him, as if the ghouls were forbidding him to deny its portent, and yet, it didn't make sense. Falcons had once lived in the Desert, perhaps fifty years ago, but could only be found in the northlands now, so where was this egg to come from? Other images were more plain: Jait's wet corpse lying on the ground, a female deer coaxing him to stand. One way or another, the old Prince was coming back, yet no instruction was given as to whether Aren should help or hinder his return. Each time he had tried to ask the ghouls if "sickness was still coming through the fawn," the images became random, and completely incomprehensible.

He sighed and pushed to his feet, his knees and back aching from leaning over the pool for so long. Liam's ascension was supposed to have ended all this. He thought about trying to talk to Maxal again, then pushed the idea away. The High Priest was being as difficult as the ghouls. Talking to Locke or Fara or anyone else would be equally difficult, leading to another round of questions as to why Aren did not share these visions, or even why he was claiming to see things that no one else had. What did they think? That he *chose* to watch dead Jait flail around in his washbasin while shaving in the morning?

"Aren, you have to come at once."

He turned and saw Fara standing flushed and breathless at the chamber entrance.

"What is it?"

"Antronos is here. He's brought back Ferril."

"By the Earth!" He ran after Fara to the outer tunnels where the ceremonial fonts were, and saw several Yrati trying to restrain Ferril, who had fallen into convulsions. He turned on Antronos, about to demand to know what he had done to the elder Yrati, then curbed his anger. The Desert-man was kneeling and hugging the child, Leod, his face contorted in what looked like grief, which made his purple eyes seem like they were bulging out of his pallid face, and Leelan annoyingly had an arm around his shoulders. Perhaps it was shame rather than grief. Regardless, fighting with Antronos now would mean another week-long fight with the other Yrati. No one could agree on anything since Maxal had withdrawn from them.

"He's feverish," said Fara, reaching out to catch one of Ferril's legs. "Aren, help!" Before he could move, Fara gasped and recoiled, her hands coming away bloody. "Look at his ankle!"

Now slick with sweat, Ferril subsided into weak moaning. Aren carefully lifted his priest-brother's robes so that he could see the angry ring of bruised and bleeding flesh of Ferril's ankle oozing pus onto the floor. It looked as if Fara had broken a huge pocket of infection. The stench of rot threatened to make him sick.

"It's from the shackles," Antronos said. "And he's gone mad. The Murdek were keeping him chained to a wall, I think until they broke him. It took me a week to find him after Vernus fled. He'd gone back to their lair at the bottom of the Royal archives, and he was just sitting there, playing with the chains. He actually asked me when the Murdek were coming back to help him wear his 'necklace.' I had to coax him to get him to leave."

"It's not like we *weren't* looking for him," Aren snapped.

Antronos looked bewildered. "I didn't mean that," he said. "I just wanted to help, because I—well, I never meant to let Meriamdan see him in the first place, but—"

"This is hopeless," wailed Fara. "We have to amputate his leg. Get him up. We can't wait." She and a group of other Yrati lifted Ferril from the floor and carried him away. Aren rounded on Antronos again, controlling the seething rage boiling up in him only because of Leelan's warning glare. The ghouls should have said, *sickness is coming through the snake*. The fawn didn't appear to have anything to do with it.

Antronos was showing no signs of leaving, now that he'd delivered his poisoned gift. "You're not planning on staying here, are you?" Aren asked him.

"I had an agreement with Maxal," Antronos said.

"*What?*"

"He promised to take me as his student, so that I could get away from Vernus. I still need a supervisor. I'm not done with my degree yet."

Aren shook his head in disbelief. "You come here, asking this now? Maxal isn't even guiding *us*, never mind you. He's been in isolation for months, and he's left us no instructions regarding another student."

"You could ask him, Aren," said Leelan. "Especially since you're the only one who says Maxal still talks to him," she muttered.

"Oh, *Earth*, don't start that again! I'm not stopping you from going to see him."

"And you know what happens when I try. When anybody but *you* tries."

"It's not my fault."

Leod broke away from Antronos, and shot into the tunnels behind them. Antronos tried to follow, before Aren blocked his path. "That's a low tactic, trying to use a child to get back in here."

"I have done no such thing," Antronos protested.

"Why is that boy still with you, anyway? Liam wanted him."

"Liam? And you accuse *me* of using children! Liam doesn't want Derik's bastard son any more than Derik did. He just thought he could use Leod to appeal to Derik. The boy's useless to him now, especially since he expects to have his own heirs."

"All right. You've given us Ferril. You've given us the boy. Our thanks. Get out."

"I'm not *giving* you Leod."

"Well, he's in our caves, and you're not following him. Leave."

"Aren, stop it," said Leelan.

"You want to keep him here?" Aren said to her. "Trouble follows him. Everywhere he goes. It's not like we don't already have problems."

"We should at least come to a consensus on this. You haven't even talked to the others, and it's not up to just *you*."

"Leelan, you stop it. If you want a discussion, fine. It doesn't have to be in front of outsiders, and Sen Antronos doesn't have to be here for it. He'll be perfectly safe somewhere else."

"But there are things I have to tell you," Antronos blurted. "I still need help."

"With what?" Aren asked impatiently.

"Alaindra."

"Oh, right. She went insane after hiring you. What did you do to her?"

"Well, I...I had to . . . ."

"Let me guess. You *inadvertently* let the Murdek get to her as well as Ferril."

Antronos hung his head.

Locke re-entered the cavern. "Aren, a little help with the antibiotics for Ferril would be nice," he said.

"Fine." Aren turned back to Leelan. "Maybe you're right, we shouldn't turn him loose on the world. You watch him and make sure he doesn't 'infect' anyone else. We'll settle this later."

Aren turned away from them, his eyes stinging with rage, as he tried to follow where Ferril had been taken without crashing into any walls. It was incomprehensible how Antronos kept worming his way in here, and he was more hurt than he cared to admit by Leelan first casting doubt on his claims that Maxal still spoke to him, then taking the side of an outsider over his. He was trying to protect them all. Couldn't she see that? Yes, they were to help others, but if they were all dead or possessed or whatever it was that the Murdek did to their victims, how could they help anyone?

Ferril was singing in old Temlochti, his head swinging from side to side, as he lay on his back on a surgery table. Fara had a hand over his brow, trying to make him still, speaking softly to him, but he seemed unaware of her. Locke was stripped down to his grey clinic shirt with his hair tied back, and was laying out trays of steam-cleansed surgery implements. He looked over his shoulder as Aren approached.

"Aren, scrub up. We need him anaesthetised."

Aren hesitated briefly before approaching one of the washbasins, not wanting the added irritation of seeing Jait again, however, as he rubbed soap over his arms, he saw nothing, which left him feeling strangely empty. *Wasn't that what you've been wanting all week? To see nothing?*

He took several vials out of the medicine cabinet, selected a series of syringes, and began loading a special mixture that would numb pain, but not result in unconsciousness. He knew Fara would yell at him for it, but the nagging doubt building in his chest was warning him not to do anything that might weaken Ferril's control over himself any further. He hoped keeping Ferril partly conscious would give him a better chance of defending himself, should the Murdek make another attempt at possessing his mind. As he leaned over Ferril and swabbed a patch of skin on his arm, his priest-brother suddenly fell silent, staring up at him in apparent lucidity and with a disturbing grin. His pupils looked like dark crystal. Aren frowned.

"Hallo, Aren," said Ferril. His hands shot up, catching Aren in the face, and he began muttering words that sounded like buzzing insects that descended over Aren's thoughts and carried them off like invading locusts, until the entire room dissolved into a swirling cyclone of grey nothing—

Ferril was laughing. Several Yrati were pinning him down on the table, but he wasn't struggling anymore. Aren found himself sprawled on the floor. Locke had one of his arms, and was trying to pull him up.

"Aren! Are you all right? By the Earth, what happened?"

"Funny," snickered Ferril. "Funny, funny. Surprised."

Aren tried to stand, but was shoved back down by a wave of nausea. He pushed himself into a sitting position, and raised his hands to his head to make sure it was still intact. "I think he...tried to jump into my mind," he told Locke.

"Ferril, what did you do?" Fara asked him.

"Murrrrdek game," said Ferril. "Funny."

"It's not funny. You hurt Aren."

"We did?"

"What do you mean 'we'?"

"That's it. Put him out, now," Locke commanded. Aren got up, re-formulated his medicine and put Ferril to sleep, cursing himself for not having some of Antronos' mind-blocker to mix in with the dose. "After we're done with his leg," said Locke, "we're probing his mind. I don't care if he hasn't given us consent. I doubt he's capable."

* * * * *

Aren strained his ears as he knelt just inside the doorway, hoping to hear the shuffling of Maxal's feet as the Yrati High Priest came to him. Locke and the others would be finishing up with the surgery soon, and would probably be collecting in the dinner chamber to discuss what to do next. Exasperated, Aren called out into the dark again.

"My Lord. We need you to come join us."

Someone giggled immediately next to Aren. He drew back instinctively, wishing he could bring a torch in here.

"You do it. You do it, Aren. I cannot go anymore. You're the one who is always running things anyway." Had Maxal been there all along?

"But I am not High Priest. Maxal, you have to come."

"So become High Priest then."

"Me? What of Ferril? He has returned. And he is senior."

"Yet Aren doesn't want Ferril for High Priest. Tainted you imagine he has become, with Murdek thinkings." Maxal giggled again. Aren hesitated. It sounded like Maxal's voice, but this conversation was so strange.

"What about Locke, then? Or Fara?"

"Locke, Fara, you. Doesn't matter. Why don't you be High Priest?"

"Your successor must be publicly chosen by you, Maxal. Why don't you just come and speak to us. It would help so much."

"It doesn't matter, Aren. You have strength and deep love inside. It will carry you. Go now, and do it. I cannot go anymore."

"Shall we have two old priests then, hiding in darkened caverns? It doesn't seem right for me to take your place while Dagnaum still lives, Maxal. Please come now. The assembly waits for you."

"I cannot go. I am sick."

"Then let us heal you."

"No, no. Ha ha. You can't do that. If I thought you could, I would let you try."

"Would you at least let me have a look?"

"Oh no. I can't let you see me like this. I'm very ashamed of it. Dagnaum is totally senile, and Maxal is stiffened. What shall become of you, my son, next in line for a series of title-related curses? Perhaps that is why you shouldn't want to become High Priest. Can't say I blame you, my boy."

"My Lord..."

"I know, I know. Aren doesn't believe in the stiffening disease. Hee hee hee. Well, it doesn't matter if you do or if you don't. Either way I'm still not fit to be High Priest. You go to your friends, and I'll go to mine."

"Maxal, *please.*" Aren waited. Silence. He put out a hand to where he thought Maxal must have been sitting, and touched only air. He reached further and felt only rock.

"Maxal?"

Sighing with frustration, Aren stood and brushed off his knees. For a moment he considered bringing a lamp into the chamber anyway, violating all Yrati custom, not to mention Maxal's direct command, find where the High Priest was lurking and drag him out to the assembly.

He stumbled out of the chamber and swore at an unevenness in the floor that caught his toe. He looked up in surprise to see a number of the Yrati had gathered outside the chamber, waiting for him.

"Well?" asked Fara. "What did Maxal say?" She stood with her arms folded. Ferril was at her side, supporting himself against her with an arm draped over her shoulders. Aren tried not to gawp at the sight of them.

"Ferril! You're awake already? How?"

"He's stronger than any of us thought," said Fara as she looked at Ferril affectionately. "He woke as we were cleaning up, and he's been making much more sense since that leg came off."

Aren shook his head in disbelief. "You should sit," he told Ferril. "Keep the swelling down." He moved forward to help the other Yrati ease Ferril back into the carrying-chair they had apparently used to bring him this far without a false leg. Cautiously, he reached out with his mind towards his priest-brother and was met with a cold wall of nothing. From Fara, a flood of rich anger. The other Yrati were just as easy to read, their faces showing the upset and anxiety they all felt. And now they were all looking at him, wanting him to share his connection with Maxal. He straightened, trying to rub the tension out of his neck. Wanting to delay, he turned and walked toward the dinner cavern, hearing the others follow him.

"Did you, uh, check?" he asked Locke quietly, while gesturing towards Ferril.

"Nah. We tried, but he blocked the entire lot of us. If he's that strong, it's unlikely any Murdek could force themselves into the old boy now. I think they only got inside him initially, because of—" Locke broke off and looked away. Aren didn't want to hear him say "Tibeau" either.

He swallowed hard before forcing out the next question. "What about Antronos? Can he see any of those double auras he was telling Liam about?"

Locke shook his head. "Antronos left. Besides, I'm sure he wouldn't have brought Ferril here if he saw the Murdek were still inside him. And he didn't set off the ward stones."

"You're assuming Antronos isn't intent on murdering the lot of us."

"Opalena doesn't seem to think so. She went with him."

"You're joking."

"Leelan packed them lunch."

"And Leod?"

"Went with them. We're going to have to decide what to do with Leelan. She's getting a little too...autonomous." They had entered the large cave with a fire pit in the centre that was filled with glowing coals. Cushions surrounded the pit, which was behind a raised stone ring that served as a communal table. Its surface was littered with empty clay bowls and forks that hadn't been cleared throughout the day. Several Yrati were busy tidying and putting out fresh bowls of water and food. A light breeze was coming in through the ceiling where the skylight panes were hanging open. Aren sat on a cushion next to Locke, and was crowded in on his other side by Fara. Uncomfortable, he tried to stand up again to help with the serving, but Fara caught his arm.

"Did you see Maxal?" she demanded.

Aren took a deep breath before speaking. "Yes."

"Why did you have that look when you came out?"

"What look?"

"Like something important had happened, and you're hiding it from us."

Aren fiddled with a spoon for a few moments. "He told me to become High Priest," he said finally. Fara glared at him.

"He *told* you? That's not how it's done. He has to announce it to all of us."

Aren shrugged helplessly. "He won't come out. I tried to get him to, but he refused. Go in and see for yourself if you don't believe me." With a disgusted look, Locke got up and left the chamber. Fara continued to stare at him.

"What else did he say? Should we hunt down Vernus or just accept his disappearance? Are we finished with that business about 'sickness coming through the fawn'? What about Alaindra? And what of Dagnaum's prophecy? Opalena has already left us, and even if she hadn't, what would she do? Present a lizard egg to Jait's corpse?"

"I have had visions—"

"*You* have? And what does Maxal think of your visions?"

"He told me to decide what to do. Look, I'm not making this up. Go in and ask him yourself!"

Locke returned. "His chamber is empty," he said. "I walked around the entire room with my arms stretched out. Really, Aren, I wonder just who it was you spoke to, when there's no one inside."

"Locke," Aren protested, "you know there's more than one way in or out of that chamber. I would never lie about something like this. I wouldn't dare." He grabbed his priest-brother's sleeve. "Look me in the eye and tell me you think I'm lying!" Locke looked at him for a few seconds, then glanced down sheepishly.

"No. I know you wouldn't lie. I just ache for Maxal. And you are the only one he's spoken to in days. It's hard for the rest of us to accept."

"What *else* did he tell you?" demanded Fara.

"Nothing, just that for some crazy reason, he thinks he has the stiffening disease."

Fara huffed with scepticism. "What do you want me to say?" Aren asked her. She just got up and left. Across the room Ferril was watching him unwaveringly, his eyes glittering with darkness.

Aren's anger rose up inside him. Maxal *had* told him to be High Priest, as indefinite as it had been. These divisions in the Yrati could no longer be tolerated. He *was* having visions, and they were just as valid as Dagnaum's. Maybe more so, since his interpretations were not impaired by senility. And as for Maxal giving him instructions, well, he had been instructed to decide what to do. In his opinion, Jait was dead; Opalena had suffered enough, and should not be forced to participate in any ritual or "destiny;"

any remaining Murdek should be hunted down like escaped swine; and he had had enough of all this bickering. Perhaps it was his own indecision that was preventing his clan from finding peace. His intentions were just. His will was strong. He was the only thing stopping himself from finding his own path to ensure "all evil things fell away."

As he looked around the room, he realized that his conversation with Fara had been overheard, and was being discussed by the other Yrati. Most of them looked upset and confused: none of them supportive. He got up and left the cavern, not feeling at all hungry, and nearly ran towards the labs, where he leaned against a wall in a quiet tunnel, trying to force his emotions back under control.

"So, new High Priest, huh?"

Leelan was slouched next to him. When had she arrived? Annoyed, he didn't answer her.

"I guess Antronos is *your* student, then."

"Earth, Leelan. You really know how to find exactly what will irritate me most and throw it in my face."

"Oh, that was nothing. You're going to need him, so it's best if you make some sort of peace with our friend from the Desert since it's unlikely that you'll be able to help Jait without him."

"*Help?* What are you talking about? Jait's dead. What is anyone supposed to do?"

"Of course he's dead. You killed him."

"*Damn it*, Leelan! You swore you'd never speak of that!"

"It doesn't matter what I promised. You killed him. Now it's your responsibility to help him, and if you don't, I'll tell the others what you did. It won't matter that Liam's given you his pardon and is willing to keep your dirty secret. It's unlikely you'll be Yrati anymore if the others know you killed somebody on purpose."

"Help him how? He's *dead*."

"Do you think you're the only one having visions?"

He stared at her. "You've been having them as well?"

"No. Opalena has. Apparently, if you don't do something about Jait, the Murdek are going to recapture his spirit, and become more powerful than ever. He can't be left disembodied. You're not finished Aren. You've only slowed down the Murdek, not stopped them."

"And how long have you known all this?"

"Just today. Antronos was helping Opalena fit together all the clues from her dreams."

"Their interpretation could be wrong."

"Well, then, My Lord and High Priest Aren, you'd better help them interpret it properly. Come on. They're waiting for us out by the 'Cliff."

25

Continuance

Rain still fell. The Desert's muddied dunes still shifted aimlessly with tufts of green marking its crests and eddies, and the occasional twisted bramble was decorated in a smattering of leaves. Antronos shifted his palm away from the wet rock of the cavern's entry, shivering in the unusual damp. He, Leod and Opalena were halfway up 'Ghoul Cliff,' part of a steppe along the north border of the Temlochti State that separated the magnetic part of the Desert Plains from the simply deserted. The underground tunnels lay three miles to the west.

Looking downward, over the tumble of boulders and shale covering the bottom of the 'Cliff, he didn't see any of the legendary brown ghouls who were supposed to mourn the loss of their lives when it rained, by climbing out of their graves and up the 'Cliff, constantly howling their misery to the sky. He wondered how Dagnaum had come up with that story in the first place. To his knowledge, ghouls preferred burrowing underground. Perhaps the old Yrati had once seen one of the stone skeletons spat out by the Desert, and had made some assumptions. Perhaps it was just a tale to keep children safely underground. He finally turned away from the slowly writhing landscape when he saw two hooded figures winding their way upwards, wearing dark grey robes edged with Yrati red and blue.

"They're coming," he told Opalena. She sat on a rumpled blanket in the corner, hugging her knees. Leod was curled up by her side, fast asleep.

"I don't think I can do this," she said.

Antronos knelt next to her. "We haven't even decided what really needs to be done," he said gently.

"It's not the egg part of Dagnaum's prophecy that scares me. Besides, it is completely impossible for me to give Jait a child now. Keeping his spirit away from the Murdek means keeping him with us. You know Vernus. It won't take him long to figure out that we're holding Jait. Whatever you want to call it. He'll come. And I don't think I can...Antronos, I can't go

197

through all that again."

"But if we don't, and if Vernus does capture Jait's spirit and his power, perhaps he won't come after us immediately, but we'll be hiding while he takes over the entire State. Maybe more. Either way we're involved. Isn't it better to face this head on? To fight while we can?"

Opalena's face crumpled as she leaned into Antronos' shoulder. He hesitated for a second, before cautiously putting an arm around her. "I'm just so tired. Bruised," she said. "I know I don't have any right to ask you this, but, would you do it? Fight, I mean. I just can't. I'm so weak right now. I'd probably give at the slightest push. I wouldn't be any good to you anyway."

"Will you at least discuss it with Aren and Leelan?"

She pushed herself upright and swept pale hair away from her face. "I can't stay that long. Once Leelan gets started, she'll hammer me into that prophecy. I'll take Leod to keep him safe."

"Where will you go?"

"I'll find somewhere. I'll come back once the Yrati have gone."

Antronos sighed. "Very well."

"I'm sorry."

"I do understand. You need to recover."

"Thank you." She leaned forward and kissed his cheek, then pressed her face against his shoulder. Antronos' heart thudded as he thought about how close she was to the scales on his neck, and that she didn't seem to mind. He turned his head slightly so that his face touched her hair. His body suddenly felt flooded with her warmth, her scent. The tip of her ear was so close to his lips...

His hand was reaching towards her; he was about to speak her name and tell her not to go, or let him leave with her, when she pulled away.

"Thank you," she said again. She scooped up Leod and a small satchel with a few of her belongings, then shuffled into the back tunnels at the far end of the cavern, leaving Antronos feeling abandoned and deflated.

He leaned against the rock wall and bumped the back of his head against it until Aren and Leelan stumbled through the outside entryway, splattering water everywhere.

"Where's Opalena?" Leelan asked.

"She left." Antronos gestured feebly toward the back exit.

"Well, is she coming back?"

"No."

"Told you not to trust him," Aren said. Leelan hit him.

"You didn't want to involve her anyway," she retorted.

"Well, I guess I won't have any chance to interpret her visions, then. It doesn't matter." Aren slipped his drenched cloak from his shoulders. "This is a waste of time."

Leelan plunked down next to Antronos. "So do we still agree that we need to give Jait a corporeal form? Something to anchor him so that Vernus can't just pluck him out of the ether?"

"A corporeal form we can throw eggs at," Aren muttered. "I'll present him with eggs if Opalena doesn't want to."

Leelan ignored him. "Antronos, you're from the Desert. You've heard all the stories about strange creatures being formed from the sand. Have you ever seen or heard anything we could use?"

"Yes, tell us how your mother made you."

Leelan smacked Aren without turning to look at him.

"Sure, I've seen quite a bit," said Antronos. "I don't know how to actually *make* anything. I suppose we could go out and *find* one of those sand creatures."

"Assuming sand people actually exist—"

"They *do*! I've *seen* them."

"—aren't all of those things supposed to be already inhabited by spirits of the dead?" asked Aren.

"Well, isn't that the point?" Antronos countered. "Jait's dead, and we need to encase him in one of them."

"If there is already a spirit in each of those creatures, you'd have to displace one to make room for Jait," Aren said with exaggerated patience. "Unless you know how to do that, we're still stuck."

The unwelcome memory of his failed attempts to rid himself of the Desert undertaker made Antronos even more irritable. Why in Earth was he wasting time with uncooperative Yrati, when all he really wanted to do was go after Opalena and tell her he was sorry for even suggesting she try to help him. She was right. They should just run into the Desert and hide. Let the tunnel dwellers fend for themselves. "Well, it's not like I can unravel a thousand years of Desert magic in five minutes! And you're supposed to be helping, not making this more difficult."

Aren started laughing. "Am I the only one who thinks this is ridiculous? Leelan, this is impossible. Dead people are dead. They don't get up and start walking around in sand bodies. I can't believe I let you talk me into coming here." He started to get up.

"What about your visions?" Leelan asked him.

Aren sat back down.

"Fine. Antronos, tell us how to make something living out of the Desert sand."

"Mix it with water."

"*What?*"

"Uh. Sorry. Just something my mother used to say." Antronos shook away the memory of his mother's hand, spread palm down over the sand, summoning water to the surface.

"Well, it's raining," Leelan pointed out.

"I think Antronos' mum was making an allegorical reference to how plants start growing when it rains," said Aren. "I don't think it's a clue that we should turn the former High Prince into a mud pie."

Antronos shifted away from the two Yrati, ignoring their banter. How *had* his mother made him? Did he ever have a father? No, he had to be real. Before she had died, before the Desert had changed his eyes, his mother had told him that he had been untouched by the Desert's magic.

Experimentally, he spread his fingers out a few inches above the dusty floor of the cavern, and made the sandy grains pile up into a tiny pillar. It was the most he had ever been able to do. He concentrated and tried to summon water as his mother had. Nothing. Aren and Leelan broke off their argument and stared as he pulled up another tiny mound of dust.

"How did you do that?" asked Aren.

"I don't know. It doesn't work underground. Just on the surface. Something to do with magnetic forces, I think." He shifted back toward the Yrati. "Tell me, why does all Yrati mysticism include water?"

Aren frowned. "It represents life," he said.

"So why did you reject the idea of mixing it with the Desert?"

"That's not...those stories are allegorical. We use water to meditate by, not make walking dead. Nobody has ever suggested such a thing. It's just water. I don't see how this is going to work."

"Well, we aren't going to get anywhere just talking about it." Leelan got up and picked through the pile of supplies Antronos had dumped in a corner. She selected two bowls and went to the outside doorway to collect rain water. Aren sighed and rubbed his temples.

"Suppose we do make this body. How are we going to get Jait into it? How are we even going to find him?"

"I was hoping you would do that," said Antronos.

"Me?"

"Leelan said you're always seeing him in your meditations."

Aren shot an angry glance at the other Yrati, who came back and placed the bowls in front of him.

"Have a look, then," she said to him.

Aren sighed again and took one of the bowls in his hands. He leaned over it and began to quietly sing a prayer over the water. He fell silent after a few lines and was absolutely still for several minutes. "I can see him," he finally said.

"In the water?" Leelan asked.

"Of course. That's the only place I'm looking."

"No, I mean, is he in the bowl?"

"Leelan, that's stupid."

"Well, let's just start trying things." She tugged the bowl out of Aren's grasp and poured the water over Antronos' sand piles. "Try making those little things stand up again," she said to him.

Antronos spread his hand over the muddied dust on the floor and concentrated. Some of the grains shifted slightly. He made a swirl shape in the muck.

"This isn't working. Jait's not here anyway," said Antronos.

"How can you tell?" asked Aren.

"I can't see his aura."

"Would you recognize him if you did see it? Does his aura look different from everyone else's?"

"Not really, but I'd still know him. Meriamdan has stuffed him into my head enough times. I know what he *feels* like, and I think I have a pretty good idea of how they've been 'shifting' him around. I felt that too. Maybe, if you could locate him, I could 'shift' him into one of these sand bodies."

"What do you mean 'shift?'"

"It's like...like he's liquid, and when they take control of him, they can ride his spirit, as if he makes it easier for them to shift out of their bodies and into the ether, and from there, into another person's mind."

"Aren, link with Antronos during a chant," said Leelan.

"No. Absolutely not."

"How else is this going to work?"

"It isn't going to work."

"After what you did to him, you'd better make it work!"

"Shut up, Leelan!"

"Did what, to whom?" asked Antronos, but a cold feeling of knowing was building up inside of him. The moment he asked the question, he *knew*. "You did it," he said quietly. "That's why Leod won't talk to you anymore."

"Opalena asked us to," Aren protested.

"'Us'? You did it too, Leelan?" questioned Antronos.

"No, Aren and Liam did it." Leelan caught hold of Antronos' sleeve, trying to pull him back down.

"You were there as well, Leelan!" Aren accused her.

"Only to tell you it was a bad idea."

"It was for mercy. Opalena didn't want him to suffer."

"That's not why you did it."

"Damn it! Jait asked for it himself!"

"You ruined everything!" Antronos ripped free of Leelan and stumbled towards the back tunnels. "I could have saved him. I could have helped him use his power against the Murdek, crushed them and freed him at the same time. You didn't have to kill him! I was so close."

"Antronos, don't leave," Leelan pleaded. "Help us set things right. Tell us more about how the Murdek controlled him. We can't do this without you."

"From what Aren's been saying, you can't do it at all. Oh, what's the use? If you hadn't killed him, Vernus probably would have eventually, and then resurrected him just the same. We haven't got a hope of keeping him away from the Murdek, so perhaps you're right. This is all a waste of time."

"I can find him," said Aren. Antronos and Leelan fell silent, watching Aren as he pulled a cloth packet from his tunic and unravelled it. The thing inside looked like a stick with dark, glossy threads wound around it.

"What's that?" asked Antronos.

"Jait's hair. This is what I used to find him and aim the sword."

"Where did you get it?"

"I told you. Opalena."

Antronos looked away, choking back tears. *How could she? Wasn't she in love with him? What of her responsibility to Leod?* Part of Antronos' mind asked him where this intensity of emotion was coming from. Jait was sick. Opalena had to get away from him and stop Vernus from finding her again. Jait's death was inevitable. His rationality was submerged by another wave of disappointment at Opalena's actions.

"Antronos, please," Leelan begged. "Let's just try. This is the best way we can help him. If we don't, the Murdek will get him again. I don't think any of us wants that."

"And you're willing now, Aren?" He watched Aren toy with the stick wrapped in Jait's hair.

"Not really," the Yrati answered after a moment. "But I will try. Not for his sake, and not for you, Leelan. I'll do it to make sure the two of you don't do something stupid on your own."

"Tell yourself whatever you like." Leelan pushed the second bowl of water in front of Aren and settled herself in a kneeling position. "Antronos, sit here and link hands with us. Aren will find Jait, hopefully you will sense it through him, and then this time, you *must* shift him into that sand pile."

Antronos swallowed the fresh wave of grief that was rising up in him and forced himself to move back towards the Yrati. He knelt and let Leelan intertwine her fingers with his. "And what will you do?" he asked her.

"Provide whatever support I can."

Reluctantly, Antronos also took Aren's hand, trying not to let his revulsion show. He wondered if Leod would ever forgive him for collaborating with his grandfather's murderers to turn Jait into a sand monster.

Aren began to sing. Antronos could feel the reluctance of the Yrati in letting their minds merge, but felt a kind of giddy exhilaration as Leelan's spirit crashed into his with almost physical solidity. He knew her passion, her life energy, her femininity in an instant, as it writhed past his own being. His awareness of what was around him was no longer visual, rather a perception of all emotion and energy being radiated from all things, both animate and inanimate, as he was swept out of his mind in a rush of will. It was so different from the brutal invasion of the Murdek. *It carries the collective life-force of the ghouls.* The knowledge of what it meant to be stiffened swept over Antronos. He saw it swirling past Aren and Leelan, who were oblivious to the content of this message. This capability of mind passage was part of the stiffening: this ability to move between the worlds of the living and the dead, watching the events of both. Stiffening was not a death. It was an evolution. Antronos felt Aren try to focus on his mind, jealous and infuriated over the understanding he could not perceive. After a moment, Aren lost himself in concentration, and the barriers around his mind disappeared. The focus and authority with which he drove the direction of their joined minds revealed to Antronos something else that had been kept from him; Aren had become High Priest. Something devastating must have happened to Maxal, something that would preclude his return to his duties to the Yrati—and the university.

His disappointment was caught up in Aren's own, as he felt the weight of the turmoil within the Yrati clan spill into his mind. His and Aren's combined frustration and anger fed each other until the power coursing through them was near unbearable. Leelan's spirit was almost drowned out in their midst. Antronos was vaguely aware of her struggling, somewhere at the end of what must have been his arm. Could she breathe?

All thoughts were lost in a blast of searing, white pain as something pierced Antronos/Aren, ripping up through their bowels, shoving their tongues out of their mouths, roiling with intense confusion as the two of them tore apart and came together again in a jumble of identities. Antronos resisted, shrinking back into himself as much as possible, trying to make sense of the confusion he found himself plunged into. This pain was not his; it had been Jait's. They had found the High Prince.

Antronos was running uphill, following the flow of water in a tiny creek bed that split the white fog of nothingness that curved around him. He was back in the Royal House, at Jait's tub with the enamel fish painted at the bottom. He sat at the side with his legs in the water, barely able to see the white tile around him because of the rolling white steam that rose up on all sides. He lifted his hands to wipe the sweat from his face, and saw the steam coil in them to form a round shape. It hardened into an egg, which slipped from his fingers. Something dark was moving through the water, and as it came closer, he could see a fawn paddling towards him, dark hair trailing in the water like delicate fins. Antronos reached down to stroke the white-spotted brown fur, amazed at how warm and solid it was. Jait struggled onto his lap, and pushed his dark, pointed snout up to nuzzle Antronos' cheek, his touch filling Antronos with a deep, calm, profoundly satisfied emotion that quenched the fire and rage that had consumed him earlier. As he closed his arms around the fawn, it felt as if everything he had ever wanted had just coalesced inside his body, making him complete and unshakeably strong. He had a vague memory that he was supposed to be doing something else, but he no longer cared. Did he not have everything he wanted or needed right here? How strange that he had never noticed before now that Jait could fill him thus.

How could you not know he was supposed to be yours? the Red Ghouls asked him. *We kept telling you.* Their bony red skulls circled excitedly in the water. *He understood! He understood not to let them permanently kill the fish!*

Antronos lifted his head as something moved at the other edge of the tub. There was a second fawn prancing there. This one was tiny and frolicking energetically, its fur a light gold. He stared at it in fascination, gradually becoming aware that Aren also sat at the edge of the pool, but he held no crossbow, so Antronos ignored the fact that he and the Yrati were still joined. A small coil of hair that rested in their palm twisted into a rope that clung around the neck of a dead man being pulled away from them by a rush of water being sucked into the gaping mouths of several grey, writhing worms. The hair was slipping out of their hand.

Antronos came back to himself and forced that hand shut, feeling Aren convulse in surprise. He ignored the Yrati's indignation at no longer being in control, and tried to slither his mind around Jait's. His excitement swelled as Jait responded to him, gently washing into Antronos' thoughts with the same liquid insinuation as before, but this time there was no Meriamdan to bring the pain, only Jait's own mild curiosity and complacency. Antronos culled together all his strength, thought of his mother, and put all the energy he could muster into forming that precious mound of sand. He thought of water flowing into the Earth to power the creation of life. He felt the Earth shifting, writhing—*Leelan screaming*—taking shape beneath his will—*Aren yelling at him to stop*—Jait's liquid soul insinuating itself into the sand to heat it with his being.

And Jait began to cry.

It was a thin wail, barely audible, and the most beautiful sound Antronos had ever heard. He revelled in the glory of his success—*we will be together again*—as he slowly came back to himself, the world being pieced back together as his senses resumed. There was no mound of sand in front of him. Confused, he touched the floor of the cavern, searching with his fingers for the miracle he knew had to be there, as he waited for his vision to fully return. Gradually, he became aware that Aren was gasping for breath. Leelan was bleeding, occasionally making small sounds of pain. Antronos shook his head and blinked. Leelan's hands were dripping blood all over the floor. Her skin, from her throat all the way down through her torn robes to her thighs, was shredded and oozing blood. A twisting cord stretched from her midriff to a tiny lump of flesh that was wriggling little bud-limbs as it cried. Antronos stared in horror, rubbed his eyes and stared again.

"By the Earth," said Aren. "What have you done?"

26

Resurrection

Vernus tried to control the shaking of his hands as he reined in his anger, and once again focused on painting the shapes of his runes on a set of stones. Jait's death had stunned him, but with Derik, his position had remained relatively secure. Now he had little strength left, and it was all he could do to cast his mind out the short distance needed to control this tiny patch of Desert without Meriamdan's assistance. The Yrati were watching for him in the underground, forcing him to keep his distance from the Faculty of Medicine. They had dismantled his lab, confiscated his reagents, read his private journals, and had provided all the testimony needed for the new King to put a price on his head, and issue warnings about the Murdek ability to possess people through touch. It was infuriating how the new regime pretended belief in mysticism, while all they really believed in was politics. Derik's old supporters had willingly thrown in their lot behind Liam on hearing they would not be ridiculed for practices they had thought only Derik would subscribe to. Those fools had abandoned the Murdek quest for real power in favour of living in easy collusion with the Royal House. Vernus had one last gambit to play, and he had to do it now, before Liam hunted him down like an animal. His current weakness sickened him.

The sky howled blue-black overhead, roiling in protest over Vernus' control. The Desert cast up another spume of sand against the barrier of wind he had formed around himself, and a few more of the stone creatures flailed uselessly at its perimeter. His Murdek sat curled up in the sand like lumps of stone, conserving the little energy they had left after he had drained them for his magic. Meriamdan prowled around him restlessly on fisted knuckles, appearing much more graceful when she walked on all fours. If this latest attempt failed, she would go hunt. They hadn't eaten in days.

Water bubbled up around the stones he had carefully placed in a specific sequence, causing them to sink into the sand or have the ink washed off.

Another of the strange red skeletons twisted up *inside* of his perimeter, jaw stretched open with the strain of pushing against his will. Vernus let his anger flare, generating enough force to shove the thing back where it came from. Where had such a creature come from? Red ghouls? It was unheard of. He had just calmed himself enough to resume painting when a set of bony red fingers shot out of the sand and grabbed one of his stones. He snatched up another rock and smashed the thing to bits. Something had to be controlling these red creatures. The other Desert forms had no such coordination or determination to disrupt his work. But what power was behind them? It couldn't be the Yrati, or they would have been here on the surface by now.

Finally placing the last of the stones, Vernus relaxed his will and was satisfied to see that his barrier held. No more skeletons, red or otherwise, entered his perimeter. He shifted forward until he could see through the blue-tinted glass skylight beneath which the corpse of Lord Jait lay. The old Prince was clearly rotted, but this did not concern Vernus. Meriamdan had no complaints about her desiccated form, and he expected Jait would also adapt. The real problem was the water flowing in all directions around Jait's plinth—Yrati magic that had replaced the Murdek sand. In their last attempt to enter the tomb, Vernus had not detected the subtle pull of the Yrati influence until Jalena's foot had slipped off the slightly raised stepping stones and touched the thin layer of water. Then the collective Yrati awareness flared in his own thoughts, and he could feel them rushing toward the tomb, screaming all manner of warnings and threats. His Murdek had fled to the back tunnels, but the Yrati were there in seconds and Taphit had been killed by the Royal Guard, who had made certain he had no chance to touch them and jump into one of their bodies. It was disturbing, how much the Yrati now knew.

Vernus called the Murdek to sit around the skylight and help him carefully brush away the sand. He knew the Royal Guard would be just outside the crypt entrance, and they would have to make as little noise as possible. Using a shard of obsidian with a razor edge, they cut the skylight free of its moulding and lifted it away. Iegat was lowered on ropes until he was close enough to loop another around Jait's neck. They pulled Iegat out, and then began to haul Jait upwards.

The mat covering Jait's face fell back onto the plinth. The red and blue cloths covering him also pulled away, but did not fall into the water. Relieved, Vernus allowed himself the smallest amount of satisfaction as the Murdek finally clutched Jait's body to lift him free of the tomb completely.

"Replace the glass," he instructed them, before turning to his prize. Meriamdan paced around Jait a few times, before chuckling and settling herself in the sand by his head.

They began the chant softly, each set of syllables uttered in pulses, weaving their voices into a wall of sound. Vernus slipped out of his body and floated forward, willing his thoughts into the High Prince's carcass. He felt for the resonance of the body's former life, and plucked it like a string to make it sound louder. If he could strengthen it enough, he would be able to use it as windlass, and drag Jait back from wherever he was.

Jait, he whispered. *Awaken.*

No response. Vernus reached deeper, threading his own spirit through the body of Jait, trying to follow where the old High Prince had gone. It felt like he was travelling miles. He paused, again sensing the Yrati influence, and held in his anger in case it brought their attention to him. *Why* could they not leave well enough alone? Not daring to call to Jait again, he tried to focus on how the High Prince's spirit had felt when it had been in his hands, supporting him with its power, hoping that the memory alone would help Jait materialize before him.

There! He had touched it. Sleepy, disoriented, naïve, Jait's soul wafted aimlessly in the ether. Vernus reached out to it and gently pulled. Jait slipped out of his fingers. Vernus carefully moved a little closer. His mind brushed against something that pinned Jait where he was. Curious, he probed at it. Someone probed back at him, then recoiled in alarm—an Yrati mind. *Damn!*

Vernus shot back the way he had come, twisting and feinting as his spirit tumbled along the dark passages of misty ether. Back in his body, he was vaguely aware of Meriamdan pacing around him restlessly. He linked into her mind, fed off her determination, tempered her emotions and used them to propel himself forward again.

The Yrati were distracted, milling about the ether in what might be panic. There were more of them now, taking up a guard formation around Jait. There was a great deal of unrest in their thoughts, and much anger. Curious.

Carefully picking his way through their formation, Vernus found Jait and folded his mind around the part of him that still wafted free. He felt Meriamdan within himself, and told her to get ready. She tightened her grip.

Now! With a sudden rush of determination, Vernus clamped onto his will to control Jait and fled, Meriamdan lending him strength. The Yrati anchor did not give, straining Jait's spirit across the ether. Furious, Vernus refused to let go, looping his own spirit back through Jait's body, and tugging Jait through as well. The Yrati hold still did not give. Vernus could not relax the force he was using to hold Jait in place; his strength was draining. The High Prince began to writhe in pain, trying to twist free. Vernus was unable to maintain his barrier against the Desert any longer, and the wind immediately tore across his distant, corporeal face. He felt Meriamdan redouble her efforts to shift Jait back into his body, to no avail. It began to rain.

The sand of the Desert heaved beneath them as the water fell in slick curtains over the surface, immediately soaking everything in its path. Beneath his hands, Vernus felt Jait's carcass soften, and with a slight jolt, Meriamdan finally pushed Jait's soul into it. They called the Desert into Jait's body to help them bind spirit to corpse, and despite the Yrati anchor still holding, the pull of the old Prince's former self was strong enough to stretch against that force, and keep most of his being within Vernus' power.

Feverish, dripping with water, Vernus allowed himself to sink back into his own body completely, and opened his eyes. Jait was still dead, his skin now looking as though it were made of sand, yet he moved feebly, and his empty sockets blinked up at Vernus. On his forehead, a grainy impression of the Murdek seal rested where Meriamdan had initially forced Jait in. The more the rain softened Jait, the more supple and malleable he became. They had him back. Vernus began to laugh. He hadn't used water magic in decades, but of course, to bring the dead to life, one would mix the Desert with water!

"We cannot rest. They will have an easier time finding us now because their hold on Jait has not been broken," said Meriamdan. "We must find a secure, easily defendable hiding spot where we can design how to gain him completely. Let's go."

Vernus let Meriamdan force him to his feet, amazed at her constant strength. She was right. They needed a safe place to rest. But was it necessary to free Jait? As the Murdek lifted him from the muddied sand, he probed the High Prince's mind to assess his power. He was too weak, stretched like this, to be of any use against the Yrati. That was good, since the same disadvantage must certainly be presented to Maxal. The Yrati would have to be just as cautious approaching the Murdek, and that would give them some time.

A howling that was not the wind erupted around them as a small army of the red skeletons burst up through the sand. The water slicking off their skulls made them look like they were coated with blood as they stumbled forward, trying to grab hold of Jait. Vernus was unable to summon the strength to blast them with a jolt of psychic energy. Meriamdan raced at them, trying to physically dismember their bones. Iegat assisted her as best he could, pulling away the ghouls that tried to drag her into the sand, and tearing apart those that would not let go.

"Take him!" Meriamdan shouted through the wind. "I will find you. We must not lose Jait!"

Trusting Meriamdan as much as ever, Vernus turned to the other Murdek and motioned them to run. It was hard going, their feet sinking into the wet sand, Jait dragging against their strength. Despite their current weakness, Vernus couldn't help grinning into the slashing rain.

Jait will soon be completely mine!

27

Giudecca

Antronos sat next to Leelan's bed, her hand firmly clasped in his as he apologized for the ninth time for what he had done. She smiled at him, not speaking, most of her concentration focused on maintaining her link with Jait. Seven other Yrati knelt around her bed, heads bowed as they also lent their strength to Leelan's hold against the Murdek. When Antronos leaned his forehead against Leelan's cheek, he could feel them: coiling, grey barbworms constantly pulling, gnawing, insinuating their way into the Yrati collective mind. It wasn't a simple matter of repulsing them, not without losing their hold on Jait's spirit. The tiny...thing that housed Jait was smothered in blankets and held against Leelan's bandaged chest. After Locke had severed the cord between them, she had refused to let go of Jait, even to sleep. Consequently, Antronos didn't want to let go of Leelan, despite the furious looks he kept getting from the Yrati, who came in and out of the chamber with medicines and fresh bandages. He didn't dare give voice to what he really thought. He wished she would just give him the strange baby, but after what he had done to her, she had more right than he did to say where Jait went.

Something had gone wrong. Why in Earth had he formed Jait's body from Leelan's flesh? Why couldn't he have used his own? Then it would have been so easy to hide Jait from anyone who wanted to harm him—*and I'd be sure I'd kept my promise to Leod*. It was a moot point. There was no way he could have gotten this far without Aren's help, and what they really needed was to block the Murdek long enough to disable them permanently. Aren was trying to find a way to use Jait to locate the Murdek, then inform Liam and let the Royal Guard take care of it. Antronos felt nervous involving the King, knowing how he felt about his father, but Jait was no threat to Liam now. Surely the King would not also want to kill this infant.

Antronos reached across a medical stand to retrieve Leelan's tisane for her, and bumped hands with Locke. The Yrati glared at him, retracted his hand and strode out of the cavern, not saying a word. He brushed past Ferril, who was leaning against the entryway with his new wooden leg, staring at Antronos with a strange hint of a smile playing about his lips. He didn't avert his eyes when Antronos stared back at him; if anything, his expression became more knowing. Antronos looked away, reminding himself that they had done this for a reason. Leelan had agreed, and if he faltered now, all this pain would have been for nothing. He was grateful that he had let Opalena leave. While he did not like what had happened to Leelan, at least she had started with all her strength. He picked up the cup and helped Leelan hold it to her lips.

At the foot of the bed, Fara sighed and tilted her head upward, putting her hands to the back of her neck. The other Yrati also relaxed, coming out of their meditation.

"What happened?" asked Antronos. He pushed aside the edge of the blankets to check on Jait's tiny, half-formed face.

"They stopped pulling," said Leelan.

"They've let go?"

"No, just stopped trying to force him from us."

"They probably need a rest, too," said Fara. She stood up and rested her hands on Leelan's blanket-covered feet. "You should really let someone else hold him for a while. We'd wake you the moment the Murdek started again."

"No," said Leelan. "Don't worry, Fara. I won't squash him when I sleep." She snuggled down into her pillows, turning onto her side and tucking Jait under her chin. Antronos moved out of the way and stood up, feeling an unwelcome rise of anger, jealously and impatience.

The Desert must have done something to my mind, he told himself. The possessiveness he was feeling didn't make sense. He should be happy. He had achieved his objectives, hadn't he?

"Well, I suppose you can sleep in one of the other side caverns," said Fara, taking him by the arm. As politely as he could, Antronos lifted her hand and gestured that she should go before him. His emotions were wound so tightly that the slightest nudge from anyone made him so irritable he wanted to jump out of his skin.

"Any chance of me talking to Maxal?" he asked.

"Not really," Fara replied. "Even if Aren didn't forbid it, Maxal isn't talking to any of us. It's unlikely he'd talk to you. Here, no one's using this room."

Antronos nodded his thanks, and watched as she walked off, stumbling a bit with fatigue. He leaned against the wall for a few minutes, asking himself why he didn't go back to Leod and Opalena. The Yrati didn't want him here, but then, did he really have a place with Opalena? *That's just an excuse. The fawn. That's what you're after.*

Inside the cave, Antronos lay down and shut his eyes. He dozed, but deep sleep was constantly pushed away by his unwillingness to abandon half-formed plans to convince Leelan to let go of her prize once the Murdek were dealt with. Finally, he sat up in the dark. Why did the ghouls give him that dream if he was supposed to just walk away afterward? He got up and stumbled through the dusty corridor, trying to follow the pulsating patterns of the insect auras to the meditating pool. If he couldn't have guidance from Maxal, perhaps the ghouls would give him some indication of what was meant to happen now. He told himself he would accept whatever direction they gave.

A strange smell was growing stronger as Antronos crept through the tunnel towards where he thought the pool was. It became so bad that Antronos had to cover his nose and mouth with his sleeve. An Yrati, not tall, but very broad, lurched into the hall a few doors down. The lighting was dim, masking his face in shadows. Antronos blinked and strained his eyes. What had happened to his Desert vision? There was no aura at all. As the Yrati moved away from him and passed under a mounted torch, he saw a mass of tangled, dark red hair, and a wet trail of slime left by the Yrati's sodden robes.

Someone had trouble cleaning out the sewer system? wondered Antronos. The Yrati was limping very badly. Perhaps he was hurt. Antronos hurried forward to see if he could help. The Yrati heard him, and casting a glance over his shoulder, also quickened his step.

"Is everything all right?" Antronos called. The Yrati laughed—a harsh, gargling sound.

"No more trouble from you, Antronos," he said. The stench of his breath hit Antronos like a foul wind. The Yrati collapsed and something like a grey wraith fled upward through the rock ceiling. Had he imagined it? He started forward when he heard a shout coming through the tunnels to his left.

"Leelan's been hurt! Jait's been taken!"

Antronos ran towards Leelan's room. Aren was there, shouting commands wildly. Locke and Fara were trying to force shut the gaping tear across Leelan's body. It looked like she had been sliced open with a blunt saw. They'd have to work fast if she were to live much longer. He raked his eyes through the room for Jait, and not seeing him, dashed out of the cave back toward the strange Yrati he had seen lurching through the halls. Aren ran after him.

"Where are you going?" Aren yelled.

"I think I saw an intruder," Antronos called back.

"Impossible! All living things in our caves are part of the Yrati collective mind. The plants and insects watch everything. We have ward stones. No outsider could have entered without our knowing."

Antronos saw the crumpled form of the fallen Yrati still on the ground in the darkened tunnel, and slowed down, again covering his mouth and nose with a cloth. He pulled a torch from its wall bracket and advanced cautiously. Aren came up beside him.

"Who is this?"

"I don't know. He's not one of your clan?"

Aren reached down and slowly turned the man over. Antronos was disturbed by the Yrati's continued lack of aura, when Aren's glowed brightly.

"Is he dead?" Antronos asked. The body fell over with a thump, and he found himself staring into the white, bloated face of Tibeau, his mouth opened and filled with black, maggot-encrusted rot. Aren shouted, tripped and fell backward.

"They wore him like a disguise," choked Aren. Antronos couldn't breathe. Tibeau's body was swollen to three times what it should have been, as if he had been soaked excessively in a swamp, or filled by one. Something was crushed in Tibeau's claw-like fist. Antronos nudged it away from the side of Tibeau's corpse, and saw a smear of fresh blood.

"Oh, no." He dropped the torch and forced open the stiff fingers. The tiny, bloody lump within was completely crushed. There was no aura. "They've killed him."

"Get out."

He turned toward Aren. "What?"

"I said, get out."

"We have to find Jait."

"There is no more 'we' Desert-man. You've cost me enough! Leelan...and now you've brought this," he jerked his head at Tibeau's corpse, "into my home."

"This is not my fault."

"*All of it is your fault! Get out!*" Aren's face was red, and his eyes spilled tears as he shouted.

Locke came running towards them. "Did you find Jait?" he asked. His face went slack when he saw Tibeau. "By the Earth." He sank to his knees next to Aren.

"Locke," said Aren, "get him out. I can't stand it anymore."

Locke tried to stand, but couldn't.

"Don't bother," said Antronos. He gently picked up what was left of Jait, and stepped past Aren and Locke. "There's nothing here for me anyway." He left the Yrati home and found the nearest stairwell to the surface. He needed to be away from all tunnel dwellers and to find a place to bury Jait in the sand.

*****

"*Herein fynde the recipy for powder that can block peruysal of the mynde by persons of the outsyde . . .*"

"*Is that what you were using, Sen?*"

"*I'm sorry I gave you too much medicine.*"

"*Hurts sometimes. I wonder where it went.*"

Shenan rubbed the gaping hole in his chest. He knelt down in the sand and began to dig.

"*I wonder why I didn't read this before.*" *Antronos kept flipping over the paper on which Vernus' recipe was written, and every time he turned it, it made less sense.* "*Oh, that's right. I never learned to read. Huh. I wonder why I thought I could.*"

"We all think that, Sen. I once thought I could fly."

Antronos also began to dig in the sand. With every handful he scooped away, it felt like a fistful of his brains was being torn out. He kept telling himself to stop, but the more he tried, the more his hands insisted on worrying at the clay he had now reached underneath the sand. His fingernails bent back painfully, but he still could not stop.

Dig, dig, dig, the Desert told him. Dig until you find me, Alaindra.

"Why?" Antronos asked. The Desert snickered at him.

I want to know what you did with her. You carry some interesting thoughts in your mind, young Sen Antronos. The last time I looked into your eyes, I could see that you'd hidden something inside Alaindra. Told Aren you did, too. I want to ssssseeeee what you did. Show me, boy.

"I can't. I can't remember," Antronos sobbed. *"This is hurting me."*

Tell me his name, boy. Tell me the name of your little secret.

"Sssss. Seph." Antronos couldn't make himself think of the name. It felt like the Desert was pouring itself into his body now, taking away his dignity as it forced its way into every crevice of his mind. *"It hurts,"* Antronos wailed again.

"I know, Sen," said Shenan. *"But sometimes, you've just got to take it. Sometimes, a man has no choice. I had no choice, but I accept what I've lost to the Desert."*

"I'm sorry I lost your heart."

"Ah, doesn't matter. I just wonder where it went. That's all. Why'd you want that powder anyway?" Shenan pointed at the paper in Antronos' hand.

"Oh. I think...I think there's someone trying to read my mind."

"You'd better wake up then."

Antronos jerked awake. His heart thudded in the early evening dimness. He was on the surface all right, wrapped in his cloak and half buried in the sand without a clue as to why he had decided to lie down for a nap in the middle of nowhere after burying Jait. Shenan wasn't there, nor any Murdek. Cautiously, he sat up and sorted through his thoughts. His mind felt bruised. There was a residual feeling of having been violated, and something told him he wasn't alone. He scanned the Desert for any visible auras, then stood and began to edge around the pile of stones he had set his back against. *There!* A faint glint of someone hiding just around the large boulder farther back. Antronos drew a dagger from the loop at his hip. It was blunt, but he had nothing else.

From behind the rock, someone started to snicker. Antronos froze, checking that he cast no shadow that would give away his position. A voice began to sing, a haunting, lilting aria that lulled his mind, making him want to sleep so very badly. He sagged to his knees, fighting it. The voice sighed in contentment as Antronos' will gave way, and his vision dulled. He twisted his head towards the noise, trying to blink away the dimness, attempting to focus on a pair of dark black eyes that were boring into his own with malicious intensity.

"Antronos," sang the voice. *"Tell me where you've buried your secret."*

"Who are you?" Antronos moaned. His skull was splitting.

"*Tell me what you would have told Aren...ah, I can see where you've hidden Sephus. I will be reunited with him now.*"

Antronos struggled furiously against the dullness that was threatening to suffocate him. This was unlike any invasion by Meriamdan. There was nothing to push back against; it was like fighting a large, partially solid fog. He couldn't breathe. Yellow stars were shooting across his vision, his throat was clamping shut, his mind was fading away. His attacker was tottering away from him in the sand, tattered robes fluttering in the wind. It was not the undertaker, who did not have one wooden leg, and a tangle of black hair falling down his back.

Antronos lost consciousness.

✳✳✳✳✳

"What makes you think it was Ferril?"

"Who else could it have been?" Aware that Leod was watching him fearfully, Antronos couldn't keep the agitation out of his voice or movements.

"But he was back with the Yrati. He can't be Murdek. They would have known." Opalena calmly handed him a hot cup of broth, which he took gratefully. She took his arm and led him to a pile of cushions in a corner of the cave. He sank down on them and stared out at the 'Cliff. "Did you see two auras in him when you tried to help Leelan?"

"No."

"Well, there you are."

"How do we know he hasn't turned?"

Opalena froze. She was by the hearth, in the middle of spooning up more broth. Her head moved to the side, but she didn't look at him.

"I can't believe that."

A dozen sharp retorts formed in Antronos' mind, but he voiced none of them. He sipped the broth, angry that his story of Ferril invading his mind was being met with doubt. Opalena handed a cup to Leod, who absently took it in his skinny hands without taking his eyes from Antronos.

"I was there when Vernus killed his student. Right in front of him. Antronos, he clearly loved that boy."

"And I saw him broken, just before returning him to the Yrati. His mind was completely shattered. He was one of the Murdek pallbearers, for Earth's sake."

"That doesn't mean he couldn't have healed. I think it will be a very long time before he forgets what Vernus did to him. There's no way he could be Murdek."

"Then I don't know what he is. Why'd he want to be reunited with Sephus?"

"Sephus was always ambivalent. Perhaps he wants an alliance, or maybe—"

"The last time *I* met Sephus he certainly knew whose side he was on."

"Antronos, none of us had any choice. You and I have both done things we can be judged harshly for."

"But neither of *us* ever gave in like Sephus did. When I carried him to Alaindra it was just the two of us. He had every chance then to ally with me, and he chose not to. If he had wanted to break free from Vernus, that was his best chance, and he *chose* not to take it. And if Ferril is looking for support against Vernus, why wouldn't he try to negotiate with me? Why abuse me like that? He certainly did not behave like an Yrati."

Opalena sighed. "It probably wasn't him. Or if it was, he can't be Murdek or he would have dragged you back to Vernus instead of just leaving you there. Is there any chance that the Desert could have distorted your perception of what happened?"

"I suppose," Antronos muttered. He didn't feel like discussing it any further. He resented Opalena's apparent calm, especially after she had refused to help Jait when she had been involved in his death in the first place; she had allowed him to be reclaimed by the Murdek when she said that she herself could not bear to face them again, and now, she was refusing to fully believe that Ferril had attacked him. Aren was brutal. If one Yrati could be, why not another?

Antronos' mind was a knot of anger. There were too many Murdek for him to handle on his own. They very probably had Jait again, he could no longer ask the Yrati for help, and there was no way Liam would back him without Aren's approval. Perhaps he should leave them to it. Perhaps they would overcome the Murdek, and perhaps they wouldn't. He couldn't feel good about the outcome either way. His promise to Leod would be broken regardless. Either the Murdek would torment Jait endlessly, or Aren would destroy him. Opalena leaned forward, and smiling slightly, tried to look into his face, making him feel guilty for sulking.

"I think I'm getting better at formulating that mind-blocker you were trying to teach me," she said lightly. "It's difficult to remember all the ingredients when you won't write anything down. I'm not sure if I made the nasty one that makes you black out, or the newer one that lets you keep your senses."

Antronos took a deep breath and pushed away from the wall. "Oh, you can tell from the scent."

"Well, if I made the right one, maybe you could use it. Then you won't have to worry about anyone getting in your head."

Antronos didn't answer for a few seconds, then relented and gave her a half smile. At least she didn't despise him like everyone else seemed to. "Thanks. That's a good idea." Leod seemed relieved at the drop in tension, as he scurried over and wriggled between them. He was cold as ice, so Antronos wrapped a corner of his robes around him. *The fawn was in his arms, warm and solid.* The image that flashed through his mind was so real it left him stricken with emotional pain, and it took a few seconds to notice that Opalena was holding out a glass dish with her concoction in it. He pulled his mouth shut, and reached for it with a shaky hand, hoping she hadn't noticed his lapse.

"Hmm. This is almost like the formulation I gave to Sephus."

Opalena seemed embarrassed. "I guess I made the bad one, then."

"Did you add the analgesic?"

"No, I didn't have it."

"I think I have some. Might fix it." Antronos pulled his bag from the corner where he had left it earlier in the week. He had filled it by the fistful from his desk drawer and shelves the last time he had been in his office, and he was sure he had grabbed all the pharmaceutical reagents he had there. He dug through it, finding a few packets made of folded paper. One of them had to have the extract he was looking for.

"What's this?" Leod had picked up a lump of wadded-up blue and red paper from his bag.

Antronos looked at it and felt a sudden spike of embarrassment. It seemed so long ago that he had stolen it from Tibeau. His embarrassment was followed by guilt, as he thought of what had happened to the boy. He gently plucked the thing from Leod's fingers.

"Can I have it?" asked Leod. He got to his knees and leaned against Antronos' arm.

"It's dangerous. I don't think—"

Leod wobbled sideways. Antronos quickly caught up Opalena's dish in his other hand in case the child accidentally spilled some of the formulation on himself.

"Why? What does it do?" asked Leod.

"Uh, I think it explodes into bright, coloured flames."

"Can I see?"

"Well..." Antronos looked from one hand to the other, thinking he should put the mind-blocker somewhere safe. He could just imagine having the contents of the dish exploding everywhere, especially when a formulation similar to this had caused Sephus' mind to completely shut down. It would paralyze them all at once. Antronos froze.

"What is it?" Opalena asked.

Antronos almost laughed. "I can do this," he told her. "I think I can rescue him."

Jait? Opalena mouthed silently over Leod's head. Antronos nodded.

"Thank you, Leod," he said, hugging the little boy and rubbing his back.

"Why?" asked Leod. "What did I do?"

Prison

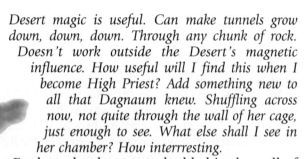

Desert magic is useful. Can make tunnels grow down, down, down. Through any chunk of rock. Doesn't work outside the Desert's magnetic influence. How useful will I find this when I become High Priest? Add something new to all that Dagnaum knew. Shuffling across now, not quite through the wall of her cage, just enough to see. What else shall I see in her chamber? How interrresting.

Burrowed down into the Earth so that he was embedded in the wall of Alaindra's chamber, Ferril watched the Lady of Dra rock herself behind the bars, peering through the gauzy curtains, trying to see past them. Herodra was standing there, smiling sadly, his fingers resting lightly upon the indentation of his hand print that had been set into the chamber wall on his wedding night. He slid his other hand into Alaindra's imprint with a caress. He looked taller, and not quite so young.

Herodra moved into the secondary chamber where Alaindra sat, shifting aside gauzy blue curtains as he did so. Ferril crumbled away a little more of the rock so that he could see better. *Careful, now. Too much and I'll fall through.* Neither of the chamber's other occupants noticed him, so enrapt they were with each other. Hero *was* older. He was dressed in a grey tailored suit, with a blue jabot and full complement of gold buttons and cuff-links. Thin sideburns traced his jaw line from his dark hair to his lips. He just stood there, gazing at Alaindra with an expression of horror. She finally turned away from him, her hair a tangled mess, and rocked again.

Sounds. Muttering sounds coming from her mouth.

"Can you imagine my *despair*, Antronos, at finding that *none of what you say is true?*"

Ferril almost laughed. Which one of them was speaking?

"*Can you imagine my despair, Antronos . . .*"

"Alaindra!"

Herodra had called to her, and was gripping the bars of her cage. She turned her head to the side, as if listening intently.

"We are angry too," she told him. Herodra's face was white and strained.

"Please," he said. "Help me understand what's happened to you."

"Antronos is a liar," she said suddenly. "Lies, lies, lies. All he says are lies."

Herodra looked disappointed with the answer.

"What did he lie to you about?"

Alaindra writhed strangely, so that Ferril caught sight of her face. She was smiling, grimacing rather, and her hand stretched out to Herodra, palm upwards.

"Touch me," she said.

Herodra began to reach towards that hand, and Alaindra watched entranced, tilting her head backwards in anticipation.

"No, don't," she said, and retracted the hand. "He wants you to, but I don't. I'm still here with him. I never died. That's what Antronos lied to him about."

"I don't know what you mean. Please Alaindra, explain it to me."

"Touch. Touch? Touch and jump. Touch and jump. That's what he wants. But he's mine. I can't let you have him."

She resumed rocking on the stool, her lower lip working as she hummed tunelessly. Herodra watched her helplessly for a moment, then tried to put on a normal face and speak to her as if everything was all right.

"I've managed to secure the last of the Dar holdings. I knew you wanted them before. And my family still with Dan hasn't been pressuring me too much about the ore sales. Your family wants to displace me, but they haven't done it yet. I promise you that they won't while you're still unwell. I'll never let them while there's still a chance that I might protect you."

Alaindra turned to him then. "I will prevail," she said. "I knew you would be strong, Hero. Wait for me?" she pleaded.

"I'll wait. I wish that I could help you somehow."

"I will only ask that you still be here when I'm free."

"Will you not tell me what afflicts you?"

She tried to answer him, but all that issued from her mouth was a low sibilant noise. She struggled for a few moments, then her eyes shut and her head snapped away, and she began muttering about Antronos again. After a few moments, she began laughing. Her arms flailed. She picked up spoons and shards of broken glass, tried to injure herself, but invariably flung the implements away before any damage was done.

"Anything you do to me, you will feel yourself!" she leered into a polished metal mirror. "Can't do it, can't do it, can you? Oh, is that what you think? You can't hide anything from me! Suicide? *I won't let you.*" More laughing.

"Alain, please. Release this madness," said Hero. "What you're saying makes no sense."

Stupid Herodra. It makes perfect sense. Ferril understood this completely. Had he not felt the same way so many times before?

"*Damn* Antronos!" Alaindra screamed. "To have to share this body with this *witch!* You were supposed to be *dead!*" she yelled at the mirror. She then burst into a new series of giggles and eventually chuckled heartily at her own rage as she growled and twisted about the chamber, trying to throw things at herself.

"I'll get you yet, you little bug-sucker!" she said to the mirror. She leaned very close to it, making sure every word was spoken clearly. "I'm very close now. You're losing control. A little more each day. What are you but some pathetic residue that thinks he is special simply because he stinks? I'll deal with you. I'll deal with you all. You will all die with your entrails stuffed into your eye sockets after you've been pithed in such a way that you'll be paralyzed, but not insensate, and each step of your dismemberment will be explained fully beforehand; one part taken off for every injury and insult you have inflicted on me, no matter how slight. I'll do it myself. I might kill Antronos too, just to make sure he doesn't overstep himself again." She backed away from the mirror, tripped over the torn hem of her gown and fell badly, striking her head against a haphazard pile of books.

"Alain!" Herodra knelt on the other side of the bars, reaching out to her. She didn't move. He rattled the cage, searching for a way to take down the barrier. Ferril tensed, suddenly worried. *Stop it Herodra, you idiot! He must not lose his quarry.*

Alaindra began convulsing violently, flipping over several times, pausing only to swear at the mirror every few seconds. She finally finished, and stretched luxuriously, laughing again. Hero gave up trying to pull down the bars and instead stretched his arms through them.

"Alain. Oh, Earth. Are you all right?"

"My Hero," she said languidly. "I am winning." Laughter. "He's giving up. He's becoming too tired to keep fighting with me. But I won't stop. Not until I've cast him *out.*" She snickered, then sat up. "Hero, I need you to do something important for me before I can come out of this cage. Do you know why I have been sick?"

"If I knew I would have found you a cure long ago."

"Antronos brought one of the—" she paused and struggled for a moment "—Murdek to me and let it inhabit my mind. I now know everything he knew. The Murdek could only pass into others by direct contact unless they used Jait. He is the key to long distance manipulation. I need Jait to send this Murdek somewhere else, into something that can be immediately killed and destroyed. It must be done quickly. I cannot tolerate living with this thing any longer."

Hero's face wrinkled further. Ferril hadn't thought that was possible.

"Alain, this is all very troubling. I don't doubt you, but Jait was killed shortly after you fell sick."

"Killed? How long has it been?"

"Over a year."

She stared at him. She drew her hands over her own face.

"Am I aged?" she asked.

"You are a magnificent lady, Alaindra."

"Am I still your wife?"

"I have insisted on it."

She sat motionless for a long while, until Hero called to her again, pleading with her not to fall back into catatonia. She turned back to him.

"A year. It's taken me far too long to win an internal battle. And now you tell me Jait is dead. There must be another way. Go to the Yrati then, and ask what they know."

"Perhaps Antronos—"

"He is self-serving and not trustworthy. He did this to me! Antronos and his Murdek will die! And not a word to the rest of the House. They have become used to my confinement. My return would upset the new balance of power and stir up assassination plots."

"As my Lady wishes."

Alaindra sat absently rubbing the dry skin of her hands. She stood, walked to the bars and stared past them, watching Hero leave. Ferril let the wall around him fall in a soft patter, then jumped to the floor. The soft layer of sand muted the noise of his movements, and Alaindra was much too occupied with the ruckus in her own head to notice much outside of herself. Feeling mischievous, he pulled a bottle of hand lotion out of his sleeve and left it on Alaindra's stool, then retreated back into the shadows. After a moment, she went back to her seat and saw the bottle.

"What?" She picked it up and looked around to see where it had come from. It took her a few moments before she registered what she saw leaning against the darkest wall of her cage.

"How did you get in here?"

He smiled and moved towards her. "There are many ways in," he said. He limped badly, and as he came into the light, Alaindra's eyes flicked to his wooden leg. "So, Antronos knew you were here all along. I wish I had found out from him sooner. I've been looking for you, Sephus."

Alaindra backed away from him. "How do you know that name?" she demanded.

"I know *all* their names. You'd better not try to run," said Ferril. Alaindra looked around the detritus on the floor, and finally snatched up the arm of a broken chair, which she pointed at him.

"What do you want?"

Ferril snickered. "No need to play hostess, Lady. I'll quite simply take what I wish."

"Are you threatening me?"

"Threatening?" repeated Ferril. "Do you mean something like having 'your entrails stuffed into your eye sockets after you've been pithed in such a way that you'll be paralyzed, but not insensate?' Why, yes. I suppose I am. So sorry, Alaindra, but you've just lost your chance at vengeance."

29
Osteolysis

Antronos sighed with the anticipation of failure as he seated himself in the sand opposite the oasis. The fact that the Desert hadn't shifted this odd spot of vegetation out of existence didn't encourage him— he cynically reasoned that if the oasis were of any use to him, it would certainly have disappeared. He took his precious cache of red finger bones from his pocket, and not really expecting an answer, casually began tossing them into the water, reasoning that he had nothing to lose, since the phalanges seemed useless in summoning the ghouls anyway.

"Anyone there?" he called out.

Nothing. He had four bones left.

Sighing again, he re-pocketed the bones and rolled up his trouser legs. His hope of rescuing Jait was futile without knowing where the Murdek were. Draping the bottom of his cloak over one arm and carrying his sandals, he carefully toed his way across the riverbed. On the other side, he strained his eyes for any hint of strange auras on the oasis ground, or any indication of the vibrancy he had noted when the ghouls had given him the first dream of Jait as a fawn. Nothing. He began to wander aimlessly, now looking for strange behaviour of insects or the few small trickles of water running over the ground. All of them seemed to be natural in their actions, the insects happily minding their own random movements, and the water obeying the laws of gravity. No strange stone temples veered into sight either.

Now there's a thought! Temples veering into sight. Just like in the Desert, subject to some inexplicable magnetic whimsy that could move a building's position. Fumbling in his pockets for magnets, Antronos managed to recover three of his old set, and began to look around for a flat surface where he could see them spin freely. Finding a lichen covered rock that was fairly level, he arranged the magnets in a triangle and waited. After a moment they began to twitch. Then their movements pulsated in unison: three quarter turns to the right, a pause, four to the left.

Earth, thank you! Now what? Antronos dug around the base of the rock, wondering if he had accidentally found a secret opening to the ghouls' lair. Well, of course not. Anywhere in the solid Earth could be their lair. Experimentally, he placed a finger bone in the middle of the triangle. Both magnets and bone twisted into a single orientation and held steady. Antronos smiled. He should have known. Deciding he would follow the bearing indicated by the tip of the finger rather than the joint, he scooped up the magnets and bone, and headed in that direction.

He went north, uphill. He was walking alongside a dried creek bed. The surroundings started to look familiar. His heart began to pound.

The gnarled tree trunks eventually gave way into an opening that looked like it may once have held the pool where he had dreamt he had seen Jait killed. However, there was no pool, and no fawn. The absence of the fulfilling emotion he had felt the last time he had touched the fawn in his dream state left him aching with an empty yearning. Some of the rocks on the ground before him looked like they might be pale and shiny if they were underwater, as they had been in his vision. At any rate, he had run into the pool to pick up the dead fawn, and that was when he had found himself running towards the stone temple.

Antronos backed up a few paces, then charged towards the centre of the opening. He remained in the opening. *Wrong angle?* He tried it again. *Hmph.*

He explored the edge of the empty might-be pool, looking for an area leading downhill. The ground was pretty much level except for a rough rock face that led upwards. Keeping a firm grip on his impatience, he searched for a way around the rock, so that he could continue in his original direction.

His foot slipped on some gravel, then the Earth gave way beneath his feet. He fell into a sink-hole with a painful jar on his left elbow and hip, a clot of Earth landing on his head. Shaking the sparkly yellow stars from his vision, Antronos tried to shift into a sitting position and groaned in pain. Putting any pressure on his left arm was a mistake. He shifted again and noticed that his pant leg was wet. He had fallen on the edge of an underground pool. He sat up eagerly, as he noticed several bright spots of aura moving in the water. They were blackfish.

Wondering if he should try tossing a finger bone into this water, he paused with the red cylinder still in his hand, watching in fascination as the blackfish suddenly pulled themselves into a series of distinct patterns. Antronos leaned forward, frowning in concentration. Aren had seen images, rather than just fish. He did not. Were the patterns symbols? Letters?

He shifted his position and the pain in his left side flared up, making him dizzy and threatening his consciousness. He rubbed at his eyes, trying to see through the cloud of pain-stars; then he relaxed as he realized that he was finally Seeing.

On campus. The university. Shelves and shelves of languishing, old, magic skeletons. A Sen working with a tiny trowel and brush. Cleaning old, magic bones. *Leave us alone!* The Sen's head twisting around unnaturally. Vernus grinning.

Antronos jerked away, gasping for breath. For a moment he had believed himself face to face with Vernus. He looked over his shoulder and around the cavern to confirm that he was alone with the fish. When he looked back into the pool, intending to ask after his mother, it was empty. Apparently, that was all he would be told.

Well. Trowels and brushes. Shelves with bones. He had a pretty good idea of where to search. The Faculty of Arts and Humanities was on the opposite side of campus from Medicine. He hadn't really thought it was important to look there before.

*****

Antronos paced restlessly in front of an open cabinet displaying the latest publications from the Department of Anthropology and Archaeology. He had found a set of non-descript grey robes, and he had cut his hair, hoping to gain some form of anonymity. He doubted the Murdek would be able to do anything if they did spot him. He was more worried about what would happen if Aren or King Liam found Jait before he did. So far, no one with hazy grey or double auras had walked past his self-appointed sentry post, and he was growing concerned that he had interpreted the ghouls' message wrong.

It had to be right. Where else on campus would it be normal to be in possession of a desiccated corpse outside of the Faculty of Medicine? And it made sense that Vernus would come back to the university where he might have a lab. It matched the historical pattern Antronos had dug up in the archives.

Deciding he had lingered too long, and was risking being noticed, he tucked the box he was carrying under one arm and sauntered as casually as he could down the hallway towards the research labs. Each time someone walked past, he kept his eyes averted so they wouldn't see his pupils.

His box contained the device he had constructed from Tibeau's flare and Opalena's mind-blocker. Once the idea had struck him, he hadn't been able to sleep until he'd finished with his poisonous creation. When he had unwrapped the red and blue paper, he had found a hive of powder-containing sections, designed to explode one after the other. It had suited his purposes perfectly. With a sense of ironic glee, he had also added a few components from the items he had accepted from the House of Dra while still in their employ. Perhaps that artistic whimsy had been unnecessary, but it provided a good disguise, and he felt he owed Alaindra at least that much of a part in his plan.

He reached the end of the laboratories and found nothing that reminded him of Murdek. Should he go back and attempt to actually walk into the labs? Was it worth the risk? *Stop*, he told himself. *Think. What else could the images have meant?*

Storage. He had seen shelves everywhere in his vision. He had just assumed that they were in a laboratory. Antronos walked back to the Department's main foyer and glanced through the directory posted on the wall to find where someone might store mummified remains. Any such rooms must have been private, as there was no listed common room.

A pair of professors entered the foyer, talking loudly and introducing a group of visitors to an administrator behind a desk at the opposite end of the cavern. They appeared to be giving a tour, pointing out everyone and everything along the way. Antronos grit his teeth and ducked back into the laboratory wing, scouting through it one last time, keeping an eye open for unmarked entryways. Again, nothing. If the ghouls knew where Vernus was, why couldn't one of them come here and lead him with its aura? He stood at the end of the hall, deciding what to do next. Students were beginning to notice that there was a stranger who appeared to be looking for someone, and were giving him friendly glances, as if deciding when to ask him if he needed help. Not wanting to risk going through the foyer, Antronos took the back exit that led out to the Arts Mall, and sighed in frustration and relief as the crowded bustle and noise of the students washed him in anonymity. Feeling hungry, he wandered to the end of the mall and into the Market Caverns, thinking that perhaps he should find some food to take back to Opalena and Leod. He would have to try contacting the ghouls again. Maybe they could be coaxed into some sort of clarification.

He was in the lowest tier of the Market, walking past the hovels of fishmongers and dung sellers. Not wanting to meet with Shenan's widow, he moved into the back access and maintenance tunnels, thinking he could go up a few tiers from there.

Earth's Bones!

Antronos pulled into a side tunnel, wincing at the scrabbling noise he made. Meriamdan, wrapped in a dark grey shawl but unmistakable nonetheless, didn't seem to notice, and kept tottering towards some cavern at the end of the passageway. *The Murdek were here?* It was so close to the outside docks of the Market Caverns. Two or three dung sellers walked through the very same tunnel seconds later, talking loudly. Well, why not? No one would expect them to hide here, and with the overall decrepit state of the humanity that normally resided in the lower Market tiers, they really wouldn't stand out that much. Antronos peeked into the tunnel again, calculating the risk of getting closer. The decision was made for him as another shadow loomed in the tunnel. He pulled back again, and caught his breath as Ferril limped past, his double aura glimmering both yellow and hazy blue. He seemed completely calm and in control. He was carrying Murdek willingly.

Without hesitation, Ferril lumbered in the same direction Meriamdan had gone. Was there another way in? Antronos waited until he was sure no one else was going to walk past, then dashed across the tunnel and crawled into a service port that led to a series of bays where maintenance workers could access the ducts that vented the Market Caverns to the surface. The bays didn't reach very far, but the vent itself stretched back into the rock in the direction Meriamdan and Ferril had gone.

Carefully sliding the box in front of him and making sure he did not shake it too much, Antronos crawled through the vent. His hand slipped and he nearly slumped noisily against the metal grate of a duct opening when he caught sight of Iegat patrolling a short stretch of back tunnel lit by a smoky torch. He held his breath and slid past the grate as quickly as he could, afraid that the smoke might make him cough. He moved over a stretch of empty cavern before reaching a second grate over a wider space filled with dank air. It was unlikely the river would have seeped into a room surrounded by hard rock, so someone must have purposefully brought a large quantity of water into this cave. The image of Tibeau's bloated face flashed through his mind.

He could see nothing, so he put his ear against the metal bars and strained for any noises at all. After a few moments, he thought he could pick out an intermittent, low moan. Almost like someone who was very weak was trying to talk. A shuffling noise told him that somebody else had entered the room and was shifting something heavy around. Water dripping. Another moan, louder this time. A ripping sound. Silence. As quietly as he could, Antronos unclipped the grate from its housing and lifted it to the side. He lowered his head through the vent opening very slowly, until he could see into the cavern with one eye.

The floor of the cave was indented into a pool, filled with water, and surrounded by damp sand. The corpse of the former High Prince lay in the indentation, completely stiff, his empty eye sockets bleak, chest cavity wrenched open by metal clamps. His aura was shining white, and gauzily wafting from a point on his forehead, as if Vernus had to pin him there somehow to stop him from drifting away. A second man, also filleted, lay discarded in a pool of blood, his chest cavity empty and gaping. Vernus turned from this man and shuffled away, holding a bloody mess of organs in his hands. He deposited these into Jait, and scooping up fistfuls of the damp sand, proceeded to smooth these over Jait's skin. He began to whisper, then his muttering became louder as he chanted in Old Temlochti. Antronos was filled with disappointed anger as he recognized some phrases his mother had used when summoning water in the Desert. Vernus knew the same magic, and was using it to do something to Jait. A dark-haired Murdek woman crept into the cave.

"It will take," Vernus told her. "Look, the Desert already weaves the organs into his body." Indeed, the sand seemed to fold over Jait's skin and fasten it as Vernus removed the clamps.

The woman leaned over Jait and touched his forehead. "Then why does he still not live?" she asked. Vernus made an impatient gesture and strode out of the cave. The woman stroked Jait's forehead, then also left.

This was probably Antronos' best chance. If he waited, he would be giving the Murdek more time to finish whatever their plans were. He slid out of the vent, painfully jarring his sore hip when he fell. He reached up, and on his toes, was able to tease the box forward enough to grab it and carefully lift it out, wincing as he almost tipped it too much to the side. Looking around for a place to put it down for a minute, Antronos decided to leave it on a table covered in surgery instruments, as it was the only dry spot in the cavern.

He moved over to Jait and saw that his aura was trapped by a strange, sandy seal bearing something like the Murdek insignia on his forehead. If he broke the seal, would Jait be set free? It seemed the easiest thing to try.

Antronos swore as the seal bent one of his fingernails back. *Earth's Guts! What did Vernus put in this stuff?* He leaned over the workbench to find a scalpel. When he turned back, Jait had risen from the pool and had advanced until he was almost within arm's reach. Antronos gawped stupidly at Jait's stumbling corpse for too many seconds, finally ducking under Jait's outstretched arm just before getting throttled. He stepped back, covering his nose and mouth with his sleeve in order to stop the stench from making him gag.

"I remember you," gurgled Jait. "Bug-eyed man who wouldn't help me swim away. I dreamt of finding you. Are we face to face at last, or are you going to leave me again?"

Seeing that Jait would follow his movements, Antronos glanced around the cavern for a way out. There were three tunnels, two of them exiting in the direction Vernus had gone, so he took the third, looking over his shoulder nervously. If Vernus were still aware of Jait's every move as he had been before, this would probably bring the old goat running. Jait stumbled after him, growling softly.

The tunnel led into a pit of sliding sand that was open to the surface. Antronos struggled through it, wondering how he was going to reach the opening twenty metres up. His hand hit against something solid, and he tried to climb onto it when it moved. A stone skeleton burst out of the sand, and clawed at him. Antronos yelled at it and thrashed in the opposite direction. Jait's waxy fingers closed over his sore wrist, bending it back painfully. Antronos couldn't break free. Instead he imagined his thoughts plunging into Jait's spirit, telling him to let go. His vision blacked out as his mind was swept away in a huge wash of Jait's power. Stunned by the immensity of Jait's soul, Antronos tried to pull away. He writhed in pain as Jait forced his way into Antronos' head and began to read the memories there. He hit on Antronos' ability to form small piles of sand, used it, and the two of them shot up into the air on a sudden pillar of grit. The force of impact broke them apart as they landed.

Antronos shook the stars from his view, trying to get himself to breathe. Jait was lying a few feet away. He flipped over, and began to drag himself towards Antronos, who forced himself to stand up and back away. Jait also stood and followed. It began to rain, and with the extended exposure to water, Jait became more supple, and more determined to catch Antronos.

His voice also became clearer. "I remember that I'm angry with you for something," said Jait, and his stride increased. Antronos began to run. It wasn't long before Jait was running too, hounding him over the 'Cliff. Antronos was struggling now, as the mud caught at his sandals and had to be kicked off before he could continue. Dead shrubs caught at his outer robe, and he shed it, hopping from boulder to boulder, while Jait howled in rage and limberly ran through the mud, almost catching him.

The oasis can't be that much farther, thought Antronos. *The ghouls* must *show me how to save him.* He slipped, and smashed his chin against the rock before managing to roll away from Jait. Still dazed, he ran raggedly uphill, hoping to find the small might-be pool where he had had the vision, and from there, maybe this time he would run onto the hill that led down to the stone temple. At the top of the hill there were no features that he recognized. Picking a direction at random, he ran down the slope, seeing neither the forest, nor the temple.

"Where are you?" he screamed. He pulled the remaining red finger bones from his pocket and threw them away from him. "Here are your bones! Come and get them! Come on! Where are you!"

He thought he saw a shifting in the ground in front of him, moving in a zig-zag pattern towards where he stood. The rain was making all the living insects and nascent plant roots glisten with aura, rendering anything new virtually indistinguishable. He paused and peered at the ground, trying to discern what he was actually seeing. Jait caught up to him, and grabbed his shoulders, digging in his stiff fingers. Antronos gasped, and started to struggle away from him, his eyes darting back and forth, as he now made out hooded figures moving cautiously towards him from the hills. They weren't the Red Ghouls. Their eerily decimated auras were that of the Murdek.

"Jait," he gasped, "we have to leave. Let me go. We can't stay here."

Jait only snarled at him, and grasped him more tightly, pulling him down. *Down?* Jait had sunk into the ground past his knees. There were red, bony hands with blinding auras tugging on Jait's limbs as he sank further into the rain-softened Earth, pulling Antronos after him. As Antronos twisted his head upwards to avoid suffocation, the last thing he saw were a set of black eyes in an enraged face, clawing at his clothing, trying to pull him back without succeeding.

30

Found

"Leod, sweetheart! You'll make yourself sick!" Opalena shouted. The child shook his head and still refused to come out of the rain. He looked skinny and frozen to the point of delirium. She stepped out into the drizzle again when Leod had his back turned, hoping that she would be able to catch him this time. Leod saw her and skipped away.

"This is where I saw him last!" he shouted over his shoulder. Opalena cursed under her breath and stepped back into the doorway.

"There isn't anyone there!" she hollered. Thinking she could coax the child back in with some biscuits, she went to the hearth and rummaged through one of the sacks Antronos had left.

Leod darted in through the door, bringing in enough water to turn the dust on the floor to mud. He just stood there, looking bewildered and upset.

"Well, nice to see you've come to your senses." Opalena picked up a blanket and started towards him.

"Opalena," Leod said loudly. "You remember the ghouly stories you told me?"

"Yes, *Haalom.*"

"Well, I think my grampa is all stiff and ghouly, too. They're out marching in the rain, just now." Leod nodded emphatically to stress his point.

Opalena laughed and shook her head. "That was just a story, Leod. I didn't mean to make you wish for your grandfather. I'm sorry. I miss him too."

"Well, actually he's outside right now, and I think he wants to come in." Leod pushed aside the door to let Opalena look into the dead, empty eye sockets of the former High Prince, and watch as he lifted his head to howl.

* * * * *

"Leod, it's about bloody time!" spluttered Antronos. "Why didn't you

229

pull us out right away?"

"I'm too small!" protested Leod. Antronos seemed not to hear him and continued ranting.

"Rotted bloody ghouls took both of us rather than just him! I was trying to get rid of him, not bloody spend the entire night buried in the ground with him! And it was close quarters, let me tell you. I mean really close! I thought I knew too much about him before; well, now I know all about his innards as well as—"

Opalena handed Antronos a blanket as he began sobbing. Trying to not look at it, she tossed a second blanket over the corpse of Jait, which had fallen over on its back once out of the rain. It was still twitching feebly.

"Earth, Antronos," she said. "What are we supposed to do with him like that?"

Antronos looked more confused than Leod. He sat sprawled on the floor of the cavern where Jait had dumped him, wearing only his inner robe, which he now tried to collect about himself into a more dignified fold.

"Uh. I don't know. I didn't think that far ahead." He turned to look at Jait. "I guess I didn't expect him to look so disgusting."

Leod stomped his foot and screamed at Antronos.

Opalena stepped away, deciding they needed to wait until they were calm enough to discuss this strange situation rationally. Rationally? What was she thinking? It was no wonder Antronos was acting insane. He probably was. One thing was certain—the last time Jait had been trapped in his body, he had asked her for release. Although Aren and Antronos wanted Jait to be safely anchored away from the Murdek, it wasn't right, him being pulled back into, of all things, a dead shell. Besides, she really didn't want him here. Steeling herself, she went to the corpse and gently lifted the edge of the blanket.

There was a fine network of blessing runes traced over the sides of Jait's face, disappearing under the collar and resurfacing at his wrists to run over the tips of each finger. Opalena was mildly amused that the blessings didn't seem to have worked. She pushed the corpse onto its side and gently lifted the burial clothes away. Prolonged exposure to water had made the tissues swell, making it difficult to see if there were any wounds on the back, especially a thin, narrow one that could have been made by a sword. Was it really true, what Aren said he had done? Was it even possible? She brushed the skin with her fingertips, unable to see much. Rolling Jait back over, she stared curiously at the odd sandy seal on his forehead. It looked like it carried a double imprint: one Murdek, the other an ancient Yrati symbol she had seen only in some of their older texts. She tentatively reached out and peeled it from his skin. As the block of sand rested in her palm, memories ran through her head at dizzying speed.

"I did want to treat you honourably, Opalena. I just never got the chance."

"Is the medicine you gave me poisoned or not?"

"Those injections are responsible for giving him bloodrot and nearly killing him in the first place!"

"I am dying. It doesn't matter how hard you try, you're treating the symptoms, not curing the disease. It is very slow and painful. One day I'll be dead, and it will just be my body walking around, a dead stiffened husk with me trapped inside."

"Jait is dying. And he is afraid. He sent me to ask the Yrati to pray for him."

"...on the Night of the Third Moon. Please Aren, do it."

Opalena broke away. She tried to stand without crying or vomiting, dropping the seal and cradling her hand to her chest like it had been burnt. She tried to stumble to the door before her nausea got the better of her, and she tripped and fell.

Antronos broke off his blubbering to stare at her.

"GRAMPA!" yelled Leod. "Look at Grampa!" They looked. The skin had softened to a warm colour. The hair looked smooth and lustrous. The eyes had filled again, and wore an achingly familiar expression of boredom and disgust. Jait breathed in, closed his eyes and seemed to sleep. Opalena struggled upright, then ran to the door to be sick.

✳✳✳✳✳

Antronos had left her alone with Jait and Leod, saying he needed to find out what had happened to his device. The confusion racing through her mind was threatening to make her stomach heave again. Jait still lay on the floor of the cavern, apparently sleeping, despite Leod's incessant chatter and pats on the face. Opalena was on her couch across from them, curled up under a heap of blankets. She had let herself believe that once Antronos had used his device, it would all be over. Now it was just sitting uselessly somewhere in the Murdek caverns, so much wasted effort. The significance of Dagnaum's prophecy, and the possibility of its being fulfilled was looming up and threatening to overwhelm her. Was Aren right? Did it mean she had to give Jait a child? How could she? The thought was unbearable.

Needing to be as alone as possible, Opalena pulled the blankets over her head and gave in to the exhaustion she felt, only for a moment. She couldn't sleep, not now, when Leod was so vulnerable. That would have to wait until Antronos returned.

Had Leod stopped chattering? Opalena peeked out from under the blankets in confusion. Had she slept? The cavern was empty.

"Leod? Leod, where are you?"

Wearily, Opalena pulled herself up. There was no way Leod could have dragged Jait anywhere. Not far, at least. She shuffled over to the doorway, stopping in shock as she realized that there were no drag marks, but rather two sets of footprints. One small, one large.

"Earth!"

Not stopping to grab a cloak, Opalena rushed out into the rain, stumbling off the narrow path and nearly falling down the sheer cliff face. She managed to catch onto an outcropping of rock and steady herself.

"Leod!" she hollered into the drizzle. She thought she could see a small, blond head bobbing somewhere towards the bottom of the 'Cliff, and began to cast about for a footpath leading down. As she turned to go around the other way, she ran right into someone who had been standing directly behind her.

"Ferril? What are you doing here?"

31

Reprisal

Vernus was fuming. His anger boiled so hot none of his Murdek would approach him. It had been days—days—since Jait had been stolen, and days since any new information had come in as to his whereabouts, and Meriamdan had gone off on one of her extended hunts, as she always seemed to choose to do exactly when he needed her council.

Jalena left a note at the periphery of his vision, not daring to hand it to him directly, then skulked away. He snatched it up and read it: Antronos had several hiding places on the surface. Jait was not at any of them. Vernus took a deep breath and forced a modicum of calm over himself. This anger was clouding his judgment. He needed his thoughts clear.

One of the idiots behind him was hovering just at the edge of his peripheral vision.

"What do you want?" he snapped.

"There's a package on your work table," rasped Iegat.

"What?"

"A package. It's addressed to Meriamdan."

Vernus whirled around. Iegat was pointing towards the hidden laboratory.

"How did it get in here?"

Iegat shrugged.

Vernus strode towards the back cavern and hunted through the clutter on his worktable until he found it. It was perhaps the size of a book, with a non-descript paper wrapping. The label on it was indeed addressed to Meriamdan. He looked down at the package suspiciously. He picked it up and gently turned it over, checking all sides. Something inside sloshed and began to seep through the paper wrapping. A faint scent wafted from it. Perfume? The paper covering the corner of the box had peeled away, revealing the blue and white packaging of an authentic cosmetics kit from the House of Dra. What in Earth was going on? Meriamdan never cared how she smelled, and she absolutely would *never* buy something from the House of Dra. He walked back to the other chamber where there was more light and put the box on a table. He wasn't so stupid as to open it.

"No one touches that!" he commanded the other Murdek. He pushed through the tangle of roots and moss that covered the entryway to Meriamdan's private chambers to see if she had returned yet. She hated having her privacy invaded, but it would be just like her to have been back for hours without notifying him.

"Meri?" She was back and had been for quite a while by the looks of it. Her desiccated, disembowelled form was pinned through the head to the soft clay wall of the cavern by a roasting spit. Her eye and mouth hung open. Several medicinal needles protruded from the base of her neck as though someone had used them to paralyse her first, before tacking her to the wall and slitting her guts.

Vernus shook his head and looked again. He couldn't believe it. Not Meriamdan. Wasn't possible. Nobody could have come in here and murdered her right under his nose. He put his hand out and touched the crusted edge of her face, feeling nothing but dry emptiness. He was too numb to think beyond the ludicrousness of her being dead. Gone. A dull thud sounded behind him, and screaming began in the lab. It jolted his anger loose and he rushed back through the corridor.

"Earth damn you all! I said no one was to touch—"

The package still sat on the desk. The outside of it had dissolved and one of the perfume bottles inside had shattered, releasing a noxious smelling smoke into the air. Several of the Murdek were lying on the floor, clawing at their eyes. A second dull thud was heard just before another bottle popped apart, sending a spray of tiny darts in all directions. Vernus tried to duck and cover his face, but a few of the darts still embedded in his fingers. Whatever was on them was potent, sending prickly numbing pain up his arm faster than he would have expected. It was a mind-blocker! He began feeling his psyche close in on itself.

"Antronos!" he hissed. Antronos was the only one skilled enough to have concocted such a thing.

The third dull thud sent a concussion throughout the lab that slammed Vernus against the floor. Jalena landed on top of him.

"Get off!" Vernus shouted.

The fourth dull thud engulfed the laboratory in flames. Vernus heard the fifth and sixth thud, but couldn't make sense of what new disasters these triggered.

32

Netting

Antronos hit the ground hard. Groaning, he pushed himself up and put a hand to his cut lip, trying not to laugh. Herodra seemed like such a runt when he wore his simpering courtier persona, but when it came down to a fistfight, he knew all the nastiest gutter tricks, and actually was quite stocky.

"You find this funny, *pachu*?"

"Oh, perhaps not funny. Just extremely ironic." Antronos shuffled onto his feet, this time managing to dodge and block Herodra's punch. He still caught an elbow in the throat, and went down a second time. Getting angry, he kicked out Herodra's feet and barely avoided a return kick in the head.

"What do you want? To kill me?" he asked. He didn't have time for this. He had to go back to Vernus' dungeon and make sure his device went off.

"Actually, yes," replied Herodra. "But I think I'll wait until after you undo whatever it is you did to my wife."

"I didn't want to do that. It was the only way I could avoid killing her outright."

"I don't care." Herodra got up and kicked Antronos in the stomach. "The little beast you put into her says you're a liar, and that's about the only thing I believe right now. I haven't been able to talk to her since she told me. She's lapsed into a coma, and if she dies, for any reason, *you will have killed her outright!*"

Between retches, Antronos managed to ask, "So now what? You beat me senseless?"

"Pick him up," said Herodra, his tone laden with disgust. A few of his henchmen dragged Antronos to his feet. When his vision cleared somewhat, he was surprised to see that Aren was seated on a wooden crate at the opposite side of the alley. *These are new tactics for the Yrati.*

A few shoppers tried to cut through the alley to the other side of the Market Caverns, and were headed off by more Dra personnel. Antronos supposed he didn't want anyone to see this anyway. He made a mock bow towards Aren, as far as the hands restraining him would allow.

"My Lord Yrati. How pleasant to see you here. Have you enjoyed today's entertainment?"

Aren smiled at him. "So. Putting Murdek into Alaindra. I was right about you all along."

"You were not."

"That's very difficult to believe."

Antronos let himself laugh this time, then spat out a mouthful of blood. "So what do you want from me?"

"How about telling us where the Murdek are hiding?"

"Sure. They have a hidden lab right here in the Market Caverns, two tiers down and out past the ninth shipping dock."

Herodra slapped him hard across the face.

"You expect us to believe that? We have spies all over the Markets. They know everything that goes on. If they had seen Murdek, they would have reported it to me." He grabbed Antronos' collar and pulled his head around roughly. "Are you saying I'm stupid? That the Murdek have been hiding right in front of me, and I'm too thick to see it?"

"Well, as tempting as that is—"

Herodra shoved him against the tunnel wall, knocking the breath from him.

"Why don't you just go look?" asked Antronos. "I'm sick of trying to protect you anyway."

"Protect *me*?"

"If you want to walk into the middle of a Murdek nest, you have my blessing. I won't stop you."

"Hero, wait."

Antronos lifted his head and saw that Aren had stood up, and was coming towards him. Herodra's fist was raised and aimed at his face. Aren braced an arm against the wall and leaned close. "Tell me something I'll believe," he said.

"Like what?"

"Like where Ferril is."

"Ferril?" Antronos' bewilderment made the suspicion in Aren's expression deepen. Did the Yrati know Ferril had turned? If they weren't sure, did Antronos dare be the one to tell them? Did he dare lie to Aren now? Herodra was slipping brass rings over his knuckles.

"I—I think he's been following me," Antronos stammered. "I don't know why."

"Is he Murdek?"

Antronos hesitated, suddenly unsure of what the double aura he had seen in Ferril meant. *He couldn't be Murdek!*

"I'm not sure. He hates them for what they did to his student. Opalena can't believe he'd go with them willingly."

"But?"

Antronos said nothing. He didn't know what he thought. Locke had said Ferril's mind was strong enough to resist any invasion, and yet *he had been carrying Murdek.*

Aren's gaze didn't waver. "Is Ferril with them?"

"I don't know," Antronos said finally.

Aren took a step back. "All right," he said. "You have one chance to convince me. We're in the Market Caverns. Let's see this Murdek hideaway you mentioned."

"I hope you're prepared for it."

"Let's imagine that I am."

"Fine. We have to go through the back tunnels."

Antronos pushed away from the wall and stumbled momentarily as the Dra men released him. Aren put out a hand to steady him. After a moment, he took a deep breath and stood on his own, then took a few painful steps towards the opening of the alley.

As they emerged into one of the busier back tunnels, the few lesser merchants (probably engaged in less than legal trading) looked stunned at first to see Herodra anywhere near their territory, then the Yrati High Priest, then Antronos, then Antronos' bloodied face. A workman stepped in front of them, holding up his hands.

"Please forgive me, Lords," he said. "But there's been some sort of accident. These tunnels are closed off until we find out what went wrong." The man took in Antronos' appearance with an expression of surprise, but didn't comment on it.

"We can't stop for an accident," said Herodra.

"It's for your own safety. Please turn around and find some other way. We think a pocket of methane built up from the dung sellers, and somehow ignited. There's been an explosion. Until we find out what went wrong with the venting system—"

My device!

Finding new energy somewhere inside himself, Antronos pushed aside the Dra men, and practically ran to where he had seen Meriamdan and Ferril, no longer bothering to plan a stealthy approach. He slowed down, stepping carefully over strewn rubble, then burnt bodies lying on the ground. Aren pushed past him and entered the cavern.

"It's quite a mess," he said. He began to gingerly turn bodies over, peering into what was left of their faces. Two bodies were stacked, and when Aren pulled one off the other, the one underneath still retained half a face.

"It's Vernus," said Antronos. He leaned over Aren's shoulder to inspect the damage.

Vernus' remaining eye snapped open.

✳✳✳✳✳

At another time, Vernus might have been gratified at how quickly Aren and Antronos recoiled at seeing him still alive, and back-pedaled when he pushed to his feet. The Yrati tried to probe his mind, but was no match for the force of his anger. Vernus shoved him out, and almost managed to climb into Aren's mind until that annoying little snake, Antronos, swung at him with a broken table leg. Vernus easily dodged Aren and Herodra, as they were loath to touch him, but was outraged when Antronos grabbed him without any respect for his powers. He twisted and clawed at Antronos, trying to throttle him quickly, but his charred hand wouldn't grip properly. Unable to kill the snake-boy first, he jumped into his mind and began the internal struggle for control. Vernus' empty body fell down dead, momentarily confusing the others.

"What happened?" Aren demanded, and kicked futilely at Vernus' corpse. Herodra also turned his attention to the body, and Vernus screamed in pain as he shoved against Antronos' will, the shards of the Desert-man's fractured mind slicing through him. Forcing himself not to relent, he managed partial control. Calculating for a split second, Vernus decided to make a dash for the door. He was summarily tripped by one of the Dra henchmen.

"He's here! He's trying to run away!"

Aren grabbed Antronos' shoulders roughly, and held on while the snake-man tried to pry him out. Antronos jabbed himself with one of his own poisoned spikes, the mind-blocker on it closing off areas of Vernus' control. He couldn't jump into Aren who was too powerful, so he tried to force control over the shards of Antronos' Desert-fractured intellect before the drug shut him down completely. He was about to worm his way into final victory, when he was distracted by one of Antronos' thoughts. *Jait! Antronos has him tucked away in some cave!*

That hesitation was enough to cost Vernus dearly. He had miscalculated Aren's ruthlessness, not expecting him to also invade Antronos' mind. The Yrati obviously was not concerned for Antronos' well-being, as he bludgeoned through thoughts and psychic barriers in a brutal search for Vernus. Staying here was not an option.

That left Herodra, but he was so far away! Vernus calculated the distance of the jump, but couldn't make it. He forced Antronos' hand to flail outwards, trying to make contact with Herodra, and the fool obligingly stepped forward, over Vernus' body to catch Antronos' hand and hold it still. At last! Through the contact, Vernus quickly slipped into Herodra, then back into his own body through the ankle that pressed against his neck, all before Herodra realized he had been passed through. He lay still, not giving himself away.

Aren released Antronos.

"Where is he?" shouted Aren. He grabbed the front of Antronos' robes, shaking him for a moment before letting go. He turned around and grabbed Herodra. "Here?" At that moment, while everyone was looking the other way, Vernus bolted from the room and managed to slow the others by flinging down a chair behind him. Herodra caught up to him, but Vernus smacked him in the face with an elbow, and ran out into the tunnels with the others in pursuit. He ran towards a section of the tunnels where he knew the floor had been worn away by the river, and jumped. He was in free-fall for a full three seconds before he was swept underground and away from his attackers by the rushing water.

33

Darkfish

Leod was at the bottom of the 'Cliff, his hand wrapped tightly around Jait's fingers as he happily dragged his grandfather towards the sea. Even though it was raining heavily again, Jait still asked for water, and the sea was the only place Leod could think of to take him. He knew it was somewhere to the south, but not how far away it was, or how long it would take to get there. All around them, the ghouls put on quite a show, their polished red bones rising endlessly in fluid motions from the softened Earth, almost like the wash of a river, as they howled at the sky. They did not sound mournful to Leod now, but rather like they were singing operatically, or cheering on champions.

Needing to rest, Leod climbed onto a boulder and sat down to watch. Jait followed him and hugged Leod to his side, momentarily beginning to shiver. Leod wrapped his arms around his grandfather, thoroughly enjoying this culmination of all the most passionate and secret things in his life.

The night grew darker, and now the ghouls were not visible until they had moved to within a foot of where Leod and Jait sat. Then it seemed that the rain and the night were parted by a hazy shaft of light to let pass a man who had once been a priest. This half-ghoul stumbled up to the boulder and fell against it, his mottled skin peeling from his red skull.

"I am," he said, as he looked up at Leod.

"You were the big Reetee with the black hair," said Leod. "Maxal."

"You are understanding that fish can live in water."

"I don't want him to leave." Leod squirmed farther onto Jait's lap, pulling at his grandfather's arms.

"Perhaps his attachment to you will anchor him for a while. But stiffening won't work, Leod. Not good to keep him so. He wasn't meant for this."

"You want my grampa to die?"

"To cycle, not to get stuck. Understand: a fish swimming free does not leave the ocean. See here."

The ghoul turned and pointed at a second shape emerging through the curtains of rain. Leod stared at the figure open mouthed but speechless. His eyes raked over the man leaning arrogantly on one leg, thumbs looped through his belt, long, tattered hair tossing limply in the wet wind. Leod stared at Derik.

Unaware of anything else, he stood up, dragging Jait with him and went after his father, filled with the overwhelming sensation that he was very close to finally having a family.

34

Nadir

Vernus dragged himself out of the river and stood there for a moment, coughing and trying to get the water out of his ears and nose. He was in an exceptionally foul mood. It was humiliating and infuriating that Antronos and Aren could be so powerful against him.

He had climbed onto the banks in a maintenance tunnel in the outskirts of the city. Checking that no one was around, he ducked into the back tunnels and wound his way towards the surface, then the 'Cliff, where he had seen Jait in Antronos' thoughts. He entered a series of natural catacombs at the base of the 'Cliff, and hunted through them, constantly climbing upward until he finally came across one that had obviously been inhabited for some time.

He searched back and forth, from one end of the small cavern to the next, finding a few items that resonated of Opalena, and the child Leod. Then he came across the sandy seal he had put on Jait's forehead, squashed and half ground into the Earth. He focused on it, trying to sense where Jait had been taken. The pull towards Jait's spirit always seemed to lead to the outer door, but that exited onto a small, unrailed balcony overlooking the sheer cliff face. There was a narrow trail, but a person would have to be completely idiotic to go down that way.

He ducked into the cave, knocked his burnt head against a rock protrusion and began an extensive string of cursing. When he looked up, he saw that Opalena was there. He stared at her in amazement.

"I have another present for you," she said, then turned and walked out into the back tunnel. *Present? What in Earth? What does she mean 'another?'* He followed her, chasing after her when she disappeared into one of the small side caves. When he entered the one he thought she had gone into, Ferril sat there grinning like an idiot. There was something about his smile, something unnervingly familiar. He thought he might recognize it, perhaps if it were in the right context. He flinched as Opalena stepped towards him from the corner of the cave.

"This is for you." She gestured towards Ferril, who didn't move. Vernus looked back and forth at the pair of them, completely confused. He took a step closer to Ferril and peered into his face. The Yrati began rocking side to side, and hissing something strange. Vernus put his ear up close to Ferril's mouth.

"Can you imagine my *despair*, Vernus, at finding that *none of what you say is true*?"

Vernus gawped at him, recognizing the voice, and deeply worried that the tone was completely unfriendly.

"By the Earth!"

Ferril's hand shot out and struck him square in the face, the Yrati's fingers sinking deep into his thoughts. Sephus slithered into him and coiled around his mind.

"An eternity!" Sephus screamed. "You promised me an eternity, but you didn't tell me it would be in hell!" He began peeling strips of Vernus away, chewing things that were still attached, grinding salt into every fester. "Let me give you a taste of my dear Alaindra's hospitality," Sephus hissed. "This is what you sent me to!"

"Opalena!" Vernus reached out to her, but she stepped away from him.

"This is to go with the wall hanging Ferril left for you," she said. "Meriamdan looks rather good as a tapestry, don't you think?"

Ferril grabbed him around the neck and spoke directly into his ear. "I enjoyed slitting your den-mother down her middle. It felt as good as when you brutalized me. When you killed my Tibeau. I enjoyed tearing Alaindra from your little pet, Sephus. And now, I'm going to enjoy watching you die."

Vernus began to fight back, but this was a battlefield he was unfamiliar with. Ferril was too strong for him to jump into, and never before had he needed to protect himself in his own mind. He had no ready defence against this torment. He stared at his opponent and saw that he had eyes as black as sackcloth *made* of hair. And there was a name written on his opponent's forehead which sounded like his own. He struck out, and knew that he wounded Sephus because he felt the pain himself. He reached out towards Opalena, trying to transfer himself into her body, where he could then kill Sephus, who would be left inside of Vernus. He should never have let his guard down! He knew not to trust Opalena! She skittered away from him, and distracted, he left a hole in his guard through which Sephus struck at him again.

They became entwined with each other, the two of them so similar that he had trouble telling himself from Sephus. Sometimes he wounded himself. He was not aware whether he was with Sephus, or he was Sephus, or he was alone, still eating himself. In the end he was not aware.

35

Healing

Aren broke the embrace before he started to cry. He was finally allowing himself to feel the full extent of how much he had missed Ferril, and regretted deeply that he had been too blind to enjoy the support they might have given each other. He stepped away from the new Yrati High Priest and genuflected before him.

"Are you sure you won't stay?" Ferril asked him.

"I can't. You saw how it ruined me." Aren could not look him in the eye.

"At least for the reinterment, Aren. It would mean a lot if you were part of the ceremony."

"I don't think so. I've seen enough of Jait to last me a lifetime."

"Will we ever see you again?"

"Perhaps. But not for a long time. I'm going away to heal."

"In the Desert?"

"Well . . ." Aren looked around the bleak landscape. "It seems there are many things for me to learn. To accept. And I think a little suffering might do me good."

Ferril watched him with a knowing glint in those eyes that seemed permanently darkened. They had both suffered, they had both killed, and they were both keeping silent. Perhaps neither of them should belong to the Yrati. Then again, one must know and understand evil in order to be able to fight it. If he were honest with himself, his own apparent humility was stained with his jealously over Antronos' success. There *was* a lot he could learn from the Desert.

"You know that I will always love you," Ferril said after a few moments.

"Likewise, brother. I wish I had been better to you."

The two men smiled at each other, unable to say more, and Aren finally turned away when Ferril's eyes began to fill with tears. He stepped out onto the open plain and looked out over the sand. He had never been on the surface for more than a few hours, yet some deep inner motivation assured him that he would not only survive but return to the Yrati with profound knowledge of not only himself, but the entire Earth.

36

Faith

Alaindra was surprised to find that she was happy. Antronos had gotten away from her, but she didn't care. She just didn't have the heart for revenge once Sephus had left her. And, she supposed, Antronos had done his best to set things right, albeit it cost her a year of her life. All she could think about was Herodra, and not letting any more time slip away from them. Her family were still busy taking over the world, but she didn't worry about them either. Leave them to the Markets, she thought, and leave Antronos to the Desert and the Plains.

Herodra came up behind her and wrapped her in his arms. They stood there together, gazing out at the skylight, watching as the night painted momentary glistening patterns in the dust of the sky.

37

Ovum

Antronos picked up his magnets from the sand and put them back in his pocket. He was beginning to understand the Desert, and was starting to predict its whimsy before its rocks moved, or some odd structure rose out of its grainy depths. He stretched his hand out over the dunes and let his own aura rise from his body. The Desert responded, the sand rising in pulsating waves, circles, lines: whatever was Antronos' whimsy. Leod laughed and clapped.

"Make a turtle!" he demanded. Antronos thought for a moment, then raised a swirling dome with the rough approximation of a protruding head and legs.

"Make a fish!" Even more easily done.

"Look!" Leod was pointing at something several dunes over. Antronos let the sand fall and saw a lone figure dressed in black walking stiltedly over the far dunes. Shaggy blond hair covered its face. A few seconds later, Antronos felt the Desert shift, and the man sunk into the sand.

"Hoya!" called Leod, waving madly. "Don't forget to cycle and come back!"

Regardless of what the ghouls had told Leod about his father, Antronos would just as soon not meet up with him. Since Derik had not stiffened and turned red, Antronos had come to the conclusion that his spirit still roamed the Earth as some sort of penance, or because he could not release the bitterness that entrapped him. At any rate, allowing himself to believe that also made it easier to accept never having found his mother in the Desert's depths—at least she wasn't trapped and suffering as Derik was.

"Come on," he said, scooping up Leod from the sand. "You've been out here long enough." Leod giggled and deliberately twisted about so that he was as awkward to carry as possible. Antronos wrapped an arm around Leod's knees and let the rest of him hang upside down.

It was easy now, to find his hut no matter where the Desert decided to move it. He walked towards it, pushed the cardboard door aside, bustled in and dropped Leod on the couch. The child immediately bounded up and ran to Opalena, climbing into her lap. Antronos caught his breath, as he always did when he saw her. Her pale hair seemed to form a shimmering, cascading halo that mixed with her double aura—one hers, one Jait's. Antronos still found it difficult to believe that she had consented to come with him into the Desert, or that he had ever had the nerve to ask her. She seemed content, and had never complained about the isolation, apparently needing the profound barrenness.

"Is Grampa here yet?" Leod asked her.

Antronos smiled. *My two fawns.*

"No," Opalena said, giving him a kiss on the nose. "And you know you can't call him that anymore."

"When's he coming?"

"It'll be a while yet."

"Is my father coming too?"

Opalena gave Antronos a look over the top of Leod's head.

"We'll see," she said.

Leod wriggled away from her. "I'm going to play with Lizard."

"All right."

Antronos sat next to her and leaned over to give her a kiss. She put her arms around him and returned it gently. Resting her head on his shoulder, she entwined her fingers with his. Antronos saw she had been reading his thesis.

"Are you ever going to finish this thing?" she asked him.

"I don't know. It hardly seems important now."

"Amphetam will be devastated. You did promise it to him before we left."

"Aww, that was just to get him off my back."

"I never thought being this happy was possible."

Antronos smiled wistfully. "There was a point where I didn't think being alive was possible."

"It's a shame about Sephus."

"He wished it. And I'm grateful to him for it."

"Still, it would have been nice if he could also have been healed."

"Hmm." Antronos didn't want to talk about Sephus. He put his hand over the swell of Opalena's belly, from which Jait's aura radiated. "Might be a girl."

"That's entirely possible."

"I think I'd prefer it."

"Really?"

"Well, we already have Leod. Would be nice to have a girl."

Antronos reached out and flipped over to the last page he had written in his thesis. It really was a lot of garbage. Even if he did send it to Amphetam, it was unlikely the Chancellor would accept it and grant a degree. He re-read the last paragraph: *Water is deadly, but a fish can live in water. If you make sure they don't permanently kill the fish, there will still be life afterwards. Although the body drowns, so long as the soul swims free, life will continue. This is true longevity.*

Don't miss these exciting titles brought to you
by Dragon Moon Press, EDGE Science Fiction
and Fantasy and Tesseracts!

Alien Deception, Tony Ruggiero (tp) ISBN-13: 978-1-896944-34-0
Alien Revelation,Tony Ruggiero (tp) ISBN-13: 978-1-896944-34-8
Alphanauts, J. Brian Clarke (tp) ISBN-13: 978-1-894063-14-2
Ancestor, Scott Sigler (tp) ISBN-13: 978-1-896944-73-9
Apparition Trail, The, Lisa Smedman (tp)
          ISBN-13: 978-1-894063-22-7
As Fate Decrees, Denysé Bridger (tp) ISBN-13: 978-1-894063-41-8

Billibub Baddings and The Case of the Singing Sword, Tee Morris (tp)
ISBN-13: 978-1-896944-18-0
Black Chalice, The, Marie Jakober (hb)
          ISBN-13: 978-1-894063-00-5
Blue Apes, Phyllis Gotlieb (pb) ISBN-13: 978-1-895836-13-4
Blue Apes, Phyllis Gotlieb (hb) ISBN-13: 978-1-895836-14-1

Chalice of Life, The, Anne Webb (tp) ISBN-13: 978-1-896944-33-3
Chasing The Bard by Philippa Ballantine (tp)
          ISBN-13: 978-1-896944-08-1
Children of Atwar, The by Heather Spears (pb)
          ISBN-13: 978-0-88878-335-6
Claus Effect by David Nickle & Karl Schroeder, The (pb)
          ISBN-13: 978-1-895836-34-9
Claus Effect by David Nickle & Karl Schroeder, The (hb)
          ISBN-13: 978-1-895836-35-6
Complete Guide to Writing Fantasy, The Volume 1: Alchemy with Words,
edited by Darin Park and Tom Dullemond (tp)
          ISBN-13: 978-1-896944-09-8
Complete Guide to Writing Fantasy, The Volume 2: Opus Magus, edited by
Tee Morris and Valerie Griswold-Ford (tp)
          ISBN-13: 978-1-896944-15-9
Complete Guide to Writing Fantasy Volume 3: The Author's Grimoire,
edited by Valerie Griswold-Ford & Lai Zhao (tp)
          ISBN-13: 978-1-896944-38-8
Complete Guide to Writing Science Fiction Volume 1: First Contact, edited
by Dave A. Law & Darin Park (tp)
          ISBN-13: 978-1-896944-39-5
Courtesan Prince, The, Lynda Williams (tp)
          ISBN-13: 978-1-894063-28-9
Dark Earth Dreams, Candas Dorsey & Roger Deegan (comes with a CD)
          ISBN-13: 978-1-895836-05-9

Darkling Band, The, Jason Henderson (tp)
        ISBN-13: 978-1-896944-36-4
Darkness of the God, Amber Hayward (tp)
        ISBN-13: 978-1-894063-44-9
Darwin's Paradox, Nina Munteanu (tp) ISBN-13: 978-1-896944-68-5
Daughter of Dragons, Kathleen Nelson (tp)
        ISBN-13: 978-1-896944-00-5
Distant Signals, Andrew Weiner (tp) ISBN-13: 978-0-88878-284-7
Dominion, J. Y. T. Kennedy (tp) ISBN-13: 978-1-896944-28-9
Dragon Reborn, The Kathleen H. Nelson (tp)
        ISBN-13: 978-1-896944-05-0
Dragon's Fire, Wizard's Flame, Michael R. Mennenga (tp)
        ISBN-13: 978-1-896944-13-5
Dreams of an Unseen Planet, Teresa Plowright (tp)
        ISBN-13: 978-0-88878-282-3
Dreams of the Sea, Élisabeth Vonarburg (tp)
        ISBN-13: 978-1-895836-96-7
Dreams of the Sea, Élisabeth Vonarburg (hb)
        ISBN-13: 978-1-895836-98-1

EarthCore, Scott Sigler (tp) ISBN-13: 978-1-896944-32-6
Eclipse, K. A. Bedford (tp) ISBN-13: 978-1-894063-30-2
Even The Stones, Marie Jakober (tp) ISBN-13: 978-1-894063-18-0

Fires of the Kindred, Robin Skelton (tp)
        ISBN-13: 978-0-88878-271-7
Forbidden Cargo, Rebecca Rowe (tp) ISBN-13: 978-1-894063-16-6

Game of Perfection, A, Élisabeth Vonarburg (tp)
        ISBN-13: 978-1-894063-32-6
Green Music, Ursula Pflug (tp) ISBN-13: 978-1-895836-75-2
Green Music, Ursula Pflug (hb) ISBN-13: 978-1-895836-77-6
Gryphon Highlord, The, Connie Ward (tp)
        ISBN-13: 978-1-896944-38-8

Healer, The, Amber Hayward (tp) ISBN-13: 978-1-895836-89-9
Healer, The, Amber Hayward (hb) ISBN-13: 978-1-895836-91-2
Human Thing, The, Kathleen H. Nelson (hb)
        ISBN-13: 978-1-896944-03-6
Hydrogen Steel, K. A. Bedford (tp) ISBN-13: 978-1-894063-20-3

i-ROBOT Poetry, Jason Christie (tp) ISBN-13: 978-1-894063-24-1

Jackal Bird, Michael Barley (pb) ISBN-13: 978-1-895836-07-3
Jackal Bird, Michael Barley (hb) ISBN-13: 978-1-895836-11-0

Keaen, Till Noever (tp) ISBN-13: 978-1-894063-08-1
Keeper's Child, Leslie Davis (tp) ISBN-13: 978-1-894063-01-2

Land/Space, edited Candas Jane Dorsey and Judy McCrosky (tp)
     ISBN-13: 978-1-895836-90-5
Land/Space, edited Candas Jane Dorsey and Judy McCrosky (hb)
     ISBN-13: 978-1-895836-92-9
Legacy of Morevi, Tee Morris (tp) ISBN-13: 978-1-896944-29-6
Legends of the Serai, J.C. Hall (tp) ISBN-13: 978-1-896944-04-3
Longevity Thesis, Jennifer Tahn (tp) ISBN-13: 978-1-896944-37-1
Lyskarion: The Song of the Wind, J.A. Cullum (tp)
     ISBN-13: 978-1-894063-02-9

Machine Sex and Other stories, Candas Jane Dorsey (tp)
     ISBN-13: 978-0-88878-278-6
Maërlande Chronicles, The, Élisabeth Vonarburg (pb)
     ISBN-13: 978-0-88878-294-6
Magister's Mask, The, Deby Fredericks (tp)
     ISBN-13: 978-1-896944-16-6
Moonfall, Heather Spears (pb) ISBN-13: 978-0-88878-306-6
Morevi: The Chronicles of Rafe and Askana, Lisa Lee & Tee Morris (tp)
     ISBN-13: 978-1-896944-07-4

Not Your Father's Horseman, Valorie Griswold-Ford (tp)
     ISBN-13: 978-1-896944-27-2

On Spec: The First Five Years, edited On Spec (pb)
     ISBN-13: 978-1-895836-08-0
On Spec: The First Five Years, edited On Spec (hb)
     ISBN-13: 978-1-895836-12-7
Operation: Immortal Servitude, Tony Ruggerio (tp)
     ISBN-13: 978-1-896944-56-2

Orbital Burn, K. A. Bedford (tp) ISBN-13: 978-1-894063-10-4
Orbital Burn, K. A. Bedford (hb) ISBN-13: 978-1-894063-12-8

Pallahaxi Tide, Michael Coney (pb) ISBN-13: 978-0-88878-293-9
Passion Play, Sean Stewart (pb) ISBN-13: 978-0-88878-314-1
Plague Saint, Rita Donovan, The (tp) ISBN-13: 978-1-895836-28-8
Plague Saint, Rita Donovan, The (hb) ISBN-13: 978-1-895836-29-5

Reluctant Voyagers Élisabeth Vonarburg (pb)
     ISBN-13: 978-1-895836-09-7
Reluctant Voyagers, Élisabeth Vonarburg (hb)
     ISBN-13: 978-1-895836-15-8

Resisting Adonis, Timothy J. Anderson (tp)
    ISBN-13: 978-1-895836-84-4
Resisting Adonis , Timothy J. Anderson (hb)
    ISBN-13: 978-1-895836-83-7
Righteous Anger, Lynda Williams (tp) ISBN-13: 897-1-894063-38-8

Shadebinder's Oath, The, Jeanette Cottrell (tp)
    ISBN-13: 978-1-896944-31-9
Silent City, The Élisabeth Vonarburg (tp)
    ISBN-13: 978-1-894063-07-4
Slow Engines of Time, The, Élisabeth Vonarburg (tp)
    ISBN-13: 978-1-895836-30-1
Slow Engines of Time, The, Élisabeth Vonarburg (hb)
    ISBN-13: 978-1-895836-31-8
Small Magics, Erik Buchanan (tp) ISBN-13: 978-1-896944-38-8
Sojourn, Jana Oliver (pb) ISBN-13: 978-1-896944-30-2
Stealing Magic, Tanya Huff (tp) ISBN-13: 978-1-894063-34-0
Strange Attractors, Tom Henighan (pb)
    ISBN-13: 978-0-88878-312-7

Taming, The, Heather Spears (pb) ISBN-13: 978-1-895836-23-3
Taming, The, Heather Spears (hb) ISBN-13: 978-1-895836-24-0
Teacher's Guide to Dragon's Fire, Wizard's Flame, Unwin & Mennenga
    (pb) ISBN-13: 978-1-896944-19-7
Ten Monkeys, Ten Minutes, Peter Watts (tp)
    ISBN-13: 978-1-895836-74-5
Ten Monkeys, Ten Minutes, Peter Watts (hb)
    ISBN-13: 978-1-895836-76-9
Tesseracts 1, edited Judith Merril (pb) ISBN-13: 978-0-88878-279-3
Tesseracts 2, edited Phyllis Gotlieb & Douglas Barbour (pb)
    ISBN-13: 978-0-88878-270-0
Tesseracts 3, edited Candas Jane Dorsey & Gerry Truscott (pb)
    ISBN-13: 978-0-88878-290-8
Tesseracts 4, edited Lorna Toolis & Michael Skeet (pb)
    ISBN-13: 978-0-88878-322-6

Tesseracts 5, edited Robert Runté & Yves Maynard (pb)
    ISBN-13: 978-1-895836-25-7
Tesseracts 5, edited Robert Runté & Yves Maynard (hb)
    ISBN-13: 978-1-895836-26-4
Tesseracts 6, edited Robert J. Sawyer & Carolyn Clink (pb)
    ISBN-13: 978-1-895836-32-5
Tesseracts 6, edited Robert J. Sawyer & Carolyn Clink (hb)
    ISBN-13: 978-1-895836-33-2
Tesseracts 7, edited Paula Johanson & Jean-Louis Trudel (tp)
    ISBN-13: 978-1-895836-58-5

Tesseracts 7, edited Paula Johanson & Jean-Louis Trudel (hb)
        ISBN-13: 978-1-895836-59-2
Tesseracts 8, edited John Clute & Candas Jane Dorsey (tp)
        ISBN-13: 978-1-895836-61-5
Tesseracts 8, edited John Clute & Candas Jane Dorsey (hb)
        ISBN-13: 978-1-895836-62-2
Tesseracts Nine, edited Nalo Hopkinson and Geoff Ryman (tp)
        ISBN-13: 978-1-894063-26-5
Tesseracts Ten, edited Robert Charles Wilson and Edo van Belkom
(tp) ISBN-13: 978-1-894063-36-4
Tesseracts Eleven, edited Cory Doctorow and Holly Phillips (tp)
        ISBN-13: 978-1-894063-03-6
Tesseracts Q, edited Élisabeth Vonarburg & Jane Brierley (pb)
        ISBN-13: 978-1-895836-21-9
Tesseracts Q, edited Élisabeth Vonarburg & Jane Brierley (hb)
        ISBN-13: 978-1-895836-22-6
Throne Price, Lynda Williams and Alison Sinclair (tp)
        ISBN-13: 978-1-894063-06-7
Too Many Princes, Deby Fredricks (tp) ISBN-13: 978-1-896944-36-4
Twilight of the Fifth Sun, David Sakmyster (tp)
        ISBN-13: 978-1-896944-01-02

Virtual Evil, Jana Oliver (tp) ISBN-13: 978-1-896944-76-0

Dragon
Moon

EDGE